She smelt like sugar and frosting and all the things he'd ever longed for. An ache gripped him so hard he had to drag in a breath.

She swayed towards him, those green eyes lowering to his lips. The pulse at the base of her throat fluttered faster and faster. Her hand tightened in his.

He gripped her chin, lifted it, needing to taste her so badly he thought he might fall to his knees from the force of it. Desire licked fire through his veins. His lips started to descend. He moved in close, so close he could taste her breath, but the expression in her eyes froze him.

They glittered. With tears.

'Don't you *dare* kiss me out of pity.'

She didn't move out of his hold and he knew then that she was as caught up in the same grip of desire as him.

'Please, Rick. Don't kiss me because you feel sorry for me.'

The tears trembled, but they didn't fall. Every muscle he had screamed a protest, but he released her and stepped back.

He swallowed twice before he was sure his voice would work. 'Pity was the last thing on my mind.'

BY

MICHELLE DOUGLAS

THE REBEL AND THE HEIRESS

BY
MICHELLE DOUGLAS

Published in Great Britain 2014
by Mills & Boon, an imprint of Harlequin (UK) Limited,
Eton House, 18-24 Paradise Road, Richmond, Surrey, TW9 1SR

ISBN: 978-0-263-91305-7

23-0814

Harlequin (UK) Limited's policy is to use papers that are natural, renewable and recyclable products and made from wood grown in sustainable forests. The logging and manufacturing processes conform to the legal environmental regulations of the country of origin.

Printed and bound in Spain
by Blackprint CPI, Barcelona

At the age of eight **Michelle Douglas** was asked what she wanted to be when she grew up. She answered, 'A writer.' Years later she read an article about romance-writing and thought, *Ooh, that'll be fun*. She was right. When she's not writing she can usually be found with her nose buried in a book. She is currently enrolled in an English Master's programme for the sole purpose of indulging her reading and writing habits further. She lives in a leafy suburb of Newcastle, on Australia's east coast, with her own romantic hero—husband Greg, who is the inspiration behind all her happy endings.

Michelle would love you to visit her at her website: www.michelle-douglas.com.

For my little brother, Kyle,
who's always been a rebel in his own way.

CHAPTER ONE

RICK BRADFORD STARED at the Victorian mansion elegantly arranged in front of him and then down at the note in his hand before crumpling the piece of paper and shoving it in his jeans pocket.

He'd checked with his friend Tash earlier. 'You're sure you got that right? Nell Smythe-Whittaker rang and asked if I'd drop round?'

'For the tenth time, Rick, yes! It was the Princess all right. And no, she didn't mention what it was about. And no, I didn't ask her.'

For the last fortnight Tash's brain had been addled by love. His lip curled. Not that he had anything against Mitch King and it was great to see Tash happy but, as far as he could tell, her street smarts had all but floated out of the window. Why hadn't she asked the Princess what this was about?

Because she was viewing the world through rose-coloured glasses, that was why. His lip curled a little more. He wasn't sure he could stand being a third wheel in her and Mitch's hazy, happy little world for much longer. It was time to move on. Tomorrow he'd head up the coast, find work somewhere and…

And what?

He lifted a shoulder.

First he'd find out what Nell Smythe-Whittaker wanted.

You won't find that out by standing here on the footpath like some dumb schmuck.

Blowing out a breath, he settled a mantle of casual, almost insolent assurance about himself. The people from Nell's world—probably including Nell herself—looked down on the likes of him and he had no intention of giving them, or her, the satisfaction of thinking he cared two hoots either way.

Would Nell look down that pretty autocratic nose at him? He hadn't spoken to her since they were ten years old. He could count the number of times he'd seen her since then—and only ever in the distance—on one hand. They'd never spoken, but she'd always lifted a hand in acknowledgement. And he'd always waved back.

It had never felt real. It had always felt somehow apart from the daily humdrum. He scratched a hand across his face. *Stupid! Fairy tales!* He was too old for such nonsense.

You're only twenty-five.

Yeah? Well, most days he felt as if he was fifty.

Clenching his jaw, he pushed open the gate and strode up the walk to the wide veranda with its ochre and cream tessellated tiles. With an effort of will, he slowed his strides to a saunter and planted a devil-may-care smirk on his face.

Up closer, he could see that Nell's fancy castle needed some attention. Paint peeled at the window trims and flaked here and there from the walls. One section of guttering leaned at a drunken angle and the wider garden was overgrown and unkempt. Here and there he caught sight of the silver wrappers of crisp packets and chocolate bar wrappers winking in the sunlight.

So…the rumours were true then. The Princess had fallen on hard times.

Ignoring a doorbell he had little faith would work, he lifted his hand to knock on the ornately moulded front door when voices from the partially open French windows further along the veranda halted him. Words didn't just drift out on the summer air. They sped.

'You won't get another opportunity like this, Nell!'

A male voice. An angry male voice. Rick's every muscle bunched in readiness. He hated bullies. And he really hated men who bullied women. He stalked down to the windows.

'You are a sleazy, slimy excuse for a man, Mr Withers.'

He paused. Her voice held no fear, only scorn. She could obviously deal with the situation on her own.

'You know it's the only answer to the current straits you find yourself in.'

'Is that so? And I suppose it's a coincidence that this particular solution is one that will also line your pockets?'

'There isn't a bank manager in Sydney who'll loan you the money you need. They're not going to touch that business plan of yours with a bargepole.'

'As you don't happen to be a bank manager and I no longer have any faith in your professionalism you'll have to excuse my scepticism.'

Rick grinned. *Go, Princess!*

'Your father won't be pleased.'

'That is true. It's also none of your concern.'

'You're wasting your not inconsiderable talents.' There was a silence. 'You're a very beautiful woman. We'd make a good team, you and I, Nellie.'

Nellie?

'Stay where you are, Mr Withers. I do not want you to kiss me.'

Rick straightened, instantly alert.

In the next moment a loud slap rang in the air, followed by scuffling. Rick leapt for the window, but it burst open before he could reach it and he found himself pressed back against the wall of the house as Nell frogmarched a man in a shiny suit along the length of the veranda, his earlobe twisted between her thumb and forefinger, and all but threw him towards the gate. 'Good day, Mr Withers.'

The suit straightened and threw his shoulders back. Rick went to stand behind Nell, legs planted and mouth grim. He folded his arms and flexed his biceps.

The suit gave the kind of smirk Rick would give a lot to wipe off his face…except he wasn't that kind of guy any more.

'I see you've your bit of rough. So that's the way you like it?'

'I'm afraid, Mr Withers, you're never going to find out how I like it.' She glanced behind her and met Rick's gaze, her green eyes…beautiful. 'Hello, Mr Bradford.'

Her voice reached out and wrapped around him like a caress. 'Hello, Princess.' He hadn't meant to call her that; it just slipped out. Those eyes widened and continued to stare into his until the breath jammed in his throat.

'Well, you needn't think your bit of rough is going to get you out of your current jam and—'

'Oh, do be quiet, you horrible little man.'

Those green eyes snapped away and Rick found he could breathe again.

And then he looked at her fully and what he saw made him blink. Nell looked as if she'd just stepped out of some nineteen-fifties movie. She wore a dress that made every male impulse he had sit up and stare. It had a fitted bodice that was snug to the waist and a skirt that flared out to mid-calf. It sported a Hawaiian beach print complete with surf, sand and palm trees.

'Mr Bradford is ten times the man you are and what's more he has manners, like a true gentleman.'

He did? In the next instant he shook his head. They were reading from different scripts here.

Without another word, Nell turned and took his arm. 'I'm so glad you could drop around.' And she led him back along the veranda, effectively dismissing the other man. 'I'm terribly sorry. I'd take you through the front door—I don't want you thinking I'm taking you in via the tradesman's entrance or some such nonsense—but I can't get the rotten thing open. I'm also afraid that you'll have to excuse the mess.'

She led him through the French windows into a large room—a drawing room or parlour or music room or something of that nature. Whatever it was, it wasn't the kind of room he'd had much experience with and, despite her words, it wasn't ridiculously messy, but there were haphazard piles of boxes everywhere and piles of papers on the only piece of furniture in the room—a small side table.

'Why can't you get the door open?' He detached his arm from hers. Her warmth was…too warm.

'Oh, I don't know.' She waved a hand in the air. 'It's jammed or swollen up or something.'

Why hadn't she had it looked at?

None of your business. He hovered by the French windows until he heard the clang of the front gate closing behind the suit. He glanced behind to make sure anyway. He turned back to Nell. 'What was that all about?'

Those green eyes caught fire again. 'He's an estate agent who wants to sell my house, only I'm not interested. In more ways than one! He turned out to be a seriously sexist piece of work too. I can tell you now, Mr Bradford, that if you try any of the same tricks you'll meet with the same fate!'

She was a slim blonde firecracker. In a retro dress. He wanted to grin. And then he didn't.

The fire in her eyes faded. She made as if to wipe a hand down her face only she pulled it away at the last moment to clasp both her hands lightly in front of her.

She was so different from the last time he'd seen her.

'I'm sorry, that was an unforgivable thing to say. My blood's up and I'm not thinking clearly.'

'It's all right,' he said, because it was what he always said to a woman.

Nell shook her head. 'No, it's not. I have no right to tar you with the same brush as Mr Withers.'

That was when he noticed that behind the blonde princess perfection she had lines fanning out around her eyes and she wasn't wearing lipstick. 'I'd prefer it if you'd call me Rick.'

The hint of a smile played across her lips. 'Are you up for a coffee, Rick?'

And, just like that, she hurtled him back fifteen years. *Come and play.* It hadn't been a demand or a request, but a plea.

He had to swallow the lump that came out of nowhere. He wanted to walk out of those French windows and never come back. He wanted…

He adjusted his stance. 'I thought you'd never ask.'

She smiled for real then and he realised that anything else that had passed for a smile so far hadn't reached her eyes. 'C'mon then.' She hitched her head and led him through the doorway into a hallway. 'You don't mind if we sit in the kitchen rather than the parlour, do you?'

'Not at all.' He tried to keep the wry note out of his voice. His type was never invited into the parlour.

Her shoulders tensed and he knew she'd read his tone. She wheeled around and led him in the other direction—back towards the front door—instead. She gestured into the large room to the left. 'As you'll see, the parlour is in a right state.'

He only meant to glance into the room but the sight dragged him all the way inside. In the middle of the room something huddled beneath dust sheets—probably furniture. It wasn't that which drew his attention. Plaster had fallen from one of the walls, adjacent to an ornate fireplace, and, while the mess had been swept up, nothing had been done about the gaping hole left behind. A rolled-up carpet leant against another wall along with more cardboard boxes. The light pouring in at the huge bay window did the room no favours either. Scratching sounded in the chimney. Birds or a possum?

He grimaced. 'A right state is the, uh, correct diagnosis'

'Yes, which is why I currently prefer the kitchen.'

Her voice might be crisp, but her shoulders weren't as straight as they could be. He followed her into the kitchen and then wasn't sure if it was much better. The housekeeper had obviously upped and left, but how long ago was anyone's guess. A jumble of dishes—mixing bowls and baking trays mostly—teetered in the sink, boxes of foodstuffs dominated one end of the enormous wooden table and flour seemed to be scattered over the rest of its surface. It smelt good in here, though.

She cleared a spot for him, wiped as much of the table down as she could and he sat. Mostly because it seemed the most sensible and least dangerous thing he could do. He didn't want to send anything flying with a stray elbow or a clumsy hip. Nell moved amid the mess with an ease and casual disregard as if she were used to it. He didn't believe that for a moment, though. The Princess had grown up in a world where others cleaned up the mess and kept things organised. This was merely a sign of her natural polish.

Or unnatural polish, depending on how one looked at it. She'd lacked it as a ten-year-old, but her parents had obviously managed to eventually drill it into her.

The scent of coffee hit him and he drew it slowly into his lungs. 'So…you're moving out?'

Nell started as if she'd forgotten he was there. She sent him one of those not quite smiles. 'Moving in, actually.'

Moving in? On her own? In this great old empty mansion?

None of your business.

His lips twisted. Since when had he been able to resist a damsel in distress? Or, in this case, a Princess in distress. 'What's going down, Nell?'

She turned fully to stare at him and folded her arms. 'Really?'

He wasn't sure what that *really* referred to—his genuine interest or his front in asking a personal question. He remembered his devil-may-care insolence and shrugged it on. 'Sure.'

She made coffee and set a mug in front of him. Only when he'd helped himself to milk and two sugars did she seat herself opposite and add milk to her own mug. The perfect hostess. The perfect princess.

'I'm sorry. I'm so used to everyone knowing my business that your question threw me for a moment.'

'I've only been back in town for a fortnight.' And he and she came from two different worlds, even if they had grown up in the same suburb.

Even amid all the disrepair and mess, she shone like some golden thing. Him? He just blended in.

'I did hear,' he ventured, 'that your father had fallen on hard times.'

Her lips tightened. 'And nearly took the livelihoods of over a hundred people with him in the process.'

Was she referring to the workers at the glass factory? It'd been in the Smythe-Whittaker family for three generations. Tash had told him how worried they'd been at the time that it'd go down the proverbial gurgler, that more unemployment would hit the area. But… 'I heard a buyer came in at the last minute.'

'Yes. No thanks to my father.'

'The global financial crisis has hit a lot of people hard.'

'That is true.' He didn't know why, but he loved the way she enunciated every syllable. 'However, rather than face facts, my father held on for so long that the sale of the factory couldn't cover all of his growing debts. I handed over the contents of my trust fund.'

Ouch.

'But I've drawn the line at selling Whittaker House.'

Her grandmother had left it to Nell rather than her father? Interesting. 'But you gave him your money?'

She rested both elbows on the table and stared down into her mug. 'Not all of it. I'd already spent some of it setting up my own business. Though, to be perfectly frank with you, Rick, it never really felt like my money. Besides, as I was never the daughter my father wanted, it seemed the least I could do.'

'But you're still angry with him.'

She laughed then and he liked the way humour curved her lips in that deliciously enticing manner. Lips like that didn't need lipstick. 'I am. And as everyone else around here already knows the reason, I'll even share it with you, tough guy.'

He leaned towards her, intrigued.

'Besides the fact he had no right gambling with the factory workers' livelihoods, his first solution was to marry me off to Jeremy Delaney.'

His jaw dropped. 'Jeez, Nell, the Delaneys might be rolling in it, but it's a not-so-secret secret that he's…' He trailed off, rolling his shoulders. Maybe Nell didn't know.

'Gay?' She nodded. 'I know. I don't know why he refuses to be loud and proud about it. I suspect he's still too overawed by his father.'

'And you refused to marry him?'

'Of course I did.'

He flashed back to the way she'd frogmarched the suit out of her office earlier and grinned. 'Of course you did.'

'So then my father demanded I sell this house.'

It wasn't a house—it was a mansion. But he refrained from pointing that out. 'And you refused to do that too?'

She lifted her chin. 'As everyone knows, I gave him the deeds to my snazzy little inner city apartment. I handed over my sports car and I signed over what was left of my trust fund, but I am not selling this house.' Her eyes flashed.

He held up his hands. 'Fair enough. I'm not suggesting

you should. But jeez, Nell, if you don't have a cent left how are you going to afford its upkeep?'

The fire in her eyes died and her luscious lips drooped at the corners. And then he watched in amazement as she shook herself upright again. 'Cupcakes,' she said, her chin at *just* that angle.

'Cupcakes?' Had she gone mad?

In one fluid movement she rose, reached for a plate before pulling off a lid from a nearby tin. 'Strawberries and Cream, Passion Fruit Delight, Lemon Sherbet, and Butterscotch Crunch.' With each designation she pulled forth an amazing creation from the tin and set it onto the plate, and somehow the cluttered old kitchen was transformed into a…fairyland, a birthday party.

She set the plate in front of him with a flourish and all he could do was stare in amazement at four of the prettiest cupcakes he'd ever seen in his life.

'I do cupcake towers as birthday or special event cakes in whatever flavour or iced in whatever colour the client wants. I provide cupcakes by the dozen for birthday parties, high teas, morning teas and office parties. I will even package up an individual cupcake in a fancy box with all the bells and whistles…or, at least, ribbons and glitter, if that's what a client requests.'

He stared at the cakes on the plate in front of him and then at the mountain of dishes in the sink. 'You made these? You?'

His surprise didn't offend her. She just grinned a Cheshire cat grin. 'I did.'

The Princess could bake?

She nodded at the cupcakes and handed him a bread and butter plate and a napkin. 'Help yourself.'

Was she serious? Guys like him didn't get offered mouth-watering treasures like these. Guys like him feigned indifference to anything covered in frosting or cream, as if a sweet tooth were a sign of a serious weakness.

He didn't stop to think about it; he reached for the nearest cupcake, a confection of sticky pale yellow frosting with a triangle of sugared lemon stuck in at a jaunty angle and all pale golden goodness, and then halted. He offered the plate to her first.

She glanced at her watch and shook her head. 'I'm only allowed to indulge after three p.m. and it's only just gone two.'

'That sounds like a stupid rule.'

'You don't understand. I find them addictive. For the sake of my hips and thighs and overall general health, I've had to put some limits to my indulging.'

He laughed and took a bite.

Moist cake, a surge of sweetness and the tang of lemon hit him in a rush. He closed his eyes and tried to stamp the memory onto his senses and everything inside him opened up to it. When he'd been in jail he'd occasionally tried to take himself away from the horror by imagining some sensory experience from the outside world. Small things like the rush of wind in his face as he skateboarded down a hill, the buoyancy of swimming in the ocean, the smell of wattle and eucalyptus in the national park. He'd have added the taste of the Princess's cupcakes if he'd experienced them way back when.

He finished the cupcake and stared hungrily at the plate. Would she mind if he had another one?

Rick stared at the three remaining cupcakes with so much hunger in his eyes that something inside Nell clenched up. It started as a low-level burn in her chest, but the burn intensified and hardened to eventually settle in her stomach. It was one thing to feel sorry for herself for the predicament she found herself in, but she'd never experienced the world as the harsh, ugly place Rick had. *And you'll do well not to forget it.*

She had to swallow before she could speak. 'Scoff the

lot.' She pushed the plate closer. 'They're leftovers from the orders I delivered earlier.'

He glanced at her and the uncertainty in his eyes knifed into her. He'd swaggered in here with his insolent bad-boy cockiness set off to perfection in that tight black T-shirt, but it was just as much a show, a fake, as her society girl smile. Still… She glanced at those shoulders and her mouth watered.

In the next instant she shook herself. She did *not* find that tough-guy look attractive.

He pushed the plate away, and for some reason it made her heart heavy. So heavy it took an effort to keep it from sinking all the way to her knees.

'How…when did you learn to cook?'

She didn't want to talk about that. When she looked too hard at the things she was good at—cooking and gardening—and the reasons behind them, it struck her as too pathetic for words.

And she wasn't going to be pathetic any more.

So she pasted on her best society girl smile—the one she used for the various charity functions she'd always felt honour-bound to attend. 'It appears I have a natural aptitude for it.' She gave an elegant shrug. She knew it was elegant because she'd practised it endlessly until her mother could find no fault with it. 'Who'd have thought? I'm as surprised as everyone else.'

He stared at her and she found it impossible to read his expression. Except to note that the insolent edge had returned to his smile. 'What time did you start baking today?'

'Three a.m.'

Both of his feet slammed to the ground. He leant towards her, mouth open.

'It's Sunday, and Saturdays and Sundays are my busiest days. Today I had a tower cake for a little girl's birthday party, four dozen cupcakes for a charity luncheon, a hen party morning tea and a couple of smaller afternoon teas.'

'You did that all on your own?'

She tried not to let his surprise chafe at her. Some days it still shocked the dickens out of her too.

His face tightened and he glanced around the kitchen. 'I guess it does leave you the rest of the week to work on this place.'

Oh, he was just like everyone else! He thought her a helpless piece of fluff without a backbone, without a brain and probably without any moral integrity either. *You're useless.*

She pushed her shoulders back. 'I guess,' she said, icing-sugar-sweet, 'that all I need to do is find me a big strong man with muscles and know-how…and preferably with a pot of gold in the bank…to wrap around my little finger and…' She trailed off with another shrug—an expansive one this time. She traded in a whole vocabulary of shrugs.

A glint lit his eye. 'And then you'll never have to bake another cupcake again?'

'Ah, but you forget. I like baking cupcakes.'

'And getting up at three a.m.?'

She ignored that.

He frowned. 'Is that why you wanted to see me?'

It took a moment to work out what he meant. When she did, she laughed. 'I guess you have the muscles, but do you have the know-how?' She didn't ask him about the pot of gold. That would be cruel. 'Because I'm afraid I don't.' She bit back a sigh. *No self-pity.* 'But no, that's not why I asked you to drop by.'

His face hardened. 'So why did I receive the summons? If you knew I was at Tash's, why couldn't you have dropped by there?'

She heard what he didn't say. *Why do you think you're better than me?* The thing was, she didn't. He wouldn't believe that, though. She moistened her lips. 'I didn't think I'd be welcome there. I don't believe Tash thinks well of me.'

He scowled. 'What on earth—?'

'A while back I went into the Royal Oak.' It was the hotel where Tash worked. Nell had been lonely and had wanted to connect with people she'd never been allowed to connect with before. For heaven's sake, they all lived in the same neighbourhood. They should know each other. She was careful to keep the hurt out of her voice. She'd had a lot of practice at that too.

There you go again, feeling sorry for yourself.

She lifted her chin. 'I ordered a beer. Tash poured me a lemon squash and made it clear it'd be best for all concerned if I drank it and left.'

Rick stared at her, but his face had lost its frozen closeness. 'And you took that to mean she didn't like you?'

She had no facility for making friends and the recent downturn in her circumstances had only served to highlight that. 'Yes, I did.'

'Princess, I—'

'I really wish you wouldn't call me that.' She'd never been a princess, regardless of what Rick thought. 'I much prefer Nell. And there's absolutely no reason at all why Tash should like me.' Given the way her parents had ensured that Nell hadn't associated with the local children, it was no wonder they'd taken against her. Or that those attitudes had travelled with them into adulthood.

He looked as if he wanted to argue so she continued—crisp, impersonal, untouchable. 'Do you recall the gardener who worked here for many years?'

He leant back, crossed a leg so his ankle rested on his knee. Despite the casual demeanour, she could see him turning something over in his mind. 'He was the one who chased me away that day?'

That day. She didn't know how that day could still be so vivid in her mind. 'Come and play.' She'd reached out a hand through the eight-foot-high wrought iron fence and Rick had clasped it briefly before John had chased him off. John had told her that Rick wasn't the kind of little boy she should be playing with. But she'd found an answering loneliness in the ten-year-old Rick's eyes. It had given her the courage to speak to him in the first place. Funnily enough, even though Rick had only visited twice more, she'd never felt quite so alone again.

That day John had given her her very own garden bed. That had helped too.

But Rick remembered that day as well? Her heart started to pound though she couldn't have explained why. 'Yes, John was the one who chased you away.'

'John Cox. I remember seeing him around the place. He drank at the Crown and Anchor, if memory serves me. Why? What about him?'

'Did you know him well?'

'I'm not sure I ever spoke to the man.'

'Right.' She frowned. Then this just didn't make any sense.

'Why?' The word barked out of him. 'What has he been saying?'

'Nothing.' She swallowed. 'He died eight months ago. Lung cancer.'

Rick didn't say anything and, while he hadn't moved, she sensed that his every muscle was tense and poised.

'John and I were…well, friends of a kind, I guess. I liked to garden and he taught me how to grow things and how to keep them healthy.'

'Cooking *and* gardening? Are your talents endless, Princess?'

She should've become immune to mockery by now, but she hadn't. She and Rick might've shared a moment of kinship fifteen years ago, but they didn't have anything in common now. That much was obvious. And she'd long given up begging for friends.

She gave a shrug that was designed to rub him up the wrong way, in the same way his 'Princess' was designed to needle her. A superior shrug that said *I'm better than you*. Her mother had been proficient at those.

Rick's lip curled.

She tossed her hair back over her shoulder. 'John kept to himself. He didn't have many friends so I was one of the few people who visited him during his final weeks.'

Rick opened his mouth. She readied herself for something cutting, but he closed it again instead. She let out a breath. Despite what Rick might think of her, she'd cried when John had died. He'd been kind to her and had taken the time to show her how to do things. He'd answered her endless questions. And he'd praised her efforts. The fingers she'd been tapping on her now cold coffee cup stopped.

'Nell?'

She dragged herself back from those last days in John's hospice room. 'If the two of you never spoke, then what I'm about to tell you is rather odd, but…'

'But?'

She met his gaze. 'John charged me with a final favour.'

'What kind of favour?'

'He wanted me to deliver a letter.'

Dark brown eyes stared back at her, the same colour as dark chocolate. Eighty per cent cocoa. Bitter chocolate.

'He wanted me to give that letter to you, Rick.'

'To me?'

She rose and went to the kitchen drawer where she kept important documents. 'He asked that I personally place it in your hands.'

And then she held it out to him.

CHAPTER TWO

EVERY INSTINCT RICK had urged him to leap up and leave the room, to race out of this house and away from this rotten city and to never return.

He wanted away from Nell and her polished blonde perfection and her effortless nose-in-the-air superiority that was so at odds with the girl he remembered.

Fairy tales, that was what those memories were. He'd teased them out into full-blown fantasies in an effort to dispel some of the grim reality that had surrounded him. He'd known at the time that was what he'd been doing, but he'd wanted to hold up the promise of something better to come—a chance for a better future.

Of course, all of those dreams had shattered the moment he'd set foot inside a prison cell.

Still...

The letter in Nell's outstretched hand started to shake. 'Aren't you going to take it?'

'I'm not sure.'

She sat.

'I have no idea what this John Cox could have to say to me.' Did she know what was in the letter? He deliberately loosened his shoulders, slouched back in his chair and pasted on a smirk. 'Do you think he's going to accuse me of stealing the family silver?'

She flinched and just for a moment he remembered wild eyes as she ordered, 'Run!'

He wanted her to tell him to run now.

'After all, I didn't disappoint either his or your father's expectations.'

Those incredible eyes of hers flashed green fire and he wondered what she'd do next. Would she frogmarch him off the premises with his ear between her thumb and forefinger. And if she tried it would he let her? Or would he kiss her?

He shifted on the chair, ran a hand down his T-shirt. He wasn't kissing the Princess.

'If memory serves me correctly—' she bit each word out '—you went to jail on drug charges, not robbery. *And* if the rumours buzzing about town are anything to go by, those charges are in the process of being dropped and your name cleared.'

Did she think that made up for fifteen months behind bars?

A sudden heaviness threatened to fell him. One stupid party had led to…

He dragged a hand down his face. Cheryl, at seventeen, hadn't known what she'd been doing, hadn't known the trouble that the marijuana she'd bought could get her into—could get them all into. She'd been searching for escape—escape from a sexually abusive father. He understood that, sympathised. The fear that had flashed into her eyes, though, when the police had burst in, her desperation—the desperation of someone who'd been betrayed again and again by people who were supposed to love her—it still plagued his nightmares.

His chest cramped. Little Cheryl who he'd known since she'd started kindergarten. Little Cheryl who he'd done his best to protect…and, when that hadn't been enough, who he'd tried to comfort. He hadn't known it then, but there wasn't enough comfort in the world to help heal her. *It hadn't been her fault.*

So he'd taken the blame for her. He'd been a much more likely candidate for the drugs anyway. At the age of eighteen he'd gone to jail for fifteen months. He pulled in a breath. In the end, though, none of it had made any difference. That was what really galled him.

Nell thrust out her chin. 'So drop the attitude and stop playing the criminal with me.'

It snapped him out of his memories and he couldn't have said why, but he suddenly wanted to smile.

'The only way to find out what John has to say is to open the letter.'

He folded his arms. 'What's it to you, anyway?'

'I made a promise to a dying man.'

'And now you've kept it.'

She leaned across, picked up his hand and slapped the letter into it. She smelled sweet, like cupcakes. 'Now I've kept it.'

A pulse pounded inside him. Nell moved back. She moved right across to the other side of the kitchen and refilled their mugs from the pot kept warm by the percolator hotplate. But her sugar-sweet scent remained to swirl around him. He swallowed. He blinked until his vision cleared and he could read his name in black-inked capitals on the envelope. For some reason, those capitals struck him as ominous.

For heaven's sake, just open the damn thing and be done with it. It'd just be one more righteous citizen telling him the exact moment he'd gone off the rails, listing a litany of perceived injuries received—both imagined and in some cases real—and then a biting critique of what the rest of his life would hold if he didn't mend his ways.

The entire thing would take him less than a minute to read and then he could draw a line under this whole stupid episode. With a half-smothered curse he made deliberately unintelligible in honour of the Princess's upper class ears, he tore open the envelope.

Heaving out a breath, he unfolded the enclosed sheet of paper. The letter wasn't long. At least he wouldn't have to endure a detailed rant. He registered when Nell placed another mug of coffee in front of him that she even added milk and sugar to it.

He opened his mouth to thank her, but…

The words on the page were in the same odd style of all capitals as the envelope. All in the same black ink. He read the words but couldn't make sense of them to begin with.

They began to dance on the page and then each word rose up and hit him with the force of a sledgehammer. He flinched. He clenched the letter so hard it tore. He swore—loud and rude and blue—as black dots danced before his eyes.

Nell jumped. He expected her to run away. He told himself he hoped she would.

'Rick!' Her voice and its shrillness dive-bombed him like a magpie hostile with nesting instinct. 'Stick your head between your knees. Now!'

And then she was there, pushing his head between his knees and ordering him to breathe, telling him how to do it. He followed her instructions—pulling air into his lungs, holding it there and releasing it—but as soon as the dizziness left him he surged upright again.

He spun to her and waved the balled-up letter beneath her nose. 'Do you know what this says? Do you know what the—'

He pulled back the ugly language that clawed at his throat. 'Do you know what this says?' he repeated.

She shook her head. 'I wasn't there when he wrote it. It was already sealed when he gave it to me. He never confided in me about its contents and I never asked.' She gave one of *those* shrugs. 'I'll admit to a passing curiosity.' She drew herself up, all haughty blonde sleekness in her crazy, beautiful Hawaiian dress. 'But I would never open someone else's mail. So, no, I haven't read its contents.'

He wasn't sure he believed her.

She moved back around the table, sat and brought her

mug to her lips. It was so normal it eased some of the raging beast inside him.

She glanced up, her eyes clouded. 'I do hope he hasn't accused you of something ridiculous like stealing my grandmother's pearls.'

He sat too. 'It's nothing like that.'

'Good, because I know for a fact that was my father.'

He choked. *Father.* The word echoed through his mind. Father. Father. *Father.* In ugly black capitals.

'And I'm sorry I've not tracked you down sooner to give that letter to you, but John died and then my father's business fell apart and…and I wasn't sure where to look for you.'

He could see now that she hadn't wanted to approach Tash to ask how she might find him.

He wasn't sorry. Not one little bit.

'But when I heard you were home…'

He dragged a hand down his face before gulping half his coffee in one go. 'Did he say anything else to you when he gave you this?' The letter was still balled in his hand.

She reached out as if to swipe her finger through the frosting of one of the cupcakes, but she pulled her hand back at the last moment. 'He said you might have some questions you'd like to ask me and that he'd appreciate it if I did my best to answer them.'

He coughed back a hysterical laugh. Some questions? All he had were questions.

Her forehead creased. 'This isn't about that nonsense when we were ten-year-olds, is it?'

He didn't understand why she twisted her hands together. She wasn't the one who'd been hauled to the police station.

'I tried to tell my parents and the police that I gave the locket to you of my own free will and that you hadn't taken it. That I gave it to you as a present.'

She stared down into her coffee and something in her face twisted his gut.

'I thought it was mine to give.' She said the words so softly he had to strain to catch them. He thought about how she'd handed her apartment, her car and her trust fund all over to her father without a murmur. So why refuse to hand over Whittaker House?

She straightened and tossed back her hair. 'That was the moment when I realised my possessions weren't my own.'

But for some reason she felt that Whittaker House was hers?

'I told them how I wanted to give you something because you'd given me your toy aeroplane.'

It was the only thing he'd had to give her.

'Which, mind you, I absolutely refused to hand over when they demanded me to.'

That made him laugh.

She met his gaze squarely and there wasn't an ounce of haughtiness in her face. He sobered. 'I've never had the chance to say it before but, Rick, I'm sorry. My mother and father were so angry. And then the policeman frightened me so much I…I eventually just told them what they wanted to hear. It was cowardly of me and I'm truly sorry if that episode caused a lot of trouble for you.'

It'd caused trouble all right. It was the first time he'd come to the police's attention. It hadn't been the last time he'd been labelled a thief, liar and troublemaker by them, though.

They'd just been two kids exchanging treasures and trying to forge a connection. Her father, the police and his background had all conspired to blow it out of proportion.

But none of it had been Nell's fault and he'd always known that. 'Don't sweat it, Princess.' He used the nickname to remind himself of all the differences between them, to reinforce them.

She sat back, her chin tilted at that unconsciously noble

angle that made him want to smile. 'Don't worry. I was let off with a caution, but I didn't know the police had questioned you too.' The poor kid had probably been terrified. He had been.

She nodded to the letter balled in his hand. 'But John hasn't hassled you about any of that?'

He shook his head and her shoulders slumped in relief. She straightened again a moment later. 'So…do you have any questions?'

She looked as puzzled and bewildered as he felt. He wondered if she was counting down the minutes until this interview ended. Did she find it awkward and wrong for him to be sitting across the table from her? Or did it feel weirdly comfortable?

He shook off the thought and set the crumpled letter on the table and did what he could to smooth it out.

'*I won't beat around the bush,*' he read, '*but you might as well know that I'm your father.*'

Nell's mug wobbled back to the table. She stared at him. Her mouth opened and closed. 'But he chased you away.' And then her eyes filled.

Rick knew then that she'd had no notion of what John's letter contained.

He glanced back at the letter and continued reading. '*I may be better served taking this knowledge to the grave as it's brought me no joy. I don't expect it to bring you any either.*'

Nell's intake of breath reverberated in the silence.

'*I have no faith in you.*'

Her hands slapped to the table.

'*But you might as well know you have a sibling.*'

She practically leapt out of her chair. 'Who?' she demanded, and then forced herself back down into her seat. 'Really?' She frowned. 'Older or younger?'

He raised an eyebrow. 'I think I'm the one who's supposed to be asking the questions.'

'Oh, yes, of course.' She sat back and folded her hands in her lap. 'I'm sorry.'

'I'm not going to tell you who it is. If it matters to you then you'll have to prove it.'

Her jaw dropped. 'But that's… How…how can he be so hard and cold? He's supposed to have looked after you and…' She swallowed and sat back again. 'Sorry.' She smiled, a weak thing that did nothing to hide her turmoil. She made a zipping motion across her mouth.

Rick shrugged. 'He ends by simply signing it *John Cox*.'

She shook herself, frowned. 'I know the questions belong to you, but, Rick, I have no idea how to answer any of them. I haven't a clue who your sibling could be. I had no idea John was your father. I've never seen him with either a woman or a child. I—'

He handed the letter to her. He watched her face as she read the remaining lines. It darkened, which gladdened his heart.

And then it went blank. Rick eased back in his chair and stared up at the ceiling, not knowing whether to be relieved or disappointed.

Nell ignored the first lines John addressed to her in the letter. *Miss Nell, if you think Rick is in any way redeemable and you can find it in yourself to help him…* She snorted. What kind of nonsense was that? What kind of father just turned his back on his child? She thought about her own father with all of his demands and bit back a sigh.

'*You'll find a clue where the marigolds grow.*' She turned the letter over, but there was nothing written on the back.

'Any idea what that might mean?' Rick asked, slouching back in his chair as if they were discussing nothing more interesting than the weather.

She opened her mouth. She closed it again and scratched her head. 'My best guess is that, as he was a gardener and this is where he gardened, it refers to a garden bed somewhere on the estate, a garden bed where he grew marigolds, but…'

'But?'

Rick sounded bored. She glanced at him, tried to read his face, but couldn't. She lifted one shoulder. 'The thing is, I don't recall John ever growing marigolds. Apparently my mother didn't like them.'

She stabbed a finger into the Passion Fruit Delight cupcake, glowering at it. 'Why couldn't he have just told you who your sibling is?' She stabbed it again. 'Why couldn't he have told you the truth from the start and been a proper father to you?' Stab. Stab. 'I'd never have guessed any of this in a million years and—'

She pulled herself up and collected herself. None of this was helping. She wiped her finger on a napkin. 'Okay, so what else could marigold mean?'

Rick picked up the Strawberries and Cream cupcake and pushed nearly half of it into his mouth. She watched, mesmerised, at the way his lips closed around it, at the appreciation that lit his eyes and the way his mouth worked, the way his Adam's apple bobbed…the way his tongue flicked out to seize a crumb from the corner of his mouth.

She wrenched her gaze back. 'It could be a girl's name.' Her voice came out strangled.

'Do you know a Marigold or two?'

The words came out lazy and barely interested. Didn't he care? She tried to focus on the question he asked rather than the ones pounding through her. She frowned, thought hard and eventually shook her head. 'I don't think so. I don't even think I know any Marys.' She leapt up, seized her address book from the sideboard drawer and flicked through it…and then searched the list of contacts in her mobile phone. Nothing.

She stood. 'Okay, maybe there's marigold wallpaper somewhere in the house or…or moulding in the shape of a marigold…or an ornament or a painting or—'

'Princess, you've lived here your whole life. Do you really need to go through this mausoleum room by room to know whether it has marigold wallpaper?'

No, of course not. She sat. She knew every room intimately. She could remember what it looked like ten years ago as if it were only yesterday. There hadn't been any marigold paintings on any of the walls. There'd been no marigold wallpaper or bedspreads or curtains. No marigolds. Anywhere.

She glanced at Rick again. She could deal with his devil-may-care teasing and that tough-guy swagger. In fact, those things gave her a bit of a thrill. Considering she didn't get too many thrills, she'd take them where she could. She could even deal with the cold, hard wall he retreated behind. She could relate to it, even if she did feel he was judging her behind it and finding her lacking. But this… This nothingness hidden behind mockery and indifference. She was having no part of it.

She folded her arms. 'Don't you care?'

'Why should I?' He licked his fingers clean.

'Because…'

'What did he ever do for me?'

'Not about John!' She could understand his indifference and resentment of the other man. On that head it was John's stance that baffled her. She leaned across the table until its edges dug into her ribs. 'Don't you care that you have a brother or sister somewhere in the wide world?'

One shoulder lifted. He reached for the last unmangled cupcake. A dark lick of hair fell across his forehead. Nell pushed away from the table to stare, unseeing, out of the kitchen window, determined not to watch him demolish it with those delectable lips, determined not to watch him demolish it the way he seemed hell-bent on destroying this chance, this gift, he'd been given.

She pressed her hands to her chest. To have a sibling… She stilled. She glanced back behind her for a second and then spun back. Rick *hadn't* left. He hadn't read John's letter and then stormed out. He *had* shared the letter with her. Rick could feign indifference and couldn't-care-less disregard all he wanted, but if he really didn't care he'd have left by now.

Her cupcakes were good, but they weren't that good.

She sat again. 'I wish I had a brother or sister.'

'And whose image would you most like them cast in?' He leaned back, hands clasped behind his head. 'Your mother's or your father's?'

She flinched. He blinked and for a moment she thought he might reach across the table to touch her. He didn't. She forced herself to laugh. 'I guess there is always that. A sibling may have provided further proof that I was the cuckoo in the nest.'

'I didn't mean it like that.'

The hell he hadn't. 'It's okay.' She made her voice wry. 'You've had a shock, so it's okay to say hurtful things to other people.'

He scrubbed a hand across his face. 'I didn't mean for it to be hurtful. I'm sorry. I just refuse to turn this into a "they-all-lived-happily-ever-after" fairy tale like you seem so set on doing.'

He didn't want to get his hopes up. She couldn't blame him for that.

He rose. 'I believe I've long outstayed my welcome.'

Nell shot to her feet too. 'But…but we haven't figured out what marigolds mean yet or—'

'I'm not sure I care, Princess.'

She opened her mouth, but he shook his head and the expression on his face had her shutting it again. 'Good girl,' he said.

Her chin shot up. 'Don't patronise me.'

He grinned a grin that made her blood heat and her knees weak and she suddenly wanted him gone. Now. 'You know where to find me if you decide to investigate this issue further.' And then she swung away to dump the used coffee grounds into the kitchen tidy. When she turned back he was gone. She sat, her heart pounding as if she'd run a race.

Rick let himself into Tash's house, his head whirling and his temples throbbing. What the hell was he supposed to do now?

What do you want to do?

He wanted to run away.

But...

He pulled up short, dragged in a breath and searched for his customary indifference, but he couldn't find it. Too many thoughts pounded at him. And one hard, implacable truth—he might not be able to do anything with the information John Cox had belatedly decided to impart. Marigolds might remain unsolved forever.

In which case he could jump in his car—*now*—and head north without a backward glance, without a single regret. Except…

What if Nell does work out what it means?

He had a brother or a sister. He rested his hands against his knees and tried to breathe through the fist that tightened around his chest.

'That you, Rick?'

Tash's voice hauled him upright. 'Yep, just me,' he called back, shoving aside the worst of his anger and confusion. Tash might be his best friend, but he wasn't sharing this news with anyone.

He just hoped the Princess would keep her mouth shut too.

He forced his feet down the hallway and into Tash's living room—still full of sun and summer, and all he wanted to do was close his eyes and sleep. One glance at him and Tash's eyes narrowed. 'What did Nell want?'

He swung away to peer into the fridge. 'Soda?'

'No, thanks.'

He grabbed a soda and then sauntered over to plant himself in an armchair.

Tash folded her arms. 'She's obviously pushed your buttons.'

'Nah, not really.' He shrugged. 'She wanted to know if I had the time and the inclination to do some work on Whittaker House.'

'Oh, Lord, you're going to make the Princess your next project?'

He stretched out a leg. 'I haven't decided yet.' He took a long drink. The cold liquid helped ease the burning in his throat. 'Mind you, the place is going to rack and ruin.'

'It's a shame. It's such a nice old place. Gossip has it that she only moved back in this week so she's not wasting any time getting things shipshape again.' Tash sent him one of her looks. 'Rumour has it that she's far from cash-happy at the moment.'

'I kinda got that impression. What else does rumour say?'

Tash managed a local pub—The Royal Oak. Lots of workers from the glass factory drank there. What Tash didn't know about local happenings wasn't worth knowing.

'Well, apparently there's no love lost between Nell and her father.'

She could say that again.

'Old Mrs Smythe-Whittaker left the house to Nell and I'm not sure how these things work, but it was left in trust for her father to manage until Nell turned twenty-five.' Tash's lips twisted. 'Nell turned twenty-five earlier in the week. She moved in and…'

'Her father moved out?'

'Bingo.'

Before he could ask any more, Mitch came striding into the room. 'Hey, gorgeous.'

'Hey, doll,' Rick murmured back, but neither Tash nor Mitch paid him the slightest attention.

Tash flew out of her chair to launch herself at the big blond detective. 'Catch any bad guys today?'

Mitch thrust out his chest and pounded on it with one hand. 'Loads.'

For a moment it made Rick grin. Mitch the shrewd detective and Tash the take-no-prisoners barmaid in love and flirting. A miracle of miracles.

He rose and set off back down the hallway for the front door. 'I'm eating out tonight,' he tossed over his shoulder.

He needed time to think.

He pushed out of the front door, his hand clenching into a fist. This whole thing could be an elaborate hoax, a nasty trick.

Or you could have a brother or a sister.

Could he really walk away from this?

He lengthened his stride but the thoughts and confusion continued to bombard him. Damn it all to hell! Why did this have to involve the Princess? She'd been trouble fifteen years ago and hard-won wisdom warned him she'd be trouble now.

There was something about her that set his teeth on edge too.

Somewhere inside him a maniacal laugh started up.

The next afternoon, Nell swiped a forearm across her brow and stared at the mountain of dishes that needed washing.

Staring at them won't get them done. If she were going to take a half-day on Mondays then she needed to use that time productively. She started to move towards them when a knock sounded on the back door.

She spun around and then swallowed. Rick. In worn jeans and another tight black T-shirt. And with that bad-boy insolence wrapped tightly around him. She didn't know whether to be relieved or something altogether different—like apprehensive.

She wiped her hands down her shorts. Instinct warned

her that the less time she spent in Rick's company the better. Better for her peace of mind and better for her health if the stupid way her heart leapt and surged was anything to go by. She tried to swallow back her misgivings. Her family had done this man no favours. She owed him for that.

With a sigh she waved him inside, kissing goodbye to the notion of a clean kitchen followed by a soak in a hot tub with a good book. 'Good afternoon.'

He just nodded as he took the same seat at the table as he had the previous day.

'Can I get you anything?'

'No, thanks.'

Neither of them spoke and the silence grew heavy. Nell moistened her lips. 'I…' She couldn't think of anything to say.

Rick's gaze speared to hers. 'Shall I tell you what occurred to me overnight?'

Her mouth dried though she couldn't have explained why. She gave a *please continue* shrug.

'I wondered if there was the slightest possibility that by staying here it meant John Cox had the chance to remain close to his other child?'

It took a moment for that inference to sink in. In a twisted way, she could see how he could make that leap. Without a word she went to her important documents drawer and pulled out a folder. She opened her mouth to try and explain its contents only to snap it shut. She shoved the folder at Rick instead. The contents could speak for themselves.

He stared at her for a moment and then riffled through the enclosed sheaf of papers. A frown lowered over his face even as his chin lifted. For a moment he looked like a devil. One who'd cajole with dark temptations that could only end in destruction and ruin. Her heart kicked in her chest.

She swallowed and looked away.

'This is a paternity test your father had done…twelve years ago.'

'That's correct. He arranged for that test when he and my mother divorced. As he said at the time, he had no intention of being financially responsible for a child that wasn't his.' Only the tests had shown beyond a shadow of a doubt that she was his daughter.

And that he was her father.

Rick slammed the folder shut. 'God, Nell, that man's a nightmare of a father!'

She turned back and raised an eyebrow. 'Snap.'

He rocked back and then a grin crept across those fascinating lips of his and a light twinkled in those dark eyes and some of the awkwardness between them seeped away. 'Okay, you got me there. I'll pay that.'

And then he laughed, and the laugh completely transformed him. It tempered the hard, insolent edges and made him look young and carefree. It made him breathtakingly attractive too, in a dangerous, thrilling way that had her blood surging and her pulse pounding.

She swallowed. 'On that head, though…' She nodded at the folder. 'I can't say I blame him. My mother isn't the kind of woman who has ever let the truth get in the way of a…good opportunity.'

Her mother was in the Mediterranean with husband number four the last she'd heard, which was about three times a year. Oh, yes, her family—they were the Brady Bunch all right.

Rick clasped his hands behind his head and leaned back. She wondered if he knew precisely how enticing that pose was to a woman—the broad shoulders on display, those biceps and the hard chiselled chest flagrantly defined in the tight black T-shirt angling down to a hard flat abdomen… and all in that deceptively open, easy, inviting posture.

She bet he did.

Even with all of that masculine vigour on display, it was

his eyes that held her. He surveyed her until she had to fight the urge to fidget. She reached for another shrug—a *pray tell, what on earth do you think you're staring at?* shrug. She was pretty certain she pulled it off with aplomb, but it didn't stop him staring at her. A ghost of a smile touched his lips. 'I'm starting to get the hang of those.'

She squinted at him—a *what on earth are you talking about?* squint. 'I'm sorry, you've lost me.'

He lowered his arms. 'For all of these years, here I was thinking you had the best of everything.'

She flicked her hair over her shoulders. 'Of course I did. I had the best education money could buy. I had designer clothes, piano lessons and overseas holidays. I had—'

'Parents who were as good at parenting as mine.'

She swallowed. 'One shouldn't be greedy.' Or self-pitying. 'Besides, they were merely products of their own upbringing…and they had their good points.'

'Name one.'

'We've already uncovered one. They didn't betray each other so badly that I was the cuckoo they thought I might be. I'm not John's secret love child and therefore I'm not your mystery sibling.'

'Just thought I'd ask.'

She hesitated. 'I did wonder…'

'What?'

'Would your mother be able to tell you anything that might be of use?'

She didn't like to ask about Rick's mother—she'd been a prostitute. Nell had a lot of bones to pick with her parents, but she'd never had to watch her mother sell her body. She'd always known where her next meal was coming from. She'd had a warm bed to retreat to. She'd been safe. She gripped her hands together. She was *very* grateful for those things.

Rick shook his head. 'She developed dementia a few years ago. It's advanced rapidly. Nine times out of ten, she doesn't recognise me these days.'

Oh. Her heart burned for him. 'I'm sorry.'

He merely shrugged. 'What are you going to do?' He said it in that casual, offhand way, which only made her heart burn more fiercely.

She clapped her hands together in an attempt to brisk the both of them up. 'Well, I had another thought too. We should go and check out John's cottage. It's been empty since he went into hospital. I mean, I know it was cleaned, but maybe it'll contain some clue.'

'It could all be a hoax, you know?'

'For what purpose?' She didn't believe it was a hoax. Not for a moment. And when she made for the door, Rick rose and followed.

They picked their way through the overgrown garden—across the terrace to the lawn and then towards the far end of the block. Whittaker House had been built on generous lines in more generous times. The house and grounds sprawled over the best part of a city block. No wonder her father wanted her to sell it.

She wasn't selling! But it all needed so much attention. She bit back a sigh. It was all she could do not to let her heart slump with every step they took. It had all been so beautiful once upon a time.

'Hell, Princess, this looks more like years rather than months of neglect.'

'John was sick for a long time before he had to go into the hospice. He had a young chap in to help him, but…' She shrugged and glanced around. Her father hadn't maintained any of it. 'There are a lot of vigorous-growing perennials here that have self-seeded and gone wild. It looks worse than it is.' She crossed her fingers.

'Do you see any self-seeding marigolds?'

He'd adopted that tone again. 'I'm afraid marigolds are annuals not perennials. They need to be replanted each year.'

'Why go to all that bother?'

'For the colour and spectacular blooms. For the scents and the crazy beauty of it all. Because—'

She slammed to a halt and Rick slammed right into the back of her. 'What on earth—'

He grabbed her shoulders to steady her, but she didn't need steadying. She spun around and gripped his forearms. '*You'll find a clue where the marigolds grow.*'

His face lost some of its cockiness. And a lot of its colour. She couldn't concentrate when he stared at her so intently. She sat on the edge of the nearest raised bed and rubbed her temples. 'When did I find out my mother didn't like marigolds? John told me when I wanted to plant some of my own.'

Rick sat beside her, crushing part of a rampant rosemary bush. The aroma drifted up around them.

'And why did I want to plant marigolds?' *Oh, but...* 'He couldn't have known, could he?'

'Couldn't have known what?'

She turned to him. 'After he chased you away that day he gave me my very own garden bed to tend.'

'And you grew marigolds?'

She shook her head. 'I wanted to, but I didn't. You see I had this old chocolate box tin and it had pictures of marigolds on it and I showed it to John and told him that's what I wanted to grow.'

Beside her, Rick stiffened. 'A tin?'

She nodded.

'What happened to the tin, Nell?'

'I put all of my treasures in it and…' But it had been a secret. John couldn't have known. Could he?

'What did you do with them?'

'I buried them here in the garden. After the policeman left. I snuck out in the middle of the night and buried them when nobody could see what I was up to.' She turned to meet his chocolate-dark eyes. 'And I never dug it back up.'

He swallowed. 'Okay, so all we have to do is try to find

where you buried it.' He leaned back on his hands as if he hadn't a care in the world, but she'd seen beneath the façade now. 'I bet you've long forgotten that?'

No. She remembered. Perfectly.

She leaned back on her hands too, crushing more rosemary until the air was thick with its scent. She drew a breath of it into her lungs. 'Doesn't that remind you of a Sunday roast?'

He didn't say anything.

'What are you afraid of?' She asked the question she had no right to ask. She asked because he kept calling her Princess and it unnerved her and she wanted to unnerve him back.

'Where I come from, Nell, Sunday roasts weren't just a rarity; they were non-existent.'

He said her name in a way that made her wish he'd called her Princess instead.

He leaned in towards her. 'And what am I afraid of? I'm afraid this isn't some hoax your gardener has decided to play and that everything he's said is true. I'm afraid I have a thirteen-year-old brother somewhere out there growing up by the scruff of his neck the way I did and with no one to give him a hand.'

Her stomach churned.

'I'm afraid he's going to end up in trouble. Or, worse, as a damn statistic.'

She pressed a hand to her stomach and her mouth went so dry she couldn't swallow.

'Is that good enough for you?'

It wasn't good. It was *horrible*. Her parents might not have been all that interested in her, but she hadn't been allowed to roam the streets unchecked or at risk of being taken advantage of. Her parents might not have been interested in her, but she had been protected.

'I remember exactly where I buried it, Rick.'

He stared and then he half laughed. 'You're full of surprises, aren't you?'

She leapt up and dusted off her shorts. 'We'd better hope John put it back in exactly the same spot or we're going to be spending a lot of time digging.'

She led the way to the garden shed. She grabbed a spade, secateurs and a couple of trowels. And gloves. Rick merely scoffed when she asked if he'd like a pair too. 'On your own head be it,' she warned. 'We're heading for the most overgrown part of the garden.'

He took the spade and secateurs before sweeping an elegant bow. 'Lead the way, Princess.'

It was crazy, but it made her feel like a princess. Not a princess on a pedestal, but a flesh and blood one.

She led him across to the far side of the garden. 'I'll trade you a trowel for the secateurs.' He handed them to her and she cut back canes from a wisteria vine gone mad. 'That's going to be a nightmare whenever I find the time to deal with it,' she grumbled. She cut some more so he had room to move in beside her. 'Believe it or not, there's a garden bed there.'

She trimmed the undergrowth around it, found the corners. It wasn't as big as she remembered, but that still didn't make it small.

She moved into the centre of it, stomping impatiens and tea roses. She closed her eyes and shuffled three steps to the right. She took a dolly step forward and drew an X on the ground. 'X marks the spot,' she whispered.

CHAPTER THREE

RICK STARED AT the spot and cold sweat prickled his nape. What the hell was he doing here?

To run now, though, would reveal weakness and he *never* showed weakness. In the world where he'd grown up weakness could prove fatal.

Not showing weakness and acting with strength, though, were two different things. When Nell took one of the trowels from his nerveless fingers, he couldn't do a damn thing about it. He couldn't move to help her. He couldn't ask her to stop.

'The spade will be overkill, I expect. The ground is soft and although it felt like I'd dug for a long time I was only ten so I expect the tin shouldn't be buried too deeply.'

It was only when she dropped to her knees in the dirt that Rick was able to snap back to himself. 'Princess, you'll get dirty.'

She grinned, but she didn't look up. 'I like getting mucky in the garden.'

She certainly knew how to wield a trowel.

'Cupcakes aren't the only things I'm good at, you know?'

'I didn't doubt for a moment that you'd be a gardening expert too.' He wondered if he should climb into the garden bed and help her. Except she looked so at home and he had a feeling he'd only get in the way. 'Can I help?'

Her grin widened. 'Nah, you just stand there and look pretty.'

He couldn't help it. He had to grin too.

'I can cook other things too. I'll cook you a Sunday roast some time and then you'll know what I meant about the scent of rosemary.'

Something hard and unbending inside him softened a fraction. Digging in the garden, grinning and teasing him, she was the antithesis of the haughty, superior woman she'd turned into yesterday. He could see now that he'd done something to trigger that haughtiness because Nell used her supercilious shrugs and stuck her nose in the air as a shield. The same way he used his devil-may-care grins and mocking eyebrows.

As he continued to stare at her, some parts of him might be softening, but other parts were doing the exact opposite. He adjusted his stance and concentrated on getting himself back on an even keel.

He wasn't letting a slip of a girl—any girl—knock him off balance.

'Princess, I admire cooking and gardening skills as much as the next man, but it's all very domestic goddessy.' A bit old-fashioned. He was careful to keep the judgement out of his voice and the mockery from his eyebrows. He didn't want her getting all hoity-toity again.

'Oh, that'd be because—'

She froze. It was only for a second but he was aware of every fraction of that second—the dismay on her face, the way the trowel trembled and then the stubborn jut of her jaw. She waved a hand in the air, dismissing the rest of whatever she'd been about to say.

He frowned. *What on earth...?*

Metal hitting metal made them both freeze. With a gulp, Nell continued digging. Rick collapsed onto the wooden sleeper that made the border for the bed and tried to ease the pounding in his chest.

Within a few moments Nell had freed the tin, brushed the dirt from its surface along with the dirt from her knees.

She dropped the trowel at Rick's feet and settled herself beside him. The tin sat in her lap. They both stared at it as she pulled her hands free of the gloves. She reached out to trace the picture on the lid.

'Marigolds,' he said softly.

She nodded.

'Why didn't John let you plant marigolds here?'

'Because my mother didn't like them, remember?'

'Nobody would've seen them all the way down the back here.'

She lifted a shoulder. 'I found it was always best not to make waves if one could help it.'

'I decided on an opposite course of action.'

She glanced up with a grin, her green eyes alive with so much impish laughter it made his chest clench. 'You did at that. I'm going to take a leaf out of your book and fill this entire garden bed with marigolds.'

Good for her.

She held the tin out to him. 'Would you like to do the honours?'

His mouth went dry. He shook his head. 'They were your treasures.' He couldn't help adding, 'Besides, you could be wrong and maybe John never knew about the tin.'

'I'm not wrong.'

Her certainty had his heart beating hard and fast.

She sent him a small smile. 'Well, here goes.' And she prised the lid off.

An assortment of oddments met his gaze. Silly stuff one would expect a ten-year-old to treasure. And from it all she detached a small gold locket that he recognised immediately. She held it out to him and his heart gave a gigantic kick. 'When I buried this I swore that if I ever had the chance I'd give it to you.'

'Nell, I couldn't—'

She dropped it in his hand. 'Even now it brings me no

joy. It reminds me of the trouble it caused. Throw it away if you want and spare me the bother.'

His hand closed about it and his heart thumped. In kid-speak their exchange of gifts had been a token of friendship. Not that the adults had seen it that way. But the locket shone as brilliantly for him now as it had back then.

'While I keep this.'

She held up the tin aeroplane he'd given her and a laugh broke from him. He took it from her and flew it through the air the way he used to do as a boy. 'You really did keep it.'

'I wasn't a defiant child. I generally did as I was told.' Her lips twisted. 'Or, at least, I tried to. This was the one thing I dug my heels in about.'

Along with this big old relic of a Victorian mansion. He wondered why it meant so much to her.

'I should've dug my heels in harder about the rest of it too, Rick. I'm sorry I didn't.'

He handed her back the plane. 'Forget about it. We were just kids.' And what chance did a timid ten-year-old have against bullying parents and glaring policemen?

'Hey, I remember those—' he laughed when she pulled out a host of cheap wire bangles in an assortment of garish colours '—the girls at school went mad for them for a while.'

'I know and I coveted them. I managed to sneak into a Two Dollar Shop and buy these when my mother wasn't looking, but she forbade me from wearing them. Apparently they made me look cheap and she threatened to throw them away.'

So instead Nell had buried them in this tin where no one could take them away from her...but where she'd never be able to wear them either. Not even in secret.

She dispensed quickly with a few other knick-knacks—some hair baubles and a Rubik's Cube—along with some assorted postcards. At the very bottom of the tin were two stark white envelopes. The writing on them was black-inked capitals.

One for Nell.

One for him.

With a, 'Tsk,' that robbed the moment of its ominousness, she handed them both to him and then proceeded to pile her 'treasures' back into the tin and eased the lid back on. 'Do we want to rip them open here or does it call for coffee?'

'Coffee?' His lip curled, although he tried to stop it.

'You're right. It's not too early for a drink, is it?'

'Hell, no. It has to be getting onto three o'clock.'

'I don't have any beer, but I do have half a bottle of cheap Chardonnay in the fridge.'

'Count me in.'

He carried the spade, the secateurs and the letters. She carried the trowels and the tin. It touched him that she trusted him with her letter. He could simply make off with both letters and try to figure out what game John Cox was playing at. But the gold locket burned a hole in his pocket and he knew he wasn't going anywhere.

Besides, Nell had been the one to decipher the clue and dig up the tin. So he helped her stow the garden tools and followed her across the weed-infested lawn, along the terrace and back into the kitchen. He set both letters onto the table. Nell washed her hands, collected two wine glasses and the bottle of wine.

He took the bottle, glanced at the label and grinned. 'You weren't joking when you said cheap, were you?'

'Shut up and pour,' she said cheerfully. 'When it's a choice between cheap wine and no wine…'

'Good choice,' he agreed, but a burn started up in his chest at all this evidence of the Princess fallen on hard times.

He handed her a glass, she clinked it with his and sat. He handed her the letter. She didn't bother with preliminaries. She set her glass down, tore open the envelope, and scanned the enclosed sheet of paper.

Rick remained standing, his heart thudding.

With a sound of disgust she thrust it at him. 'I don't like these games.'

Rick read it.

Dear Miss Nell,
If you think he's worth the effort, would you please pass these details on to him?
Yours sincerely,
John Cox.

She leapt up and snatched the letter back. 'He calls you "him" and "he's".' She slapped the sheet of paper with the back of her hand. 'He doesn't even have the courtesy to name you. It's…it's…'

'It's okay.'

She stared at him. She gave him back the letter. 'No, it's not.' She took her seat again and sipped her wine. She didn't grimace at its taste as he thought she would. In fact, she looked quite at home with her cheap wine. He'd have smiled except his letter burned a hole in his palm.

'And just so you know,' she added, 'the details there are for his solicitor.'

Rick didn't think for a moment that John had left him any money. It'd just be another hoop to jump through. Gritting his teeth, he slid a finger beneath the flap of the envelope addressed to him and pulled the letter free.

At least it was addressed to him.

Rick
If you've got this far then you have the approval of the only woman I've ever trusted and the only woman I have any time for. If you haven't blown it, she'll provide you with the information you'll need for the next step of the journey.

It was simply signed *John Cox.*

He handed the letter to Nell so she could read it too. It seemed mean-spirited not to. She read it and handed it back. 'Loquacious, isn't he?'

Rick sank down into his chair.

'The solicitor, Clinton Garside, is wily and unpleasant.'

'Just like John Cox.'

She shook her head and then seemed to realise she was contradicting him. Based on all the evidence Rick had so far, 'wily and unpleasant' described John to a T. 'I never knew this side of him. He was quiet, didn't talk much and certainly wasn't affectionate, but he was kind to me.'

Maybe so, but he still hadn't let her plant marigolds.

Nell glanced at Rick and it suddenly hit her that he was only a step or two away from abandoning this entire endeavour.

She didn't know why, but instinct warned her that would be a bad thing—not bad evil, but bad detrimental. That it would hurt him in some fundamental way. As the messenger of the tidings she couldn't help feeling partly responsible.

You have enough troubles of your own.

Be that as it may. She owed Rick. She owed him for what had happened fifteen years ago. She owed him for letting herself be browbeaten, for not being strong enough to have defended him when that had been the right thing to do. She might only have been ten years old, but she'd known right from wrong. She had no intention of making the same mistake now.

She straightened. 'Clint will give you the runaround. He'll tell you he won't be able to see you for weeks, and that's not acceptable.'

'Nell, I—'

'If you have a sibling out there who needs you—' she fixed him with a glare '—then it's unacceptable.'

His lips pressed together in a tight line. He slumped back in his seat without another word.

Nell pulled her cellphone from her handbag and punched

in Clint Garside's number. 'Hello, it's Nell Smythe-Whittaker. I'd like to make an appointment to see Mr Garside, please. I know he's very busy, but it's rather important and I was hoping to meet with him as soon as possible.'

'I'll just check his appointment book,' the receptionist said.

'Thank you, I appreciate that.' She searched her mind and came back with a name. 'Is that you, Lynne?'

'It is, Ms Smythe-Whittaker.'

'Please, call me Nell. How's your husband coming along after his football injury? Will he be right to play the first game of the season? All the fans are hoping so.'

'We think so, fingers crossed. It's nice of you to ask.'

Exactly. And in return…

'There's just been a cancellation for Wednesday afternoon at three-thirty. Would that suit you?'

'Wednesday at three-thirty,' she repeated, glancing at Rick. He shrugged and nodded. 'That's perfect! Thank you so much, Lynne. I really appreciate it.'

She rang off and stowed her phone back into her bag. 'Three-thirty Wednesday,' she repeated.

'So you're intent on holding my hand?'

An edge had crept into his voice. She sat a little straighter and lifted her chin. 'It'll speed things up.'

'Why are you so intent on helping me get to the bottom of all this?'

She reached out to clasp the stem of her wine glass, twirled it around and around on the table. She lifted a shoulder. 'There are a few different reasons. Guilt, for one. Your father has been dead for eight months and I've only found the time to give you his letter now.'

'If he was my father.'

If.

'You had no idea what that letter contained. If you did…'

'I'd have tried to deliver it the same day! And I'd have quizzed John to within an inch of his life, but that's beside the point. I should've found the time to deliver it to you sooner.'

'You've had a lot on your plate these last eight months. You've no need to feel guilty.'

'The locket,' she whispered. 'It caused you so much trouble.'

'We were just kids, Nell. None of it was your fault.'

That wasn't true. 'I still feel badly about it.'

He reached out and for a moment she thought he meant to take her hand; at the last moment he pulled his hand back. 'I wish you wouldn't.'

He hadn't touched her but warmth threaded through his eyes. His mouth had lost its hard edge, replaced with a gentle sensuality that threatened to weave her under its spell. She knew in her bones that Rick would know how to kiss a woman and mean it.

It took all her strength to suppress the thrill that rippled through her. She fumbled to find the thread of their conversation again. 'The police labelled you a thief and a liar,' she forced herself to say. 'They thought you bullied me into handing the locket over. Those labels stuck.'

'Not my fault, Nell. And not yours.'

Because he seemed to want her to, she nodded.

'Anything else?'

'John,' she sighed. 'I can't help feeling he'd want me to help you and…I don't owe him, but he was kind to me.'

He shot back in his chair, his eyes cold.

Her heart thumped. 'I'm not trying to justify his behaviour to you. That's shocking and unforgivable.' But Rick would never have found the marigold tin without her help and what if there was further nonsense to be endured during the solicitor's appointment?

All of the hard angles had shot back into Rick's face. A lazy devil's smile hovered about his mouth, but it didn't reach his eyes. She pulled herself up, lifted her chin and gave the most speaking shrug in her armoury. 'Of course, if you'd prefer I didn't attend the appointment on Wednesday, obviously I won't.' She reached for her glass and took a sip, pretending it was something French and priceless.

Just like that, Rick laughed and the devil leached out of him. 'What a pair we are.'

'What are you talking about?'

He dismissed that with a flick of his fingers. 'If you think it'll make the meeting more profitable then I'd appreciate your presence.'

She took another sip, glad this time that it was just plain old Chardonnay. 'Okay.'

'What's more, I'll thank you in advance and mean it. Thank you, Nell.'

'You're welcome.'

'This, however—' he lifted his glass and drained the last mouthful '—is awful.'

She feigned outrage, but he only grinned. 'I know where Garside's office is. It's on the high street, right?' She nodded. 'Would you like to grab a coffee beforehand?'

'Oh.' Her face fell. 'That's a really nice idea, Rick, but—'

'You have other plans. No sweat.' He rose as if it were of no consequence. She wished it felt that way to her. Coffee invitations had been few and far between these last few months. 'I'll see you out the front at three-twenty-five.'

She rose too. 'Right.'

'Correct me if I'm wrong, Nell… You don't mind if I call you Nell, do you?'

Nell suppressed a shudder at the wet smile Clint Garside turned on her. 'Not at all.'

'I was under the impression that the business you wished to discuss concerned yourself.'

She forced her eyes wide. 'Oh, but it does, Mr Garside. It's just before we get to that I was hoping we'd be able to clear up this little matter for Mr Bradford and my family's former employee, the late Mr John Cox. It's been such a weight on my mind.'

'Well…of course, of course.'

He smoothed his hair back and sent her another greasy smile. He barely glanced at Rick. She'd forgive him the smarminess, but she wouldn't forgive him for ignoring Rick. He had no right to his snobbery. He had no right thinking he was better than Rick.

'You have to understand, however, that it may take my staff and I some time to locate the file. It's an older case and I'm sure you appreciate—'

'Oh, I do hope not.' Nell crossed her leg and smoothed a hand down the bodice of her dress. 'Once that document is found I was hoping to discuss the possibility of selling Whittaker House with you. I wanted to know if you'd be interested in handling the conveyancing of the property for me?'

She traced fingers along the V-neck of her dress, drawing the solicitor's eyes there, and she could've sworn that beside her Rick was trying not to laugh. She didn't dare glance at him for fear that a fit of giggles might overtake her.

She tossed her hair back and assumed the most superior posture she could. 'Of course, I couldn't possibly consider that while I have loose ends like this one hanging over my head.' She sighed and made to rise. 'Perhaps you'll be so kind as to call me once you've found the relevant documentation and then we can take it from there.'

'Oh, please sit, Nell. Let's not be too hasty.' Clint Garside rushed around the desk and urged Nell back into her seat. 'Let me just have a quick look to see if they're near at hand after all.'

'Why, of course.' She beamed at him. 'I can't tell you how much I appreciate all the trouble you're taking.'

Rick snorted. Clint glanced at him sharply and Nell reached out to touch the solicitor's arm and recapture his attention before elbowing Rick in the ribs. 'The file?' she reminded him gently.

'Oh, yes.' He was all smarmy smiles again. He patted her hand before trotting over to a filing cabinet on the other side of the room. *Ugh!* Behind his back, she wiped her hand down her skirt. The man had a touch like a dead fish.

'Bingo!' Clint turned with another wide, wet smile and held a file aloft. And for no reason at all her heart started to hammer. Was this the moment Rick would discover the identity of his sibling?

'So...' Clint sat across from her at his desk again, the file closed in front of him '...about Whittaker House...'

Beside her, she could feel Rick bunch up with tension. 'Yes, it's such a responsibility owning a house like that, but...' She gave a delicate little cough and glanced sideways to indicate Rick. 'Perhaps we can take care of this matter first and then...talk in private?'

His eyes gleamed. 'Why yes, of course.'

He opened the file and glanced at what she supposed must be John's instructions. 'There's nothing too difficult here. The late Mr Cox left a letter for Mr Rick Bradford should Mr Bradford ever come to collect it. The letter will need to be signed for, of course.'

'Of course,' she echoed.

'But, before that can happen, Mr Bradford has to provide a password.'

The air left her in a rush. Her entire body slumped like a deflated balloon before she had the foresight to shake herself upright again. She turned to Rick, trying to swallow her panic. *A password?*

'You will only get one chance, Mr Bradford.'

Acid burned her throat. 'Oh, Rick...'

He merely grinned at her, those dark eyes dancing. 'Don't sweat it, Princess.' He turned to the solicitor. 'The password will be Marigold.'

'That's correct.'

Marigold? He was a genius!

'All you now need to do is sign here.' Clint handed Rick

a pen without looking at him and indicated where he should sign. His lack of courtesy grated on her. Hadn't the people around here heard that Rick's name had been cleared?

Ah, but there's no smoke without fire. Her lip curled at the narrow-minded pettiness of it all.

Rick read the short statement, signed and took the letter from Clint's outstretched hand. He clasped her shoulder briefly. 'Thanks, Nell.'

And then he left. She wondered if she'd ever see him again.

Seven and three-quarter minutes later Nell made her escape from Clint Garside. With what she hoped was a breezy wave to Lynne, she shot outside to drag a breath of air into lungs that had cramped.

'Hey, Princess.'

She spun around to find Rick leaning against the wall just outside the door. One leg slightly raised, knee bent so his foot rested on the wall behind too. The epitome of casual indolence and she had to swallow to contain the leap of joy her heart gave at seeing him.

Slowly, she eased a breath of air out of lungs that had cramped up in an entirely different way. Rick wore a pair of dark denim jeans and a white business shirt, top button undone—no tie—and with the sleeves rolled up to his forearms. He looked like a model for a jeans commercial.

'Everything okay?'

She should be the one asking that. She swallowed and nodded and tried not to swoon in relief that he'd waited. 'I wasn't sure if you'd still be here.'

'Why not?'

That intent dark gaze watched her as if…as if she were worth watching, she realised. As if he liked not just what he saw, but…her. As if he liked *her.*

No doubt it was all just a trick of the light. And if it wasn't it'd just be smoke and mirrors. Rick had a reputation where women were concerned. Flirting would be as natural as breathing to him.

'I thought you might like to be alone to read John's letter.'

He glanced away and she took a step closer. 'What did it say?'

One of those broad shoulders lifted. 'I haven't opened it yet.'

She stared at those shoulders and bit her lip. A hum started up in her blood. She stretched out her toes to prevent them from curling.

'The street didn't seem like the right place. I'd prefer more privacy than that.'

Did he want to go home? Or maybe he wanted privacy, but didn't want to be totally alone? 'You could come back to Whittaker House with me if you like.'

One corner of his mouth hitched up. It made her blood chug. 'You're dying of curiosity, aren't you?'

'Absolutely,' she agreed. 'But there are cupcakes at my place. There's a Salted Caramel with my name on it.'

'Is there one for me?'

She gave an exaggerated roll of her eyes. 'Of course there is. I would never be so cruel as to eat one in front of company without offering them around first. You can have the Cherry Cheesecake and the Bubblegum if you like.'

'Sold!' He pushed away from the wall and fell into step beside her. 'Did you drive?'

She shook her head. 'It's only a five-minute walk—did you?'

'Nah, it's only about two minutes from Tash's.'

They walked along in silence. She was aware of the heat and magnetism he gave off, of the grace with which his tall body moved and the confidence in his strides—shortened to match hers at the moment. With each step she took, her awareness of him grew.

'You were magnificent back there, you know?'

'Me? You were the one who guessed the password!'

'You had that slimy solicitor eating out of the palm of your hand.'

She snorted. 'That was nothing more than him being overtaken by his own greed.'

'You played him to perfection. I went into that meeting determined to stamp my mark on it, but…'

She pushed a strand of hair behind her ear and dared to meet his gaze. 'But?'

'You were an absolute delight to watch and I didn't want to interrupt you. I can't remember the last time I enjoyed myself so much.'

Her cheeks warmed. 'I was pretty good, wasn't I?' she said because she didn't want him to see how much his words touched her.

He threw his head back and laughed. 'Did you crush him like a bug when I left?'

'I was tempted to, but no.'

He eased back to survey her. 'Why not?'

She kept her gaze straight ahead. 'It doesn't do to make enemies.' She had enough of those as it was. 'He thinks I'm exploring my options and that he's number one on my go-to list. Besides, I didn't want to burn our bridges where he was concerned until after you'd read your letter.' Who knew when they might have to consult with him again?

He didn't say anything so she forced herself to smile up at him. 'I'll save squashing him for another day.'

Her heart started to thump. Hard. She had to tread carefully—very carefully. She was in danger of turning this man into her Sir Galahad. Just as she'd done as a ten-year-old…and throughout her early teens—the fantasy boy who'd ride up on his white charger and rescue her.

She scowled and picked up her pace. Well, she was no damsel. And Rick Bradford wasn't a Sir Galahad in anybody's language.

CHAPTER FOUR

NELL BUSTLED ABOUT the kitchen, putting the coffee on to percolate, arranging some of those sugary confections with their over-the-top frosting and decorations onto a plate and setting it on the table.

While Rick was aware of Nell's activity, all he could focus on was the letter he'd placed on the table. Sun poured in through the windows over the sink and a warm breeze wafted through the wide open back door and the kitchen gleamed in spotless—if somewhat crowded—cleanliness. And yet none of it could hold his attention.

The envelope sat on the table and the black capitals seemed to sneer at him. He deliberately turned to Nell. 'When did you move back in here, Princess?'

'Friday.'

His head snapped back. 'Friday? As in five days ago?'

'That's right.' She poured out two mugs of steaming coffee. She wore another frock. This one was white with cherries printed all over it and she had a red patent leather belt cinched at her waist.

She'd moved in on Friday, met all of her weekend orders, had dealt with the suit *and* had found the time to help him out too? And she hadn't complained. Not once. She hadn't made him feel as if he were in the way or as if she had more important things to do.

Why?

Because of a silly incident fifteen years ago and a sense

of responsibility to a dead man? He dropped into a chair, his chest heavy.

She sat too. She glanced at the letter, but she didn't ask about it. Instead, she selected a cupcake and cut it into quarters, sliced one quarter in half and with the crumb delicately held between thumb and forefinger she brought it to her mouth. Her lips closed about it and she let out a breath, her eyes half closing.

He swallowed. If the taste and texture of salted caramel did that to her, he wondered what she'd look like if she licked whipped cream from his—

He shot back in his chair, hot and hard. Hell! Where had *that* come from? Gritting his teeth, he tried to shake his mind free from the scent of sugar. He gulped coffee instead and scalded his tongue.

'Ignoring it won't make it go away.' She broke off another crumb. He averted his gaze as she lifted it towards her mouth. She was silent for a moment. 'You really aren't sure yet if you do want a brother or a sister, are you?'

He'd already told her that. 'You don't get it?' Why he'd expected her to understand he couldn't begin to explain. They might've grown up in the same neighbourhood, but they came from completely different worlds.

'I think I do. You're afraid this unknown sibling will reject you.'

Her candour sliced into the heart of him. He held himself tight so he couldn't flinch.

'I'd be afraid of that too.'

The simple admission eased some of the previous sting. 'Who in their right mind would reject you, Princess?'

'I know. It's inconceivable, isn't it?' She lifted her nose in the air and gave an elegant shrug, but it was so over the top he found himself biting back a grin.

He let a part of the grin free and reached for a cake.

'You're afraid your history—having been to jail and

whatnot—will mean they won't want anything to do with you.'

He bit into the cupcake, barely tasting it.

'And yet you're also afraid your sibling could be on the same path you were, that he or she may need help.'

It took all of his strength to swallow without choking. Acid churned in his stomach.

'There's no easy answer to any of that, is there?'

He couldn't bear to look at her. He wasn't sure he could stand the sympathy he suspected he would find in her face. He pushed his chair back and sat side on to the table.

'You do know you don't have to address those concerns yet, though, don't you?'

Very slowly, he turned back to her. Her face wasn't full of sympathy, but rather no-nonsense practicality.

'You can find out who this sibling is and then make the decision about whether to approach them or not.'

She had a point. In fact she made a very good point. He straightened. If all was well and good in his sibling's life, he could walk away without a pang.

Liar.

If all weren't well, maybe he'd find a way to help them anonymously.

Or maybe he'd introduce himself. Maybe he'd give family another shot and—

He clenched his eyes and closed his mind to that possibility. It was too soon to think about it, too soon to get caught up in the fairy tale Nell harboured—that this would end well for everyone. This was the real world and, more often than not, in the real world things didn't work out.

That didn't change the fact that on this point she was right—he didn't need to make every decision at this current moment in time. He went to reach for the envelope when she said, 'It's also occurred to me…'

She bit her lip. It made her look incredibly young. He pulled his hand back. 'What?'

She grimaced. 'What if John left a letter for your sibling with sleazy solicitor Garside—to be opened at some future date?'

He stiffened.

'What if at some time in the future this sibling turns up on your doorstep? Wouldn't it be better to…' She trailed off as if she didn't know how to finish that sentence despite all of her surface polish.

His hand clenched to a fist. 'You're saying forewarned is forearmed?'

They stared at each other for a moment. Eventually she shook her head. 'I don't know what I'm saying.'

Her chin lifted. 'Yes, I do. I'm saying read the darn letter, Rick, and then maybe you'll enjoy your cupcake.'

It surprised a laugh out of him. The Princess had changed from the shy little kid and the awkward teenager. He wanted to ask her about the transformation, only he suspected she'd chide him for changing the subject and avoiding the obvious.

And she'd probably be right.

He tore open the letter. He tried not to think too hard about what he was doing. It didn't stop the skin of his scalp tightening over until it became one big prickling itch.

The envelope contained a single sheet of folded paper. His hand trembled—just for a fraction of a second—and that sign of weakness make him want to smash something. He glanced at Nell to see if she'd noticed, but she was intent on reducing her cupcake to a pile of crumbs. He let out a breath and unfolded the sheet of paper.

He stared and stared.

And then he let loose with the rudest word he knew.

Nell jumped. Her chin shot up. 'I beg your pardon?'

'Sorry,' he growled. Not that he felt the least bit remorseful.

She moistened her bottom lip and he was suddenly and ravenously hungry. For a moment it seemed that if he could lose himself in her for an hour he'd find the answer to ease the burn in his soul.

As if she'd read that thought in his eyes, she drew back, but pink stained her cheeks and her breathing had grown shallower. If he wanted, he could seduce her. Right here, right now.

If he wanted...

A harsh laugh broke from him. Oh, he wanted all right, but there was always a price to pay for seducing a woman. The price for this woman would be too high.

He leapt out of his chair and wheeled away, his hands clenched to fists.

'Please don't punch a wall. I already have enough holes to mend.'

Her words couldn't drag even a ghost of a smile from him.

'I take it, then, that you recognise the name John has given you?'

Name? *Ha!* He wheeled back and thrust the letter at her. With a wary glance up at him she took it. She stared at him for two beats more, looked as if she wanted to say something, and then with the tiniest of shrugs turned her gaze to the letter.

She frowned. She turned it over and then back. She held it up to the light. The frown deepened to a scowl. She slammed it down to the table. 'But this doesn't make sense!'

'It's obviously some kind of code.'

'A code?'

She swore then too and it surprised him so much his head rocked back.

'Of all the mean-spirited pieces of spite!' She leapt up, hands clenched and eyes narrowed, as she paced up and down beside the table. 'Not only does he spend your *entire* childhood ignoring you—' she flung an arm out '—but now he plagues you with nonsense and taunts you with a carrot he keeps whisking out of reach.'

She ended on an incoherent growl of frustration. Rick eased back to lean against the wall. The Princess wasn't just cross—she was hopping mad. In fact, she was a great big ball of boiling rage.

She stabbed a finger in his direction. 'If I could get hold of him now I'd make his ears burn, let me tell you.' She slammed a hand to the table. 'Well, we'll just crack that code! And to hell with him!'

She glanced at Rick, stilled and then rolled her shoulders. 'What?'

'Who are you really angry with, Princess?'

The colour leached from her face. 'I don't know what you're talking about.' She took her seat and crossed her legs, polished and smooth once more.

He sat too. Even though he knew he should leave.

She pushed the sheet of paper back across to him. 'All of these letters and numbers—they have to mean something.'

Did he really want to bother with any of this? He raked both hands through his hair and fought the exhaustion that washed over him. If he walked away now, what would be the worst-case scenario?

The answer came to him too swiftly. He reached for a cupcake, needing the sweetness to counter the bitterness that rose up through him. The worst-case scenario would be at some point in the future to come face to face with a younger version of himself—a kid he could've helped. A kid he'd chosen to reject in the same way John had rejected him. How could he justify walking away to that kid when he'd had the chance to discover the truth?

Could he live with that?

Maybe, but in his bones he knew he didn't want to.

Damn it all to hell!

He came back to himself to find Nell copying the code onto a notepad. 'What are you doing?'

'Making a copy.'

'Why?'

She'd taken this too personally—as if John had lied to her.

'I'm going to do an Internet search on codes tonight to see what I can find out.'

'Nell, this isn't your problem.'

'That's not what it feels like.' She finished and pushed the letter back towards him. 'Besides, it won't hurt to have a copy.'

He supposed not.

'C'mon.' She rose. 'We haven't checked John's cottage yet. There might be a box or two of his belongings left behind, something that might give us a clue.'

He rose. What he should do was thank her for her help, and tell her this was no longer her problem. Except…it wouldn't hurt to check out where John Cox had spent over thirty years of his life. It might give him a sense of the man. He'd take anything to gain some leverage in this wild goose chase.

And then he could leave.

For good.

He couldn't prevent a sense of déjà vu when they stepped out of the back door and made their way across the terrace. The yellow heads of dandelions waved in the breeze. Nell pointed to one. 'I've always kind of liked them. They're cheery, don't you think? I must've spread a whole forest of them throughout the garden. I loved it when they turned puffy and I could blow their seed heads and set them free. I used to think if I could blow the entire seed head off in one breath and make a wish it'd come true.'

'Did your wishes ever come true?'

She lifted an eminently elegant shoulder. 'I expect one or two must've, I made so many. Law of averages would suggest so.'

She was lying. He wasn't sure how he knew. Maybe it was the way she lifted a hand to her face to brush an imaginary strand of hair back behind her ear. Maybe it was the way she studiously avoided meeting his gaze.

And maybe he was watching her just a little too closely? Gritting his teeth, he forced his eyes to the front.

They passed the garden shed. They moved beyond Nell's first flowerbed until they reached the very back of the property. Nell pushed open a gate in a six-foot-high bamboo fence to reveal a cottage on the other side. Rick followed. 'You'd have no idea this was here if you didn't know about it.'

'That's the point. Heaven forbid that one should catch a glimpse of where the hired help live.'

He couldn't tell from either her voice or her bearing whether she subscribed to that view or not. She didn't give him the time to figure it out either, but strode up the two steps leading to the cottage's veranda and reached for the door handle…and then came up short when it didn't budge. She turned back to him with a shrug. 'Locked. I wonder where the set of master keys for the property can be?'

He knew how to pick a lock…

Nell moved back down the steps, dropped to her knees and reached beneath the veranda. When she drew her hand back she held a key.

It hit him then that he wouldn't be able to just walk away. Nell knew his father and this property like no one else did. If he wanted to solve this mystery he was going to need her help.

Nell was going to be the key.

Nell tossed the key to Rick.

He caught it as if he'd been catching curve balls all of his life. Which was probably true. She bit back a sigh. She couldn't change Rick's past any more than she could change her own.

'You can do the honours,' she told him.

'Why?'

She blinked. 'What on earth do you mean—why?' She didn't feel like explaining her ambivalence. 'Because you're closer.'

'Was closer,' he corrected.

How was it possible for this man to divine her private moods so accurately? *Who are you really angry with?* She shied away from that one. 'As far as I know, this place hasn't been disturbed in months. If there're any creepy-crawlies in there you can encounter them first.'

'I'm not buying that for a moment, Princess. I just saw the way you stuck your hand beneath the veranda. You're not afraid of spiders or insects.'

'What about ghosts?' The words shot out of her before she could pull them back. She grimaced at his raised eyebrow. 'Not a literal one. Ghosts from the past.'

She ruffled out the skirt of her dress to give her an excuse not to look at him. 'This area was always out of bounds to me when I was a child. I'm still not feeling a hundred per cent easy being here.'

'Princess, you own this cottage. It's yours. You have every right to be here.'

She lifted her chin and considered him. He raised that eyebrow then, as if daring her. She plucked the key from his fingers, stuck it in the lock and turned it. 'I don't even know if the power's still connected.' She swung the door open, but when she tried the switch, light flooded the room.

She stepped inside with Rick at her heels. The door led straight into the living room. 'I've never been in here before,' she murmured, 'so I don't know the layout.'

This room and the adjoining kitchen were sparsely furnished but, other than a faint layer of dust, it was remarkably clean and tidy. She strode across to the kitchen area and hunted through the cupboards. 'There's some crockery, cooking utensils and cutlery, but there doesn't seem to be anything personal,' she said, turning back to the living area.

'Not much in here either,' Rick said, closing the drawer of the sideboard.

'Maybe we'll have more luck in the bedrooms.'

But, other than a bed, a mattress encased in plastic—presumably to protect it from the dust—and some linens, they found no trace of John Cox's presence in either of the two bedrooms. It was as if he'd been washed away when the cleaners had come in. Whoever her father had hired, they'd done their job to perfection.

Nell dropped to the wooden chair that sat at the desk in the smaller of the two bedrooms. Had John used this room as a study? If so, what had he studied? What, other than gardening, had he been interested in?

Other than avoiding his paternal duties, that was.

She glanced at Rick. She couldn't tell what impression the cottage had made on him. If any.

He turned as if he'd felt the weight of her gaze. 'You were hoping we'd find something.'

'Of course I was. Weren't you?'

'I thought it a fool's mission from the beginning.'

Oh, great. She glared at the ceiling. So not only was she a spoiled little rich girl, but she was a fool too? She straightened when she realised what she was staring at. 'A loft hatch.' She rose and set her chair beneath it and then gestured for Rick to investigate further.

'If there's anything at all up there, Princess, it'll only be porn magazines.'

'Look, I'm not tall enough to reach it properly so just humour me, okay?'

He didn't move. He just stared at her instead. She lifted her arms and let them drop. 'If I have to go and get the ladder from the shed to do it myself I will.'

With a smothered something she was glad she didn't catch, Rick hauled himself up on the chair and pushed the loft cover to one side. Pulling himself up, he peered inside.

Nell surveyed the way his forearm muscles bunched

and the promise of bulging biceps. Not to mention the long clean line of his back. Her heart pitter-pattered. Her fingers curled into her palms, even as her tongue touched the corner of her mouth.

Rick had been a good-looking youth, but it was nothing to the man he'd become. And in those jeans there was no denying that he was all man.

And the stupid fluttering in her throat reminded her that she wasn't the kind of woman who was immune to Rick's particular brand of masculinity. Not that she had any intention of doing anything more than looking.

'There's something up here.'

That snapped her to. 'What is it?'

If only it'd give them another piece of the puzzle. Or, barring that, a clue as to how to solve that stupid coded message.

'I'm going up.'

With that, he disappeared completely into the ceiling space. Nell paced down below. 'What is it?' she called up again.

'Some kind of box.'

'Are there any photos in it? A family tree or birth certificates or—'

His face appeared at the hole and he laughed down at her. 'You really are the eternal optimist, aren't you?'

Her face fell.

'It's locked,' he said. 'Here—I'll pass it down to you.'

She had to stand on the chair to reach it. When she was on the ground again, he swung himself back down beside her. 'Don't worry, Princess. I'm a dab hand at picking a lock.'

She couldn't drag her gaze from the box.

'Nell?'

She swallowed and forced her gaze up to his. 'We won't need to pick the lock.' She handed him the box and reached up to open the locket at her throat. She removed the tiny key it contained.

His gaze narrowed. 'Where did you get that?'

She touched the locket. 'This was my grandmother's. And that—' she nodded at the box '—is her jewellery box.'

He stared at her and the lines around his mouth turned white. 'John Cox stole your grandmother's jewels?'

She laughed. It held little mirth, though it was better than sitting in the middle of the room and bawling her eyes out. 'I don't think he stole them. I think he probably saved them.'

Comprehension dawned in his eyes. 'From your father?'

'From my father.' Before she'd died, her grandmother had owned a couple of nice pieces. Nell had thought them long gone.

He slung an arm about her shoulders and led her back into the living room. He placed the box on the tiny kitchen table and pushed her into one of the two chairs. He sat in the other. Even though he'd removed his arm she could still feel the warm weight of it and the lean coiled power of his body as he'd walked beside her. He smelt like dust and something smoky and aromatic like paprika.

'Aren't you going to open it?'

Of course she was. It was just…she'd never expected to see this box again. She missed her grandmother. Seeing this only made her miss her more.

His face darkened. 'Or would you prefer to take it back to the big house and open it in private?'

Her spine stiffened. Her chin lifted. 'I never once thought you a thief, Rick Bradford!' A temptation, definitely, and one she fully intended to resist, but a thief? No.

For a moment his slouch lost some of its insolence. 'Goes to show what you know, Nell Smythe-Whittaker. My teenage shoplifting is on police record.'

'I'm not even going to dignify that with an answer.' She pulled the box towards her, unlocked it and lifted the lid.

Her breath caught. 'Oh, her rings! I remember her wearing these.' She had to swallow a lump. 'My grandfather gave her this one.' She touched a large diamond ring. 'And this emerald belonged to her grandmother. The gold signet belonged to her mother.' She lifted them out one by one and passed them to Rick.

'The diamond and the emerald might fetch you a bit.'

'I couldn't sell them!'

She knew he wouldn't understand her sentimentality, but…her grandmother was the only person in her life who'd loved her unconditionally.

'How old were you when she died?'

'Seventeen.'

'That must've been tough.'

Sure, but it was nothing compared to all Rick had been through in his life. 'Oh, look.' She lifted a shoulder in a wry shrug. 'John has left me a letter.'

He rolled his eyes. 'He's turning out to be the regular correspondent.'

Dear Miss Nell,

If you've found your grandma's box then I expect you know why I hid it. I'm sorry I couldn't rescue it all before your daddy got a hold of the diamond necklace.

She stopped to glance into the box. 'Yep, gone,' she clarified.

'We only have John's word it was your father who took it.'

'And my knowledge of my father.'

Rick straightened. Unfortunately, it didn't make his shoulders any the less droolworthy. 'Hell, Nell.'

'Hell's bells, Nell, has an even better ring to it,' she told him, resisting the sympathy in his eyes and choosing flippancy instead.

Who are you really angry with?

She cleared her throat and smoothed out the sheet of paper.

I know the old lady meant these for you, and I know you'd want to pass them on to your own daughters when the time comes.
Regards, John.

She folded the letter and put it back in the box. Silently, Rick put the rings back on top. Nell locked it. She pulled in a breath and then met his gaze. 'Rick, would you please put this back where you found it?'

His head rocked back. 'Why? You should at least wear this stuff if you're not going to sell it. You should at least enjoy remembering your grandmother.'

In an ideal world…

She moistened her lips. 'The set of master keys for Whittaker House are nowhere to be found. Until I find them I can't…' She halted, swallowed. 'What I'm trying to say is that I can't think of a safer place to keep them than where we found them.'

'You're forgetting one thing.'

'What's that?'

'*I* know where they are.'

'I've already told you that I don't believe you're a thief.'

'No, but I do mean to make you a proposal, Princess, and that might change how you feel about things.'

CHAPTER FIVE

NELL'S HEART STUTTERED at the casual way Rick uttered the word *proposal.* It held such promise and she knew that promise was a lie.

Oh, not a lie on his behalf, but on hers. She wanted to invest it with more meaning than he could ever hope to give it—a carry-over from her childhood fantasies of making things right over the locket.

The childhood fantasy of having one true friend.

But Rick didn't know any of that. The man in front of her might look like the boy who'd starred in her fantasies, but inside she didn't doubt that her boy and the real Rick were very different people.

Life hadn't been kind to Rick Bradford.

And she needed to remember he had no reason to think kindly or act kindly towards her.

He stared at her with those dark eyes and she drew a long breath into her lungs. 'Proposal?' She was proud her voice didn't tremble.

'I was going to leave Sydney at the end of the week.'

That didn't give them much time to crack John's code.

'I've holidayed long enough and it's time to be doing something.'

She couldn't help herself. 'What do you do for work?' Did he have a regular job?

'I usually pick up some building labourer's work here and there.'

So, that'd be a no then.

He grinned—a lazy insolent thing, as if he'd read her mind. 'I don't like being tied down to one thing for too long.'

She knew then he was talking about women and relationships too.

'I like my freedom.'

Given how his freedom had been curtailed in prison, she could understand that.

A prison sentence he should never have had to serve, though. A prison sentence he had served because a woman had taken advantage of him.

'What are you thinking about?' he suddenly barked and she jumped.

'How awful jail must've been.' It didn't occur to her to lie, but when his face turned grey she wished she had. 'I'm sorry you were sent to jail for something you didn't do, Rick.'

'It's all in the past.'

The words came out icily from between uncompromising lips and Nell had to suppress a shiver. He'd carry the scars of jail with him forever. She glanced down at her hands before lifting her chin. She had no right picking the scabs off those wounds. 'You said you *were* planning to leave Sydney, as in past tense. Have you changed your mind?'

His eyes blazed. He stabbed a finger to the table and dust rose up in the air around him. His crisp white shirt, his hands and hair all sported streaks of dust and cobwebs. She guessed the skirt of her dress wasn't in much better shape. It was the kind of carelessness that as a child had earned her rebuke after rebuke from her mother.

She forced her chin up higher. Well, her mother was off somewhere with husband number four and Nell was old enough to do what she darn well pleased. She didn't have to answer to anyone.

But those dirty streaks on Rick's shirt reminded her that while he'd been convicted of a crime he hadn't committed, it didn't necessarily make him a law-abiding citizen.

It didn't mean he wasn't a heartbreaker who'd take advantage of weakness when he saw it in others.

And you're weak.

She swallowed. Correction. She had been weak. Past tense.

He continued to glare at her with those blazing eyes but he didn't say anything. She made her voice as impersonal as she could. 'You were saying?'

He pushed away from the table and paced to the other side of the room before striding back. 'I'm going to get to the bottom of this bloody mystery!'

He spat out his *bloody* with so much anger she couldn't help wincing.

He dragged a hand down his face, glancing back at her with hooded eyes. 'Sorry.'

She shook her head, cursing her own prissiness. 'You don't have to apologise. I understand your venom.'

'You know what, Princess?' He took his seat again. 'I believe you do.'

She didn't want to follow that conversational thread so she merely said, 'I think it wise to try and discover who your sibling might be.'

'Except I've overstayed my welcome at Tash's.'

She doubted that.

'Besides, she's in love. I'm cramping her style.' He grimaced. 'And I can't stomach much more of her and Mitch's lovey-dovey stuff.'

That sounded more like it.

For some reason, the skin on her arms started to chill.

'So what I was going to suggest is that you let me use this cottage rent-free for the next few weeks. I mean, it's just sitting here doing nothing.'

The chill spread up her neck and down her spine.

'And in return I'll do some work on the big house.'

The chill disappeared. He didn't mean to take advantage of her after all?

'What kind of work?'

He lifted one lazy shoulder. 'Whatever repairs I manage to get to and maybe even some painting.'

That would be brilliant! She opened her mouth to snap up his offer before he could retract it, but a glance in his direction had her closing it again. Rick had a look in his eyes that she recognised. A look she'd seen in her father's eyes—an *I'm going to get my own way and I don't care by what methods* look.

She wasn't a pushover any more. Her father had discovered that and now Rick could too. She pushed her grandmother's jewellery box towards him. 'Put that back where we found it.'

'Is that a yes or a no to my proposal?'

'It's negotiations are underway but, regardless of the outcome, it doesn't affect the fate of the jewellery box.'

He leaned back and folded his arms. For a moment she thought he was going to refuse. And then she started. 'Heavens, where are my manners? Would you *please* put the box back in the ceiling?'

One side of his mouth hooked up. 'I wasn't waiting for a please, Princess.'

'I know, but there's no excuse for bad manners. Have you seen enough of the cottage to satisfy your purposes?'

'Yes.'

'Then I propose we go back up to the house and see if we can come to some arrangement that will satisfy mine.'

He laughed at that. She wished he hadn't. He looked younger, nicer, when he laughed and it had the potential to turn her to jelly.

She didn't need jelly but steel.

Without another word, Rick rose and placed the box back in the ceiling. Nell locked the door behind them and pocketed the key. Rick watched her, but he didn't say anything. In fact, neither one of them spoke on the walk back to the house.

When they reached it, Nell cleared her throat. 'I'd prefer to nail you down to specifics, Rick. How long do you think you'll stay?'

He shrugged. 'Can we start with a month?'

'Absolutely.' She pulled her no-nonsense business voice out and dusted it off. 'We can agree to a week-by-week arrangement if need be after that.'

'Fine.'

Was he laughing at her? She glanced across but couldn't tell. 'So, included in your four weeks' worth of repairs…' she walked through to the front of the house to the grand hall with its staircase that curved up to the first floor and pointed to the front door '…can you fix that?'

'Check.'

She didn't care if he was laughing at her. She tossed her head and walked into the grand parlour with its enormous bay window. 'Can you fix the hole in the wall?'

He walked over to it, tested it with his fingers, bent over to examine it more closely and the denim of his jeans stretched across those powerful thighs and taut butt and Nell had to swallow as her saliva glands kicked into overdrive. *Oh, my word.* Rick Bradford filled out a pair of jeans to perfection. Her fingers fluttered about her throat. Her eyes widened in an effort to take in as much of the view as they could. A hunger, deep and gnawing, that no number of cupcakes would assuage, racked her.

Rick turned. 'This doesn't—'

He broke off, a grin bold and sure spreading across his face. Folding his arms, he leant a shoulder against the wall. 'See anything you like, Princess?'

Heat scalded her face. She wished the floor would open up and swallow her. 'Don't be ridiculous.' But her voice came out at a squeak, which only made his grin widen.

She gestured to the wall. 'You were saying?'

Very slowly, he sobered and straightened. 'I'm not on offer, Nell. I'm not part of the bargain.'

'I never for one moment considered you were.' How could he cheapen not only her but himself like that? And then she remembered his mother had been a prostitute.

She closed her eyes and swallowed. If she hadn't been weak fifteen years ago, if she'd stood up for Rick, she could walk away from all of this now and…

Oh, who was she kidding? It didn't erase her sense of responsibility towards John. The way he'd treated Rick was beyond the pale, but there had to be a reason for all of this—something they couldn't see yet.

She forced her eyes open. 'Can we please get back to the task at hand?'

His lips twisted. 'Gladly.' He gestured to the wall. 'This looks like damage caused by something hard or heavy being banged against it.'

That'd be the removal men her father had hired to pillage the house of its expensive antiques.

'I can replaster it and then paint the entire room.'

That was even worth putting up with Rick's mockery!

'Then you have yourself a deal.'

He laughed. 'You have no idea, do you?'

'What are you talking about?'

'So far we've nailed down about a week's worth of work.'

Was that all?

'I'll fix the guttering that's falling off the outside of the house—that's another day's work.'

Wow. Um… 'What about painting the outside of the house?' It was badly in need of it.

He shook his head. 'That's too big a job for one person. Given the style and heritage of this place, it'd be best left to the professionals. Besides, I'm not sure you could afford the materials at the moment if money is tight.'

Her mouth dried. 'How much would it cost?'

'For paint, scaffolding and labour? I wouldn't expect you to see any change from twenty grand.'

So much? She needed to sit down. Only there wasn't a

stick of furniture in the room. And yet if she were to put her plan into action it would need to be done.

'I can ring around and get some quotes for you if you like?'

She nodded. 'I'll need it for the business plan I mean to take to the bank.'

'I know this is none of my business…'

She glanced up at him.

'But is this place really worth going into so much debt for?'

'Yes.' She'd made a promise—a promise she had no intention of breaking. Her hands clenched. She could make this work!

Rick walked across to her with that indolent loose-hipped stride that could make her mouth dry in a millisecond. He stopped less than two feet away. His hands went to his hips—lean, sexy hips—and he leaned in towards her with narrowed eyes. 'What are your plans for this place?'

A husband and babies—a family. Lots of laughter. And love. But until then…

'I'm going to turn Whittaker House into the most in-demand venue for high tea parties that Sydney has ever seen.'

He blinked. She waited for him to laugh and tell her she was crazy. Instead, he turned back to survey the room. 'That's a nice idea for an old place like this. What rooms are you planning to use as public rooms?'

'These two front reception rooms—the parlour and the drawing room—the dining room as it opens onto the terrace, and the library. They're all large rooms. For more intimate gatherings, there's the morning room and the conservatory.'

She took him through each of the rooms. They ended the tour in the dining room—a grand room with French windows that led out to the terrace. Rick walked around the room's perimeter, checking skirting boards, picture rails and the windows and doors. 'Everything looks in pretty good nick, just the odd minor repair here and there—nothing that some putty and a screwdriver wouldn't fix.'

She let out a breath.

'It could do with some freshening up, though.' He pursed his lips. 'I could paint the two front rooms and this dining room in a month.'

Her heart didn't leap with the same unadulterated joy as it had earlier.

He shuffled his feet. 'Actually, throw the library in too—there's not much to do in there.'

She bit her lip. 'How much will the materials cost?'

'Depends on the kind of paint you want. You'll need something durable. What colours were you after?'

'The Victorians weren't afraid of colour and these rooms are big enough to bring it off. I thought a peacock-blue and a jade-green for the two front rooms, maybe coral in here. The library is lined with bookcases and there's not a whole lot of wall to paint so maybe just a cream to prevent it from becoming too dark in there.'

How much would it all cost, though?

'This room opens onto the terrace and lawn. You might want to consider making this the green room to fit in with the garden theme and have the coral room at the front.'

'Oh, that's a nice idea.' She pulled in another breath. 'But how much is this going to cost me?'

He tapped a finger against his jaw before straightening and naming a figure that made her wince. She nodded. 'Okay, I can manage that.' Just. 'Rick, it looks as if you have yourself a deal.'

He sent her a sly smile. 'Not so fast, Princess—negotiations aren't over yet.'

They weren't?

'You drive a hard bargain.'

He'd have had an easy one if he hadn't been so honest.

'In exchange for all of this slaving away on your house, I now have an additional demand.'

She folded her arms. 'Which is?'

Just for a moment his gaze lowered to her lips. Her breath stuttered. Oh, he couldn't mean…?

They both snapped away from each other at the same time.

'That you provide me with half a dozen cupcakes a day. A working man needs to keep up his strength.'

She planted her hands to her hips. 'Rick, you can't eat six cupcakes a day. You'll rot your teeth and make yourself sick.' She stuck out her jaw. 'How about two cupcakes a day and I'll throw in some sandwiches?'

'Four cupcakes and some sandwiches.'

Did he eat properly? Tash was probably taking care of that at the moment. How was he off for money? Not that she could talk, but she was making enough to cover the food bill and she still had some in her savings account, which would cover the cost of paint and materials. Sure, he might be getting rent-free accommodation, but he wouldn't be earning while he was here. She blew out a breath. 'And I'll throw in a Sunday roast.'

'Now you're talking.'

'C'mon.' She led him back into the kitchen. Taking a seat at the table, she dragged a notepad towards her and wrote out a brief contract outlining what they'd agreed to. She signed it and then pushed it across to him.

'You think this necessary?'

'I've learned not to take chances.'

His eyes darkened. 'You're prepared to trust me with your Gran's jewels, but not take my word about our deal?'

'I told you already—I don't believe you're a thief.' She glared because he made her feel self-conscious. 'It doesn't necessarily follow, though, that I trust you.'

Rick's heart burned for her, mourned that wide-eyed little girl who'd smiled at him with such open-heartedness it had made him believe there were better things in the world than he'd experienced up to that point.

'That sounds like hard-won wisdom, Princess.'

She didn't answer. He signed her contract because he wanted her to trust him. For good or ill.

'You've changed, Princess. A lot.'

She snorted. 'You mean I'm not fat any more?'

'Don't use that word!' His voice came out sharper than he intended, but he couldn't help it. Reverberating through his head, all he could hear were insults—*You're a fat piece of useless lard! How could anyone love you? You're fat and ugly!* Horrible things flung at women by men who'd meant to wound.

Nell eyed him warily. He glared at her. 'You were never fat!'

Her gaze slid sideways. She lifted a shoulder. 'I was plump, and I was awkward and almost chronically shy.'

Those things were true. 'I always thought you were kind of cute.'

That made her look back at him. She tried to hide it, but he could tell she wanted to believe him. 'If that's the case,' she said eventually, 'then you were in the minority.'

He still thought her cute, but he had no intention of acting on it. She was still trouble. And he avoided trouble wherever he could. And power games. And complications. He pushed his shoulders back. 'So how'd you go from shy and awkward to polished and sophisticated?'

She waved that away. 'It's too boring for words.'

Her reluctance intrigued him. 'I'd like to know.'

She blew out a breath before jumping up to put coffee on to percolate. He was about to tell her she drank too much caffeine but then she proceeded to set out some of her extraordinary cupcakes and he decided to keep his trap shut.

'Blueberry Delight and Tutti-Frutti,' she said, pointing. She made coffee and sat again.

He raised an eyebrow. 'Well?'

'As you've probably gathered, I wasn't precisely the kind of child my parents had been hoping for.' She blew on her coffee. 'They'd hoped for some pretty, delicate little thing who did ballet and uttered childish whimsies that charmed everyone.'

He winced. Nell hadn't fitted that picture.

'When I became a teenager, my mother hoped I'd become a fashion plate who'd be eager to accompany her on her many shopping expeditions.'

'And your father?'

'Who knows? He'd have probably been happy if his golf buddies made comments about me becoming a heartbreaker and that he'd have to beat the boys away with a big stick.'

Did she know that was exactly how she could be described now?

'When my grandmother found out how miserable I was she set about helping me.'

'How?'

'She took me to a therapist who helped me overcome my shyness. She took me to a stylist who trained me in what clothes and make-up best suited me, and she found me an up-and-coming young hairdresser who was an absolute whizz.' She sipped her coffee. 'Obviously, it didn't all happen overnight.'

Rick unclenched a hand to reach for a cupcake. 'You know your parents were wrong to have such expectations?' They should both be horsewhipped for making her feel like a failure, because she hadn't met their specific designer mould. People like that shouldn't have kids.

'I do now.'

He took a savage bite of cake and frosting. 'I mean, would you ever do that to a kid?'

Her eyes flashed. 'No!'

He set the cupcake back on his plate and eyed her for a long moment. 'Why all this determination to avoid self-pity?'

Something inside her eyes hardened. 'Because, regardless of my gripes about my parents, I never had it as tough as you or Tash or even Crazy Cheryl who you went to prison for.' She gave a half smile. 'Cheryl used to throw stones at me whenever she saw me in the garden.'

It didn't surprise him. Cheryl's home life had been beyond shocking. But…there was more than one way to damage a kid.

'It's not a contest, Princess.' She was entitled to her pain and disappointment.

'Tell that to my parents.'

Exhaustion hit him at the expression on her face. 'It didn't work, did it?' He slumped back. 'Did they notice at all?'

'They noticed. It just took me a long time to realise that it didn't make any difference, that it didn't make them love me more. It just meant they didn't mind parading me around their friends so much.'

He wanted to swear, but he knew she wouldn't like it so he didn't.

'And then I realised I was wasting all of this time going to parties I didn't enjoy, buying clothes I didn't want and doing coffee on a weekly basis with women who called me their friend but who haven't had the decency to return my phone calls since calamity came calling.'

He did swear this time.

She transferred her glare to her coffee. 'That was when I decided to be done with all that and focus on something more important.' Her lips lifted. 'Like cupcakes.'

He'd have laughed except he suddenly saw it all too clearly, could see now why she'd done what she had.

'You handed your trust fund, your apartment, and your car over to your father because you wanted to make a clean break with your past.'

'Bingo, tough guy.' She might sound sophisticated and self-assured, but she couldn't hide the vulnerability that flickered through her eyes. 'Do you think that's stupid of me?'

'I think it was smart and brave. You don't need to be beholden to people like that.'

'Thank you.'

She smiled and for a moment he swore he saw glitter flickering at the edge of his vision. He blinked it away. 'There's one thing I don't get.'

'What's that?'

'Why are you fighting to keep this old relic of a house? Why don't you rid yourself of the responsibility?' And rake in some much-needed moolah while she was at it?

'This house belonged to my grandmother. She's the only person who loved me unconditionally. And she loved this house.'

She wouldn't have wanted it to become an albatross around her granddaughter's neck, surely?

'My parents lived here once they were married, not because it was convenient for the factory but because they wanted to be seen living in the Big House, as you call it. They never loved the place. They look at it and all they see are dollar signs. I look at it and…'

She didn't finish the sentence.

'And you see a Victorian teahouse.'

'You think that's dumb?'

'I think it's an interesting business plan with definite potential.'

She leaned towards him, her face alive. It was the way she'd looked at him fifteen years ago when she'd given him her locket. Only she wasn't a little girl any more but a woman. And he was a grown man.

Heat circled in his veins to pool in his lap. He surreptitiously tried to adjust his jeans, reminding himself about trouble and complications and grief and misery. He was *not* going to travel down that road with Nell. This wasn't a fairy tale. It wouldn't end well. He gritted his teeth. Business—this was just business.

'I've done my homework. High teas have become big

business in Sydney. Lots of clients are looking for themed party venues—something a bit different. I think Whittaker House will fit the bill perfectly. I predict my Victorian teahouse will become a big hit, not only for birthday parties, but for hen parties, bridal showers, anniversaries and family reunions too.'

He didn't doubt her for a moment.

'I know Whittaker House isn't Downton Abbey, but it does have its own charm and I happen to think other people would enjoy the location too.'

'Absolutely, but…'

Her face fell. 'But?'

He hated being the voice of reason. 'It'll take a lot of start-up capital to get the business off the ground.' The house would need a lick of paint both inside and out. The grounds would need to be not only wrestled into shape but manicured to within an inch of its life. She'd need to kit out the entire operation with suitable tables and chairs, pretty linens and crockery. It wouldn't come cheap.

'Which is why I'm preparing a business plan to take to my bank manager with projected costs, profits et cetera in the hope I can secure a business loan.'

'Which, unless you have some other asset you've not told me about, will mean putting Whittaker House up as collateral.'

He watched the fire leach out of her eyes. 'How'd you know that?'

It wasn't an accusation but a genuine bid for knowledge. 'I did a business course when I was in prison.'

She chewed her lip and nodded. Her glance sharpened. 'Do you have your own business?'

He shook his head.

'If you're as handy as you say, then maybe you should start up your own building business.'

He choked. 'Me?'

'Why not?'

'There have to be at least a million reasons!'

'And probably just as many why you should,' she said in *that* tone of voice. 'Well, I'm still going to put my proposal together and make an appointment with my bank manager. If I get no joy there then I'll have to find investors.'

'Which means the business is no longer your own.'

'Which isn't ideal, but it's better than nothing.'

He could click his fingers and make the money appear for her. If he wanted. For a moment he was tempted. He cut the thought off. He hadn't told Nell he was rich for the simple reason that he didn't want the news getting about.

She tossed her head. 'I bet there must be some kind of government initiative to assist fledgling businesses. I'll check into that too.'

He had to give her credit. She wasn't sitting around waiting for Prince Charming to swing by and rescue her.

She lifted her chin. 'And if it takes longer to get off the ground than I want, so be it.'

In the meantime she'd be stuck with the upkeep of the place. 'You know your grandmother's rings would bring in the kind of money you need.'

'Out of the question.'

Stubborn. He respected that, but it wouldn't pay the power bills.

She dusted off her hands. 'In the meantime, you're going to do some work on the place in return for rent-free use of the cottage.'

'And cupcakes.'

Her lips twitched. 'And sandwiches and a Sunday roast or two.'

Her eyes narrowed and he recognised the calculation that suddenly flashed in their brilliant green depths. What amendment to their deal would she try and come up with now? He folded his arms and waited.

She moistened her lips. 'If I help you crack that code

of John's, would you consider glancing over my business plan once I've written it?'

He grinned. 'Princess, if you can crack that code I'll write the darn plan for you.'

Her hand shot across the table. 'You have yourself a deal.'

He closed his fingers around her hand. His hand completely encompassed hers, but her grip was firm. He didn't want to let go.

'When do you want to move into the cottage?'

He kept hold of it, even though he knew it was dangerous. 'Tomorrow.'

She glanced at the clock. 'Oh, dear Lord!' She pulled her hand from his. 'I'll need to get my skates on if I'm to get it into any fit state to live in.'

'It's fine the way it is, Princess.'

'It most certainly is not!'

'There's absolutely no need to drag your cleaning lady out at this late hour.'

Her head lifted, her chin jutted out—so unconsciously haughty that it couldn't be feigned—and for some reason it made him want to laugh. 'I'll leave the key in the same spot. Will you be able to find it?'

'I'm sure I'll manage.'

Amazingly, she bundled up the remaining cupcakes into brown paper bags. 'Take them home with you.'

'An early down payment?'

'It'll stop me snacking on them. Besides, Tash and Mitch might like one or two.'

He couldn't have said why, but his heart started to burn. He almost did something foolish like invite her to have dinner with him, Tash and Mitch that evening. A crazy, foolish impulse.

Why on earth would the Princess want to have dinner with him? He rose, thanked her for the cupcakes and left.

CHAPTER SIX

RICK HAD JUST finished his last cupcake and a mug of coffee when Nell walked through the back door. She stopped short when she saw him. 'Hey.' She swallowed. 'How's it going?'

Lines fanned out from her eyes and her *frock*—yellow with big purple polka dots—looked rumpled and tired. He wondered what she'd been up to all day. She dropped her handbag on the table, glancing at his plate and mug. Before her face could twist up with suspicion he said, 'You can start using the front door if you like.'

A smile lit through her, banishing the lines around her eyes. 'You fixed it?'

He swallowed. A woman like her could make a man like him feel like Superman if he wasn't careful. 'It was no big deal. The wood had swollen. I filed it back, rehung it and it's as good as new.'

He tried to pull himself back. She might be a damsel in distress…or not. But he was no hero. He knew that and so did she. 'I did promise to earn my keep,' he reminded her.

'Well, yes, but I didn't expect you to start working the moment you moved in. I thought you'd take a day or two to settle in.'

Settle in? It didn't take much 'settling in' to unpack a single suitcase.

'You left cupcakes and sandwiches for me at the cottage.' The cottage had been spotless too—not a speck of dust to be seen. He wondered who she'd had come in and clean it at such late notice.

'Oh, that was just a neighbourly gesture. If I'd thought you'd want to start work today I'd have left you a key.' She stuck out a hip. 'Which rather begs the question—how did you get in?'

His stomach burned acid and he waited for that soul-destroying suspicion to wash over her face, for her to rush off and count the family silver. Ever since he'd been released from jail it was how people treated him. They didn't believe a man could pay his debt to society and then move on and make something of himself.

If he'd known at eighteen what he knew now, would he have still taken the rap for Cheryl, claimed the drugs were his rather than hers? He stared at the Princess and had a feeling that answer would still be yes.

Which meant he hadn't learned a damn thing.

Which meant he was still as big a sucker as he'd ever been.

He'd gone to prison a boy but he'd come out a lot wiser and a whole lot harder. He couldn't draw comparisons between Cheryl and Nell—their lives were too different—but the same protective instincts rose up in him whenever he looked at Nell now.

Ice washed over his skin. He had no intention of getting that close to anyone again—no intention of taking the blame for anything that would land him back in jail. Ever. Regardless of who it was.

'Oh, get over yourself, you idiot!'

He blinked at Nell's rudeness.

'If I trust you with my grandmother's jewels I'm going to trust you with the contents of my house. For heaven's sake, there's nothing left worth stealing anyway. My father long made off with anything of value.'

Genuine irritation rather than suspicion chased across

her face and he jolted back into the present. He rolled his shoulders.

'Is my security that bad?'

'It's not brilliant. You should install an alarm system. I, uh, got in through the back door.'

'But I locked it.'

'You need to remember to use the deadbolt.'

She sighed. 'An alarm system? I'd better put it on the list.'

She bustled about making coffee. She eyed the jar of instant he'd bought with distaste. 'Would you like another?'

'No, thanks.'

'Why didn't you make yourself a proper coffee? It's worth the effort, you know.'

'That coffee is yours.'

Very slowly she turned. 'And I'm guessing there's milk in the fridge with your name on it too and sugar in the cupboard?'

He shifted. 'People can get funny about things like that.'

She pointed her teaspoon at him. 'Let's get one thing clear right now.' She raised her voice to be heard above the gurgling of the percolator. 'You're welcome to help yourself to tea, coffee, bread, biscuits and whatever else is in the pantry while you're working. And—' she thrust out her jaw '—if I feel like having instant coffee I mean to help myself to your jar. You have a problem with that?'

He grinned. 'None at all, Princess.'

'Hmph.' She made coffee, sipped it and closed her eyes as if it were the first chance she'd had to relax all day. He wondered again what she'd been up to—hobnobbing with society types hoping to find an investor or three?

'Oh, I meant to ask. Is that your car out front?'

'Yup.'

'There's room to park it in the garage if you want.'

'There's a garage?'

'Come with me.'

With coffee cup in hand, she led him out into the garden. About halfway between the house and the cottage she veered left. Hidden behind strategically placed trees and shrubs squatted a substantial wooden building with three large wooden doors. She walked across to the cast iron fence, fitted a key into the lock and slid the fence back. The fence slid along on a kind of roller. From the footpath it'd be impossible to see that this part of the fence also acted as a gate.

'I had no idea this was here.' And he must've walked past this section of fence a hundred times. He turned to survey the garage. 'What did that used to be?'

'The stables, once upon a time.' She slid the gate shut again. It barely made a sound. 'They were converted eons ago, which is why the gate and the garage doors aren't automatic. Maybe down the track. Mind you, these big old doors have a certain charm I'd be loath to trade in merely for the sake of convenience.'

She took a sip of coffee. 'This bay here is free.' She lifted a latch and walked backwards until the door stood wide open.

He entered. And then stopped dead. A van, a bit like the ice cream vans that had done the rounds of the neighbourhood during the summers of his childhood, stood in the next bay along. Only, instead of ice creams, the van's sides were decorated with cupcakes. 'Candy's Cupcakes' was written in swirly pastel lettering.

He turned back to her, folded his arms and leant against the doorframe. 'Your business is obviously bigger than I thought.'

She drained her coffee. 'Yes.'

'Why didn't you tell me?'

For a moment her gaze rested on his shoulders. She shook out her arms as if an itch had started up inside her. His heart started pounding to a beat as old as time then too.

He gritted his teeth. He and the Princess were not going to dance that particular tango. 'Nell?'

She jumped. 'Sorry, I—'

She averted her face, but that didn't hide the colour on her cheekbones. Rick gritted his teeth harder.

'Sorry.' She turned back. 'I'm tired. Concentration is shot.' She gestured to the van. 'Everyone expects me to fail. Some have said so outright. Some have laughed as if it's a joke. Others have smiled politely while raising sceptical eyebrows. I don't need that kind of negativity in my life.'

'And you thought I'd react that way.'

She met his gaze. 'You did.'

'I…'

'You thought my little cupcake business was limited to a few deliveries on the weekend and nothing more. You didn't even begin to entertain the idea that I might also work Monday to Friday. But I do. I have a weekly schedule and I head out in Candy for the CBD to take cupcakes and coffee to the masses.' She lifted a shoulder and let it drop. 'Or, at least, to office workers. You won't believe the number of people who now treat themselves to a weekly cupcake for morning or afternoon tea.'

Wow.

'I thought you'd know better than to pigeonhole me like you did.'

Everything inside him stilled.

'You've been in jail. I know what people say about you. They think once a criminal always a criminal. They think a man like you can't be trusted and is only out for whatever he can get. And they're still going to think that when your name's cleared because it doesn't change the fact that you were in prison.'

Each word was a knife to the sorest part of him.

'*I* haven't treated you like that.'

She hadn't, but he kept waiting for her to. His stomach

started to churn. That was hardly fair, though, was it? She'd shown him nothing but…friendship.

'I also happen to know what people think of me—the pampered society princess who has never had to lift a finger one day in her life.' She strode over and stabbed a finger to his shoulder. 'Well, I'm not useless and I'm not a failure and I'm not…I'm not useless!'

He grabbed the finger that kept jabbing at him and curled his hand around it. 'You're not useless, Princess. You're amazing. Completely amazing and I'm sorry I misjudged you.'

She tried to tug her hand free but he wouldn't let her. 'You really are skint?'

She stopped struggling to frown at him. 'Yes.'

'Yet amid all of your own troubles you've found the time to help me.'

'Help or hound?'

He chuckled and a warmth he'd never experienced washed over him. 'Thank you for cleaning my cottage.'

'You're welcome.'

God, such vulnerability in those wide green eyes, such softness and sweetness beckoned in those lips. She smelt like sugar and frosting and all the things he'd ever longed for. An ache gripped him so hard he had to drag in a breath. 'Princess…' The endearment scraped out of him, raw with need and longing.

She swayed towards him, those green eyes lowering to his lips. The pulse at the base of her throat fluttered faster and faster. Her hand tightened in his.

He gripped her chin and lifted it, needing to taste her so badly he thought he might fall to his knees from the force of it. Desire licked fire through his veins. He moved in close—so close he could taste her breath—but the expression in her eyes froze him.

They glittered. With tears.

'Don't you dare kiss me out of pity.'

She didn't move out of his hold and he knew then she was as caught up in the grip of desire as him.

'Please, Rick. Don't kiss me because you feel sorry for me.'

The tears trembled, but they didn't fall. Every muscle he had screamed a protest, but he released her and stepped back. He swallowed twice before he was sure his voice would work. 'Pity was the last thing on my mind, Princess. So was guilt and feeling apologetic.'

It was just…he'd allowed himself to see her properly for the first time and it had blown him away. He needed to get away from her, to find a sense of balance again. 'I just…' he dragged a hand back through his hair '…I just think it'd be a really bad idea to kiss you.'

'Definitely.'

He glanced at her sharply, but he couldn't see any irony or sarcasm in her face.

She tossed her head. 'Besides, I don't want you or anyone else to think I'm taking advantage of you.'

He almost laughed. 'Take advantage of me?' That'd be the day.

She waved an impatient hand in the air. 'You know what I mean—seducing you so you'll fix up my house all spick and span.' She glared. 'I can stand on my own two feet.'

He glanced at Candy. 'I don't doubt that for a moment.' Did she ever take a day off?

'Right.' She smoothed down her skirt. 'Good. I had some keys cut for you—the front and back doors and the gate here in the fence.'

There was an awkward moment where she held them out to him and he tried to take them and they danced around each other, trying not to touch. In the end she tossed them in the air and he caught them.

'Now, if you don't mind…' She collected her coffee mug from where she'd set it on the ground. 'I'm going to go have a much-needed shower.'

'There's something else we need to talk about, Princess.'

She turned back.

'Those jewels can't stay in the cottage while I'm living there.'

'But—'

'I've been to prison, Nell, and I'm not going back. If those jewels go missing the finger will be pointed at me.'

'Not by me!'

She said that now. 'You need to put them in a safety deposit box, because I'm not risking it.'

The shadows in Rick's eyes told Nell exactly what prison had been like. Oh, not in detail, perhaps, but in essence. She suppressed a shiver. 'I didn't think of that,' she finally said.

When really what she wanted to say was *kiss me, kiss me, kiss me*. Not that kissing would do either one of them any good.

She stroked her fingers down her throat. It might help iron out some kinks…scratch an itch or two.

Oh, stop it! Be sensible.

She cleared her throat. 'Is it okay if I collect them first thing in the morning? As soon as it opens I'll take them to the bank for safekeeping.'

For a moment she thought he might insist on her taking them now, but eventually he nodded. 'First thing.'

With a nod, she backed out of the garage and fled for the house, leaving him to close up, or to drive his car around, or whatever he pleased.

She sat, planted her elbows on the kitchen table and massaged her temples. Dear Lord, she had to fight this attraction to Rick because he was right—kissing would be a bad, *bad* idea. It'd end in tears—hers. The minute Rick discovered his sibling's identity he'd be out of town so fast she wouldn't see him for dust.

As a kid she'd dreamed of Rick riding up and rescuing her—like the prince rescuing Rapunzel from her tower.

That had all been immature fantasising mixed up with guilt, yearning and loneliness. It hadn't been based on any kind of reality.

It hadn't factored in Rick going to jail.

It hadn't factored in that she could, in fact, save herself.

She shot to her feet. 'I am a strong woman who can make her dreams come true.'

She kept repeating that all the way to the shower.

During the next week Nell marvelled at the progress Rick made on the house. He transformed the parlour from something tired and battered into a room gleaming with promise. He'd done something to the fireplace—blackened it, perhaps—that highlighted the fancy tile-work surrounding it. The mantelpiece shone.

It didn't mean they became cosy and buddy-buddy, though. They edged around as if the other were some kind of incendiary device that would explode at the slightest provocation.

When Nell returned home in the afternoons she and Rick would chat—carefully, briefly. Rick would either continue with whatever he was doing or retire to the cottage. She'd start watching one of the spy movies she'd borrowed from the video store or would investigate code breaking on the Internet. To no great effect.

'Oh, for heaven's sake! This is a waste of time.' She slammed down the lid of her laptop. Biting her lip, she reached out to pat it. The last thing she needed was to have to go out and buy a new computer.

'Not having any luck?'

She glanced up to find Rick in the doorway. Wearing a tool belt. Her knees went a bit wonky. She swallowed first to make sure her voice would work. 'I've trawled every website and watched every darn movie ever made about codes and code breaking and yet I'm still none the wiser.'

She pulled the piece of paper on which she'd scrawled the code towards her.

'LCL 217, POAL 163, TSATF 8, AMND 64, ARWAV 33, TMOTF 102,' she read, even though she'd memorised it.

'I don't get it, not one little bit, and I'm tired of feeling stupid!'

He didn't say anything.

She leapt up. It took an effort of will not to kick the table leg. 'Why on earth did he make it so hard?'

'Because he doesn't want me to find the answer.'

'Why tell you at all then?'

'To chase away his guilt? To feel as if he were doing the right thing and giving me some sort of chance at figuring it out?'

To chase away his guilt? In the same way he'd chased Rick away? Her stomach churned. And then she frowned. 'Rick, it's Saturday.'

'Yup.'

'You don't have to work weekends.'

'Why not? You do.'

She blinked.

'I want to attach the new locks I bought for the parlour windows. I've been trying to work that code out all morning and now I want to hammer something.'

She blew out a breath. John's code had evidently left him feeling as frustrated as it had her. 'You haven't given me the receipts for those locks yet.'

His gaze slid away. 'I can't find where I put them. I'll hunt them up tonight and give them to you on Monday.'

That was what he'd said on Wednesday.

'I might not be rolling in money, but I have enough to cover the work you quoted me.' Besides, he couldn't exactly be rolling in it himself. 'Fixing up this house is exactly what I choose to do with my money.' Well, that and eat.

'And I had some questions about the library,' he added as if she hadn't spoken. 'If you have the time…'

Something shifted in the darkness of his eyes, but she couldn't tell what, only that it made her pulse quicken. She scowled. 'Are they questions I'll be able to answer?'

He grinned. It was swift and sudden and slayed her where she stood. 'Colour schemes and stuff.'

She stuck her nose in the air. '*That* I can do. I've been trained by the best. Piece of cake.'

'Speaking of cake…' His gaze searched the table.

She rolled her eyes. 'Yes, yes, there're cupcakes in the cake tin. Help yourself.' It suddenly occurred to her… 'I didn't make you any sandwiches. Would you like me—?'

'Nope, not necessary. Sandwiches Monday to Friday was the deal.'

'Was it?' When he grinned at her like that she forgot her very name and which way was up. She had no hope of recalling anything more complicated. She swung away. 'Nell,' she murmured under her breath. She pointed to the ceiling. 'Up.'

'Talking to yourself, Princess.'

The warm laughter in his voice wrapped around the base of her spine, making her shiver. 'Library,' she muttered instead, pointing and then leading the way through the house.

'It's a nice room,' Rick said from the doorway.

She tried to stop her gaze from gobbling him up where he stood. 'I used to spend a lot of time in here as a child. It was my favourite room.' She hadn't disturbed anyone in here.

'You were a bookworm?'

The look he sent her had her rolling her shoulders. 'Uh-huh.'

He moved into the room. 'Do you mean to keep all of these books in here when you open for business?'

She hadn't thought that far ahead. 'All of the leather-bound collections will probably remain in here—the room wouldn't earn the term library if there were no books.' She trailed her fingers along one wall of glass-enclosed bookcases. 'But I'll take my old worn favourites upstairs. They're a bit tatty now. I suppose I could put some pretty ornaments on the shelves here and there for interest and—'

She stopped dead and just stared.

'What?' Rick spoke sharply and she suspected the blood had all but drained from her face.

'*POAL*,' she managed faintly.

'*POAL 163*,' he corrected.

She opened one of the bookcase doors and dropped to her knees in front of it. She ran a finger along the spines. 'I'd have never got it. Not in a million years.'

'What are you talking about?' He strode across to her, his voice rough and dark. 'Don't play games with me, Nell.'

She grabbed his arm and dragged him down to the floor beside her. 'Look.' She pointed to a book spine.

'*Lady Chatterley's Lover*,' he growled. 'So what?'

'*LCL*.' She pointed to the next spine along. '*Portrait of a Lady—POAL. The Sound and the Fury, A Midsummer Night's Dream, A Room with a View, The Mill on the Floss.* These are my first-year literature texts from university. She pulled out *Lady Chatterley's Lover* and handed it to him. 'Open it at page two hundred and seventeen.'

She had no idea if she were right or not, but…

He turned the pages over with strong, sure hands. They both caught their breath when the page revealed a single sheet of folded paper.

He handed her back the book and she could have sworn his hand trembled. 'It could just be some note or other you made.'

Her heart burned as the conflicting emotions of hope and pessimism warred in his dark eyes. 'It could be,' she agreed, though she didn't think it was. There'd only be one way to find out—if he unfolded it—but she didn't try to hurry him. She couldn't imagine what it must be like to suddenly discover you had a sibling you'd never heard about before.

He leapt to his feet and strode away. She swallowed back the ball of hurt that lodged in her throat. He wasn't obliged to share the contents of John's message with her. She stared instead at the book and waited for him to say something, her heart thumping and her temples pounding.

'A *T*.'

She turned to find him holding up the sheet of paper bearing the single letter. His lips twisted. 'He did say he wasn't going to make it easy, didn't he?'

She gathered up the other five books. 'Obviously it's going to spell something out. Maybe a name.' This room was devoid of any furniture so she took the books back through to the kitchen and set them on the table before walking away.

'Where are you going?'

He spoke sharply and she spun around. 'I thought you might like some privacy.'

He cocked an eyebrow, all tough-guy badness in a blink of his eye. 'Aren't you curious?'

She wished she could say no. 'Of course I am. I'm burning up with it.'

'Then stay. We'd have never got this far if it weren't for you.'

She didn't need any further encouragement. She moved back to the table and watched silently as he laid the six letters out. When he was done they both stood back and stared at it.

T H E S U N

A growl left her throat. 'What the bloody hell is that supposed to be and what's all this nonsense of *X*, *C* and *M* on the last card?'

'Roman numerals,' Rick said, leaning over to look at them more closely. 'I think it's a date.'

He straightened. Nell stiffened. '*The Sun*,' they said at the same time, referring to a Sydney newspaper.

'I'm not good with Roman numerals.' Nell moved back around to her computer. 'But there's bound to be a site on the web that can tell us what that date might be.'

Rick didn't move. 'It's the twenty-sixth of May in the year of two thousand and thirteen.'

That was almost a year ago now. 'The paper is bound to archive its back issues online.' She went to the newspaper's homepage, flicked through several screens and found the paper issued for the twenty-sixth of May. All the while she was aware of Rick standing on the other side of the table, unmoving, and it started to worry her. 'Rick!'

He started and glanced her way. It hit her that inactivity wasn't good for him. 'Here, I found the right paper. I think. You do the search while I organise cake and coffee.'

Searching would keep him focused. Organising afternoon tea would give her something to do with her hands other than fidget.

He took her seat. 'What do you reckon—search the personal classifieds for some coded message?'

She growled. 'It better not be too coded.'

He laughed and turned his attention back to the computer screen.

She measured out coffee and set cupcakes on a plate—Citrus Burst, Pine Lime, Vanilla Cream and Café au Lait. She almost swiped a finger through the frosting of the coffee cupcake, but pulled back at the last minute. It had taken her a lot of work to lose her teenage puppy fat. As soon as she had her Victorian teahouse up and running she meant to enjoy the fruits of her labours to her heart's content and to hell with her waistline. But until then…

Her nose curled. It was a well-known fact that slender women received more chances and better opportunities than plump women. It wasn't fair. In her opinion it was downright scandalous, but she didn't have too many assets—a big house that was threatening to crumble down around her, her ability to cook the best cupcakes on the planet and a trim figure. She meant to make the most of all of them while she could.

Behind her, she sensed Rick's sudden stillness. She swung to him. 'Well?' Her voice came out choked, as if she had an entire cupcake lodged in her throat.

'There's a message here…for me.'

Her heart gave a giant kick. 'Does he tell you…?'

'No. The message reads: *Rick Bradford. Many Happy Returns.*'

The twenty-sixth of May was his birthday?

'*You've exceeded expectations. For she's a jolly good fellow.*'

'She?' That couldn't be right, surely?

'She,' he repeated.

'Do you think that's some oblique way of saying your unknown sibling is a sister?'

'I think he's referring to you.'

Her?

'*Return on the thirteenth of March.*'

She slammed the plate of cupcakes to the table. 'Return where?' she shouted.

'I think he means to the classifieds in the newspaper.' He leaned back. 'Which means he put some thought into all of this before he died—paid for these ads well in advance. I wonder how many years' worth he organised.'

The intricacy of John's scheme stunned her. 'The thirteenth of March is only a couple of weeks away.' She bared her teeth. 'That is if he's referring to this year. There's no guarantee of that, of course.'

'*All will be revealed then if you have the eyes to see it.*'

She opened a kitchen cupboard just so she could slam it shut again. 'That's what I think of that!'

'And it ends with *Hip Hip Hooray!*'

'Oh, and that's worth its weight,' she snarled.

He laughed. 'He was right about one thing. You are a

jolly good fellow. I'd never have got this far if it hadn't been for you.'

'Well, of course you wouldn't!' she exploded, pacing up and down. 'That's the whole stupid point, isn't it? How could you ever have possibly traced that stupid code to bits of paper in *my* books? How would you have ever known about *my* stupid marigold tin? How dare he risk everything on something so…so tenuous! How could he risk… All of it hangs on such a thin thread that could've broken at any time.' She slashed a hand through the air. 'How could he know I'd keep helping you? How could he know you'd even stick around? How could he know that I hadn't sold the house?'

'He couldn't.'

She stared at the plate of colourful cupcakes and made a fist. Rick dragged the plate towards him out of harm's way.

'Princess, it's not worth getting all hot under the collar about.'

'Not worth…' She started to shake.

'You're really furious at him, aren't you?'

She had a feeling they weren't talking about John any more. 'Yes,' she gritted out. Because whether they were talking about her father or his, it was true on both counts. 'How dare he drag me into his nasty little game!'

Again, that counted on both heads.

'What right did he have? What…'

The air went out of her and she sat with a thump.

Rick leaned towards her, his eyes wary. 'Uh, Nell… you okay?'

She swallowed. 'Earlier you said that he might be trying to make himself feel better…to make amends.'

'Yeah, so?'

'That's what this is about. He wants me to make amends too.'

CHAPTER SEVEN

RICK PULLED UP short when he strode into the kitchen to find Nell drinking coffee and eating cupcakes.

At ten on a Wednesday morning.

He counted two cupcake wrappers, which meant she was steadily making her way through a third. He frowned. That wasn't the way to eat one of those cupcakes! Every mouthful should be savoured to the full.

She didn't look up. He rubbed the back of his neck. 'Good morning.'

She continued to glare at the table. 'Morning.' Bite. Chew. Swallow.

Okay, take two. 'I ducked out to grab a few supplies. I ran out of sugar soap and sandpaper.'

'You don't need to justify your movements, Rick. I believe you'll keep your side of the bargain. The how and when is entirely up to you.'

He should leave her be and get back to sanding and painting, keep it all on a work footing. He hesitated and then pulled out a chair and sat. 'You don't need to justify your movements to me either, but what on earth are you doing at home—' eating cupcakes as if they were nothing more extraordinary than a digestive '—when peak morning tea time is about to hit Sydney's CBD?'

She ate more cupcake. Her shoulders hunched. 'Candy has broken down.'

He grimaced. 'She's at the garage being repaired?'

More cupcake and more shoulder hunching. 'No.'

'Why not?'

Finally she looked at him. He tried not to wince at the lines of strain that bracketed her mouth. 'Because of these.' She held up a pile of opened letters. 'Bills.' She then proceeded to set each one down onto the table, barking out the amount due. 'It adds up to more than half of what I have left in my account. At the moment I'm not sure I can afford to get Candy fixed.'

Yet without Candy on the road she wouldn't be able to earn the money to pay those bills.

If there was something he'd learned in the last fortnight—other than the fact he really wanted to kiss her—it was that Nell worked like a Trojan. If anyone deserved to cop a break, she did.

'How much money are you expecting to come in from your party orders and how much do you have outstanding?'

She blew out a breath, pushed her plate away and pulled her laptop towards her. 'Let's see…' Her fingers danced across the keyboard.

He came around the table to peer over her shoulder. What he saw made him frown. 'Princess, there're half a dozen orders here—' big orders too '—from over three months ago and the bills are still outstanding.'

If her shoulders drooped any further they'd be on a level with the table. He pointed to her spreadsheet. 'Look—here, here and here.' The movement brought him in close so her hair tickled his jaw and the sugar-drenched scent of her made his mouth water. He moved back a few inches to stop himself from doing something stupid. 'These three orders on their own would cover the cost of your bills.'

'I know, but…'

She leapt up and he shot back, dodging her chair before it could do him a serious injury. She paced to the end of the table and then spun back, flinging an arm in the air.

'How do you make people pay? I've sent each of them

at least three reminder letters. I've spoken to them on the phone and each time I've been assured the cheque is in the mail. Funny thing is, though, none of those cheques have yet materialised.'

'Do you know if any of these people are in financial difficulties?'

'No! That's the thing. I mean I have written off a couple of debts because I found out…'

She'd written those debts off because she knew what it was like, hadn't she? Because she had an amazing ability to empathise with others—something he'd have never expected in someone from her background. But then he'd misjudged her on so many levels.

It didn't change several salient facts. 'Do you think it's either reasonable or responsible to order a party load of cupcakes if you can't afford it?'

For a long moment she didn't say anything. 'I shudder to think how many bills my father didn't pay.'

'They weren't your responsibility, Princess.' And in the meantime people with the wherewithal to pay took advantage of her. He ground his teeth together.

She merely shrugged. 'You want to know something funny?'

From the tone of her voice he suspected he wasn't going to find whatever it was either amusing or humorous. 'What's that?'

'Each of those people—' she gestured to the computer '—with the outstanding debts; I thought they were my friends.'

It took an effort of will to keep his shoulders loose and relaxed. Two things were certain. Firstly, these people were not friends and secondly, she couldn't afford to write those debts off.

'What you need to do, Princess, is hire a money collector.'

She gazed at him blankly.

'And, as you currently have me at your disposal...'

She stilled. For a glorious moment her eyes gleamed that extraordinary emerald-green that made him want to kiss her all over again. 'Ooh, I couldn't...'

'You have no choice.'

He'd had experience of money collectors from the other side of the fence—they'd visited his mother and grandmother on a too regular basis. But it meant he knew the grim and forbidding demeanour, and he knew how to come across as threatening without actually threatening someone illegally. He'd threaten this lot with exposure in the local paper if they didn't cough up.

She shifted from one foot to the other.

'You worked hard for that money.'

'I know, but...'

'Nell, if you don't have the stomach for this then maybe you need to rethink your plans for Whittaker House.'

She stiffened at that. Without another word she printed off those three bills and handed them to him. He glanced at them and nodded when he saw they contained all the information he needed—names, addresses and amounts outstanding.

'Please don't frighten them.'

'Of course not.' He crossed his fingers behind his back. After he was done they'd think twice before failing to pay a bill again.

'I mean...this will be seriously humiliating for them.'

He'd make sure of it. These people hadn't just humiliated Nell—they'd hurt her, had tried to bully her. They were supposed to be her friends, for goodness' sake!

'And just so you know...' she moistened her lips '...the Fenimores have a Rottweiler.'

He tried not to focus on the shine of her lips. Or on the sweet curve of her lower lip and the way it seemed to swell under his gaze. He snapped away.

This attraction between him and Nell was crazy. It

couldn't go anywhere. Acting on it would be a stupid thing to do.

But glorious.

He ignored the insidious voice and tried to concentrate on the conversation. 'Is he vicious?'

'Not in the slightest. He's a big softie. Call their bluff if they…' She lifted a shoulder.

He almost laughed at that, but it wouldn't have been a pretty laugh. He didn't bother telling Nell that he didn't respond well to threats. He'd deal with the Fenimores.

Before he left, however… 'Nell, sit. We need to have a tough talk.'

She eyed him uncertainly, but did as he asked. He knew these bills were merely the tip of Nell's financial troubles. He'd been working on that darn business plan of hers and there wasn't a bank manager in Sydney who'd lend her a red cent unless she put Whittaker House up as collateral. He told her that now in plain unvarnished English.

'But—'

'I'm not telling you this because I want to make your life difficult, but you need to know the truth.' The panic that raced through her eyes clutched at his heart. 'Nell, I know you loved your grandmother.'

'Yes, of course, but…'

But what did that have to do with anything? He could see the question in her eyes even if she didn't ask it out loud. 'How badly do you want to save Whittaker House? How badly do you want to turn it into a Victorian teahouse?'

She shot to her feet and clenched her hands so hard she shook. 'It's the most important thing in the world to me.'

Because she wanted to honour the memory of the only person who'd shown her unconditional love? Because she wanted to prove she wasn't useless and that she could make a success of her life? Because she had nothing else in her life? *Oh, Princess, you deserve so much more.*

The last thought disturbed him. He shook it off. 'You really want it more than anything?'

'Yes.' Her chin lifted.

Stop thinking about kissing her! 'So you're prepared to make sacrifices?'

'Of course I am!'

His heart grew heavy in his chest. 'You have a source of income that will get you started and keep you out of trouble for a long while. Nell, you need to sell your grandmother's diamond ring.' And probably the emerald as well.

The last of the colour leached from her face. She sat.

He found himself crouching in front of her and clasping her hands. 'It's not a betrayal of your grandmother.'

'Then why does it feel that way?'

'If she were here now, what would she tell you to do?'

'I...'

'Did she place more value on things rather than people?'

'No! She...' She gave a half-laugh full of love...and loss. 'She'd just want me to be happy. If she'd ever had to choose between her diamond ring or this house she'd have sold the ring in an instant.'

He waited and eventually she lifted her chin and squeezed his hands. 'You're right. It's time to be practical. My grandmother's spirit doesn't reside in a few pieces of jewellery.'

He stood and moved back. Holding Nell's hand when she was upset was one thing. Holding it when she fired back to life was altogether different.

Different and compelling and bewitching.

'Besides, those jewels would've been more trouble than they're worth. I'd have had to be constantly looking over my shoulder waiting for my father to try and take them.'

Rick had grown up among people like that, but it made his gut clench that the Princess had experienced it too.

'For heaven's sake, look at me! Sitting around here comfort eating and feeling sorry for myself. How pathetic!'

She was a lot of things, but pathetic wasn't one of them.

He shifted his weight. 'If someone offered you a pot of gold to get you out of this fix…and it'd mean you'd get to keep your grandmother's rings, would you accept it?'

She bit her lip and then shook her head. 'No.'

He breathed easier.

'I want to do this under my own steam.'

Good.

'So while you go and play bailiff I'm going to get my grandmother's ring out of the safety deposit box and make an appointment with a jewellery evaluator. An antique piece like that…it might even be worth placing in an auction.'

A coil of tension in his chest loosened at the colour in her cheeks and the sparkle in her eyes. *Way to go, Princess.*

'I think it might be a good idea for me to attend that appointment with you.'

She stared at him and then a Cheshire cat grin slanted across her face. 'While I have absolutely no intention of being taken advantage of, I think that's an excellent plan. I dare anyone to even think of it while you have my back.'

Exactly. 'I'll see you back here in a couple of hours.'

'Won't you need more time?'

The addresses were all within twenty minutes of Nell's house. 'I don't think so.' He made for the door.

'Rick.' She bit her lip. 'Don't let any of them make you feel like a second-class citizen. You have more true honour in your pinkie finger than any of them have in their entire bodies.'

Something inside him expanded. He couldn't utter a word.

'And you—you who have every reason to bear me a grudge—have shown me more true friendship than just about anyone.'

As she spoke she moved towards him. All he could do was watch. Common sense told him to back up, but his feet refused to move. Reaching up on tiptoe, she kissed his cheek, drenching him in all of her sweetness. A groan rose in his throat, but he swallowed it back.

'Thank you.'

The sincerity of it shook him loose. 'No sweat, Princess.' He had to break the moment or something would happen—something earth-shattering that had the potential to break both of them.

It doesn't have to.

But it would. Guys like him didn't end up with girls like her.

He cleared his throat. 'I don't suppose you could spare a cupcake or two for a hardworking bailiff on his weary travels?'

She laughed at that, retrieved a large cardboard box of them and pushed it into his hands. 'Maybe you could leave one with each of them as a gesture of…goodwill.'

He grinned. 'Behind that pretty face you're evil, you know?'

She blinked.

'Because we both know one cupcake is never enough.'

That slow smile spread across her face again. 'Give them hell, Rick.'

He tipped an imaginary hat at her and left. He fully intended to.

Rick returned to find Nell waiting for him. She immediately leapt up to put the kettle on to boil. 'How did it go? Were they horrible to you? Did they say mean things to you?'

Not: *Did you get my money?* Not: *Was the mission successful?* But: *Were they horrible to you?* He stopped dead and just stared.

Her face darkened. 'They were.' He watched in a kind of bemusement as her hands clenched. 'I'm sorry! I shouldn't have asked that of you. I should've done my own dirty work and—'

'I had a ball.'

She eyed him warily. 'You did?' she finally ventured.

He could see she didn't believe him. 'Ever since I got out of jail, people like those clients of yours have made me feel like scum. I can't tell you how satisfying it was to turn the tables. Do you have any more outstanding debts I can deal with?'

That surprised a laugh out of her—as it was meant to. She pushed him into a chair, set a plate of sandwiches in front of him and grabbed him a beer. 'One thing's for sure. You've earned lunch.'

She stood over him then with arms folded. He glanced up, a sandwich halted halfway to his mouth. 'What?'

'I don't think you should let anyone make you feel like scum.'

That was easier said than done, but… It struck him then that Nell had only ever treated him as an equal—someone deserving of respect and consideration.

The realisation tightened his chest. He bit into the sandwich then took a swig of his beer. Neither loosened the tension growing inside him. He pulled three cheques from his pocket and handed them to her.

She flicked through them and her eyes widened. 'You managed to get them to sign cheques for the *entire* amounts outstanding?'

He wanted to puff out his chest at the delight bubbling up through her. 'What were you expecting?'

'More promises. Part payment at best.' She perched on a chair across the table from him and crossed a leg. 'It couldn't have been easy.'

'Princess, it was a piece of cake.'

Nell stared at him. It might've been simple for him, but there was no way on God's green she'd have been able to manage this same outcome. She checked the amount on the cheques again. 'This is amazing.'

He was amazing.

'This will keep the wolf from the door for a little while.' Enough to give her some breathing space at least.

'Were you really friends with those people?'

Some of the golden delight leached out of her. 'I thought we were.' If a single one of those people had found themselves in the same desperate financial straits that she had, she wouldn't have dropped them. She might not have been able to give them financial aid, but she'd have offered them moral support. She'd—

'Princess?'

She snapped to. Although she tried to keep her face composed she couldn't stop her lips from twisting. 'It seems my entire life has been a series of very poor judgement calls.' Letting her parents browbeat her into saying Rick had taken her locket; working so hard to earn her parents' love and approval to discover that they'd never been worth the effort, that they didn't know the meaning of the word love; spending her free time with people who only liked her when she was successful—shallow, callous people who enjoyed playing power games with those less fortunate than themselves.

It wasn't noble, but… 'I hope you gave them a seriously hard time.'

'I can assure you that they didn't enjoy the experience.'

The warmth in his eyes almost undid her. She leapt up to pour herself a glass of water. 'Oh, here.' She pulled a velvet pouch from her handbag. 'My grandmother's ring. You might like to keep a hold of it.'

'No.'

She frowned. 'I thought you were going to be my muscle, my brawn…my hard man.' It'd be safer with him than with her.

'You keep hold of the ring and I'll guard you.' There wasn't an ounce of compromise in his eyes. Slowly she pocketed it again, recalling his words when he'd demanded the jewels be removed from the cottage. *I've been to prison, Nell, and I'm not going back.*

Bile churned in her stomach. Jail must've been hell. Pure hell. She wished he'd been spared that.

'Did you make an appointment for a valuation?'

'Yes, we're to meet with the evaluator in an hour.'

He stopped eating to stare at her. It felt as if his gaze reached right down into her soul. She swallowed and wanted to look away, but she couldn't. 'You sure you're okay with this?' he said.

Was he afraid she'd become hysterical partway through negotiations?

'I wish things could be otherwise, but that's just not possible. So, yes, I'm okay with this.'

And because she didn't want him to read any of the other thoughts rising up through her, she backed towards the hallway. 'I'll just go powder my nose and get ready.'

He didn't call anything teasing after her and she wondered if he'd read her thoughts despite her best efforts. Thoughts of kissing him, of the need that pummelled her whenever he was near…of how close she'd come earlier to throwing herself at him.

Oh, that would've been another sterling example of her brilliant judgement. Rick might want her. She knew enough to know what the heat in his eyes meant when he looked at her a certain way. She knew that these days men found her attractive. And she knew she found Rick attractive, but where would it lead? To heartbreak, that was where.

Rick wasn't a criminal, but he was a heartbreaker. He'd made it clear that he had no intention of sticking around once he solved the mystery his father had set him. And she didn't fool herself that she'd be the woman to change his mind.

She was through with fairy tales. From here on she dealt in reality.

* * *

'I'm sorry, Ms Smythe-Whittaker, but this ring is a copy… a fake.'

The room spun, the ground beneath her feet bucked, and Nell had to reach out and grip the countertop in front of her.

'Mind you, it's a very good copy. It wouldn't have been cheap to have had this made.' The jeweller peered at the ring through his eyeglass again. 'But there's no doubt about it. The stone is just a very cleverly cut crystal and not a diamond.'

It was Rick's hand at her elbow that finally stopped the room from spinning. It took all her strength, but she gathered the shreds of her composure around her. 'How disappointing.'

'I am sorry, Ms Smythe-Whittaker.'

'I am too, but I do thank you for taking the time to look at it. I can't tell you how much I appreciate it.'

He handed her the ring. 'Any time. It's been a pleasure.'

Nell, with a silent Rick at her back, left the shop.

'Could he have been mistaken…or lying?'

She shook her head. 'The man has an impeccable reputation. He would never consider taking a bribe from my father to suggest the ring was a fake. He wouldn't risk his professional standing like that.'

'Nell—'

'Please, not here. Let's wait till we get home.' A home she might not be able to keep for much longer. A lump lodged in her throat. She swallowed, but that only shifted the heaviness to her chest.

Could she give up the idea of her gorgeous Victorian high teas and get a real job?

Doing what? Who would employ her? And even if she could get a job, the likelihood of making a wage that could manage the upkeep of Whittaker House was so slim as to be laughable.

She didn't realise they'd reached home until she found

herself pushed into a chair with a glass of something foul-smelling pressed into her hand. 'Drink,' Rick ordered.

Obeying was easier than arguing. She tipped the glass back and swallowed the contents whole.

'Omigod!' She gasped for air. She choked and coughed and struggled to breathe.

'That's better.'

'Better? What are you trying to do? Poison me!'

'You've at least some colour in your cheeks again.'

She bit her lip. *Dear Lord...* 'Have I gone pathetic again?'

'There's nothing pathetic about you, Princess. You've just had a nasty shock.'

She held her glass back out to him. 'May I have another one of those? It was very…bracing.'

He took the glass with a laugh and handed her a soda instead.

'I see we're being sensible now,' she grumbled.

'If you want to get roaring drunk we'll need to find you something better than cooking brandy.'

He had a point. Besides, she didn't want to get roaring drunk. Not really. She hunched over her can of soda, twirling it around and around on the spot.

'So…obviously my father ransacked the jewels before John hid the box.'

'But why have a copy made? Why go to that bother?'

She stared at him. 'That's true. He didn't go to the same trouble for the diamond necklace, did he?'

'Unless John moved the box before he had a chance to.'

She turned the question over in her mind. 'No,' she finally said. 'He wouldn't go to that effort just for me. He'd simply laugh as if he'd bettered me, got one up on me. He'd tell me to suck it up.'

On the table Rick's hand clenched. 'I'm fairly certain I don't like your father.'

Ditto.

She blew out a breath. 'He must've pawned that ring while my grandmother was still alive. He's not afraid of me, but he'd have been afraid of her retribution.' She twirled her can around a few more times, running a finger through the condensation that formed around it. 'Which means I'd better not pin my hopes on anything else in that box.'

'Nell…'

She glanced up at the tone of his voice. She immediately straightened at the expression on his face. 'What's wrong?'

'You're aware that I had both the means and the opportunity to take something from that jewellery box and to have had a copy made.'

'Oh, right, in all of your spare time in the what—one night it stayed there?'

'I knew about it for two nights.'

She folded her arms. All the better to resist the urge to pitch her soda at him. 'I've already told you more than once that I don't believe you're a thief. How many more times do I have to say it before you believe me?' If her glare could blister paint, the wall behind him should be peeling by now. 'Why are you so determined for me to think badly of you?'

He dragged a hand down his face and her chest cramped and started to ache. He *didn't* want her to think badly of him, but he kept expecting her to because that was how people treated him. She didn't blame him for this particular chip on his shoulder, but she wasn't 'people'.

He held up a hand to forestall her. 'If a complaint were made, I'd be a major suspect.'

'Oh, for heaven's sake, who's going to make a complaint? I can assure you that I won't.' Though it'd serve her father right if she did and the scandal was splashed all over the papers. But it wouldn't bring Grandma's ring back. 'And the only other interested party—my grandmother—is dead. I think you can rest easy on that head, don't you?'

He sat back as if she'd punched the air out of him. 'You really believe I'm not a thief.'

She pulled out her most supercilious shrug. 'I refuse to repeat myself on that head ever again.'

He laughed. 'You're an extraordinary woman, you know that?'

'Uh-huh, extraordinary and broke.'

He grinned, a sexy devil of a smile that made her heart lurch and her pulse beat like a crazy thing. She should look away, be sensible, but it seemed as if the fire from the brandy had seeped into her blood.

'Would you like a cupcake?' she offered.

'I'd love one, but I better not. You'd read me the riot act if I told you how many of those things I've eaten today.'

'With Candy breaking down, it's not like I didn't have plenty to spare,' she mumbled.

His grin only widened.

'Oh, okay!' she snapped. 'I'll take the bait. How come are you so darn happy when my life is imploding around me?'

He leaned towards her. 'Let me lend you the money, Nell.'

Her jaw dropped.

'I have the funds. Doing your business plan, I've calculated how much you need.' He named a sum. 'I've more than enough in the kitty to cover it.'

Her jaw dropped lower.

'And, believe me, if there's one person who can make a success out of a crazy Victorian teahouse, then, Princess, that person is you.'

CHAPTER EIGHT

Nell stared at Rick. For a moment she didn't know what to say. She moistened her lips. 'I can't let you risk your money like that.'

'Taking risks is how I've made my money. As far as I'm concerned, this is the safest risk I've taken with it so far.'

Did he mean that? For some reason his certainty only brought her insecurities rushing to the surface. 'You can't know that! You can't know that I'll pull this off. It may all end in disaster and—'

'I've yet to meet anyone who works as hard as you.'

His dark eyes fixed on her with an intensity that dried her mouth and sent her heart twirling and jumping with the kind of exuberance that made it impossible to catch her breath.

He rose, went to the sideboard and pulled the file containing all her clippings and notes from a drawer. 'I stumbled across this last week. I wasn't snooping. I was looking for string.'

She swallowed and pointed. 'Next drawer along.'

'I know that now.'

She stared at the folder and shrugged. 'That's just a whole bunch of pictures and ideas I've collected and…' She trailed off.

He reached across the table and took her hand. 'It's a whole lot more than that.'

Okay, there were recipes and menus and table settings

and names of businesses she might be able to use. There were colour schemes for Victorian houses, teapots, and anything else that had taken her fancy that she thought might prove inspirational for her own venture. She'd have to get a bigger folder soon because that one was bursting at the seams and she was adding to it all the time.

'This helped me visualise your dream.'

His hand on hers was warm and it seemed to be melting her from the inside out.

'Rick, I—'

'It made me see your Victorian teahouse wasn't some last-ditch plan to save your skin, but…'

She tried to pull her hand away, but his grip only tightened. 'Nell?'

She couldn't resist him. Not when he said her name like that. She lifted her gaze to his.

'This is a dream of long standing. It's something you've thought long and hard about. You have the drive and the work ethic to make a success of this business.'

His thumb stroked her wrist in lazy circles. She wanted to stretch and purr at his touch.

'I'm cynical enough to know that's not necessarily a recipe for success.'

'Well, of course not,' she said, because she had to say something and that slow circling of his thumb was addling her brain.

'But you have an X factor.'

His thumb stopped its stroking and the cessation added weight to his words.

'An X factor?' *What on earth…?* Had he had too much sun today?

'Talent.'

Everything inside her stilled.

'Your cupcakes could make grown men weep.'

'Oh, anyone can learn to do that.' She pulled her hand from his to wave it in the air. She'd reclaimed it deliberately.

Rick was treading on her dreams—admittedly very carefully—but if he suddenly became lead-footed she wasn't sure she could bear it.

He shook his head. 'Nobody makes cupcakes like you. Why are you determined to dismiss that as if it's of little value?'

Not holding his hand didn't help at all. She reached across the table to lace her fingers through his. 'The thing is, Rick, it doesn't actually seem like much. After twenty-five years of privileged living it seems the only talent I've acquired is to make cupcakes. I know they're pretty good, but…' She shrugged. As much as she tried to channel nonchalance, she'd never felt more naked in her life.

'They're not just good. They're spectacular. They're the kind of cupcakes people travel hundreds of kilometres for.'

She laughed. 'Now you're just being silly.'

'And you're wrong. You're good at lots of things. You're running your own small business, aren't you?'

'Not very successfully if today is anything to go by.'

'You troubleshot that.'

He'd troubleshot that.

'You have social poise and that's rarer than you know. It'll hold you in good stead as the face of the business when the teahouse is up and running—you'll need it. You also have vision and courage and you're not afraid of hard work or sacrifice.'

She opened her mouth, but he held up a hand to forestall her. 'Sorry, Princess, but you're not going to talk me out of believing in you.'

Unconsciously, her hand tightened in his. 'You believe in me?' she whispered.

'Heart and soul.'

Her heart leapt.

'I believe in you so much I'm willing to lay out the money you need to get your business off the ground.'

A lump the size of a teapot lodged in her throat. Nobody had ever told her they believed in her before.

'So will you accept my loan and make this dream of yours a reality?'

She really wanted to say yes, but the lump refused to dislodge. She stared at him and his face gentled as if he could read what was on her mind. He reached out his fingers as if to touch her cheek. She held her breath…

He snapped away.

They shook their hands free.

Bad idea. Touching of any kind. They both knew it was a bad idea.

'I'd best warn you, though, that there'll be some stipulations that come with the loan.'

Finally she was able to harness the strength to swallow deeply enough to clear her throat. 'Like?'

'It won't be interest free.'

'Of course not!'

Though she had a feeling that was just a sop thrown to her pride. Still… 'This can't be charity, Rick. It's business. I will be paying you back at business loan interest rates.'

'You bet it's business and I want it to succeed. It's in my best interests that it succeeds, which is why I want you to drop back to three days on the road with Candy.'

'But—'

'You need to start focusing some real energy on the new venture or call it quits right now.'

'I…'

'Between your weekend orders and three days out in Candy, you'll still be making enough to live on while you get Whittaker House ready. Your personal expenses are incredibly low…for a princess.'

They both knew her living expenses were incredibly low full stop. Circumstances demanded it. He might call her a princess but she lived like a pauper in her rundown castle.

'And you'll have the loan to cover the larger expenses like land rates and power bills.'

He was taking a risk and he was demanding that she take a risk too.

'Well?'

Her heart thumped. 'Yes, thank you, Rick. I would very much like to accept your offer.'

When Nell reached out a hand Rick shook it. He didn't keep hold of it like he wanted, though. The more time he spent in her company the more he wanted to touch her.

You only need to hold out for another couple of weeks. Once he found out the identity of his sibling he'd leave.

And go where?

Who cared? Just somewhere different where the people didn't know him, where they didn't whisper behind his back.

Nell's not like that.

Yeah, but Nell was one in a million. The fierce gladness that had gripped him when she'd accepted his offer of a loan, though, had taken him off guard.

But…

It was just…

The Princess deserved a break.

He leaned back in his chair, assumed his usual swagger. 'I'll organise to have the funds transferred into your account early next week.'

She peered down her nose at him. 'You need to have a contract drawn up.'

Whatever. He trusted her. His grin widened when she didn't ask the question he could see burning in her face. 'You're just dying of curiosity, aren't you?'

She lifted her chin. 'I have no idea what you're talking about.'

He laughed. 'You want to know how I came to have so much money.'

He watched her manners wrestle with her curiosity.

'Okay, you win. Yes, I do. I want to know how you came to have so much money that you can offer to help…' her lips twisted '…damsels.'

'You're no damsel, Princess. If you were some helpless woman looking for a man to make it all right I wouldn't still be here. Damsels are afraid of independence, hard work and taking risks. None of those things apply to you.'

She leaned back and folded her arms. 'It doesn't answer the question of how you made your money, though, does it? Or why you live even more cheaply than I do.' She frowned. 'Are you lending me all of your money?'

'No.'

Behind the glorious green of her eyes her mind raced. 'Have you left yourself enough money to cover emergencies and the like if they crop up?'

'Yes.'

She pursed her lips and he almost laughed out loud when he realised she didn't believe him. Did she really think he'd be as Sir Galahad as all that? The thought had him shifting on his chair.

'What percentage of your savings have you just lent me?'

And because he could see she was on the brink of pulling back he told her the truth. 'About five per cent.' And that was a conservative estimate. He had so much money he found it hard to keep specific figures in mind.

She stared. She seized a pen and piece of paper and did the maths. She held up the amount she came up with.

'That'd be about right.'

'You're a millionaire. Several times over.'

It wasn't a question so he didn't say anything.

She blew out a breath. 'That's a relief. I can stop worrying that I'll be leaving you short.'

Something muddied the green of her eyes. For reasons he couldn't begin to explain, a bad taste coated his tongue. Was she going to try to hit him up for more money? Would she—

'I'm glad you have money.' Those incredible eyes met his. 'How did you do it?'

Her surprise rankled. 'Shocked?' he taunted.

'To the soles of my feet,' she returned, evidently undaunted by his glare.

'Not to be expected of the jailbird?'

She maintained his gaze and it was so steady it made his heart thump. 'You're the one who keeps reminding everyone that you were in jail.'

Yeah, well, it was better to get in first than be taken by surprise when your guard was down.

'And you never qualify it with the fact your name has been cleared.' She frowned then glared. 'What is that about?'

Her question hit too closely to the sore spots inside him. 'When I was in prison a fellow inmate taught me how to count cards.'

Her eyes turned a murky green like a sea churned up by a storm. 'Was it horrible?' she whispered. 'Prison, I mean. Was it awful?'

Nobody had ever asked him that before. Nobody. And it ripped all his defences from him.

'Rick?'

The sympathy in her eyes, the care in her face, tore something in him. 'It was worse than awful.' The words burst from him before he could stop them. She reached out with both of her hands to grip one of his. 'There are men in there so terrifying they freeze your blood. I didn't think I would get out of that place alive.'

Memories, dark and powerful, pounded at him, one after the other. He rested his head on his free hand and gripped Nell's hands tightly, ordered himself to keep breathing. 'The things you have to do in there to survive… I thought anything in me that was good and kind would be gone for good.'

'But that didn't happen.'

That was when he realised her touch anchored him. He lifted his head and met her gaze. 'I'm not convinced about that, Princess.'

'I am.'

Her belief pushed back some of the darkness. 'How can you be so sure?'

'Tash is still friends with you. She wouldn't be if you'd changed that much. You've been kind to me. You want me to have the opportunity to follow my dream. Someone with no good left in them wouldn't care about that. And someone with nothing good or kind in them wouldn't care if they had ten unknown siblings who needed them or not.'

'I don't know if I do care about that yet.'

'You care enough to find out what their circumstances are like.'

His heart thumped.

Her gaze refused to release his. 'I'm sorry you went to prison. I'm sorry you had to suffer through all of the horror of it. But, whatever else you believe, know this. It didn't destroy who you are. It didn't destroy your honour and integrity. It didn't even destroy your sense of humour or your ability to appreciate the little things. I don't doubt that prison left you with scars, but you're a man in a million and don't let the naysayers convince you otherwise.'

He wanted to believe her with everything he had. He pulled in a breath, unable to deal with all of the confusion raging through him, the pain of remembering that time and all it had stolen from him. He pushed it all away to some deep inner depth where he hoped it'd never see the light of day again. 'I guess it did have its silver lining.'

She choked. 'I beg your pardon?'

'Like I said, I learned to count cards. When I was released from jail I was hired by a building firm. It was one of those parole programmes the powers that be are so gung-ho for. Anyway, I took my first pay packet to the casino and trebled it. Next fortnight I did the same. Within six months I'd made ten times my original winnings.'

'You made your money gambling?'

'I moved from one form of gambling to another. Once I had enough money I traded in blackjack for the stock market. I started making some decent investments, took some risks which paid off.'

'Where did you learn about the stock market?'

'One of the benefits of prison is access to education. I did a business course. Like I said, silver linings.'

Nell leapt up, poured herself a glass of water and drained it. 'You're saying that if it wasn't for prison you wouldn't be rich.'

'That's exactly what I'm saying.'

'What do you think your life would've been like if you hadn't gone to jail?'

He shrugged. 'I'd have ended up working in your father's glass factory or one of the auto parts factories. I'd probably have played on the local football team and I guess I'd have eventually settled down—got married and had a couple of kids.'

She stared down into her glass. 'That sounds kind of nice.'

Yeah, it did.

'But you speak as if none of that's possible now.'

It wasn't.

'You have all this money and yet this is how you choose to live—drifting around like a vagrant as if you don't have two dimes to rub together?'

'I'm not hurting anyone.'

She stared at him. Eventually she nodded. 'You're a good man, Rick—you're kind and you'd rather help than hinder—but prison did steal something from you.'

He stiffened. 'You want to explain that?'

'It stole your courage.'

His head snapped back.

'Before you went to jail you had dreams. Now…' She shrugged. 'Now you're too scared to dream.'

Her words sliced through him.

'Because if you did, you wouldn't choose to live your life the way you do.'

A film of ice covered him from head to foot. 'How I live my life is no concern of yours.' He stabbed a finger at her for added emphasis. 'It's no business of yours.'

Nell shrugged as if his coldness couldn't touch her. 'You're a hypocrite too.' She turned away to wash the dishes in the sink.

His jaw dropped, but he doubted she'd noticed. 'I'm lending you a ludicrous amount of money and all I get is abuse?'

She glanced over her shoulder and raised an eyebrow. 'You want me all doe-eyed and grateful?'

Actually, if he were honest, he wanted her hot and sweaty and horizontal.

'I don't think so,' she snorted. 'I have a feeling doe-eyed would have you running for the hills, tough guy.'

He ran a finger around the collar of his shirt.

'If you intend to concern yourself with my affairs then you can jolly well put up with me concerning myself with yours.'

He thrust out his jaw. 'I'll take back that offer of a loan.'

She turned and planted sudsy hands on her hips. They made damp patches on her dress and he found it hard to look away. 'Go on then,' she said.

He opened his mouth. He stared at those sudsy hands and swore. Nell merely laughed. 'You can't because you're too nice a man.'

Nobody called him nice.

'It's called friendship, Rick.'

He stilled. She went back to washing the last of the

dishes. Friendship. Had the Princess just offered him friendship?

Actually, he saw now that she'd offered it the moment he'd shared John's letter with her.

Back-alley guys like him didn't end up with uptown girls like the Princess, but… But it didn't mean they couldn't be friends, did it?

He rolled his shoulders. He stretched his neck first one way then the other. 'You never told me what was wrong with Candy.'

She pulled the plug and reached for a tea towel. 'The roadside assistance guy who got me started again said something about…points and plugs? Are they something that belong in a car?'

He bit back a grin. 'Yep.'

'Well, apparently they need replacing and so does my… alternator?'

She asked the last as if checking she had that word right too.

'Is that all?' His shoulders rolled suddenly free. 'I can fix that for you. I'll need to grab some parts, but all up it should cost less than two hundred dollars. Mind you, the shop would charge four times that to cover labour.'

She tossed the tea towel and slammed her hands to her hips again. 'Is there anything you can't do?'

He found himself laughing. Nell made him feel young—young and alive and free. 'You can deal with sleazy solicitors and smarmy estate agents and I can debt collect and fix cars.'

'You haven't seen under Candy's hood. What makes you so sure you can fix her?'

'I spent a ludicrous amount of time in my misspent youth with the guys in the neighbourhood trying to keep our rust-bucket cars on the road. I even helped restore a couple.'

She took a step towards him, her face alive. 'From scratch?' He nodded and her smile widened. 'What fun!'

The Princess was interested in cars? 'C'mon—' he hitched his head in the direction of the door '—let's go take a look.'

When they reached the garage, Rick popped Candy's bonnet. 'Tell me what you know about the engine.'

She wrinkled her nose. 'I'm afraid it's not much.'

She looked so pretty in her 1950s-style dress and heels peering into the workings of the old van it was all he could do not to kiss her. 'That doesn't matter.'

'I don't know what any of it does, but I know that's where I put in water if it's running low.' She touched the radiator cap. 'And that's where I put in the oil.'

'You put in your own oil?'

'A man at the garage showed me how. It's a cinch. Way easier than making cupcakes.'

All he could do was stare.

'So what are plugs and points and an alternator? What do they do?'

He pulled off the distributor cap and pointed to the plugs and points and explained how they worked. She asked questions—intelligent questions—and before he knew what they were about they'd dismantled the alternator from the van and had it spread on the floor of the garage.

'It's fascinating!'

She went to brush a strand of hair from her face, but he caught hold of her hand before she could. He turned it over and pointed. 'I'm thinking you don't want to smear grease all over your face or through your hair.'

She stared at both of her hands in astonishment. 'Heavens, this is messier than gardening…and just as much fun.'

The grin she shot him almost slayed him where he crouched.

'I think it'd be wonderful to be able to repair a car.'

'I can teach you how to change plugs and points. When we get a new alternator I'll show you how to install it. And if you want I'll even teach you how to do a grease and oil change. I warn you, though, it's a mucky business.'

Nell stared at Rick and was almost too afraid to breathe. 'You will? Really truly?'

'Sure I will.'

She'd get covered in grease, she'd break fingernails, and it'd be one more step towards becoming independent and not useless.

And it'd be fun!

It hit her then that she'd been so busy trying to plug all the holes in her life that she'd forgotten about fun.

She couldn't stop herself from beaming at Rick. 'Thank you!'

He grinned that slow grin that could turn a woman's world upside down. Her heart pounded up into her throat and back again to bam-bam in her chest and she couldn't have reached into her wardrobe of shrugs and pulled one on now for all the money in the Reserve Bank.

She didn't care about shrugs. She cared about learning new things and making a success of her life and…

And she cared about Rick.

As a friend.

Somewhere inside her a metaphorical eyebrow lifted. She swallowed and glanced back over at him. His smile had faded. Those dark eyes fixed on her with an intensity that froze everything—even the air—and then it all rushed back, wind roaring in her ears, and she swayed.

Rick reached out to steady her, but she shot to her feet and stumbled. He rose too—as if attached to her by some invisible string—and again he reached out a hand to steady her. 'You're a bit wobbly on your feet there, Princess.'

She didn't know if it were the touch on her arm or the way his teasing swagger didn't quite reach his eyes, but the ability to lie had deserted her. Either that or she'd flung it away recklessly. And she hadn't done anything reckless in fifteen years.

'I've been off balance ever since I saw you standing on my front veranda, Rick.'

All signs of teasing fled. 'Princess…'

One of his fingers slid up her arm. She glanced down at it. 'That's not helping.' But the finger didn't stop—it moved back down from her elbow to her wrist, tracing a path along the inside of her arm.

She wanted to dash herself against him like a wave against a rock and encompass him completely. And still that finger trailed paths of spiralling heat and delight across her skin.

'That makes both of us, Princess, because I find it hard to remember my own name when I'm around you.'

They'd cast pretence aside. She lifted her chin. 'I know you find me attractive sometimes.'

'All the time.'

'And I know there's a lot of reasons why I shouldn't kiss you and you shouldn't kiss me.'

'Uh-huh.'

'But I can't remember any of them at the moment so you better start reciting them to me, Rick, because…'

'Because?'

They moved an inch closer to each other. 'Because kissing you is the only thing I can think of.'

They reached for each other…and stopped at the same time. Nell glanced at her greasy hands. Rick glanced at his. She didn't want to ruin his shirt, but… 'I don't care about my dress,' she whispered.

His mouth hooked up in *that* way. 'But I like that dress. The things I dream of doing to you while you're wearing that dress would make you blush, Princess.'

She hadn't known her heart could beat any harder. She hadn't known her skin could flare with so much heat.

'I care about the dress…' But his words emerged on a

rough growl and they wrapped around the base of her spine until she trembled with the force of it.

His hand reached for hers, their fingers lacing. One tug brought them chest to chest. He glanced down at her and his eyes darkened. Very slowly she slid against him, relishing the feel of his hard chest against her softness.

His quick intake of breath curled her toes. 'It seems we don't need hands,' he murmured.

His thumb brushed against the sensitive pulse point of her wrist. Very slowly she turned her hands so his spooned them before dancing her fingers across the backs of his fingers and then lacing them through his again. 'I like hands.' The words came out on short, jerky breaths.

His hands tightened about hers. She tried to glance up at him, but her gaze caught on the pulse pounding at the base of his jaw. She ached to touch her lips to the spot. She wanted—

'Princess?'

She looked up at his hoarse rasp.

Very slowly his lips descended towards hers. She held his hands tightly as the world tilted and, leaning her weight against him, she reached up on tiptoe to help close the distance between them.

And finally their lips touched.

CHAPTER NINE

THEIR LIPS TOUCHED, their mouths opened, and the world spun away from Nell as the taste and feel of Rick filled her. The only thing that mattered was the way his mouth moved over hers—tender but firm, slow yet sure, practised but with a hint of tentativeness that spoke of his desire to please. It told her that the same stunned delirium that coursed through her veins coursed through his.

He nibbled her bottom lip and she moaned, arching against him, feeling anything might be possible in this moment, feeling she could be anything she wanted to be in this moment and that would be okay.

His lips slanted over hers again, less tentative, more urgent, and she met him kiss for kiss, deepening it at the same moment that he did—tongues dancing, teasing, awakening.

She'd thought he'd taste dark and dangerous…like the shadows she sometimes saw in his eyes, but he tasted like cupcakes—all vanilla and spice—and her sweet tooth sat up and begged. He tasted of every good thing she'd never had in her life before. He tasted of all the good things she wanted to be in her life—smart, capable, competent. He tasted like…life.

She wanted to crawl inside his skin or to pull him inside hers. He kissed her back as if he wanted that too. They kissed until they had no oxygen left and then very slowly they eased away from each other, fingers still entwined.

She touched her tongue to her bottom lip and sucked it

into her mouth. He watched with those dark eyes. 'Wow, that was something,' she said when she could finally speak.

He frowned. 'Yeah, it was.'

She frowned then too. 'There's a problem with that?'

'Kisses like that feel like promises and I can't make you any of those, Princess.'

Can't or won't? Reality slammed back into place. She shook her hands free of his and snatched up a clean rag to clench them in. 'I told you there were a lot of reasons we shouldn't kiss.'

She backed up to lean against Candy's side, needing the support for knees that threatened to give way. 'I don't do short-term flings.'

He adjusted his stance and blew out a breath. 'Yet they're the only kind of relationships I have.'

'Strike One.'

She stared down at the rag, shut her eyes for a moment before lifting her chin and tossing back her hair. 'Everyone thinks I'm going to solve my current financial difficulties by finding a rich husband or boyfriend. You're rich. Strike Two.'

He slammed his hands to his hips. She opened her mouth to remind him about the grease and oil, but it was too late. His glare made her mouth dry. 'You're counting me out because I'm rich?'

She pushed upright from the van. 'I'm counting you out because you're rich *and* you can't commit. I'm not going to let you try to buy me off to salve a guilty conscience.'

His jaw clenched so hard she thought he might snap teeth. She pulled in a breath, held it for the count of three and released it.

'It's three strikes before I'm out. What's Strike Three?' he demanded.

She reached for, and found, her most supercilious shrug. 'What? Do you want me to do all of the hard work? Can't you possibly come up with a reason or ten of your own?' She made her voice deliberately scornful.

His eyes narrowed. Very slowly he sauntered to where she stood. Every instinct she had screamed for her to run. Except for those rogue ones that told her to grab him and kiss him again.

She squared her chin, forced herself to meet his gaze.

'You're confusing me with your lily-livered, pretty society boys, Princess. You won't get gallant manners from me. I'm debating the benefits of simply taking what I want—what, in fact, may be freely on offer—and to hell with the consequences.'

He slanted a deliberately insolent gaze down the length of her body and, to her horror, her nipples tightened and her thighs softened. How could he be so ruthless?

'Taking it and enjoying it…over and over—and, believe me, Princess, you'd enjoy it too—until I was sated.'

Her body responded to the smoky seduction of his voice.

'I know how to make a woman want…how to make her respond and to yield.'

She didn't doubt that for a moment.

'And what I want right now is you writhing beneath me, begging for release and calling my name as you come with the kind of orgasm that would blow your mind.'

Her breath caught and her stomach clenched. 'Why?' The word croaked out of her.

'The Princess submitting to the local bad-boy and begging for more—how satisfying would that be? What a triumph.'

She wanted him. His words set her body on fire. But they chilled her too. She didn't doubt that, if he put his mind to it, he could seduce her. She'd succumb. And it'd break her heart.

She met his gaze. 'If you do that, I will put you through as much hell as you do me. You might, in fact, be able to seduce me, but don't doubt for a moment that I have the ability to make you pay.'

They stared at each other for long fraught moments. He lifted his hand as if to touch the backs of his fingers to her cheek, but he stepped back with a low laugh and let his hand drop. 'We're not all that different after all, are we, Princess?'

'No.' But she didn't know if that were a strike against them or not.

They didn't speak again. Nell headed for the door of the garage. Rick turned back to Candy's engine. It didn't stop the burn in her body. It didn't stop the burn in her mind. It didn't stop the insane urge she had to throw herself face first onto the nearest available garden bench to cry.

She didn't. She just kept walking towards the house.

The money Rick promised arrived in her bank account the following Monday. Her bank manager rang to tell her the good news—and to try and pump her for information. She didn't tell him anything, but she frowned as she snapped her cellphone shut. Her father and the bank manager were still as thick as thieves. It'd mean her father would now hear about the upswing in her fortunes.

She should've taken the time and trouble to switch banks, but with everything else going on…

She shook the thought off. She'd deal with her father when she needed to and not before.

She and Rick were careful not to spend too much time in each other's company. He fixed Candy. He painted the drawing room and the library. She baked and delivered orders and went out in Candy—on Monday, Tuesday and Wednesday.

She waited till Thursday before approaching him. 'You haven't given me a contract to sign yet,' she reminded him.

'Do we really need something that formal?' He didn't look at her as he painted the library wall a soft, lush cream.

'Yes.'

'I'll get onto it.'

She made a sceptical, 'Hmph.' No doubt he'd get onto it the same way he'd got onto those receipts for building materials. She'd yet to see a single one.

The problem with Rick was that he had all of this money, but he simply didn't care about it. He probably wouldn't even notice if she paid him back or not. What he needed was a reason to care.

Her feet slowed. *Maybe...*

She came to a complete stop. *Well, why not?*

She made a beeline for the telephone to call her lawyer.

Rick started at the knock on his door on Friday evening. He glanced at his watch. It'd just gone six. *Who on earth...?*

Nell.

For a moment he was tempted to pretend he wasn't in.

Prison stole your courage.

With a muttered oath, he stormed over to the door and flung it open. Nell stood on the other side. Holding a bottle of champagne. Holy Mother of God! She wasn't going to try and seduce him, was she? Damn it, he wouldn't stand a chance and—

'Hello, Rick.'

It took all his strength not to shut the door in her face. 'What are you doing here, Nell?' He didn't have to work hard at making his voice unwelcoming. It came out that way. His only other option was to drag her into his arms and kiss her until neither one of them could think straight.

It'd taken all of his strength not to seduce her last week—every single ounce of it. He hadn't been able to recall anything he'd wanted more than to lose himself in her sweetness, to forget himself, to let himself believe in fairy tales if only for a few brief moments, to see if she could help heal the dark places inside him. He still wanted that with a fierceness that shocked him. And a man had only so much strength.

He hadn't seduced her then and he couldn't seduce her now. Nell deserved better from him. She deserved better from the world.

'Aren't you going to invite me in?'

'Do you think that wise?'

'I don't mean to stay long.'

He glanced at the champagne bottle and raised an eyebrow.

She laughed. 'I don't have shenanigans in mind. I just wanted to deliver this.' She held up an official-looking A4 business-size envelope.

Biting back a sigh, he moved to let her in, careful to keep his distance. 'What is it?'

She handed it to him. 'Open it and see.'

She sauntered across to the kitchen as if she owned the place. Which, technically speaking, she did. She reached up into the cupboard for two glasses. She didn't seem to mind that they were old food jars rather than champagne flutes. The cork of the champagne left the bottle with a pop. She didn't send it flying across the room, nor did she let a single drop of champagne fizz out of the bottle and onto the floor. She poured the bubbly, lifted both glasses and turned back to him.

'Well, open it.' She nodded at the envelope he still held. 'It's not an evil omen or bad news. I promise.'

God give him patience. He lifted the flap and slid out the single sheet of paper inside. He read it.

His heart stopped. The edges of his vision darkened. He blinked and read it again. His throat started to ache. She pushed one of the glasses into his hands, clinked it with hers and took a sip. He couldn't move.

'I wanted to say thank you, Rick.'

But...

'You've lent me the money that will allow me to follow

my dream. I doubt there's anything I can do or say to tell you what that means to me. But I want you to know my gratitude is real, that I don't take your financial assistance for granted and that if, in the future, I can ever do you a good turn then I'll do my absolute best to deliver on that.'

He couldn't move and he couldn't speak. The ache in his throat travelled to his arms, his chest, his temples.

She set her glass on the tiny kitchen table, wiped her hands down the skirt of her Hawaiian frock. 'Well, that's all I wanted to say. I'll be off now. Enjoy your evening.'

'Nell…' He managed to croak out her name before she reached the door.

She turned.

'You've…you've…' She'd given him a thirty per cent share of her business! 'You can't do this.'

She frowned. 'Yes, I can.' Her frown deepened. 'Why not?'

'It's too much.'

Her face cleared. 'No, it's not. I talked it over with a lawyer. He assures me that's fair.'

'But I don't care about the money I'm lending you!'

She gave a little laugh, but there was more sadness in it than joy. 'I know, but I do. I care about it hugely. It means so much to me and I…I want to try and show you how much.'

She'd managed that, but…

'And I wanted…' her fingers clutched at the air as if trying to find the words to explain '…I wanted to give you something back that might mean something to you. That's all.'

He rustled the paper entitling him to thirty per cent of her business under her nose. Was she crazy? 'You're giving me power over your dream!'

'Yes.'

She said that simply, as if it were no big thing, when it was the biggest thing he knew.

'I could destroy it!'

'Without you, my business had no chance of getting off the ground in the first place.'

'You shouldn't give anyone this kind of power over you.'

She moved forward and clasped his face in her hands and bizarrely it felt as if she held his heart instead. Those amazing green eyes blazed at him. 'I keep telling you that I trust you. Maybe now I've shown you how much.'

She pulled her hands away slowly, as if she'd have rather left them there. He stamped on the primal, savage impulses pounding through him. Impulses that ordered him to grab her and kiss her and to make her his.

She backed up a step as if she sensed the fight taking place inside him. Her eyes spoke of her own primal battle. He bit back a groan. She shot him a brave little smile. 'Enjoy the champagne.' And then she was gone.

Rick stumbled over to the sofa and collapsed onto it. He knocked back a generous slug of champagne, coughing when the bubbles hit the back of his throat. He stared at the paper in his hands entitling him to thirty per cent of her business.

I trust you.

Thirty per cent!

Maybe now I've shown you how much.

Oh, she'd done that all right. Nobody had shown this much faith in him. Not ever. And he didn't know what to do with it. Just as he didn't know what to do with the conflicting emotions coursing through him—a mixture of dread and elation, fear and satisfaction.

Enjoy the champagne.

With a laugh, he took another sip. It was good stuff. The Princess didn't skimp at the big moments.

He paused halfway through his third sip. Maybe she had some ulterior motive, maybe…

His shoulders sank back into the softness of the sofa. She didn't have an ulterior motive. She wasn't playing some deep game. Nell had a heart as big as Sydney Harbour.

Something around his heart loosened then and some dark thing slipped away. Nell wanted to give him something important because she believed he deserved it, because she didn't believe he was a no-hoper or a loose cannon, but because she saw something in him that no one else saw.

And it gave him hope.

Not that he knew what he was hoping for.

The next morning—the thirteenth of March—Rick knocked on Nell's back door where before he'd have just strolled in. Before—as in before that kiss. His groin tightened at the memory.

Nell glanced over her shoulder and gestured him in. 'The paper's arrived.'

It sat on her table, still rolled up. She hadn't even had a peek, though he knew her curiosity must be eating her alive. She finished packing up a box of the most mouth-watering-looking cupcakes and set it on the end of the table with a host of other boxes. Pouring mugs of steaming hot coffee, she pushed one into his hand and sat at her usual spot at the table. She rolled the paper across to his usual spot.

A bad taste rose up in his mouth. He gulped coffee to chase it away. Nell stared at the paper and her nose curled. 'C'mon, then, there's no point in putting it off. We may as well find out what wild goose chase John means to send us on next.'

Us? He tried to resist the warmth the word threaded through him. 'Nell, you know you don't have to—'

'Yeah, right. Blah-blah fishcakes. You'd have never got this far without me, and you're not cutting me out of the game now.'

How was it this woman could make him grin at the most unlikely moments?

'And, look, I know it's not a game. I'm not trying to trivialise it.'

He knew that. He raised an eyebrow. 'Blah-blah fish-cakes?'

'It's a wonderful phrase, don't you think? I mean to do my bit to bring it back into the common vernacular.'

She'd donned her prim and proper, hoity-toity princess manners, but he knew her well enough by now to know it for a sign of nerves.

'I'm not going to push you out of this, Princess. Rest easy. I just wanted to give you the chance to back out if that's what you'd prefer.'

She snorted in a very un-princess-like way. 'Get over yourself, tough guy. Sit. Turn to the classifieds.'

She was right. Putting it off was pointless. With a sigh, he did as she bid.

He pushed his coffee to one side. He didn't want it. He'd had one earlier. The Princess drank far too much of the stuff. He opened his mouth, only to shut it again. Now mightn't be the time for that particular lecture. Instead, he ran his fingers down the line of classifieds. On a Saturday morning the paper was full of birthday and anniversary announcements, of births, deaths and marriages, and personal ads.

His finger stopped. '*Rick*,' he read.

'What is it?' Nell demanded.

'*Freemont Park. Two p.m. Wear your party clothes.*'

'What on earth…?' She leapt out of her chair and came to stand behind him to read over his shoulder, her hand resting lightly against his back. His heart rate kicked up at the warm feel of her. She read John's message, harrumphed and went back to sit in her chair. Rick closed his eyes and pulled in a breath. 'He's proving just as chatty in death as he was in life.'

Rick laughed. Nell flipped open her laptop. 'Okay,

Freemont Park. It's in the south-eastern suburbs. It'll take us the best part of forty minutes to get there.'

Rick thrust out his jaw. 'I'm not wearing party clothes.'

Nell leapt to her feet. 'I'm off to do my deliveries. I'll meet you in the garage at one o'clock sharp. Right?'

He scowled. 'Right.'

Nell and Rick stood on the edge of the park and glanced around at the assorted picnickers and walkers.

'Where in the hell are we supposed to start?'

Rick's face had gone as tight as his shoulders. She clutched a box of cupcakes and pulled air into her lungs. 'It's not a ridiculously large park.'

'It's big enough!'

'We'll just amble for a while.'

She hooked her hand through his elbow and propelled them forward, setting them on a path that led diagonally through the park. They must look an odd couple. She wore her cherry print dress with a red patent leather belt and heels. Rick wore his oldest jeans—torn at the knee—and a tight black T-shirt. He hadn't shaved.

In defiance of John's strictures?

She didn't mind. That T-shirt showed off the breadth of his shoulders to perfection and did rather nice things for his biceps. If he'd stop scowling at their surroundings he'd be downright hot and handsome.

Oh, who was she kidding? He was devastatingly and dangerously delicious, regardless of what expression he wore. And that day-old growth…

She had a vision of being stretched out beside him and running her tongue across his jaw and…

'Any particular reason you're pinching me, Princess?'

Oh! She relaxed her grip and swallowed. 'Sorry.'

She forced her gaze and mind from Rick's, uh, finer points, to focus on their surroundings until her breathing returned to within the realms of normal. The park was lush and green, with distant views of the harbour. Gum trees and Norfolk Island pines swayed in the breeze, providing shade for picnic blankets and camp chairs. Oleanders in lush blooms of pink, white and red added a riot of colour. At one end stood a rotunda amid a rose garden.

The bright sunshine, blue sky and chatter from a flock of nearby rainbow lorikeets spoke of summer, holiday fun and relaxation and something inside her yearned towards it all.

A rowdy and boisterous happy birthday chorus had them both turning to their right. They moved off the path and onto the grass, stopping by an oleander in full pink flower to watch.

'Happy birthday, dear Poppy…'

She couldn't help smiling. There had to be a crowd of at least twenty people—of varying ages—and everyone was smiling and jolly. An ache started up inside her chest. 'I always wanted a family like this,' she whispered. People who loved each other—enjoyed each other's company—and wanted to spend time together.

'Me too.'

Of course he had. She had no right to moan when one compared her childhood to his.

They continued to watch. Small children danced around, elderly folk sat in chairs, and everyone else stood as they hip-hip-hoorayed. What must it be like to be the focus of all that love? The birthday girl cut the cake, but her back was mostly to them. She mightn't be able to see it, but Nell could imagine the breadth of the girl's smile.

Oh, if only this could be Rick's new family!

'Poppy is a botanical name,' she offered.

'Grasping at straws, aren't you?'

Probably. With a shrug, she turned back to survey the party. And then the birthday girl swung around and Nell's breath jammed in her throat.

Oh, my God!

Oh! My! God!

When she was able to tear her gaze away she glanced up at Rick. Had he seen it? The family resemblance was unmistakable.

Rick's eyes had fixed on the girl's face. His jaw clenched tight and his chest rose and fell as if he'd been running. 'How old do you think she is?'

The words growled out of him and Nell had to swallow before she could speak. 'Eighteen or nineteen.' She had no idea what to do.

A woman, probably in her late forties, turned at that moment and saw them. With a smile, she set off towards them. With a curse, Rick turned and strode away, his long legs eating up the distance.

'Oh, Rick, wait! I—'

'Hello?'

Nell turned and hoped her smile didn't appear as sick and green as she felt. 'Um, hello. I… Well, we…I…kind of received an invitation.' It wasn't precisely a lie.

'You must be one of Poppy's friends. I'm her mother, Marigold Somers.'

Marigold! She reached out to steady herself against the oleander.

'Is everything okay with your friend?'

Oh, dear Lord. 'He…he had to take an urgent phone call.'

'Never mind, come and join the party.'

'Oh, I don't think I can.'

The woman stared at her.

Um...what to do? 'You see, my invitation came from a rather unusual source and…' She bit her lip. 'My name is Nell Smythe-Whittaker and I don't know Poppy, but I believe you knew my late gardener and…'

The woman blanched. 'Oh, please, no!'

The distress in Marigold's face tore at her. She reached out to clasp the other woman's hand. 'Oh, please, I haven't come to cause you any trouble, but…'

'But?'

'Did you know John died?'

She swallowed and nodded. 'Yes.'

'Did you know he left behind another child?'

Her jaw slackened. 'You?'

'Not me.'

'Your friend?'

'I...'

Others in the group were starting to glance in their direction. Nell didn't want to create a scene. It wasn't her scene to create. She wanted to find Rick. That was what she really wanted to do. She pushed the box of cupcakes into Marigold's hands. 'Say they're from a secret admirer. My card is taped to the lid. Please call me?'

The other woman nodded and, before anyone else from the party could approach, Nell turned and made her way back the way she'd come—as quickly as she could on grass in heels.

So...

They'd found Rick's sibling. Finally. She didn't blame him for his shock, but... *Oh, my word.* To be a part of such a family! Her heart pounded against her ribcage, the blood raced through her veins. Still, there were so many variables. Did Poppy know she was John's child? And how would she react to discovering she had a brother?

And, of course, there was Rick.

He was waiting for her in the car. She slid into the passenger seat, turned to him and opened her mouth.

'Don't.'

She winced at the darkness in his eyes.

'Put your seat belt on.'

Once she had he pulled the car onto the road and roared away from the park. She glanced once more at him before keeping her eyes fixed to the front. Swallowing, she tried to put herself in his shoes. It had to be a shock to come face to face with someone who looked so much like you.

The shock she understood, but the anger…?

After a moment she shook her head. No, she understood that too and Rick was entitled to it. How dared John and Marigold keep such secrets? How dared John taunt Rick with a vision of a life that had been closed to him his entire childhood?

And how dared John father children he'd had no intention of nurturing!

When they arrived home, Nell leapt out of the car to open the gate to the garage. Rick drove in, just as silent as he'd been for the entire trip back.

She folded her arms and leant against the doorway as he emerged from the car.

He barely met her gaze. 'I'm leaving. Today.'

What the...? She didn't move. 'The hell you are.'

He swung to her with a glare that should've reduced her to ash, but she rushed on before he could blast her with a barrage of abuse. 'You promised me until the end of next week. We signed an agreement. You *will* keep your word.'

He stabbed a finger at her. 'That agreement is not some binding contract! And—'

'Regardless of any of this other nonsense, you owe me.'

'I owe you nothing!'

She agreed with that but had no intention of telling him so. 'I've kept my word to you. In fact, I've more than kept it. You can jolly well do the same.'

'What the hell for?' he shouted at her.

She gripped her hands in front of her. 'Because we're friends and that's what friends do.'

He stilled

'And because none of this situation is of my making.'

He dragged a hand down his face. 'You're right. You don't deserve this from me.'

'The situation isn't of your making either, Rick. You're entitled to your anger.'

He fixed her with that hard gaze. He stalked over to her,

intent outlined in every muscle. 'You promise me right now that you won't interfere any further in this godforsaken mess.'

'What are you going to do about this godforsaken mess?'

'Nothing.'

Her jaw dropped.

'That girl's life is perfect.'

'You can't know that after five minutes of spying from the bushes!'

'And she sure as hell doesn't need someone like me coming in and ruining things.'

'Ruining?' Her jaw worked. 'You're her *brother*.'

'We're strangers.' He fixed her with a glare. 'And you either butt out or I leave now.'

She held up her hands. 'Fine, whatever.' But if he thought this situation had finished playing out he was seriously mistaken.

'And, Nell, I will be leaving at the end of next week.'

She didn't bother trying to disguise the way her face fell. 'I'm sorry about that. I'll miss you, Rick.'

He froze for a moment, closed his eyes and dragged a hand down his face. Nell turned and left. She didn't wait to hear what sop he meant to throw her. It wouldn't help to soften the blow.

Blinking hard, she made her way across the garden…to find the kitchen door open. She had locked it, hadn't she?

She went to call for Rick when a figure appeared in the doorway. 'Good afternoon, Nell.'

Her heart slithered to its knees. She forced her legs forward. 'Hello, Father.'

CHAPTER TEN

NELL MADE COFFEE out of habit. She set a mug in front of her father. She was too tired for games. 'I expect this isn't a social call?'

'I want the money you made from pawning your grandmother's diamond ring.'

It took all of her strength not to throw her coffee at him. She pulled in a breath, held it and then slowly let it out. 'I know you already pawned it and replaced it with a copy, a fake. Why are you playing this game with me?'

He leapt out of his chair so fast it fell to the floor, his face twisting in purple fury. 'It's a what?'

She stilled. For a moment she almost believed him and then she remembered what he was like. 'You're afraid I'll go to the police and that the theft of the jewels will be traced back to you.'

'Those jewels should've been mine!'

'But they were left to me. What a scandal it'd be if it was known you'd hocked your mother's jewels—jewels that rightfully belonged to your daughter. It'd serve you right if I did go to the police.'

He stared at her. Very slowly the ugly colour faded from his cheeks, replaced with a calculating gleam in his eyes that was twice as ugly and had acid burning in her stomach.

She set her coffee down, folded her arms and leaned back against the sink. 'Who told you I'd found the ring?'

'I know you found more than just the ring.'

It took an effort not to sneer. 'I'm getting a new bank manager.'

'I know who you have living here.'

'What business is it of yours?'

'Rick Bradford's a thief, a drug addict and a jailbird.'

Her composure vaporised. Coffee sloshed over the sides of her mug. 'He's a hundred times the man you are!'

He laughed. He actually laughed. He righted his chair, sat and sipped his coffee. 'Daughter, here's how it's going to be. You're putting this house on the market.'

It was her turn to laugh. Oh, this should be good. 'How do you propose to convince me of that?'

'If you don't, I'm going to lodge a complaint with the police. I'm going to tell them your grandmother's jewels were stolen and replaced with copies and where do you think suspicion will fall?'

'You!'

'I'll make sure it falls on your little friend, Rick Bradford.'

Her heart flew up into her throat. She fought for breath. 'It'll never stick. He's innocent!'

He laughed again, and too late she realised her mistake. She'd shown weakness, had bared her Achilles heel.

'I know when he started living here. I know when you placed those jewels in the safety deposit box. I know he had the opportunity.'

No!

'And, given his background, he'd have had the means.'

Rick was innocent!

'He'll be hauled in for questioning. I will bribe men to say he took the rings to them for copies to be made. I will make sure he goes down for it.'

Her heart pounded. She couldn't speak. Would her father really stoop so low? He knew people. He still had connections, but would he really...?

He shook his head, his eyes hard. 'I wasn't born to be a

poor man, Nell, and I have no intention of remaining poor. The sale of this house will get me out of trouble and give me a chance to rebuild my business.'

'And you really don't care who you hurt in the process?'

'It's a dog eat dog world.'

'You really don't care that if you do this I will disown you? That I will never speak to you again?'

He laughed. It was an ugly sound that made her stomach churn. 'You'll come crawling back when you see the money come rolling in, demanding your share. Just like your mother. Yes, you're your mother's daughter. Mind you, I'll be generous.'

She stared at him. Had she ever really known him? 'What a sad life you must have.'

He stiffened.

'You judge your value by the amount of money you have rather than anything more substantial like how good you are at certain things or the good you do or the friends you have. I…I wouldn't want to be like you for all the jewels in Grandma's jewellery box.'

'Excellent.' He rose. 'Then you won't mind handing them over when I return tomorrow with the estate agent. There'll be a sale contract for you to sign.'

Her heart pounded. Sell the house? The house counted for nothing beside Rick's freedom, but… *Oh, Grandma, I'm sorry.*

'You can make all the pretty little moral speeches you want, daughter…'

He said that word as if he owned her. Her chin snapped up. He didn't own her. Nobody owned her. She was her own woman.

'But I don't see you making a success of yourself from whatever it is you're good at. I don't see you doing any good in the world. I don't see you surrounded by loving and loyal friends.'

She forced herself to meet his gaze. 'Maybe not, but

I'm a hundred times the person you are.' And she knew that now, deep down in her bones. 'At least I can sleep at night.'

He blinked.

'You might regain your riches, but you're going to be a very lonely man if you insist on this course.' She gestured to the house. 'If you have any feeling for me whatsoever turn back now and there may still be a chance we could forge some kind of relationship. If you don't…' she pulled in a breath, all the while maintaining eye contact with him '…when I marry, you won't be invited to my wedding. When I have children, you will not be allowed to meet them. And don't bother calling for me when you're on your deathbed because I will not come.'

His gaze hardened. 'You always were a stupid and useless girl.'

The old taunt had her shoulders inching up to her ears. She forced them back down. She wasn't useless.

'I'll bring the estate agent around at eleven on the dot. Be here.'

'It's a Sunday!'

The smile he sent her was pure smug self-satisfaction. 'There are buyers interested, and some people who still jump when I ask it of them.'

Unlike an ungrateful, useless daughter?

He left. Nell limped over to a chair and lowered herself into it. If she didn't do as he ordered, he would send Rick to prison. She didn't doubt his ruthlessness…or how much he wanted the money the sale of Whittaker House would bring. And it wasn't just ruthlessness, but spite. Spite directed at her for not jumping when he demanded it, for not marrying money when he'd ordered it, for not getting him out of his financial straits.

Signing over her apartment and sports car and her trust fund—none of that counted as far as he was concerned. Apparently she was still useless!

She ground her teeth together. She wasn't useless. In fact, that had been a darn fine ultimatum she'd given him. And she'd meant it. Every word. Not that it had done any good. She swallowed, battling nausea. She rubbed her temples. What guarantee did she have that her father wouldn't go after Rick once the house was sold anyway, just to punish her? She might not be useless, but she needed advice.

But who could she turn to?

She tapped her fingers against the wooden table top. Who wouldn't go tattling to her father the minute her back was turned—the sleazy solicitor? Not likely.

The thing was, her father had been right on that head. She wasn't surrounded by an army of loving and loyal friends. She had one friend in the world—Rick—and she wasn't telling him about this. She wasn't giving him the chance to be noble. She didn't need noble.

One friend… She pushed a hand back through her hair. *Useless…*

A moment later she straightened. She mightn't have any friends, but Rick did.

She reached for the phone book, searched and then punched a number into the phone. 'Tash? Hello, it's Nell Smythe-Whittaker. I was wondering if I could possibly trouble Mr King—uh, Mitch—for a quick word?'

'He's not here at the moment. Would you like me to have him drop by some time?'

'Oh, no, not here.' She didn't want Rick to see.

'Would you like to make an appointment at the station?'

'God, no!'

Tash didn't say anything for a moment. 'Nell, are you in some kind of trouble?'

'I…I don't know. And please don't mention this to Rick. I don't need a white knight—I just need some advice.'

'Okay.'

But she drew the word out and Nell knew Tash would

talk to Rick eventually. Her loyalty did reside with him, after all.

She swallowed. 'Would it be possible…I mean would you mind if I came over to your place at a time convenient to both you and Mitch?'

'Sure, why not? Mitch should be here within the next half an hour if you're free this afternoon.'

'Thanks, Tash.'

She knew the other woman didn't think much of her, and she didn't blame her. But at that moment she could've hugged her.

Nell sat opposite Tash and Mitch at Tash's kitchen table and her mouth went dry. What if they accused her of ruining Rick's life? She'd have no answer for that.

'Would you like me to leave the two of you alone?' Tash eventually said.

Nell shook her head. Tash should know what was in the works in case Rick needed her. Besides, it didn't take a genius to work out that Tash and Mitch were besotted with each other. And not just besotted but a team. If Tash left now, Mitch would only fill her in later.

She was the outsider here. And as long as she made sure nothing bad happened to Rick because of her father then it didn't much matter what either Tash or Mitch thought of her.

She lifted her chin. 'I guess I better start at the very beginning so you get the full picture.'

'Sounds like a plan.' Mitch nodded his encouragement and his calm sense helped ease the racing of her pulse and frightened leaps of her heart. She could see why Tash had fallen for him.

She told them how she and Rick had searched John's cottage. She didn't tell them about John's letter, though. That was Rick's secret to tell. She told them about finding the jewellery box and how she'd asked Rick to put it back, thinking it'd be safe there. She told them about the deal she and Rick had come to—rent-free accommodation in return for maintenance work on Whittaker House—and how after one night in the cottage he'd refused to keep the jewels there and how she'd put them in a safety deposit box at the bank.

As she spoke, Tash's face grew darker. Mitch merely listened, his eyes intent, his face revealing nothing of his thoughts.

And then she told them about her father's threats and demands. Tash's face darkened further. She leaned across the table towards Nell, but Nell held up a hand. 'I know, okay, I know. My father is a nasty piece of work. I'll do what he demands…I'll sell my grandmother's house.' Her voice cracked. She swallowed and cleared her throat. 'But none of that will ensure Rick's safety. I mean, once the house is sold and my father has the money, what's to stop him from attempting to press charges against Rick anyway?'

Hell, if her father found out how much money Rick had… The thought made her temples throb.

Tash slumped back. 'You believe Rick is innocent then?'

'Of course he's innocent!' Surely Tash hadn't thought—

'Who do you think is responsible?' Mitch broke in.

'My father, of course.'

Mitch frowned. 'But you said he demanded the money you made from the sale of the ring.'

'No doubt to cover his tracks. He has no right to that jewellery. It was left to me. I could press charges against him if I chose to.' Not that she would.

'The rest of the jewellery is still in the bank?'

'Yes.' First thing on Monday she was changing banks.

'Would you trust me with it?'

She gazed at Mitch. 'Of course I would, but, Mitch, I don't want to make any of this official.'

Tash straightened. 'What do you want?'

'I want to ensure Rick is free from any of this. I want to make sure my father can't go after him.'

Mitch nodded. 'You said you're signing a contract with some estate agent tomorrow?'

'Yes.' She could barely get the word out.

'You're not doing that on your own. I'm sending my solicitor along.'

'I'll pay.'

Tash shook her head. 'We'll sort all of that out later.'

Nell swallowed and fished the diamond ring—the fake diamond ring—from her pocket and set it in front of Mitch. 'I'll retrieve the rest of the jewellery first thing Monday—I expect they'll all be fakes.'

Mitch surveyed the ring. 'Whittaker House is in your name, right? That means, even if a buyer is found immediately, we have six weeks before the property officially changes hands and the bulk of the money is transferred into your account.'

Which she'd then have to transfer to her father.

'That means for at least the next six weeks, Rick is safe.'

A sigh eased out of her. Six weeks of knowing Rick couldn't be hauled in and charged with a crime he hadn't committed. But what then…? All the tension shot back into her.

'If we have to,' Mitch said, 'we'll force your father to sign a clause to the effect that he won't press charges against Rick.'

That could be done? Nell sagged in relief. 'Thank you.'

There didn't seem to be anything else to say after that, so Nell left.

'Damn!' Tash muttered as she and Mitch watched Nell drive away.

Mitch rested an arm across her shoulders. 'What?'

'She's in love with him.'

'Lucky man.'

Tash snorted. 'As soon as he realises he'll bolt.'

'Why?'

She shook her head. 'He just will. It's what he does.'

'She's prepared to make a hell of a sacrifice for him.'

Tash glanced up. 'Will we be able to get him off the hook *and* save her house?'

'We'll give it our best shot.'

She reached up on her tiptoes to kiss him. 'Have I mentioned lately how much I love you?'

Nell wasn't sure what to do when she returned home. Start packing boxes in preparation for her imminent eviction?

She fell into a chair, pulled a box of cupcakes towards her, opened the lid, stared at them for a few moments before pushing them away again. Eating cupcakes wouldn't make her feel better.

She could hear Rick hammering something in the dining room, even though it was past six o'clock on a Saturday evening. She should tell him not to bother. She should tell him…

She dropped her head to the table. How was she going to explain selling Whittaker House to him? She'd have to give him his money back too, of course. The dream of a Victorian teahouse wasn't going to come to fruition any time soon.

She frowned. Had her bank manager traced where that money had come from? If so, had he informed her father? She lifted her head…

To find herself staring at a woman in the doorway.

Marigold.

Marigold shifted her weight from one foot to the other. 'Have I come at a bad time?'

Nell stared and then shot to her feet. 'Of course not. I… Please! Come in.'

She thought about Rick thumping away in the dining

room and swallowed. Dear Lord, all of this could end in tears. Lots of tears.

Mostly hers, probably.

She swallowed, but the uncertainty in the other woman's face caught at her. 'Please, sit down. Can I get you a coffee or a soda?'

Marigold perched on a chair, twisting her hands together, her eyes wide in a pale face and Nell shrugged—nothing practised or elegant, but simply a shrug. 'To heck with that, let's have some wine.'

She pulled a bottle from the fridge, grabbed two glasses and poured. 'You'll have to excuse this—' she handed Marigold a glass '—but it's cheap and cheerful rather than elegant and expensive.'

'If it's alcohol, bring it on.'

'Amen, sister.'

They clinked and drank. Rather deeply. Nell topped up the glasses and then wondered what to do…what to say.

'I remember when you were a little girl.'

Nell's glass halted halfway to her mouth. 'You do?'

'I went to school with your mother. I came to a few parties and afternoon teas here over the years. You'd have not been more than six or seven when I fell pregnant with Poppy.'

'And that's when you stopped coming round?'

Marigold took a gulp of her wine and nodded. 'I met John at one of those parties.'

'And you had an affair?'

Marigold stared down into her wine and a tiny smile touched her lips. 'We did, yes. It was rather short-lived, but intense. We were very careful to keep it secret. If we'd been discovered John would've lost his job and my friends would've…well, they wouldn't have understood.'

Wow! 'And you fell pregnant?'

She nodded and they both gulped wine. 'That's when things turned bad. John wanted nothing to do with a baby.'

Nell swallowed. *Double wow.* 'Do you know why?'

'Not really. I glimpsed something extraordinary in him, but there was a hardness there too. Maybe it's because he grew up in a boys' home and from what I understand it was a rather brutal place. He never said as much, but I don't believe he trusted himself around children. Or maybe he didn't want to be reminded of the childhood he'd had.'

'Does Poppy know he was her father?'

Marigold nodded. 'I told her when she turned fifteen. You see, she knew the man who she calls Dad—my husband Neville, who she adores and who adores her back—wasn't her biological father; we met when she was two. But she really wanted to know who her biological father was… and it only seemed fair to tell her.

'She sent him a letter that he never answered, and she insisted on sending him an invitation to her birthday party every year—the party in the park is an annual tradition. But he never did turn up.'

Nell stared into her glass of cheap wine and recalled the way he hadn't let her plant marigolds. Was it because they'd have reminded him of this woman and a vision of a different life, a different path he could've taken? None of them would ever know now.

A sigh escaped the other woman. 'But if Poppy has a brother…'

Nell glanced up.

'Well, of course, she has every right to know him. I can't prevent that and I wouldn't want to. All I ask is that you give me a chance to tell her about him first, that's all.'

'But of course!'

'I'm sorry I panicked earlier and—'

'Nell!'

Rick's voice boomed down the hallway, his footsteps growing louder. 'Where the hell have you put the masking tape?'

He stopped dead in the doorway. Across the table from

her, Marigold gasped. 'Dear heaven, you're the spitting image.'

Those dark eyes fixed on Nell with an accusation that cut her to her very marrow. Very softly he said, 'Deal's off.' He walked through the kitchen, out of the back door, and she knew he headed for John's cottage to pack. To leave. For good.

'What just happened?' Marigold whispered.

Nell blinked hard. She reached for her wine and tried to force a sip past the lump in her throat. 'Rick is… I don't think he means to make himself known to Poppy. He thinks it'll complicate her life.' *And he thinks I betrayed him.*

Marigold rose. 'I mean to tell Poppy about him. She has a right to know and I don't want there to be any lies between us.'

Nell rose too. Marigold pushed a card into her hands. 'I sincerely hope you can convince that young man to reconsider his decision. Perhaps you'll be kind enough to give him this?'

Nell stared down at the card—a business card with Marigold's phone number and address. 'Yes, of course.'

Marigold left. Nell grabbed her glass of wine and drained it. Then she headed outside for the cottage. She knocked twice—a quick rat-tat—and then opened the door and walked in.

Rick whirled around from throwing things into a holdall. 'I didn't say you could come in,' he snarled.

'Oh, for heaven's sake, shut up and listen for once, will you?'

He glared. She merely thrust her chin up a little higher. 'You need to know some things.'

'If it's anything to do with Poppy or John-bloody-Cox then no, I don't.'

'Back at the park after you raced off,' she said as if he hadn't spoken, 'I told Marigold that John Cox had another child.'

'You had no right!'

She snapped herself to her full height. 'If you'd hung around I'd have let you deal with it, but you'd raced off! You left me to improvise the best I could.'

His glare didn't lower by a single degree.

'Marigold—that's Poppy's mother—went pale at the news. So I pushed the box of cupcakes at her, told her my business card was taped to the lid and asked her to contact me. And then I left. That's what happened in the park and that's why Marigold was in the kitchen this afternoon. She didn't ring or give me any warning.'

'You were drinking wine together!'

'I wasn't going to turn her away! Besides, she was nervous…and so was I. Wine seemed like a good idea.' She thrust her chin out, daring him to challenge her. 'And it still does.'

Rick dragged a hand down his face.

'And now you can jolly well listen to what she had to say.' And then she outlined the conversation she and Marigold had just shared, leaving nothing out.

'I don't care,' he said when she finished.

Her heart stuttered. 'But—'

'I'm leaving.'

Just as she'd known he would, but it didn't stop the blow from nearly cutting her in half. Given her father's threats, it'd probably be better if he did leave. If he left Sydney and went far, far away, but…

But it didn't mean he had to turn his back on his family!

'Do whatever you damn well please!' she hollered at him. She strode forward to poke him in the shoulder. 'We can't choose our families. You and me, we're perfect proof of that except…'

She whirled away from him. 'Except in this case you can choose—you can decide to choose your sister!' She swung back. His face had gone pale and wooden. 'Poppy seems lovely. Marigold seems lovely. Her husband Neville sounds lovely. They all seem lovely, but you're not going to choose them—you're going to reject them instead. Just like John did!'

Rick's jaw worked for a moment, but no words came out. 'Reject?' he finally spat out. 'Their lives are perfect!' He wasn't going to waltz in there and ruin it for them.

He'd met people like that before—good, decent people who wouldn't turn him away. But their lives would be that bit worse for knowing him, their happiness diminished. They didn't deserve that. That lovely girl—his sister! She didn't deserve that.

Nell glared at him. 'Who's to say their lives wouldn't be more perfect with you in it?'

He stepped in close to her, pushed his face close to hers and tried to ignore the sweet scent of cake and sugar and spice. 'Fairy tales don't come true.'

'You have a sister. *That's* a reality. This *isn't* a fairy tale.'

Her belief in happy ever afters was a fiction, though, and he had to take a step back before some of that magic took hold of him. 'This is my decision to make.'

Her head snapped up. 'You're going to walk away?'

He glanced heavenward. 'Finally she gets the message.'

'Fine!'

He glanced back down.

'Marigold asked me to give you this.' She took his hand and slapped a business card into it and then dropped his hand as if she couldn't bear to touch him. 'Now get the hell off my property.'

Rick scowled and pounded on Tash's door. Tash opened it. 'Is it okay if I bunk here tonight?' he asked without preamble.

'Sure.' She pushed the door wide. 'I take it you and Nell have had words.'

'What?' He rounded on her.

Tash didn't even blink at his growl. She gestured for him to dump his stuff in the spare bedroom and then continued through to the living room. Mitch sat at the table. He and Rick nodded their greetings to each other. Tash turned. 'You ought to know she was here earlier.'

He slammed his hands to his hips 'So she told you about John Cox and Poppy and the whole mess of it, I suppose, and tried to enlist your help?'

Mitch opened his mouth but Tash took the seat beside him, elbowing him in the ribs, and he shut it again. 'Something like that. She made a good case.'

'Can it, Tash.' He couldn't believe she'd be on Nell's side. 'I don't care if that girl is my sister.' And it didn't matter what Nell or Tash or Mitch had to say about the matter. 'There's no law that says I have to meet her.'

'Holy crap!' Tash's jaw dropped. 'John Cox, the gardener, is your father?'

He stilled and then swore. She'd played him to perfection. If Nell hadn't riled him up so much he'd have never fallen for one of Tash's tricks.

'*And* he fathered more than one child?'

He closed his eyes.

'That wasn't the mess she told us about.'

Obviously. He waited for Tash to grill him further, but she didn't. A wave of affection washed over him then. Tash knew how to give a guy the space and privacy he needed. His face darkened. Unlike some others he could name. He glanced up, but the expression on Tash's face made his blood chill. He straightened. 'What the hell was she here for then?'

Tash and Mitch shared a glance. 'You might want to sit down to hear this, Rick,' Mitch said.

CHAPTER ELEVEN

RICK LISTENED TO the tale Tash and Mitch recounted with growing disbelief. 'You have to be joking? You're telling me she's going to sell her house—the house she's done everything in her power to hang onto—in an attempt to keep me out of jail?'

'That's exactly what we're saying.'

Oh, Princess. 'She knows that's crazy, right?'

'No,' Tash said, as if it were obvious it wasn't crazy. Or as if it should've been obvious to him that Nell wouldn't think it crazy. She had a point.

'And she'd be right,' Mitch said. 'It's not crazy.'

Ice filtered through his gut. He wasn't going to prison again for anyone. Ever. Again.

Except…

Except he wasn't letting the Princess sell out on his behalf.

'She picked a fight with me on purpose. She kicked me out to get me out of the way.' Because Nell could twist him around her little finger and if she'd wanted him to stay, if she'd argued with him to stay, if she'd promised no more interference on the Poppy and Marigold front, he'd have stayed.

'That's my best guess,' Tash said. 'It's what I'd have done in her shoes.'

Rick's mouth opened but no words came out.

'She has a point, Rick. It might be best if you do disappear.'

And leave Nell to bumble along as best she could? 'No way, I'm not going anywhere.'

Tash fixed him with a look that made him fidget. He rolled his shoulders. 'I'll buy the bloody house.'

'No you won't!'

Tash and Mitch both said that at the same time. He scowled at them. Mitch leaned towards him. 'It wouldn't be a good idea at this point in time for Roland Smythe-Whittaker to know you have money.'

Rick slumped back in his chair, silently acknowledging the truth of that.

Mitch glanced at his watch. 'I've gotta go.' He rose, kissed Tash and left.

'Do you have enough money to buy Whittaker House?'

He nodded.

'How?'

He lifted a shoulder. 'It's amazing how much money you can make playing poker, Tash.'

She closed her eyes. 'Oh, Rick.'

He didn't know why, but her words burned through him. He shifted on his chair. 'I could buy the house anonymously.'

Tash grabbed two beers from the fridge and tossed him one. 'No.'

His hand tightened around the can. 'This is not your decision to make!'

She snorted at him. 'What would you be doing tomorrow if we hadn't told you about the situation?'

He didn't answer.

'You'd jump in your car and head up the coast without a backward glance, right?'

She was spot on. As usual. The thing was, she had told him about the mess Nell was in and—

'She came to us for help—me and Mitch—not you. It's not even help but advice she asked for. All Mitch and I plan to do is arm her with the information she needs to make her next move.'

He opened his mouth, but she cut him off. 'She said she doesn't want some white knight riding in and saving the day.' Tash took a long slug of her beer. 'She's not some helpless woman you can ride in and rescue to ease your damn guilt, Rick.'

'What guilt?'

'The guilt at leaving.'

He stared at her. He could barely breathe, let alone speak.

'She can save herself. What's more, I think she needs to do this on her own so she can prove exactly that.'

The Princess was resilient—strong. It was just…

He wanted to be her white knight.

Why? To ease his guilt, as Tash said? His stomach churned. 'She thinks you don't like her, you know?' It would've taken a lot of courage for her to approach Tash.

'I don't really know her, but I like her just fine. I *really* like what she's prepared to do for you.'

That only made his stomach churn harder. 'It harks back to when you made it clear she should leave the Royal Oak after one drink and kept such a close eye on her the entire time.'

Tash stared at her beer. 'I didn't want any trouble. I didn't want anyone hassling her. Her father wasn't a popular man at the time.'

'I knew it'd be something like that.'

'She's in love with you, Rick.'

His beer halted halfway to his mouth. His heart pounded.

'Don't play games with her.'

He wanted to jump up and run.

'You have two choices as far as I can see. You either get up in the morning, get in your car and drive off into the sunset.'

He thrust out his jaw. He wasn't leaving. Not until he knew Nell and her dreams were safe.

'Or if you're so hell-bent on sticking around you better start doing something to deserve her.'

Tash rose then and left the room. He realised his beer was still stranded at that crazy angle and he lowered it to the table, his heart pounding. Why wasn't he already in his car, tearing away from Sydney as if the hounds of hell were at his heels?

Because Nell was about to sacrifice everything that most mattered to her for him.

For him!

He couldn't let her do that, because…

He stared at the wall opposite as it all fell into place. He loved Nell. He was in love with the Princess.

Somewhere along the line her dreams had become his dreams. She'd given meaning to his hobo existence and he didn't want to go back to drifting aimlessly through life.

He wanted…

He swallowed and tapped a finger against his beer. He wanted the dream he'd had before he'd gone to prison. He wanted the wife and kids and a regular job. He wanted a place in the world and he wanted that place right by Nell's side.

You better start doing something to deserve her.

On Sunday her father and Byron Withers, the estate agent, arrived promptly at eleven a.m.

Byron smirked at her with so much I-told-you-so satisfaction it was all Nell could do not to seize him by the ear and toss him back out of the front door. It took an effort to pull all of her haughty superiority around her, but she did. She wasn't giving these two men the satisfaction of knowing how much she cried inside.

Besides, she was doing this for Rick. He didn't deserve

what her father had planned for him and that gave her strength too.

Both men, though, faltered when they found the solicitor Mitch had organised for her already ensconced at the kitchen table.

'This isn't necessary,' her father boomed.

'Nevertheless, I am having Mr Browne read over the contract before I sign it. That's non-negotiable.' She wasn't afraid her father would walk away in a huff. She knew how much he wanted the sale of Whittaker House to go through. 'So the sooner Mr Withers hands the contract over the sooner my solicitor can read it and the sooner you can both be on your way.'

With a curt nod from her father, Byron Withers did as she'd suggested. She'd provided Mr Browne with coffee and cupcakes when he'd arrived. Her father eyed the cupcakes hungrily. 'Coffee, daughter?'

'No, Roland, I'm afraid there's none on offer.' She'd never called him by his Christian name before and the shock in his eyes gave her little pleasure. But she wanted him to know that she'd meant what she'd said to him the previous day. If he insisted she sell Whittaker House, if he persisted in his threats against Rick, she would never acknowledge him as her father again.

The solicitor glanced up. 'We are not signing this clause, this clause or this clause. Mr Withers, these are not only immoral but they're bordering on illegal.'

Her father's cheeks reddened and his face darkened.

The solicitor turned to her. 'If it's okay with you, I'd like to take this to the authority that is, in effect, the Estate Agents' watchdog. This kind of thing shouldn't be allowed.'

Thank you, Mitch.

Byron came bustling up between them. 'I'm sure there's no need for that! It'll have merely been some innocent oversight by the contract department.'

'But—' Her father broke off at Byron's shake of his head. He took to glowering at her instead.

She folded her arms and glared back while her solicitor forced Byron to initial the changes and insert clauses that had apparently gone inadvertently 'missing'. 'I've had a lifetime of that look,' she informed him. 'But I find I'm impervious to it now.'

His jaw dropped.

They both glanced back to the table when Byron groaned. 'But that means she can pull out of the sale at any time without making any financial recompense to the agency for advertising or…or…anything!'

Nell lifted her chin. 'As my father claims he already has a buyer for the property, pray tell me what advertising you'll actually be doing? I mean, of course, if you'd prefer we took this to the authority Mr Browne mentioned earlier then by all means…'

'There's no need to be so hasty,' Byron muttered, scrawling his signature at the bottom of the newly formed contract. He pushed it across to her.

She almost laughed when Mr Browne winked at her. 'This is now a document I'm prepared to let you sign.'

She signed it.

She turned to her father and Byron. 'The two of you can leave now. I'm busy. And I don't see any point in the two of you lingering.'

'I'll need to contact you when I have clients to show through the property,' Byron said.

'Yes, of course, but you'll do that without Roland present if you please.'

Her father's head came up. He stared at her as if he'd never seen her before.

'I'm afraid I don't trust him not to steal from me any further.' Something flickered behind his eyes and if she hadn't known better she'd have almost called it regret. 'Now, good day to you both.'

They left. She walked back to kitchen and to Mr Browne. 'Thank you for your advice. I have a feeling it was invaluable.'

'They were trying to rob you blind.'

No surprises there, but… 'You helped me gain back a little of my power. I'm very grateful.'

'It's all part of the service,' he said, gathering up his things. 'Besides, I haven't had that much fun bringing someone to their knees in a long time.'

She grinned and handed him half a dozen cupcakes. 'Make sure to send me your bill.'

He merely winked at her again and left.

Nell sat at the kitchen table with burning eyes and rested her head against the wooden table top. She gripped her hands in her lap. She pulled in a deep breath and then another. She kept deep breathing until she was able to swallow the lump lodged in her throat. When she'd done that she forced herself to her feet. There was work to be done—another two orders to fill. And then boxes that she would need to start packing.

Mitch turned up on her doorstep on Tuesday morning, just before she was about to set off in Candy. Candy who was now running like a dream thanks to Rick.

Rick.

A burn started up in her chest, at her temples and the backs of her eyes. He'd be hundreds if not thousands of kilometres away by now. She hoped so—she dearly hoped so. She wanted him well and truly beyond her father's reach.

Oh, but how she ached to see him, hungered to hold him, yearned to know he was safe.

'You okay?' Mitch asked.

Nell shook herself. 'Yes, sorry. Please come in. Can I get you a coffee or a—'

'No, thanks, Nell, I only have a few minutes before I have to get to work.'

Right. 'I want to thank you for sending Mr Browne on Sunday. He was superb.'

'I heard. I've also spoken to him about your father's threats against Rick and he assures me that he can draw up a clause that prohibits your father from bringing any action against Rick.'

She fell into a seat and closed her eyes. 'Thank God,' she whispered. They flew open again. 'Is it watertight?'

'As watertight as these things can ever be.'

Right.

'I've also hunted up some other information that might be of interest to you.'

She gestured for him to take a seat. He did and then pulled her grandmother's ring from his pocket and laid it on the table in front of her. 'I've found out who really had this copy made.'

Her lips twisted. 'I know—my father—but he'll bribe people to lie for him and I'm not putting Rick through a trial. He's suffered enough grief due to my family.'

'It wasn't your father.'

She stared at him. 'Not…' She swallowed. 'Then who?'

Mitch glanced down at his hands and she stiffened. 'If you tell me it's Rick I won't believe you. He's not now nor has he ever been a thief. If that's what your informers have led you to believe it's because they're on my father's payroll.'

Mitch smiled then. 'You think a lot of him, don't you?'

She nodded. She loved him.

'It wasn't your father and it wasn't Rick. This fake was made almost thirty years ago.'

Her eyes felt as if they were starting out of her head. Mitch pulled several receipts from his pocket and handed them to her. She read them, blinked and then she started to laugh. 'These are signed by my grandmother.'

'During the recession in the eighties, your grandfather's business took a bit of a beating.'

'So my grandmother sold her jewels to help him out?'

'That'd be my guess.'

She stared at the receipts, she stared at the ring and then she stared at Mitch. 'This is proof.' The import of that suddenly struck her. Her shoulders went back. 'I…I don't know how to thank you.'

'No thanks necessary. It only took a little digging to find the truth. I was glad to be able to do Rick a good turn.'

She nodded.

'And it means, as far as all this goes, the ball's now in your court.'

She could now ensure Rick didn't go to jail. She could save Whittaker House. She could make her dream of a Victorian teahouse a reality. And she could make sure Rick's investment paid him back fourfold.

She straightened. She lifted her chin and pushed back her shoulders. 'I feel dangerously powerful.' And very far from *useless*.

'If you want me here when you confront your father or if you want me to haul him in on blackmail and attempted extortion charges, just say the word.'

'No, thank you, Mitch. I'd like to deal with this on my own now.'

The moment Mitch left, Nell rang Byron Withers and took her house off the market.

'But,' he blustered, 'it's only—'

'It's non-negotiable, I'm afraid, Byron.'

'Your father will be most displeased!'

She smiled. 'Yes, he will.'

Then she rang her father. 'I've just taken the house off the market,' she said without preamble. 'If you wish to discuss this any further then you're welcome to drop over at five this afternoon.'

She hung up. She switched off her phone. And then she went out in Candy to sell cupcakes and coffee.

* * *

Her father was waiting for her when she returned home that afternoon. 'You changed the locks!'

'Yes, I did.'

'I've been waiting over half an hour!'

'I told you what time I'd be here,' she returned, not in the least perturbed, unlocking the door and leading the way through the house. *Her house*. She'd become immune to her father's demands and anger. Her body swung with the freedom of it.

'Would you like coffee and cake?'

'No, I wouldn't! I want to know the meaning of this!'

'Would you like to take a seat?'

'No!'

Fine. She shrugged. 'I found out it wasn't you who had the copy made of the ring after all.'

'I told you it wasn't.'

'I didn't believe you. I also discovered it wasn't Rick Bradford who had it made either.'

The skin around Roland's eyes sagged, making him look a lot older than his fifty-seven years.

'It was Grandma herself. It seems she did it to help Granddad out of some financial difficulty at the factory.'

Roland closed his eyes, but she refused to let pity weaken her. This man had bullied and harangued her all her life, had made her feel she'd never measure up. He'd threatened the man she loved.

She lifted her chin. 'I have the receipts to prove it. So now I'm going to tell you for the last time that I am *not* selling Whittaker House. I promised Grandma I would cherish it and that's exactly what I mean to do. You can demand and yell all you like.' She shrugged—a straight from the heart *I am not useless* shrug. 'But none of that will have any effect on me.'

'I'll be ruined!'

'Maybe so, but I'm not the one who ruined you.'

He sagged, looking older and more helpless than she'd ever seen him.

'When you demanded it, I gave you my trust fund, my apartment, my sports car and I didn't even say a word when you took the majority of my designer wardrobe, but not once did you ever say thank you. You just wanted more and more. Nothing I have ever done has been good enough for you. I'm through with that. I'm not giving you anything else.'

His face turned purple. 'This house should be mine!'

'But it's not. It's mine. And I'd like you to leave now.'

He called her names, but none of them hurt. He threatened her, but it merely washed over her like so much noise. And then he left and a weight lifted from her shoulders. She would never have to deal with his demands, his threats and his ugliness again.

At nine o'clock on Thursday morning a registered package arrived; Nell had to sign for it. It was from the solicitor, Clinton Garside.

Clinton's enclosed note merely said: *Following the instructions of the late Mr John Cox.* Inside was a letter from John. Her heart picked up pace as she read it.

Dear Miss Nell,

I left instructions with my solicitor to have this sent to you if Rick should ever turn up to claim his letter. I know you won't understand my attitude to my children or why I've spoken now after so long keeping the secret. You were about my only friend and you added the only sunshine I had in my life, so I'll try to explain it to you.

The truth is, when I was a young man, I killed someone. I was charged with manslaughter and went to jail for eight years. I've always had a temper. I was never afraid you'd be in any danger of it because you were too well supervised, but I couldn't inflict it on my children. I didn't dare. That's why I stayed away from them.

Her jaw dropped. The words blurred. Nell had to swallow hard and blink before the page came back into focus.

I could've loved the woman who had my other child, but I would've had to tell her the truth about my past and I couldn't do that.

'Oh, John,' she whispered, wiping her eyes.

So why haven't I told Rick who his sibling is outright? I stayed away in the hope it'd protect him, but he turned out too much like me anyway. He needs to prove himself and that's why I set him the test. I involved you because... Well, you were such a shy, quiet little thing but I saw the way you two connected when you were just little tykes. You'll know now why I chased him away. Maybe you'll become friends after all.

'In my dreams, John.'

I wish you well and very happy and I hope you don't think too badly of me.
Your friend, John.

She folded the letter and stared at the wall opposite for a long time, wishing she could share its contents with Rick.

Standing, she moved to the door and picked her way through the overgrown lawn and wild garden down to John's cottage. Rick's cottage. A path had been worn through the undergrowth to it during the last few weeks.

With her heart in her throat, she reached beneath the

step and her fingers curled around the key. She rose and inserted it into the lock. She pushed open the door and…

Her eyes filled with hot tears. Her throat burned. Rick was gone. As she'd known he would be, but…

Some crazy thread of hope had remained alive inside her, hoping to still find him here, hoping he'd ignored her demand that he leave.

She halted on the threshold for a few seconds before forcing herself inside the room. She immediately pressed her hands to her eyes and pulled in a breath. If she inhaled deeply enough, concentrated hard enough, she could still catch the faintest trace of him in the air—a scent she couldn't begin to describe, but it had his teasing dark eyes and wicked grin rising up in front of her.

A breeze wafted through the door behind her, disturbing the scent and amalgamating it with the perfume of warm grass and native frangipani instead.

No! She leapt to slam the door, but it was too late. All that registered now were smells from the garden.

She wanted to drop to the floor and pound her fists against it. She didn't. She forced herself to inspect the entire cottage—all of it neat and clean. She didn't even have the garbage to take out. Rick had done it before he'd left.

Nothing.

Not even a note.

'What on earth did you expect?' she whispered.

This was always how it was going to end—with Rick riding off into the sunset.

Without her.

With stinging eyes, she walked back through the cottage and locked the door behind her. She didn't replace the key beneath the veranda. There didn't seem to be any point.

Rick paced through Tash's currently deserted house and tried to make sense of the conflicting impulses raging through him—the urge to run and the urge to stay. The urge to jump into his car and drive until he was too tired to drive any more. Or the urge to race over to Nell's house, take her into his arms and kiss her until she swore she'd never send him away again.

His chin lifted. He started for the door.

What can a guy like you offer a girl like Nell Smythe-Whittaker?

He slid to a halt with a curse and went back to pacing.

Do something to deserve her.

Like what? He planted his hands on his hips and glared about the room. How on earth could he do that? How the hell could he prove to her that he meant to stick around? How—

For a moment everything stilled and then he slapped a hand to his forehead and planted himself in front of Tash's computer. He typed 'How to start a business' into the search engine.

And he started making notes.

It took Rick two days to register Bradford's Restorations with the business bureau, to obtain an Australian Business Number and to have business cards printed. He bought a van and organised for a sign writer. He bought tools. He hired someone to design him a website. He barely slept three hours a night.

Surely a business would convince Nell he meant to stay, would prove to her he was serious about making something of himself?

She'd believe it more if you had family ties in the area.

He swallowed and turned to the phone. Family? Poppy? What if Poppy rejected him? He swung away to throw himself down on the sofa and drag both hands back through his hair, his lungs cramping.

What if she doesn't?

The voice that whispered through him sounded suspiciously like Nell's. He stared at the phone again. Swallowing, he pulled Marigold's business card from his wallet and dialled the number.

'Hello?'

The voice was female and he had to fight the urge to slam the phone down. 'I, uh…' He cleared his throat. 'May I speak with Marigold Somers please?'

'Yes, speaking.'

He swallowed again. 'Mrs Somers, my name is Rick Bradford and I…' How did one say it—*I'm your daughter's brother*? 'You met my friend Nell Smythe-Whittaker at the park the other day.'

'Rick!' He heard the catch in her voice. 'I'm so glad you called. I've told Poppy all about you and we're dying to meet you.'

His throat tightened at the warmth in her voice. 'I'd like that.'

'Come for dinner, please? We'd love you to.'

Her eagerness and sincerity made his heart thump.

'Promise you'll come. Tomorrow night?'

His eyes burned. He stared up at the ceiling and blinked hard. 'I…you're sure?'

'Positive.'

They made a time. He rang off and then he didn't know what to do. He knew what he wanted to do. He wanted to go and find Nell and tell her what he'd done and have her assure him it was the right thing to do.

You haven't earned her yet.

He pulled a receipt from his pocket—a copy of the one Mitch had retrieved for Nell. It was time to see a jeweller about a ring.

CHAPTER TWELVE

NELL GLANCED THROUGH her dream folder, sipped a glass of wine and tried to find the tiniest hint of excitement.

And failed.

Closing the folder, she rubbed her fingers across her brow. Her zest for life would return. Other people recovered from broken hearts, didn't they?

She glanced at the kitchen clock. Was six o'clock on a Saturday evening too early to go to bed?

A knock sounded on the front door. She glanced towards the hallway without the tiniest flicker of interest. Maybe whoever it was would go away if she ignored it.

Another knock.

Ignoring it won't help you get over a broken heart.

She pulled a face, but all the same she forced herself to her feet to answer it.

Smile.

She pasted one on before opening the door.

The smile slid straight off again. Her heart gave such a big kick she had to reach out and cling to the door to remain upright. 'Rick?' she whispered.

'Hey, Princess.'

Those dark eyes smiled down at her, the mouth hooked up, and all she wanted to do was throw herself into his arms.

Now there was a sure-fire way to embarrass herself.

'I… I…' She swallowed. 'I thought you'd left Sydney.' Why had he come back?

For her?

Oh, don't be deluded and pathetic. Nonetheless her pulse raced and her palms grew slick. Very carefully she released her grip on the door and wiped them down the sides of her yoga pants.

Her rattiest yoga pants. Why couldn't she be wearing one of her fifties-inspired dresses?

He shifted his weight. 'I never left. I've been staying with Tash.'

'Oh.'

Oh!

So he knew then? She swallowed and gestured him inside. 'Come on in. I was just having a glass of wine. Would you care for one?'

It took a superhuman effort, but she found her manners and managed not to sound stilted. Well done her!

'That sounds great.'

Now, if only she could pour him a glass without her hand shaking.

She didn't believe she could pull that off so she poured it with her back to him while managing a breezy, 'Take a seat.' She turned. 'Oh, and help yourself to a cupcake.' And she gestured to the tin on the table, which averted his gaze from the way her hand shook when she set his wine in front of him.

She sat. She twisted her hands in her lap. She didn't want to talk about her father. She didn't want to find out that Rick felt beholden to her in some way. 'How long are you planning to stay in Sydney?' she asked instead, determined that her stupidly optimistic heart should know the truth asap.

His grin lost its cockiness. He swallowed. It made her swallow too. 'I'm, um…planning on sticking around.'

Her fingernails dug into her palms. *He's not hanging around for you!*

'Why?' The word croaked out of her. She didn't want it to. She'd do anything to recall it, but she couldn't.

His eyes darkened. 'Damn, this is awkward.'

He could say that again.

He drew in a breath. He stood. He came around the table to where she sat and dropped to one knee in front of her. She almost fell off her chair. 'Nell, I love you and I want to spend the rest of my life with you.'

He pulled a small velvet box from his pocket and opened it. Her grandmother's diamond ring winked back at her and some instinct told her this was no copy.

'Will you do me the great honour of marrying me?'

He was offering her everything she wanted!

She closed her eyes, counted to three and opened them again. The ring still hovered there, winking at her with all of its promise. Her throat and chest burned. Her eyes stung. 'No,' she whispered. 'No, Rick, I won't marry you.'

Rick stumbled to his feet, a darkness he'd never experienced before threatening to descend around him. He stumbled around the table and back into his chair because he didn't have the strength to make it all the way to the front door.

'Tash was wrong.'

He couldn't believe his voice could emerge so normally while everything inside him crumbled.

'Tash?'

Nell's voice didn't come out normally at all, but strangled and full of tears. *Damn it all to hell!* He wished he could rewind the last five minutes and erase them. But he couldn't and he was too tired to lie. Nell might not love him, but she'd never be cruel. 'She told me you were in love with me.'

'She wasn't wrong.'

It took a moment for him to make any sense of that.

When he did a shaft of light pushed the darkness back. He straightened. 'What did you just say?'

Her green eyes suddenly flashed. She leapt up and slashed both hands through the air. She paced to the sink, gripped it till her knuckles turned white and then swung back to stab a finger at him. Her hand shook and he wanted to capture it in his and never let it go.

'If you've been staying with Tash then you know what my father threatened.' Her hands slammed to her hips, the long line of her leg clearly defined in those stretchy pants, and his mouth dried. He tried to keep his mind on what she said rather than how she looked…and how much he wanted to ravish her.

'Which means you know I put Whittaker House on the market.'

'To save my skin!'

'Which means you also know,' she went on as if he hadn't spoken, 'that Mitch provided me with information to finally, once and for all, defeat my father.'

He didn't know where she was going with this—just that the pain in her eyes tore at him. He gave a wary nod.

'Damn it, Rick! I don't want a husband who marries me because he feels beholden to me.'

His jaw dropped. 'I don't feel beholden to you.' He loved her!

She gave a laugh. 'Oh, right.'

He opened his mouth.

'You've been playing white knight all your life. As a boy you tried to protect all the kids in the neighbourhood, you took the blame and went to prison for one of those friends. Heaven only knows how many women you've rescued from untenable situations since then. You specialise in damsels.'

He swallowed. Everything she said was true, but…

'I'm just the latest in a long line. Well, I don't want to be a defenceless female. I want to be strong enough to deal with my own problems.'

'You are. You have!' He didn't see her as someone who needed rescuing.

'And I don't want a white knight!' she shouted. 'When I marry I want it to be an equal partnership.'

'Damn it, Nell.' He leapt to his feet. 'Can't you see that I'm not the white knight here? You are!'

Her jaw dropped. He passed a hand across his eyes. 'You are,' he muttered, falling back into his chair.

Her mouth opened and closed but no sound came out. She stood there, staring at him as if she didn't know what to do, what to say or if to believe him.

'I've spent the last week trying to do things to earn you—to prove to you that I'm worthy of you.'

She plonked down on her chair as if the air had left her body. She reached for her glass of wine, but she didn't drink from it.

'I'm in the process of establishing my own restoration building company. I'm hoping to interview potential employees next week.'

She blinked. 'I… Congratulations.'

'Thank you.' He nodded. 'I rang Marigold and I've met Poppy. In fact I've met the whole family.'

Her glass slammed to the table. She leaned towards him. 'How did it go?'

It almost made him smile. 'Pretty well. She's great. In fact her whole family is great.' His gaze captured hers. 'She's not a damsel either.'

Nell sat back. 'No, she's not.'

Steel stiffened his backbone. 'And neither are you. You're a lot of things—maddening, stubborn, generous to a fault and optimistic in the face of all evidence to the contrary—but the one thing you're not is useless.'

Her eyes filled with tears and he ached to go to her, to pull her into his arms, but then she smiled and it was like a rainbow. 'I know.'

Something inside him unclenched.

She frowned. 'You aren't either.'

He rested his elbows on the table and dropped his head to his hands. 'Princess, I've always been able to save other people, but I've never been able to save myself.'

'Oh, Rick!'

And then she was on his lap and in his arms. He pressed his face into her neck and breathed her in. 'You saved me, Princess.' She ran a hand back through his hair and then her arms went about his shoulders and she held him so tight he could feel the broken bits of himself start to come back together.

He drew back to touch a hand to her face. 'You believed in me so strongly that you made me believe in myself again.'

She pressed a kiss to the corner of his mouth. 'You're wonderful! You *should* believe in yourself.'

'Nobody has ever been so completely on my side before you came along.'

'There are lots of people on your side.' Her eyes flashed. 'Tash and Mitch and all your friends, and now Poppy and her family. You just won't let yourself see it. You're afraid of not being the strong one everyone else can rely on.'

Was that true?

'I went to Tash and Mitch for advice about the fake ring. Do you think that makes me weaker or less strong?'

'Hell, no! It shows how smart you are to approach the people who have the expertise you need.'

She raised an eyebrow.

His heart thumped. Slowly he nodded. 'There can be strength in reaching out and asking for the help you need.'

'Precisely.'

In that moment a spark of light lit him up from the inside, so bright it almost blinded him. He ran his hands slowly up her back and she shivered. 'Princess, you're in my lap.'

She grinned at him. 'Would you like me to get up?'

'Not a chance.'

She laughed and then gasped when he shifted her a fraction so she could feel what she did to him. 'Oh.' Her eyes widened. She wriggled against him. 'Ooh.'

He bit back a groan. 'Steady, Princess. Not yet.'

Her face fell. 'Why not?'

He tried for mock stern but probably failed. 'There's another couple of things we need to clear up.'

She bit her lip and then nodded. 'Okay.'

'You gave me the courage to reach for my dream again.'

'It only seems fair. You're giving me the chance to chase mine.'

'I want to have a family that's the polar opposite from the one I had growing up. I want to do that with you, Nell. Not because I feel I owe you or because I think you need a man in your life to look after you, but because I love you.' A tear hovered on one of her eyelashes. He wanted to kiss it away. 'I need to know if you believe me.'

She took his face in her hands and stared into his eyes. He felt exposed in a way he never had before, but he didn't look away. 'Yes,' she said. 'I do believe you. I never thought I'd be the kind of girl who could convince you to settle down. You kept telling me how different we were and—'

He touched a finger to her lips. 'I was fighting what I felt for you.'

She nodded. 'I know that now, but when you proposed I was too afraid to believe it was for real.' She brushed his hair back from his forehead. 'But I'm not afraid any more, Rick.' And then she leaned forward and touched her lips to his and they kissed so fiercely and with all of their hearts that they were both breathing hard when they finally broke apart.

He tried to get the racing of his blood under control. 'So you'll marry me?'

'Yes.'

He slipped her grandmother's ring onto her finger. She

stared at it and then covered it with her other hand and pressed it to her heart. 'How did you find it?'

'I approached the jeweller who'd sold it on behalf of your grandparents and tracked down the buyer. I made an offer to buy it back and he accepted.'

'I bet you paid twice what it was worth.'

More or less. 'I wanted to give you a ring that meant something special to you.'

She twisted around to face him more fully. 'I don't need fancy rings or fast cars or pretty clothes.'

She mightn't need them, but he meant to lavish her with all that and more.

'I don't even need this house.'

He had every intention that it remained in the family.

'I love you, Rick. All I need is you.'

'Princess, you have me for as long as you want me.'

'Forever,' she breathed.

'And beyond,' he agreed. 'Now, can I have a cupcake to keep up my strength before I take you upstairs to ravish you?'

She laughed and the sound of it filled him. 'I can see we're going to have to find ourselves a good dentist.' She reached over and lifted the lid on the tin and offered them to him.

'On second thoughts…' He replaced the lid, lifted her in his arms and headed upstairs instead. There'd be time for cake later.

EPILOGUE

MITCH RUSHED UP and clapped Rick on the shoulder. 'I have it on good authority that the show's about to start. Ready?'

'I've been ready for eight months!' Rick shot to his feet and glanced down the red carpet that led from the ornate wooden rotunda to the terrace of Whittaker House. Rows of red and white roses created an avenue for Nell to walk down. Once she appeared, that was.

Mitch took his place beside Rick, tugging at the jacket of his tux. 'I can't believe how much you guys have transformed this place.'

It'd taken a lot of hard work, but he and Nell had relished every second of it. And it had paid off. Whittaker House gleamed, apricot and cream in the warm November sunshine, the deep red accents providing a perfect contrast. His chest swelled. He'd done that. *Him!* His gaze moved to the garden—a riot of spring colour—and his pulse quickened. This was the real triumph, though, and all Nell's doing.

Nell.

He glanced at his watch and then back towards the house, his fingers drumming against his thighs. The wedding guests murmured quietly among themselves on chairs arranged beneath a red and white striped awning whose bunting danced joyfully in the breeze. A group of less than thirty people that included Poppy and her family, some of his old school friends, Nell's employees and his, as well as friends they'd made in the course of setting up their businesses—an intimate and generous-minded group. On nearby trestle tables covered in fine white linen was a wedding tea fit for a princess. In pride of place was the cupcake tower—the wedding cake—that Nell had baked and assembled herself.

It was all ready.

He touched unsteady fingers to his bow tie and then swung to Mitch. 'I thought you said it was about to—'

The band kicked up with *'Here Comes the Bride'*.

Rick turned to find Nell standing at the other end of the red carpet. His breath jammed. A fist squeezed his chest. *She was beautiful.*

She started down the avenue towards him in a magnificent 1950s frock in white silk. A scarlet sash circled her waist. Her white satin heels sported scarlet bows. In her hands she held a bouquet of marigolds. He stared and stared and his heart hammered.

She was walking down the aisle to him. *To him!*

Everything blurred. He had to blink hard. Swallow hard. 'I'm marrying a diamond of a woman,' he croaked to Mitch.

'Me too,' Mitch choked back.

Tash, Nell's bridesmaid, looked pretty in scarlet. She and Mitch had booked a date here in February for a garden wedding of their own.

Nell was setting a trend—high tea weddings.

When she finally reached him he took her hand, kissed it and held it fast. 'You look beautiful, Princess.'

'So do you,' she whispered back, her green eyes sparkling, her lips soft and her grip as tight as his.

He wanted to kiss her, but the wedding celebrant cleared her throat and he and Nell turned to her. They made the vows that would bind them together for life. They kissed—a solemn, almost chaste kiss. They signed the register. His heart grew so big he thought he might burst.

Nell leaned in against him, drenching him in the scent

of sugar and spice. 'Once upon a time a girl met a boy and fell in love, but she lost the boy.'

He touched a finger to her cheek. 'Many years later the boy met the girl again and fell in love.'

Nell turned to face him, her hand resting against his chest. 'And they lived happily ever after.'

'I'm counting on it, Princess.' His throat thickened and his breath bottled in his chest. 'You've made me believe fairy tales can come true.'

'I'm going to spend the rest of my life proving it to you,' she whispered before reaching up on tiptoe to kiss him.

Warmth washed through him. She didn't need to prove anything. His arm snaked around her waist and he pulled her closer. She'd made a believer out of him. He believed in her. Most of all he believed in them. And he made sure his kiss said as much—he and Nell, together forever.

* * * * *

[illegible]

his thumbs [illegible]
[illegible]

“Let’s dance.”

Liz felt a spurt of adrenaline as Connor pulled her into his arms and drew her close to his hard-muscled body. His hat nudged hers, but he didn’t let that stop him from pressing his cheek against hers. She was burning up. He couldn’t help but notice.

When the song ended, he didn’t let go. “This is nice,” he whispered in a husky voice.

So nice she could hardly breathe. He continued to rock her in his arms until another song began. “I like your gold barrel-racer earrings. They’re unique.”

Liz lost track of her surroundings. The whole time they clung to each other, his warm breath tickled the ends of her newly cut hair, sending rivulets of delight through her body. It was uncanny how they moved as one person.

"Let's dance?"

Liz felt a spurt of adrenaline as Connor pulled her into his arms and drew her close to his hard-muscled body. His feet nudged hers, but he didn't let that stop him from pressing his cheek against hers. She was burning up. He couldn't help but notice.

When the song ended he didn't let go. "This is nice," he whispered in a husky voice.

So nice she could hardly breathe. He continued to rock her in his arms until another song began. "I like your gold barrel-racer earrings. They're unique."

Liz lost track of her surroundings. The whole time they clung to each other, his warm breath tickled the ends of her newly cut hair, sending rivulets of delight through her body. It was uncanny how they moved as one person...

A COWBOY'S HEART

BY
REBECCA WINTERS

Published in Great Britain 2014
by Mills & Boon, an imprint of Harlequin (UK) Limited,
Eton House, 18-24 Paradise Road, Richmond, Surrey, TW9 1SR

ISBN: 978-0-263-91305-7

23-0814

Harlequin (UK) Limited's policy is to use papers that are natural, renewable and recyclable products and made from wood grown in sustainable forests. The logging and manufacturing processes conform to the legal environmental regulations of the country of origin.

Printed and bound in Spain
by Blackprint CPI, Barcelona

Rebecca Winters, whose family of four children has now swelled to include five beautiful grandchildren, lives in Salt Lake City, Utah, in the land of the Rocky Mountains. With canyons and high-alpine meadows full of wildflowers, she never runs out of places to explore. They, plus her favorite vacation spots in Europe, often end up as backgrounds for her romance novels, because writing is her passion, along with her family and church.

Rebecca loves to hear from readers. If you wish to e-mail her, please visit her website, www.cleanromances.com.

Many thanks to three remarkable ladies who were kind enough to give their time and answer some of my questions about the rodeo world:

Leslie DiMenichi with the WPRA, professional horse trainer, barrel champion rodeo competitor and breed show trainer.

Sue Smith, 2x NFR Qualifier, Circuit Finalist & Year End Winner, Calgary 100k Winner, Multiple Futurity and Derby Winner, Amateur Rodeo Barrel Racing and Breakaway Roping Winner.

Martha Josey, WPRA, AQHA and NBHA World Champion Barrel Racer, Cowgirl Hall of Fame in 1985, representing the United States in the 1988 Winter Olympics in Calgary, Canada.

Chapter One

November 28 and Mother Nature had decided to dump new snow over the Pryor Mountains on both sides of the Montana–Wyoming border. Ten inches during the night. Their biggest storm so far this year.

Liz Henson, the top barrel-racing champion in both the Montana Pro Rodeo Regional Circuit and the Dodge Ram pro finals in Oklahoma, left the barn astride Sunflower. She headed toward the covered arena behind the Hensons' small house that sat on Corkin property. With this snow she was glad she'd had the farrier in White Lodge check both her horses' shoes yesterday.

Both she and Sunflower enjoyed the invigorating air as her horse made tracks in the pristine white fluff past the Corkin ranch house. Liz's parents had worked for the Corkins since before she was born. Sadie Corkin was Liz's best friend, and both families had shared the barn over the years.

Every dawn, like clockwork, Liz got up to put her horse through a practice session before she left for work as a vet at the clinic in White Lodge twenty minutes away. Sometimes it was a trail ride, other times flat work in the arena. She tried to vary the experience for Sunflower.

Every night at dusk she went through another practice session. Barrel racing required months of progressively harder and more challenging work to build up her horse's tolerance to intense acceleration and turning. She needed to spark her horse out of some rollbacks, yet keep her soft and relaxed.

Today she wanted to work on her horse's shoulders. Mac Henson, her father, idol and mentor, had explained that the more control you had over the shoulders, the easier it would be to steer Sunflower. He'd warned Liz about everything that could happen during competition.

Her horse might be too hot and nervous, or refuse to rate or stop. It might dive into the barrel and knock it over, or misbehave in the alleyway and balk at entering the arena.

Liz had received a five-second penalty in a competition when Sunflower had dropped her shoulder at the barrel. Since then they'd been practicing correct body arc and position around the barrels.

A horse was generally left-sided, just as most humans were right-handed. The trick during the lope or canter was to shape your horse for either turn by using reverse-arc exercises and riding serpentines. She needed to teach her horse to lift the shoulder away from the pressure of the inside rein.

If the problem couldn't be mastered, she wouldn't have a prayer of winning at the Pro National Finals Rodeo in Las Vegas in December. The Mack Center on the University of Nevada campus hosted the top rodeo competitors in the world.

She might have made it to number two out of the top fifteen money winners in her event, but without constant practice and staying in excellent physical form to make her legs strong, she couldn't expect to come out with the overall win. Sadly, this would be her last competition before she gave it up to devote herself full time to her career. Dr. Rafferty needed a partner who wasn't off every few days barrel racing in another rodeo to stack up wins.

Her seven-year-old quarter horse had been a runner from the beginning and was well proportioned. Liz had trained half a dozen horses, but felt she couldn't have found a better horse for the sport than this one.

Polly, the other quarter horse Liz trained and took with her to every rodeo, wasn't as reliable as Sunflower. But if something happened to Sunflower during competition, Liz needed a backup.

Her third horse, Maisy, she left behind. She wasn't as teachable and hadn't learned to body rate or lower her head when Liz pulled on the reins. The ability for a horse to slow its speed at the first barrel in response to light rein pressure was crucial. Only then could you position it for a precise first turn and properly align it to change leads for the other two turns, thus shaving off time.

When Liz's body relaxed, Maisy should have related that to the movement. She tried to teach Maisy, but the horse was slow to respond. Nevertheless, she was a great horse for riding in the mountains.

Since Liz used dressage in her training regimen, snaffles were the best bit to use. This morning she was using training reins and had picked the square mouthpiece O-ring to teach control and collection. This bit kept her horse's mouth moist without damaging it.

Liz had about ten different bits, but didn't have a favorite competition bit. No matter which one she used, she rarely rode Sunflower in the same bit she was running and changed it frequently to keep the horse's mouth soft.

Liz trained with four barrels, arranged in what was called the cloverleaf pattern, even though there were only three for competition. Her dad had taught her that if you went for the diamond pattern, the horse wouldn't know which barrel was first, thereby reducing the excitement so her horse would stay controlled. A clever trick that worked.

Once inside the arena, Liz spent time making perfect circles with Sunflower, starting at fifty feet and diminishing to twelve, so the horse would get used to going in circles using a little inside leg. Her horse's back feet needed to go in the same track as her front feet. Liz worked Sunflower in one direction, then the other, making as many circles as necessary to get that control, sometimes walking, sometimes jogging, sometimes loping and trotting where Liz could stand in the stirrups to strengthen her legs.

Barrel racing was all about speed transitions, stops and then backing up. But Liz had learned that "all go and no whoa" wasn't fun. An effective warm-up was everything. She walked Sunflower over to the fence, stopped, backed up, then went in the other direction, using the "whoa" to alert her horse to stop. This exercise built up her horse's hindquarters. Practicing at the fence caused Sunflower to use her back hocks and stifles to turn around, building vital control.

When the moment came, Liz walked her horse along the wall, using her right hand to tip the horse's nose slightly toward the wall. She kept her left hand low and moved it out in the direction she wanted to move the shoulders.

Then she pressed the horse up by the girth with her right leg to push its shoulders away from the wall. When she felt Sunflower take two steps off her leg, she released the pressure and let the horse walk out straight.

"Good girl, Sunflower."

Liz repeated this process in the other direction, and eventually Sunflower progressed to the trot and canter stages.

The sound of clapping caused her head to jerk around.

"You're looking on top of your game, Liz."

To her surprise, it was Connor Bannock from the neighboring ranch. Coming from him there couldn't be a greater compliment. At her first junior rodeo competition years earlier, she'd blown it so badly she'd wanted to die. But Connor, who was a year older and already on his way to a world championship, had sought her out. In front of a lot of people he'd told her she had real talent and shouldn't let one loss be a reason to give up. His encouragement, plus the way he'd smiled and tipped his hat, had lit a fire in her that had never gone out.

"I'm working on it." She walked Sunflower toward him. "As usual, your fame precedes you. I just heard about your latest win. Congratulations."

"Thanks."

He and his hazer, Wade Torney, had already returned from the rodeo in Kalispell. Wade, who rode parallel to the steer as it left the chute to keep it traveling in a straight line, had been Connor's partner for years. They must have driven hard through the snow to make it back this fast.

Now the twenty-seven-year-old world steer-wrestling champion sat astride one of his stallions, wearing a shearling sheepskin jacket and his trademark cream-colored Stetson. The man was a legend.

In his teen years, Connor had been Montana's high school all-around steer wrestling and team roping champion two years in a row. Early in his career he'd stacked up dozens of awards, among them the PRCA Overall and the Steer Wrestling Resistol Rookie of the Year.

To the envy of the other competitors, last year he won his fifth world title, placing in seven out of ten rounds at the Wrangler NFR, winning the fourth round in 3.3 seconds. The list of his achievements over ten years went on and on. She knew all of them.

Beneath his cowboy hat, a pair of piercing brown eyes studied her with a thoroughness that puzzled her. Without his hat, his overly long dark-blond hair was gilded at the tips by the sun.

What was the divorced, hard-muscled rancher doing over here? Nature had played all sorts of surprises this morning. First the snow, and now the powerfully built man who'd made the cover of a dozen Western magazines naming him the sexiest cowboy of the year.

No doubt about it. The six-foot-three, two-hundred-pound bulldogger attracted a huge share of buckle bunnies who followed him around the circuit. When she was a young and impressionable teenager, the sight of him used to make Liz's heart bounce like a Ping-Pong ball.

But Liz was a twenty-six-year-old woman now,

who'd had relationships with several great guys. At the moment she was dating Kyle James, a pilot with an air charter service out of Bozeman. He'd flown in some supplies for Dr. Rafferty on an emergency. Liz had met his plane at the airfield outside White Lodge.

His good looks and friendly nature appealed to Liz. He ended up flying to White Lodge several times to take her to dinner. She'd driven to Bozeman twice to spend time with him. He was growing on her, but when he'd offered to drive with her to Las Vegas, she'd turned him down, explaining that she'd made other arrangements.

Not to be discouraged, he'd told her he planned to fly down for the last event on the fourteenth. Though she hadn't told him not to come, she wasn't sure she wanted him there. Her hesitation to let him into her life to that degree proved she wasn't ready for a full-blown relationship yet.

As Connor continued to study her, she started to grow anxious. Over the past eight years he'd only stepped on Corkin property twice that she knew of. The first time was the day of Daniel Corkin's funeral in May, when all the Bannocks showed up, except for Connor's father, Ralph, who'd been too weak to come.

The second time was the night, a month later, when Connor and his brother Jarod had rescued Sadie from their mentally unbalanced cousin, Ned Bannock. He'd trespassed on Corkin property and attacked Sadie in the barn. For the present, Ned was being treated in a special mental health facility in Billings.

Her body tautened. Connor would never have come to the ranch, especially this early, if something weren't wrong that could affect her on a personal level. "You must have bad news, otherwise you wouldn't be here. Has something happened to my father?" Her dad was the Corkin foreman and had left the house early to talk business with Zane Lawson, Sadie's stepuncle. He was the new owner of the Corkin ranch.

"If it had, do you think we'd still be here talking?"

She blinked. "But—"

"It's not your mom, either." He read her mind with ease. "This has nothing to do with your parents."

Though relieved, she bit her lip. "Then, is your father ill again? Do you need help?" Liz adored Ralph Bannock, the patriarch of the Bannock family. A great rodeo champion himself in his twenties, he'd always encouraged her and Sadie in their barrel racing. But he'd suffered a serious bout of pneumonia last spring that had put him in the hospital. Since then he'd recovered, but he was getting older and more frail. So what was *wrong?*

CONNOR WAS TAKEN aback by the questions, and the look of alarm in Liz's eyes told him how much she cared for his father. He found himself touched by her concern. "He was fine when I left him after breakfast."

"Thank goodness. When I visited with him a couple of days ago, he seemed well." She looked anxious. "What aren't you telling me?" She was really worried.

Liz was all business. It shouldn't have surprised him. She had every right to be suspicious of his unexpected presence. If it hadn't for Daniel Corkin, who'd warned the Bannocks off his property several decades ago—which meant staying away from the Hensons, too—Connor would have invited her to use the Bannock facilities for training whenever she wanted. It had taken Daniel's death for everything to change.

She was an outstanding rider who'd been trained by her father. No barrel racer Connor had seen on the circuit this year had her speed and grace. He'd spotted her exceptional ability years earlier. Though she'd had a poor showing at her first professional rodeo, a lot of it had to do with the wrong horse.

Mac Henson, her father, had been an expert bull rider, but without financial support he hadn't been able to realize his dream of becoming a world champion. He had, however, turned his daughter into one by investing in a proper horse for her. Sunflower was a winner and could bring her a world championship.

"How would you like to drive to Las Vegas with me for the finals?"

Her lips broke into a sunny smile. "Ralph put you up to this."

No. His grandfather had nothing to do with it. Connor's invitation was his alone, but since she thought Ralph was behind it, what could it hurt? Maybe he'd have a better chance of getting her to say yes. He'd been planning to ask her for several months, but had to be careful not to give the impression he saw her as a charity case where money was concerned.

"In case you didn't know, he's sweet on you." That was only the truth.

Liz Henson was a brilliant horsewoman and had worked hard to get where she was. The least he could do to show support for a neighbor was to drive Sunflower there for the big event. Her dun-colored quarter horse had great speed. He liked her unusual yellowish-gray coat, which was set off by a black mane and tail. An original, like Liz herself.

Mac and Millie Henson hadn't made much money as foreman and housekeeper for that scrooge, Daniel Corkin, before he'd died. Now that they worked for Zane, there still wasn't a lot of money. Liz did have a job as a vet, but the practice wasn't lucrative. Even with the money she'd won so far this year, he knew she could use some physical help to get her to Las Vegas. He happened to know her equipment was ancient and liable to break down at any time along the way.

Connor realized his life had been blessed with many gifts. It would ease some of his guilt to use his means to do something for Liz, who had incredible talent. He was proud of her for making it to the national pro finals in Las Vegas. That was where they were both headed, since their wins at the Dodge Ram finals for the U.S. circuit region winners in Oklahoma City.

His grandfather was betting on her to win. So was Connor. With Daniel Corkin out of the way, Connor had decided he wanted to make things easier for her in the only way he knew how.

"That's very nice of both of you, but I've already made my arrangements. I'll be driving my truck and trailer."

Her answer sounded definitive. Connor figured she'd fight him at first, because she had spirit and was independent, like her folks, who were the salt of the earth. Connor had always liked the Hensons, too. But where Liz was concerned, it came to him that he'd have to fight fire with fire to get her to drive with him.

They'd been neighbors from birth, yet in all the intervening years he'd never spent time alone with her.

In fact, he'd never seen her when she wasn't wearing a cowboy hat and had a braid hanging down her back.

"If you don't accept my offer, it'll hurt my feelings."

She chuckled. "Since when?"

"You think I don't have any?"

Her brows formed a delicate frown. "I didn't say that."

"Good. It would mean a lot if you'll drive with me. Over the past few years I've seen you at a lot of the events and thought it ridiculous we didn't travel to them together. But because of Daniel's ban against all Bannocks, including you, I never tried to arrange anything."

"I'll admit he was a scary man, but that's over now."

"Since you said it, why don't you bury the proverbial hatchet and accept my offer. It'll be nice to have the company. We'll talk shop on the way down and celebrate our wins on the way back."

He was pleasantly surprised when her eyes lit up. "I like the way you think."

So far, so good. "I've made reservations at the RV park near the Mack Center. It has equestrian accommodations, and indoor and outdoor swimming pools. For the twelve days we're there, you and I will live out of my trailer while we're competing, whatever you want." It was the least he could do for his neighbor, and hopefully, friend.

Live WITH HIM? "I'm scheduled to stay at the Golden Nugget with the other barrel racers."

"I know, but you might like to be away from the others after your nightly events. I learned early I prefer being alone so nothing else gets into my head."

That was exactly the way she felt. The other competitors would be a distraction because they always wanted to go over the evening's events with a fine-tooth comb. Not staying with them might seem antisocial, but Connor had read her mind and had just given her priceless advice she'd be a fool not to take. "I hardly know what to say."

"Just say yes. But it's up to you. In case you didn't know, this is going to be my last event. After Las Vegas I'm through with competition."

"Sadie told me as much." Liz's best friend was married to Connor's brother and often confided in her.

"My new sister-in-law informed me this is going to be your last event, too."

Looks as if the confiding went two ways. "Yup. I've got to get serious about my career, but I have to admit I'm surprised about your decision." She smiled. "There are more good years left in the king of the bulldoggers."

"Those good years need to be spent doing more worthwhile things."

"That's an odd thing for you to say."

"The fact is, I've lived a selfish life so far, Liz."

She studied him for a moment, not understanding a comment like that. "What about Wade? You won't have room for three of us."

"Wade will be driving his horses down in his own trailer with his girlfriend, Kim. My traveling partners Shane and Travis will bring your second horse, Polly, and my other horse, Phantom, in my older rig with them. When they reach Las Vegas they'll stall them at the Mack Center tent for the rodeo. The guys will be over to pick up Polly whenever you give the word. We all like our own space."

He patted his horse's neck. "Since we need to be in Las Vegas by the third to attend the welcome celebrations before the first event on the fifth, I'm leaving early the day after tomorrow. Please say yes, otherwise I'm going to think Daniel did permanent damage to the relationship between our families."

He turned his horse to leave. When he reached the entrance, he looked over his shoulder at her. "I'll be listening for your call tomorrow. Just phone the ranch and I'll get back to you. Don't disappointment me. I'd rather not be alone with my own thoughts during the drive down and back, let alone throughout the competition." Without waiting for an answer, he left the arena.

Liz thought about his invitation all the rest of the day.

"Yoo-hoo!" she called to her mother when she got home from work.

"Is that you, honey?" Millie Henson always said that when Liz arrived.

"Who else?" she teased, and walked through the house to the kitchen.

"You're late. Your dad and I had Zane over for dinner an hour ago."

"I'm sorry."

"I was afraid something might have happened to your truck in this snow."

Liz stood at the sink to wash her hands. "I had to help with a birth at the Critchlow ranch. Mother and foal are doing well."

"That's good."

She turned to kiss her mom's cheek. "Something smells wonderful."

"Sit down and I'll serve you some roast chicken. I

tried that new recipe with the lemon and garlic from the food channel. The men said it's a winner."

"That's no surprise. You've never fixed a bad meal in your entire life."

Her mother drank coffee at the table with Liz while she dug into her meal. "This really is delicious, Mom."

"Thank you. Now, I want to talk to you about something serious. I'm worried about you driving all the way to Las Vegas in that old truck."

"It has enough life in it to get me to Nevada and back before it dies. But what if I told you I could drive there in total comfort?"

When Connor had told Liz he'd rather not be alone with his own thoughts, the statement had sounded lonely, troubled even. Before that he'd snapped, *You think I don't have feelings?*

Those two unexpected revelations in their conversation had made her decide to take him up on his offer, but telling her mom would only escalate her motherly concern. Still, they always talked things over. No matter what, there was honesty between them. Might as well get this over with right now.

Her mother put down her coffee mug. "Is Kyle taking you?"

"No."

"No?" She sounded disappointed. Her mom kept hoping Liz would meet the right man and settle down. "Then Sadie must have prevailed on Jarod to drive you."

Sadie's world had been transformed since she'd married Jarod Bannock six months ago. "They offered to take me, but I said no."

"That leaves Dr. Rafferty. Did he offer you the loan of his truck?"

"Yes."

"But you turned him down, too."

"I don't like being beholden to anyone."

"So you decided to rent a new truck. That's awfully expensive. I happen to know you've been saving your winnings to pay back your vet school loan."

"No, Mom." Liz put a hand on her mother's arm. "Early this morning Connor came by the arena and asked me to drive with him."

Like clockwork a shadow crossed over her mother's face. "Connor…as in Connor Bannock."

"Mom…"

Liz knew that came as a huge shock to her mother, who got up from the table. "You mean in his fancy hotel on wheels?"

"Unless he has to fly, it's the way he's been getting around for the past four years. It's not nearly as luxurious as some you see at the events. His handlers will bring Polly and his second horse down in his older rig. He's not a show-off, Mom, that much I do know about him."

He was all cowboy, tough and daring to the point that she often chewed her nails watching him shoot out of the barrier on his horse. He was so fast, his event was over before you could blink. Any pictures the journalists got of Connor had to be taken while they ran after him, because he never hung around after the required autographing sessions and photo shoots for his Wrangler sponsor. She and Sadie had often commented that both Bannock brothers were the least vain cowboys they knew.

"After all these years, why would he suddenly ask you now?"

Liz wanted an answer to that same burning question, but she said, "Ralph put him up to it. You *know* he did."

"I'm sure you're right about that, honey."

If Liz went with him, then she'd find out why he'd decided to honor his grandfather's wishes, but she'd known this would be her mother's reaction. Without hesitation she spent the next few minutes telling her the gist of their conversation at the arena. When she'd finished, Millie started to clear the dishes.

"Mom?" she prodded her.

"You're a grown woman, honey, and don't need my permission about anything."

Picking up her water glass, Liz took it over to put in the dishwasher. "I wasn't asking for permission," she said quietly.

Her mom turned to her with a sober expression. "You want my approval, otherwise you would have let me find out after the fact. But I don't want that responsibility. For years I watched you and Sadie grow up, both of you dying for love of the Bannock brothers. In Sadie's case, her love was reciprocated, whereas—"

"Connor hardly knew I existed and married someone else," Liz finished the sentence for her. Although they'd been neighbors, she'd never spent time alone with him, not even at the competitions. "Even having gone through a divorce, I doubt he's ever stopped loving her. Wasn't that what you were going to say?"

"Only that your infatuation with him has never ended," her mother murmured.

"You're right. I've been thinking about that all day. Infatuation isn't love. It's a crush I never outgrew. After all these years of being haunted by him, I have an opportunity for the first time to get a real dose of him, one-on-one. I'm convinced that driving to Las Vegas with him will be a revelation and provide the cure I've been needing."

"And if it isn't?"

Liz took a deep breath. "If it isn't, then I'll have to take a serious look at my life and make changes."

Her mother turned to look out the window. "That's what has me worried. Bannocks never pull up roots. That means you'll be the one who leaves us and move somewhere else."

"You're so sure of that? I'm thinking this will be my one and only chance to see who he really is and get over what has prevented me from moving on with another man."

A sigh escaped Millie's lips. "I only know one thing. I'm afraid to tell your father. He hasn't wanted anything to distract you before the competition. When he hears about this…"

Liz hugged her mom for a long time. "I'll talk to him and make him understand."

Chapter Two

Connor's black-and-silver horse trailer, hitched to his four-door black truck, contained everything you needed for comfortable living on the road. Two horse stalls with an extrawide floor and nonslip rubber matting, a niche with a bed and a sofa/pullout bed, a living/dining room, satellite TV, kitchen and bathroom, all in a nutmeg-colored wood with a ranch motif.

While Connor stashed her bags on board and showed her parents around, Liz took Sunflower's temperature one more time, and checked her eyes and nose before putting her in bell boots for protection during the journey. Now that the horse was ready to travel, she led Sunflower from the barn and loaded her into the trailer stall next to Firebrand.

Liz threw light rugs over each of them. Who knew whether the big sorrel gelding loaded in the roadside stall would like Sunflower's company or not? They were as unused to each other as Liz was to Connor. Despite the long journey ahead, Liz wasn't nervous and couldn't figure out why.

When she'd told her father she was going to drive with Connor, he'd been surprisingly supportive. "I'm glad you'll be with someone who's been hauling himself and his horse around for a long time. More snow is forecast over the whole intermountain region for the next few days. He's got the kind of equipment you need to keep you and Sunflower safe and comfortable."

Between the lines she read all the things he didn't say or warn her about. He didn't have to. She saw it in his eyes. Liz had the greatest parents on earth.

After she'd loaded her lightweight, high-horned saddle, she put the collapsible pop-up barrels she used for practice in the tack room of the trailer. She'd brought protein feed for her horse, wanting to keep a balance between forage and grain. Once she'd gathered her medical bag and stored it with everything, it was time to go.

She hugged her mom and then turned to her father. "I'm going to give it everything I've got to win, Dad. Thanks to you and Mom, and all your expert help, I think I have a chance."

"I know you do, Lizzie girl. Since Connor wants to win, too, I think you two are the best kind of company for each other. You already know what it's like to be in each other's skin, so to speak. You'll be able to offer each other the right sort of tips and comfort. Anyone not competing wouldn't know what you're facing, particularly when this competition will be the last for both of you."

Her dad understood everything.

"I can't believe this day is finally here."

He gave her that endearing lopsided grin. "Either you're growing up way too fast, or I'm getting too old."

"You're not getting old." She hugged him hard. *Please don't ever get old.*

"Your mom and I will fly down on the fourteenth

for the big night. Call us when you have a moment here and there."

"I'll call you when we get to Salt Lake tonight."

Connor had been standing close by and shook his head. "If the weather forecast is correct, we'll be lucky if we make it to the Utah border."

Her mom grabbed her one more time. "We'll be waiting to hear from you."

"I promise to stay in close touch."

"I love you, honey."

Tears stung Liz's eyelids. When she looked in her mother's eyes, she saw a whole world of love, fear, concern and pride. "Not as much as I love you," she whispered before climbing into the truck cab.

"I made some chili and rolls for you to enjoy on the way down. I put everything in the fridge."

"Thanks, Millie. We'll love it!" Connor called to her before she shut the door. His friends had already come to the barn to pick up Polly. Liz had given her a complete checkup first, and a treat, promising to see her soon. There was nothing left to be done.

Connor, wearing a green plaid shirt, jeans and well-worn boots, was already behind the wheel, ready to go. Minus the Stetson he'd tossed in the backseat, his hair had a disheveled look she'd seen often enough when he was wrestling a steer to the ground. That look suited him.

She wouldn't describe Connor as handsome in the traditional sense. *Authentic male* was what came to mind when she looked at the arrangement of lines and angles making up his hard-boned features.

Striking when the sun blazed down on his tanned skin.

Beautiful in motion when he mounted his horse bareback for a run.

Unforgettable when he flashed a quick smile or broke out in laughter, usually from some remark his friend Wade murmured at the gate so no one else could hear.

The kaleidoscope of pictures stored in her mind was there for good. Hopefully on this trip she'd see what was on the inside, the intangible traits that truly mattered and shaped the inner man. Was his inner self equally worthy of such admiration? If the cover of the book was better than the story, now was the time to find out.

Deep in thought, she didn't realize they'd pulled to a stop in front of the Bannock ranch house until Connor said, "Grandpa asked me if we'd come in so he could say goodbye and wish you luck."

"How sweet of him. I'd love to."

She jumped out into the snow and headed for the front porch. The temperature had to be close to thirty-two degrees. She zipped her parka all the way. It looked as though they'd be driving under an overcast sky most of the way today.

Connor opened the door and they headed for the den where they found his grandfather at his desk. The blaze from the fireplace gave out delicious warmth. The older man looked up with a smile and got to his feet. "Well, Liz."

"Hi again, Ralph." She hurried across the room to give him a hug. Liz had been here many times over the years.

"Connor told me you agreed to drive with him. Is he taking good care of you?"

"Of course. I'm a very lucky girl."

"It pleases me that my two favorite champions will be together. I have a little gift for the two of you." He pulled a small leather pouch out of his shirt pocket. "Avery picked it up for me on her way home from work yesterday."

Avery was Connor's sister. Liz couldn't imagine what the pouch could hold.

Connor's gaze shot to hers. "Go ahead and open it."

From inside the pouch she pulled out what looked like a silver charm bracelet. "You hang it on the rear-view mirror of the truck to bring you luck. I chose the charms myself for this red-letter moment in your lives. See that horseshoe? Both of you have beaten me at the game any number of times. The next charm is a boot for riding. There's a cowboy hat. The others are a horse in motion, a bulldogger on his horse, a cowgirl barrel racing, and a heart with wings for love of country."

Liz was so touched that, once again, her throat swelled. "This gift is priceless, Ralph."

She noticed that Connor's eyes took on a haunted look when he glanced at his grandfather. *Why?*

"We'll treasure it."

"If Addie and your parents were here, son, they'd tell you and Liz to take it with our prayers and blessings. We've always been proud of both of you and know you'll do your best at the competition. We'll all be watching the Great American Country broadcast on cable. Whatever happens, come back safe. That's all I ask."

Full of emotion, Liz clutched the bracelet in her hand before reaching for him once more. "All we ask is that *you* stay well. I promised my folks we'd stay in close touch. We'll make the same promise to you. Without your help, I would never have made it this far. Whenever I got discouraged, you would never let me stay down."

"Ditto," Connor said in a husky tone of voice, and gave his grandfather a bear hug.

The older man whispered, "Good luck," to him, and a tear rolled down his cheek.

She waved to Ralph from the doorway. "See you soon." Without waiting for Connor, she hurried out of the house to the truck. He needed a minute with his grandfather, and she needed to treasure this special moment in private. Both she and Sadie had always loved Ralph and Addie. Like her own parents, she thought they were just about perfect.

Carefully she undid the chain clasp so she could hang the bracelet. To make certain it was visible, she draped it over the mirror. The little charms tinkled as they dangled.

A minute later Connor strode toward the truck and climbed in behind the wheel. He fingered one of the charms, and then flicked his gaze to hers. "Grandpa thinks the world of you to have given you this."

"Didn't you notice it's for both of us? Whenever he talks about you, his eyes light up."

An odd silence followed her remark. She didn't understand and wondered what he was thinking as he started the engine.

"Before we leave, is there anything you've forgotten?"

"If I have, it's not important."

"Bless you." Spoken like a man. She chuckled before he said, "Let's go."

They drove away from the ranch to the highway, cleared of snow since the storm the other night. "I'd like to reach North Salt Lake by evening. I made a reservation at the RV park on the outskirts with easy access."

"Sounds good to me. In case of more snow, I'd planned to drive as far as I could through Wyoming before finding a motel. I'm really grateful you asked me to come with you."

"Did you have someone to drive with you if I hadn't asked you?"

A vision of Kyle passed through her mind. She looked out the passenger window. "Yes. I had several offers from friends and family, but this is one trip I wanted to take alone. Knowing it's my last one, I didn't feel like sharing the experience with anyone else."

He sat back in the seat. "So how come you came with me?"

"Honestly?" she answered with another question.

"Shoot."

"Because you're not anyone else. When I told Dad I was driving with you, he said we were the best kind of company for each other since we already know what it's like to be in each other's skin."

"He was right."

"You've been to nationals and have won back-to-back world championships five times. Now you're trying for your sixth! This is my first time and you know exactly how vulnerable I'm feeling on the inside. I'm full of doubts and ambitions no else could understand, no one but someone like you, who's already experienced all those emotions and triumphed."

"That's the problem," he muttered. "No matter how many triumphs, you're only as good as your last one."

"I know. I find that out every time I compete at another rodeo."

"If you know that already, then you know a hell of a lot more than ninety-nine percent of your competition who believe their own hype."

His unexpected burst of emotion showed he felt as vulnerable as she did. Maybe more, because this would be his last competition. The need to prove himself one more time had to be testing his mettle in ways she couldn't fathom. No one would ever suspect that of Connor Bannock, the picture of confidence personified.

"In all honesty, I'm afraid, Connor," she admitted under her breath.

"Of failure?"

"A lot more than that. No matter what happens, I don't know what the future's going to be like without having a goal. I've been pursuing this dream for so long, it's taken up the hours of my world, consciously and subconsciously for years. Of course, I have my career, but that's different. I can't imagine what it will be like to wake up on December 15, knowing it's truly over...and the rest of my life is still ahead of me," she whispered.

"Lady, you just said a mouthful."

Liz turned her head toward him in surprise. "You *too?*"

"In spades."

SO FAR, NO snow had fallen, but it was coming. Connor felt the icy wind from a bleak sky while he and Liz walked their horses at their first roadside park stop. Two hours at a time was as much as their animals could handle riding in the trailer. Their muscles got tired of trying to maintain their footing and needed the rest.

With them tied up outside, he and Liz ate sandwiches and drank hot coffee in the trailer. Her earlier admission about thinking she'd be at a loss once the competition was over was so in tune with his own feelings, they seemed to have achieved a level of understanding that didn't require a lot of conversation. He didn't feel the need to fill the gaps of silence. Neither did she.

By late afternoon, they'd made their fourth stop to exercise the horses. Inside the trailer they both made calls. He checked with Ben, the ranch foreman. Connor had hired a new hand to keep all the equipment on the ranch in top shape. That had been Ned's job. Ben sounded hopeful this new guy would work out. As they talked, Connor could hear Liz talking to Dr. Rafferty about a sick horse.

Once their phone business was done, they cleaned up the stall floor before watering the horses and replenishing their hay nets. Soon they'd brought the horses back inside and were on their way again.

Since his quickie divorce from Reva Stevens two years ago in Reno, he'd dated women, but he'd never taken any of them on the road with him. This was a first since the disastrous marriage in Las Vegas that had only lasted a year. His grandfather had never said anything, but Connor knew the older man hadn't been happy about his impulsive marriage to the L.A. TV anchor.

They'd made their base at her condo in L.A. When

he wasn't spending time with her, he traveled the rodeo circuit and worked on the ranch. She stayed on the ranch with him for a week after their honeymoon, but ranch life didn't hold her long. Both of them were too driven by ambition to put the other person first. The long separations took their toll, and divorce had seemed the only solution.

Though they hadn't been able to make it work, Reva called him from time to time. He kept their conversations short. He missed her in his bed. That had never changed, but it was everything else.

Liz's comment about being afraid of the future had resonated with him big-time.

Out of the corner of his eye he noticed her reading something on her iPad. "Anything interesting?"

"Yes. I've been checking stats. Dustine Hoffman just won the barrel-racing event at the Tom Thumb Texas Stampede in 13.71 seconds. She's everyone's competition."

He whistled. "That arena gives you faster time than the one in Las Vegas with its special soil."

She rolled her eyes at him. Between the dark lashes, they were as green as lime zest. He'd never seen eyes that exact color. "Thanks for trying to make me feel better. The truth is, she's a great athlete."

"So are you." Connor discovered that Liz had a great mouth, too. Soft and full, not too wide, but he couldn't afford to take his eyes off the road. "Didn't you do a 13.70 at Bakersfield?"

"I doubt I'll see a number that low again, but I can dream."

He knew all about that. "Did you read anything else interesting?"

A sly smile broke the corner of her mouth. "There must be a hundred blogs devoted to Connor Bannock. Your fans stretch around the country and back. Jocko Mendez from the Southeastern circuit in Arkansas is your closest competition, but word is out that Las Vegas is betting on you. Have you ever read any of them?"

She tried to get him off the subject of her.

"I don't have time." He let out a sigh. "Do yourself a favor and forget about Dustine Hoffman's stats. Concentrate on your routine with Sunflower. I watched you working with her the other morning. I'm impressed how well she body rates and changes leads between the first and second barrel."

"But I hear a but. What aren't you telling me?"

Liz was such a quick study, he needed to stay on his toes. "Am I that transparent?"

"Yes!"

He laughed. It was refreshing to be with someone who was too guileless to be anything but honest… unlike Reva, who'd harbored hurts and suspicions, then exploded at an unexpected moment.

"I notice you were working with wax reins, but they can be sticky. You have to really watch your hands with those. When they stick, you're pulling your horse around the barrel when you should be guiding her."

"Was that what I was doing the other morning?"

"No. I happened to notice it at your competition in Great Falls."

"You did?"

"Liz—we're not always at the same rodeos, but when we are, I make it a priority to watch my neighbor's performance."

She stirred in the seat. "I had no idea."

"When we get to Las Vegas, try using a knot rein at practice. They still slide when needed, but you might like the feel of them better. It's just a thought."

"But valuable input, coming from you. I'll try it."

One eyebrow lifted. "You're not offended?"

"By advice from *you?* What else did you see I can improve on?"

Connor decided she was like her dad, who didn't have a resentful, paranoid bone in his body. "Not a thing."

"Liar," she said with a smile, but it soon faded when stronger than usual gusts of wind buffeted the trailer. "Whoa—"

"Another storm front is moving in, but we're making good time so far. I'm glad we've reached Kemmerer. There's an RV park a mile away where I made a reservation, just in case. We may have to spend the night in Wyoming after all. I don't want to take chances with priceless cargo."

"You're right, of course. Our horses are precious."

"I was referring to you," he murmured.

Though she didn't dare take him seriously, her heart jumped anyway. "You sounded like your grandfather just then. Between your father and Ralph, you've had remarkable role models in them and it shows."

She saw his hands grip the steering wheel a little tighter. "You don't know my history. I'm afraid Grandpa has about given up on me."

There he went again. Something was going on where his grandfather was concerned, and she was curious. "Why would you say that? While he was hugging you, he had tears in his eyes, he's so proud."

"Those were tears of disappointment. I should have

quit the circuit several years ago in order to help him and Jarod."

Liz decided to take a risk. "Don't tell me your cousin Ned got to you, too, before he was put in that mental health facility—"

She heard his breath catch and knew she'd hit a nerve. "Sadie told me he about destroyed Jarod's confidence before they got back together. It sounds like he did a pretty good job on you, too. What did he tell you? That you didn't have what it took to run the Bannock ranch? Or did he make digs that you were running away from your responsibilities by letting the rodeo take over your life since your father's death?"

Connor stiffened. "I don't want to talk about it."

"You need to talk about it! Don't forget your grandfather was a rodeo champion in his day. He's in heaven watching you rack up the gold buckles."

Snow started to pelt the windshield, but she hardly noticed. "No doubt Ned accused you of leaving the work to your brother. Ned Bannock caused more trouble than Sadie's father ever did. Don't you know how jealous he was of you?"

Liz was all wound up and couldn't stop. "Ned never had your horsemanship and couldn't keep up with you. You were given a special gift. After you won your first buckle, why do you think he quit competing in rodeos so quickly? All he could do was undermine you, so you would feel guilty. He probably had a coronary when you married Reva Stevens, who looks like a movie star."

The windshield wipers were going full force while she kept on talking. "I'll bet he loved baiting you when you were divorced. Ned always did like to kick a man when he was already down. Well, I'd say he did a pretty fantastic job on you to make you feel like your grandfather is disappointed in you. But you would be wrong!

"Ralph adores you! I ought to know. I've been friends with him for years. If he's disappointed, then it's because he's afraid you've believed Ned. Shame on you, Connor!" Her rebuke rang in the cab.

By now, he'd turned into the RV campground and drove to the first place where they could stop. They were in a whiteout. But for the din of her voice, there was an eerie quiet. When she dared to look at him, his shoulders were shaking in silent laughter.

He turned in the seat, resting his head against the window where the snow was piling up and stared at her. "And here I thought you were a quiet little thing. But I should have known better after watching you on a horse. There's a spitfire inside of you. Feel better now that you've gotten it off your chest?"

Heat washed over her body in waves. "I'm sorry. I don't know what got into me."

His eyes played over her. "I don't think you left a thing unsaid. In fact, you mentioned a few things I hadn't even thought of that went straight to the gut."

She wanted to crawl in a hole. "Who would have thought Liz Henson from the Corkin ranch, who's always in her own world, had so much insight?"

Always in her own world?

"I'm afraid Sadie and I spent a lot of time on the backs of our horses discussing Ned, who never left her alone. Worse, he never wasted a chance to berate his cousins in front of us and any audience who happened to be around. It wasn't just Jarod he hated. He had plenty to say about you.

"When you trained Firebrand, a feral no one else could handle, he was furious at your success. Worse, every girl on the Montana circuit would have given her eyeteeth to go out with you and *he* knew it."

"Not every girl," he said in a quiet voice.

"You mean Sadie, but we both know why."

"I meant *you,* Liz."

"Me—?"

Connor cocked his head. "Don't you remember the time I asked you if you wanted to celebrate with me after you won at the Missoula Stampede?"

Liz blinked. "I figured you asked me for Wade's sake in order to set us up."

"He has a girlfriend now."

"I'm glad. He's kind of shy. Though I've always liked him, I was never interested in him that way."

"Ouch. Now you've wounded him *and* me."

"What do you mean *you?* You were married."

"Nope. Divorced. If you'd agreed, I would have told you I was single again, but you didn't give me the time of day. Before you shut me down cold, I figured we were far enough away from home that old man Corkin wouldn't find out the off-limits neighbors were getting friendly."

Her heart thudded. "Even if I had known the change in your marital status, I wouldn't have said yes. Being in love with the woman you married doesn't go away because of a piece of paper. Jarod and Sadie were still head over heels in love after eight years, even after she wrote him that awful goodbye letter he actually believed, and all because of Ned!"

"That's a fact." Connor reached to shut off the engine. "I think your explanation for rejecting me has helped a little."

"Give it up, Connor," she teased with a chuckle.

"I'll keep everything you told me in mind and cogitate on it."

"You do that."

"What do you say we go back to the trailer and enjoy some of your mom's chili while we see how long this storm is going to last."

WHILE SHE WARMED up their food, Connor put on his hat and jacket before walking back to check on the horses. The wet snow was coming down fast. The horses were better off inside their stalls where it was warm. He didn't want them catching a cold and made sure they had what they needed before he headed for the trailer.

He shook off the snow before entering. When he saw her seated at the kitchen table, a sense of guilt swept over him. Not for the things she'd deduced about his troubled psyche, which were right on, but because he hadn't given her life the same amount of thoughtful attention she'd given his. Most of the time he'd been too immersed in his own problems to think of others. He was the opposite of his grandparents.

They knew all about Sadie's and Liz's dreams, but they'd never divulged the essence of their conversations with Connor. His grandparents were saints who worried about everyone and did the little things that endeared them to friends and family. Take that charm bracelet. Connor had seen the loving expression on her face for Ralph. It came from the heart.

After hanging up his hat and jacket, he moved to the table. She immediately got to her feet to wait on him and pour him a mug of hot coffee. The one time he'd traveled with Reva in his trailer, to an event within California, she'd sat there waiting for him to take care of her. Even then, she'd insisted on staying nights at a hotel with room service.

She'd told him she really didn't like the trailer. It was too claustrophobic for her. Reva liked to eat out. So did he, once in a while. He excused her because he knew it simply wasn't her lifestyle. But the time came when just about everything he did or suggested didn't appeal to her.

They didn't grow together in their marriage. Through no true fault on either part, their physical attraction couldn't take care of everything else that was wrong. Starting a family had been out of the question. But enough dredging up the past he preferred to forget.

After eight hours of driving it was still so pleasant being with Liz, he kept wondering when the spell would wear off and she'd turn into someone else.

"Eat while the chili's hot. Mom made some rolls, too." Liz passed the plate to him. He took three.

"Thank you. I've been salivating for this all day."

"Me, too. How are our children by the way? Do you think they're getting along all right in such close quarters?"

Connor chuckled at the charming way she'd put it. "They were both quiet."

"They've never been stalled together. Sunflower is probably missing Polly and vice versa."

"This is a new experience for Firebrand, too. I don't know if they're being shy or bored."

"Wouldn't it be interesting if horses had romantic feelings…"

When he looked into her eyes, they were smiling. "Since when did White Lodge's newest vet delve into horse psychiatry?"

"Since the time Sadie told me about Chief, Jarod's stallion. He had a harem when he ran wild in the mountains. That got me thinking."

A burst of full-bodied laughter broke from him. "Maybe by the time the rodeo's over, we'll find out Firebrand and Sunflower have become inseparable."

She grinned. "You have to admit it would be amazing. I'd write it up in the *Journal of American Veterinary Medicine.* At our last stop, I noticed Firebrand sniffing around Sunflower's dung. Did you know feral horses like yours are fascinated by the dung piles of other horses?"

He tried not to laugh, but couldn't help it. "I have to admit I didn't."

"It's true. Dung and urine from other herds act as newspapers from one herd to another. Just what is communicated through urine and dung is unknown, but it may communicate how healthy the herd is, what mares are in season and even what types of food is available in the area."

"Let's be thankful her heat cycle ended after September. Otherwise, we'd know it by now."

Liz laughed gently. "Never fear. When I compete at the wrong times, I give her a medication so there's no problem. So…if these two get interested in each other, it won't be because of hormones."

Connor eyed her thoughtfully. "Just pure chemistry."

"Wouldn't *that* be something." She sounded bemused.

"Indeed it would." But his mind wasn't on the

horses. The woman seated across from him had drawn his attention. She wore her usual braid, but it lay forward over her shoulder, brushing against her flushed cheek while she drank her coffee. He could pick out the sun streaks in her light chestnut hair.

The collar of her tan Western blouse lay open at the throat. It came to him she had no idea how truly lovely she was. There was nothing artificial about her. If she wore makeup right now, he couldn't tell. She didn't need it.

"More chili?"

He handed her his bowl. "Please."

"You don't know how happy it will make Mom to hear you liked it." She got up from the table, giving him a profile view. Liz had to be five foot seven, with a supple body filling out her blouse and jeans in all the right places. With those long legs, she made quite a sight astride her horse during a competition.

His thoughts flicked to Reva, who was five foot four and more voluptuous. But she didn't move with the same grace as Liz, who was in fabulous shape from working and riding horses all her life.

Connor wouldn't be a man if he hadn't noticed, but it had always been at a distance. His grandfather had begged him to stay away from the Corkin ranch so there'd be no trouble. He had obeyed him, effectively putting Liz out of reach over the years.

Since then, she'd become a doctor of veterinarian medicine. No doubt she'd have to work years to pay off her loan for medical school. Besides the gold buckle, she'd win the big money, so maybe she could buy a new truck. More than ever he wanted her to be able to take those prizes home. No one deserved them more than she did. The relic she'd been driving was on its last legs.

He was glad she'd come with him. The storm hadn't let up. It could snow another hour or two, but they and their horses were safe and cozy inside the trailer. His mood had been dark for the past few months despite his wins, but right now he felt a lifting of his spirits and liked the feeling.

Connor got to his feet and took his dishes over to the minikitchen. "What do you say we give the horses a little exercise now?"

"I can see you're dying to find out how they're getting along."

"Aren't you?"

She flashed him an intriguing smile before putting on her parka and gloves. Her black cowboy hat came last. After he put on his gear, they walked out into a white world. The snow wasn't coming down as hard, but it was steady. Like a child, she put her head back to catch some snowflakes on her tongue, reminding him of his youth. He hadn't had this much fun in a long time.

Connor opened the back of the trailer and they walked inside. Both of them spoke in low tones to their horses as they led them outside for some exercise. After they'd gone a distance, they stopped.

"It feels like we're in wonderland." She half laughed the words. "Look, Connor. Did you see what Sunflower just did when Firebrand smelled her breath?"

He couldn't say that he had because he'd been looking at the expression of delight on her face. "What did I miss?"

"Sunflower's head lifted in the air and she lowered

her ears. See how she's chewing on the air? That's a submissive gesture in front of Firebrand because she recognizes his higher rank. Her foal-like behavior is so sweet. I think they really do like each other!"

Connor patted his horse's neck. "Is that true, buddy? Are you falling for Sunflower?"

A nicker came out of his horse, followed by one from hers.

"I swear he understood you!"

"Maybe they've been giving each other tips."

Her amused gaze met his, sending an emotional response through him he hadn't expected. How was it that Liz had been his neighbor for twenty-six years, yet it had taken until now to start seeing inside this attractive woman who he already knew had the heart of a champion?

"You mean about racing?"

"And other things..."

Gentle laughter escaped her throat. "You think they're making plans for after we leave them alone for the night?"

"Something like that. Firebrand hasn't been around such a fetching little mare in a long time. Being gelded doesn't mean he's forgotten anything."

Her eyes sparkled through the falling snow. "Come to think of it, Firebrand's Spanish heritage is pretty exciting, with those horizontal zebra stripes on the backs of his forelegs. His coloring is unique, even among ferals. It gets a female thinking."

He moved closer to her. It brought the horses closer together. "And here I thought it was only the male who was a leg man."

"You'd be surprised what captures the attention of the female."

"What else, for example?" he drawled.

"Oh, the white star on Firebrand's forehead and his dorsal stripe. And he's a powerful size. Makes a female feel protected. Notice how she's been scratching him on the rump with her teeth? She likes being around him."

"He likes a good scratch."

Her arched brows lifted. "Well, he's getting one. Amazing she knew where he itched."

"Lucky him. Who would have thought being stuck out in the back of beyond during a blizzard he would find such bliss?"

"It proves pure chemistry can work anywhere, but I think we'd better take them in. I want to check their gums and temperatures."

"If they both have a fever, we'll know romance is definitely in the air."

As she walked ahead of him with Sunflower, her laughter rippled back to tease his senses. He followed her into the trailer. After they'd dried off the horses, she gave them a thorough checkup while he cleaned the floor and put out fresh water and hay.

They worked as a team. No unmet expectations. No trauma of any kind. No deadlines. All that lay ahead of them was the rest of the night together. Nothing could have suited him better.

"It's still coming down, Liz. We're going to have to stay here until morning. By then the highway will have been plowed and we'll have a straight shot to Salt Lake. Depending on the weather tomorrow, we might make it to Las Vegas by nightfall."

"I'm glad we're not taking chances. Our horses need

special handling at a time like this if we expect the very best from them in the arena."

"Amen."

She threw the light rugs over them. "They look good and are probably wishing we'd leave them alone. Okay, guys. Treat time." She reached in her parka for some Uncle Jimmy's Squeezy Buns. She gave a few to Connor to give his horse.

"Did you see that? Sunflower starts talking when she hears the wrapper being opened. I swear she'd drool if she could."

Another chuckle came out of Connor, who fed Firebrand. After they'd finished their chores, he followed Liz out of the back. Just before he closed things up, he heard more nickering between both horses. Liz's mouth curved into a mischievous smile. "I'd say all is well."

Yup. Everybody was happy. It surprised him how much he was looking forward to more time alone with her.

The ringing of his cell phone broke the magic of the moment, preventing him from responding. He pulled it from the pocket of his jeans to check the caller ID.

Reva? He might have known. She knew how to choose her times.

Damn.

"Go ahead and take it while I clean up the kitchen." She hurried around the end of the trailer. Liz couldn't have known who was calling, but good manners stopped her from asking questions or lingering. Not that he'd been trying, but so far he hadn't found anything wrong with her. Quite the opposite, in fact.

He could talk to his ex-wife now or call her back later. The choice was his. But in that moment, while he was deciding what he wanted to do, he realized more than ever how much his feelings had changed since they'd been divorced. The old Connor wouldn't have let it ring a fifth time.

Before long she'd left him a text message.

Connor? Know u r on the road. Want u to know I'll be in Las Vegas tomorrow.

No way. He had no desire to see her while he was there to compete. There was no time for her. He and Wade had their horses to exercise and take care of.

I took off work. Have reserved honeymoon suite at the Mirage. Hope to give our marriage another try.

Where was this coming from? Something new had to be going on in her life. Maybe she'd broken up with the television producer she'd been dating since their divorce. Some kind of change was in the works. He knew Reva. For them to reconnect, she'd have to leave Los Angeles, because ranching was his life. She hated ranch life. If he didn't know anything else, he knew that.

She'd had two years to think about it. So had he, but he wasn't sure if he wanted her back, even if she gave up her television career and agreed to live with him on the ranch. Two years had changed him, and would have changed her. It would mean starting over again.

He doubted she would ever get the show biz bug out of her system. Connor couldn't blame her for that, any more than he could stamp the rodeo bug out of his blood. She was pursuing her dreams. With the right marriage she could go on doing it.

Key at front desk. Let yourself in. Middle of night doesn't matter. Dying to see you, lover. Miss u more than ever.

Connor couldn't honestly say the same. What was going on with her?

The snow kept falling.

Shielding his phone, he replied with his own text message.

Reva? May not make Las Vegas by tomorrow. Can't stay at Mirage. Give u a call later.

The Mirage was home to the NFR steer wrestlers, but she knew he preferred staying in his own trailer. After he put the phone back in his pocket, he walked around to the entrance. Shaking more snow off everything, he stepped inside and hung his things up. No sign of Liz, which meant she was in the bathroom. She'd cleaned up the kitchen. Her appeal was growing on him in ways he hadn't anticipated.

He washed his hands and poured himself another cup of coffee. While she was busy, he phoned Wade. He and Kim had made it to Evanston. So far, so good. They talked about the weather for a minute before hanging up.

He made one more call, to his grandfather, who sounded relieved to hear Connor's voice. After assuring him that he and Liz were fine, Connor asked how Ralph's day had gone. That was when he learned Ned would be coming home tomorrow for a supervised overnight visit. His first since being at the mental health facility.

Connor put his coffee down. "Does Jarod know?"

"Yes. I told him that he and Sadie ought to go out to the reservation while he's here."

"Good plan. You don't want anything to go wrong that could set him off."

"According to the doctor, Ned is making a turnaround. We're all keeping our fingers crossed."

"I will, too."

"Bless you, son. What you need to do is keep concentrating on the competition. Tell me about the little princess." That was what Ralph had always called Liz.

"She's a great vet and terrific company." All of it true. But he'd already found out she was a lot more than that.

"That's what I needed to hear. I assured her father you were taking good care of her."

"We're taking good care of each other. Let him know Millie's chili and rolls were a sensation."

"I'll tell him." After a silence, "Son?" Connor heard him hesitate. "Reva called the house earlier. I told her you were already on your way to Las Vegas."

He gripped his phone tighter. "She texted me." Connor could hear the question his grandfather didn't ask. It was the question Connor couldn't answer.

Ralph never pried. That was what made him so lovable.

"I'll call you tomorrow night, Grandpa. Maybe by then you can tell me how the visit went with Ned. Sleep well and don't worry about a thing."

"Ha! Just wait till one of your grandchildren tells you the same thing."

That last comment stayed with him as he hung up the phone. Since the divorce, he couldn't see himself having children, let alone grandchildren. Much to his grandfather's disappointment, as well as Connor's own personal pain, that didn't appear to be in his future.

Right now he didn't want to think about it.

Chapter Three

"Connor? Is everything all right?"

His head jerked up.

Liz had just come out of the bathroom in her new nautical-design pajamas in navy with polka dots on the bottoms. She'd washed her hair and had braided it again.

"Perfect," he said automatically, but she didn't believe him. "Where do you want to sleep? Up in the niche or near the floor? Both are comfortable."

"I think the sofa pullout bed." It was closer to the bathroom and the kitchen if for any reason she had to get up in the night. In the back of her mind she imagined Connor had probably slept with Reva in the niche with its pull-down ladder.

"Good. I'll take my shower now. By the way, I had keys made for you to open the trailer and the truck. I put them there on the counter."

"That was very considerate. Thank you."

"Anything to oblige."

By his tone of voice, something was wrong and it worried her.

She turned on the TV to the weather channel and then made her bed. To her surprise, his low-profile satellite dish was still allowing transmission despite the snow. The forecast predicted more intermittent flurries through Wyoming and the northern half of Utah tomorrow, but the southern half would be warmer and might see a little sun. Las Vegas was enjoying sixty-three–degree weather during the day and lower forties at night with some wind.

Liz still couldn't understand why she didn't feel uncomfortable in this situation. Maybe it was because they both knew so much about each other's lives, there was no mystique. Connor didn't feel like an acquaintance or a confidante, brother, cousin, best friend or boyfriend.

He existed outside those categories, though he wasn't a figment of her imagination. She didn't know what he was, but so far the inside of the book matched the cover. That didn't bother her, either. Curious.

Once under the blanket, she made a call home and thanked her mom for the food. Liz assured her parents that she and Connor were snug as a bug in his trailer while they waited out the storm in Kemmerer. The horses were in great shape. Connor was an expert—behind the wheel or mounted on his horse.

"Good night, you two. Thank you for being the greatest parents on earth."

When she clicked off, she discovered Connor standing there in a pair of navy sweats. Their nightwear more or less matched. She could smell the soap he'd used in the shower. She'd left hers and he'd used it.

"Your parents are very trusting, you know that?"

"Besides the fact that you're one of *the* famous Bannock brothers, don't forget I was away at vet school for a long time and am not exactly a little girl anymore."

"No, you're not." His emphatic tone sent a shiver through her before he picked up the remote and flipped the channels to an old creature-of-the-lagoon movie. After tossing it to her, he turned out the light and climbed into the niche using the same masterful agility with which he threw a steer. She laughed when he got comfortable and looked down at her over the edge. "Monsters don't scare you?" His mood had improved.

"Not really, if that was your intention. I'm laughing because I meant *this.* I'm having fun. Being in the trailer is like we're in a little hut deep in the forest of some mysterious kingdom."

"With satellite TV, no less." His sudden smile turned him into the most attractive man she'd ever laid eyes on. "In truth, I'm having more fun than I've had in years, stranded with a vet who's writing a romance article about the mating rituals of horses. After it's in print and you've won the prize for the world champion barrel racer, what do you plan to do for an encore?"

She raised herself on one elbow. "Mind if I try something out on you?"

"What do you think? Go ahead."

"Well, the Crow council in Pryor has asked me if I'll be one of the vets for the reservation. Even if Jarod had everything to do with the offer, it's such a great honor I can hardly believe it. But I haven't given them my answer yet because I'm committed to Dr. Rafferty at the vet hospital. I'd have to stretch myself thin to do both."

He rested his chin on his hard-muscled arm. "And here I thought you were worrying about what you were going to do with the rest of your life once the rodeo was over. Winning money to buy a new truck is going to come in handy with you driving back and forth from White Lodge to the reservation."

"Don't I wish! In order to win it, I'll have to beat Dustine's time along with several other unknowns at the moment. That's a tall order."

"You're the best barrel racer on the circuit this year, Liz. In my official opinion, you're a shoo-in. To the winner goes all the pickings."

"Thanks for the morale boost, Connor." She patted her pillow. "As long as we're talking about the future, after you've won your sixth title, have you thought about getting involved with the Pryor Mountains National Wild Horse Refuge?"

He laughed. "*What* did you say? I don't think I heard you correctly."

"Oh, I think you did." She egged him on. "When you rescued and adopted Firebrand, you got yourself a real prize. The horse refuge needs people like you. Your voice would carry a lot of weight, politically."

A look of surprise crossed his face. "Are you a lobbyist, too?"

"I'm just a vet who's an interested bystander and would love to see someone like you, with real clout, protecting Montana's natural resources. It's the second feral horse refuge in the U.S. Gus Cochran, one of the leading equine geneticists, concluded that the Pryor herd may be the most significant wild-horse herd remaining in the States. These animals don't exist anywhere else, and they need advocates."

He held himself so still, she realized she had his attention.

"Do you remember Wild Horse Annie, a secretary at an insurance firm in Reno?"

"I know of the Wild Horse Annie Act."

"Well, she was obviously a wild horse advocate who lobbied for passage of a federal law to prevent hunting the herds from helicopters, and motorcycles that terrorized the horses and caused extreme cruelty."

"Amen to that."

"Because of her, the Hunting Wild Horses and Burros on Public Lands Act was passed in the late fifties, banning the hunting of feral horses on federal land using aircraft or motorized vehicles."

"You learn something new every day. Tell me more," he urged with a genuine smile.

His honest interest pleased her. "Seven years ago, the last three slaughterhouses in the U.S. were closed, all because certain interested parties discovered that some of the excess wild horses being sold had been sent straight to the slaughterhouses and killed."

He shook his head, signaling his disgust.

"When they intervened, the BLM had to suspend the sales program. After investigating, they resumed the sales, but only after implementing new requirements to deter buyers from killing the animals.

"There's a ton of work to be done for their preservation. Your grandfather has a huge ranching reputation in the state. For his prominent grandson, Connor Bannock, to get involved in the fight to preserve the very kind of horse that will bring you another victory in the arena... It would be doing a great thing for man, horse and country. Of course, you'd have to do that work along with your regular ranch work. It would be stretching you to the max, too."

The next instant Connor swung himself to the floor with masculine ease and hunkered down in front of her. His brown eyes searched hers for a full minute. "What's behind all this?" He was asking a serious question.

"Ever since you started working with Firebrand, I've wanted to talk to you about it. He's a very special horse, and you knew it right away. Not everyone has an eye for good horseflesh like you. Ralph said your father was the same. It seems you inherited that trait. I understand it was while he was looking over the best horses on the reservation that he met Jarod's mother."

"That's true."

"If you were to salvage a couple more stallions like Firebrand, you could start your own stud farm. The filly Jarod gave Sadie came from Chief, another feral. Think about it!"

His brows furrowed. "Where did that idea come from?"

"From you! Before your parents died, Sadie and I were over in your backyard throwing horseshoes with Ralph. We happened to overhear you tell Jarod you wanted to establish a stud farm to bring in more money. I thought it was a fabulous idea, but then your folks were killed. I could see you had your hands full with the regular ranch work and your grief."

"That was a terrible time," he whispered.

"I know, but I've thought about your idea ever since. Do you realize your stud farm would be unique if you advertised that you only used adopted feral stallions? There are horse lovers everywhere who'd be excited for a foal from a sire like Firebrand. You'd be preserving the bloodline of horses that have roamed these mountains for centuries. It gives me chills just to think about it."

"You're not the only one." He showed her his arms with raised bumps. She couldn't believe it. "I had no idea you heard me," he murmured, "let alone that you would still remember."

"We hadn't meant to eavesdrop, but both of us thought you should do it. You wouldn't have any competition."

He cocked his dark blond head. "Where have you been all my life, Liz Henson?"

"Right next door, working on my dream to be a barrel racer."

"You worship your dad, don't you?"

He could see right through her. She nodded. "He should have been able to realize his dream to be a pro bull rider, but it didn't happen."

"So you're doing this for him."

"Probably somewhere inside I am. He had to work so hard for everything all his life. Daniel Corkin was not an easy taskmaster."

"No."

"My parents couldn't have more children. I was it, and I was a girl. He needed a son. All I could do was be the best at something and decided to try barrel racing. Mom encouraged me because she knew what it meant to him. Sadie raced with me."

"Don't take me wrong, but your talent surpassed hers and everyone else's at those early rodeos. All you needed was the right horse."

"Thank you."

"There was never any jealousy between the two of you, was there?"

"Or between you and Jarod. If you must know, my mother suffered over not being able to have another baby. That's why she was so happy when Sadie turned to her for everything after her parents' divorce. With Sadie's mom in California, there was no one else to love her except our family. Sadie was a sweetheart. Still is."

Connor's eyes grew suspiciously bright. "I agree, but I have to say you've been blessed with exceptional parents, Liz. There's nothing I'd like more than to see their little girl take the prize in Las Vegas. I'm here for you in any capacity you need." His voice throbbed with emotion she could feel clear through to her insides. "Ask anything of me and I'll do it if it's within my ability."

"Connor—" she put a hand on his arm "—driving me to Las Vegas is the greatest thing you could have ever done for me. You've taken away the burden of getting my horse there by myself. Now I can concentrate."

"That's good. You need to feel relaxed." He checked his watch. "I'm keeping you up when you need sleep. Do you want the TV on?"

"If you want to watch a program, that's fine with me. If not, turn it off." She let go of his arm to hand him the remote.

He clicked off the TV and put the remote on the table before returning to his niche.

Liz lay there in the dark, wide-awake. The wind had died down. All was quiet. Her thoughts drifted to Connor. She'd never slept in the same room with a man before. When she'd accepted his invitation, she'd done it to find out what the real Connor was like.

Already she'd discovered he was thoughtful and kind in ways she wouldn't have expected. Hidden in the many layers was a sense of humor. Buried even deeper lived a sensitive, vulnerable man. All this she'd learned, and it was only the first day.

As for the damage his divorce had done to him, she didn't know, but she envied the woman who was loved by him….

"Liz?"

Her pulse raced. "Yes?"

"Who's the lucky guy in your life?"

She smiled. "Dad says they're all lucky."

"All?" After a pause, "Why aren't you with your favorite?"

"They're all my favorites for different reasons, but as I told you this morning, I wanted to be alone this trip. The fact that I'm with you doesn't count."

"Why?" He sounded a little tense.

"Because in my mind you're not animal, vegetable or mineral."

"Thanks a lot."

"I haven't finished. You're beyond all that."

"In other words, you view me as an extraterrestrial."

"No. You're an entity who has always floated around in the background of my life. I think that's why I don't find it strange being with you."

"You mean I'm like the specter that never went away."

A chuckle escaped her lips. "No. *You* have substance and form."

"I'm feeling better already."

"Go to sleep, Connor. You need it much more than I do."

"Hey—I'm not an old man yet."

"Age has nothing to do with it. You've done all the

driving. I'm beholden to you. The only way to pay you back is to feed you and let you rest."

"Did you bring any treats?"

"If I give you one, will you promise to go to sleep?"

"I can't promise to do that, but I'll stop talking."

"Hallelujah!"

He burst into laughter as she got out of bed and padded over to the kitchen. After retrieving a Snickers candy bar from the sack, she hurried back and lifted it to him. "Enjoy. You can work off the calories later."

Connor grabbed her hand and held on. "Want to split it with me?"

"I can't. I just brushed my teeth."

She tried to get away but he tugged harder. Liz had a hunch she was going to pay for teasing him.

"You can brush them again. I don't like having a midnight snack by myself. Come on up." Before she knew what had happened, he'd lifted her onto the edge of the bed so her feet dangled. His strength in throwing steers accounted for the ease with which he'd brought her up to his level.

"Here." He broke the bar in half and handed her a piece. "Partners in sin." Between the adrenaline rush he'd given her and the sugar, she'd be awake for the rest of the night. "Good, huh?"

Liz's mouth was full of chocolate. She made a sound of assent.

"As you can see, I not only have form and substance, I can eat, too."

"I'm convinced!" she finally managed to say.

"Then I'm making progress."

Yes. Way too much.

"Good night, Connor." She jumped down before he could stop her. One more second up there…

She didn't dare think about it. Her father had commented that it would be good for them to travel together because they knew what it was like to be in each other's skin.

But once under the covers, she had one more thing to add to this day of revelations. He'd almost charmed her right out of hers.

SMOKEY'S STEAK HOUSE in St. George, Utah, lay straight ahead. Connor looked over at Liz. "Hungry?"

"Starving."

"So am I. They serve a great steak. I've been here dozens of times."

After being on the road all day with stops to take care of the horses, they needed a hot, filling meal. Because of the snow, they'd gotten away from Kemmerer later than he'd wanted. The highway had looked like a snow-covered pasture instead of a road in spots, which had cost them a couple of hours in time. However once they got past Cedar City, Utah, the highway was clear.

They could make it to Las Vegas tonight, but it would be eleven at night before they pulled in. Connor preferred to spend the night at an RV park here and arrive tomorrow during daylight. Reva was probably at the Mirage now, expecting he would break down and come to the hotel, but that wasn't going to happen.

To his surprise, for the first time in years he felt as if he was on a real vacation and wanted it to go on and on. The ten days of competition coming up hadn't caused his stomach muscles to cramp. Maybe there was something wrong with him to feel this relaxed.

Liz had brought a couple of books on tape that they listened to during the drive. It was a nice change from music he got tired of listening to. He'd enjoyed both books very much and had finished off another Snickers bar during their lively discussions about the new theories behind Kennedy's assassination. There was always another version of what really happened.

When he'd parked their rig, Liz excused herself to use the restroom inside the restaurant, and he watched her walk toward it. Cowboy boots on the right pair of long shapely legs along with hips encased in jeans were a sight to behold all on their own. Her braid swung back and forth against the back of her fitted suede jacket. He noticed she'd drawn the eyes of several interested males in the parking area.

The temperature here was sixty-one degrees, so he didn't bother with a coat. His sweater would do. Putting on his hat, he walked back to check on the horses. Their ears pricked the moment they heard noise.

"Hi, guys. How's the romance coming?" More nickering out of both. He smiled. "After our dinner, we'll take care of you."

He closed the door and headed into the crowded restaurant. Liz had found them a booth by a window. Cozy, just like the trailer. Their eyes met. "I'll wash my hands and join you."

"Take your time. How are the children?"

"They told me to hurry."

She laughed. "I think they can't wait to be outside together."

"It wouldn't surprise me." His good mood stayed with him until he was returning to their booth and saw a couple of guys talking to Liz. One of them turned in his direction.

"Connor! We saw you pull up in your rig."

If it wasn't the Porter brothers from Rock Springs, tough competitors on the circuit in team roping. As siblings they had instincts that guaranteed them another championship. Both were friends of Wade's from their college days and had spent part of an evening with Connor and Reva in Las Vegas after they were married.

"Hey, guys." They shook hands. "I take it you've met this year's soon-to-be barrel-racing champion, Dr. Elizabeth Henson."

"We're working on it," Monty said with a grin.

Derrick asked, "You mean, besides chasing the cans, you're a doc? I've got a sore leg I'd like you to look at."

"She's a vet," Connor inserted before Liz could. Odd that he felt so territorial.

"That's good, too," Monty commented. "Our horses need a good going-over." His brows lifted. "Is Reva still out in the trailer?"

Time to get this over with. "We're divorced," he said.

"Whoops." Monty looked embarrassed. "I'm afraid we didn't hear about that," he murmured.

"How could you have known?"

They probably hadn't because they competed in the Mountain States circuit. But the fact that Wade hadn't gossiped about Connor's private life to other people raised the man even more notches in his estimation.

"We were going to ask if you wanted to join us, but under the circumstances we'll find ourselves another booth."

"Thanks, Monty." Connor didn't feel like sharing Liz. "Good to see you, too, Derrick."

"Going for your sixth title has already made you a legend. Good luck, Connor."

"The same to you. This could be your third."

"We're hoping."

He turned to Liz. "Ma'am. If Connor says you're a winner, then you can believe him." They tipped their hats to Liz, their eyes lingering on her before they walked off.

The moment he sat down across from her, the blond waitress came to take their order.

"They were nice," Liz said after the woman walked away.

"Wade met them in college."

"I saw them in action at the arena in Oklahoma. They're fast."

"In a lot of ways," he informed her. His comment produced another chuckle. "If you want, I'll find them. They wanted to join us, but I didn't know how you'd feel about that."

"I'm glad you didn't take them up on it."

He squinted at her. "I bet you get hit on all the time."

"I don't get the attention *you* get. So far, every waitress in here has passed by our table, even when it isn't their area. They all know who you are. Ours was salivating over you. No doubt she'll serve you a free dessert and invite you for drinks later."

Connor started to laugh. "The things you say, Liz Henson, and the times you pick to say them."

"If the truth fits... Please do what you want."

His jaw hardened. "I don't party or drink except for an occasional beer with Jarod or Wade. Ned's alcoholism cured me of that problem early in life."

Her eyes softened. "I didn't mean to upset you, Connor. I just wanted you to feel free to do whatever you want."

"You're too good to be true, you know that?"

"Is *that* what I am? I thought traveling with you in your trailer was a pretty daring move on my part."

"How could it be daring when you only think of me as an entity?" He hadn't forgotten how she'd shocked him when she'd jumped down from his bed last night before he could think.

"With substance, form and an appetite for candy bars," she added with a twitch of her lips, enticing him. "At this point I have to add deep-seated feelings to the list I'm making on you."

"A list?" Connor liked the sound of that.

His cell phone rang, intruding on his personal thoughts. Much as he wanted to ignore it, he didn't dare in case something was wrong with his grandfather. He reached in his pocket and pulled it out to check the caller ID. One look and he put it back.

By now, their dinner had arrived. He thanked the waitress without looking at her. He'd been happy until they'd come into the restaurant. Now everything felt out of kilter. They ate in silence. When he saw the waitress coming again, he asked Liz, "Do you want dessert?"

"Oh, no. That steak did it for me."

"Then let's get going."

He pulled out his credit card and handed it to their server without waiting for her to talk. She'd looked as though she was about to say something, then thought the better of it. "I'll be right back."

A glimmer of amusement lit Liz's eyes. "You disappointed her."

"She'll get over it."

"Connor—you can't blame a gal for trying."

"How come you didn't have that compassion for me when you turned me down flat in Missoula?"

A shadow broke out on her face. "That was different. I thought you were a married man, but you already know that."

"It still hurt. We were neighbors." He wrote the tip on the receipt the waitress had brought back with his credit card. When she left the table he pocketed it.

Liz got to her feet and put on her jacket. "Have you forgotten you were a Montague and I was the closest thing to a Capulet?"

He put his hat on. "I haven't forgotten anything about that nightmarish situation."

"But it's over now." They left the restaurant and headed for the truck. "Do you want to know something Sadie told me? It's very sad."

"I'm all ears."

"When she was writing the obituary on Daniel for the paper, she said she almost wrote, 'Ding-dong, the wicked witch is dead.' Her own father..."

They'd reached the passenger door side. He looked down at her. "That's tragic."

"Isn't it?" Her eyes had filled with sorrow. She climbed in the cab. He walked around and got behind the wheel to start the engine.

"Thank God everything came right in the end. My brother would never have come back to life otherwise. Sadie's his whole world. Always was." They took off and headed for the RV park, where he'd made reservations.

"All the time she was in California she was in mourning for Jarod. I think she sobbed through half our phone conversations over those years. Theirs is a great love."

Connor supposed that if he envied his brother anything, it was that. Connor hadn't been so lucky and had missed the mark. He and Reva had been a mismatch. He knew it as surely as he was sitting there, and nothing would ever change it. "I guess you know that since Sadie's successful heart operation they're trying for a baby. She doesn't keep anything from you."

"There are a few things, I'm sure." Liz's eyes closed tightly. "Oh, I hope they get pregnant soon. That nursery they built in their new house needs a little body in it."

"I have a feeling Grandpa is going to hang on until it happens. He can't wait!"

"I can't, either. Mom and I are crazy about Sadie's half brother, Ryan. Can you imagine having two little angels to squeeze and love?"

Connor had been in an emotional abyss for a long time. But looking over at the radiant face turned to him, he could imagine it and a lot of other things. Before he did something that would shock her senseless and get them in an accident he said, "Let's go take care of *our* lovebirds."

"Good idea."

Once they'd parked for the night, she entered the trailer and grabbed two bananas. "They love these, skins and all."

He grinned. "I prefer my Snickers."

"I've found that out."

They walked back to the end of the trailer. "I'm sure

they can hear us talking," she said before going inside. When they led the horses out of their stalls, Sunflower nibbled her with affection, causing her to laugh gently. Connor wouldn't mind doing that to her himself, but he'd have to wait until the time was right.

"How's my buddy?" He rubbed Firebrand's forelock before giving him a banana.

His horse snarfed it down. When he looked over, he could see Sunflower was making short work of her treat. They walked their horses away. Then an amazing thing happened. Firebrand moved next to Sunflower, who rested her head on his neck.

"Do you see what I'm seeing?" Liz whispered.

"I bet you can't wait to get this down for your article."

"I'm going to title it 'Lovebirds at the Arena.'"

He threw back his head and laughed into the air. It was a mild winter night in St. George. There was no snow here and it was pleasant beyond words. Then his cell phone rang again. The horses' ears pricked in response. He was sure Liz's did, too, but he let it go on ringing.

A half hour later they'd put their horses to bed for the night and could go themselves. His phone rang again as they entered the trailer. Liz turned to him. "Whoever is trying to get you isn't going to go away until you answer. I'll shower first to give you privacy."

He didn't need privacy. Once she'd disappeared in the bathroom, he listened to his voice mail. Reva was at the hotel waiting for him.

He texted her that he wasn't in Las Vegas. When he arrived tomorrow, he'd call her at the hotel.

By now he should be feeling some rush of excitement at the thought of seeing her again, but nothing could be further from the truth. He resented her intrusive phone calls. Something had been happening to him since Liz had agreed to come to Las Vegas with him. Tonight he felt as though he'd been spirited away to a different place and point in time with nothing to do with his past life.

Concern for his grandfather prompted him to phone the older man he loved. He wondered how Ned's visit had gone. Once he got him on the line, Connor told him about the horses and Liz's speculation about them experiencing romantic love.

"That girl's a horse whisperer. If anyone can figure it out, she can."

"Well, so far they're acting sweet on each other. Now, tell me about Ned. Did you see him?"

"No. He went straight to his parents' house and spent time with the family. Your great-uncle Tyson called me and told me what went on. It wasn't good. They've got Ned on a medication that has calmed him down, but he's not himself and very quiet. He's going to need a lot of therapy, but at least he was able to come home for a first visit."

"That's something. As you've always told me, time is the great healer."

"Yup. How's that working out for you?"

When he looked around, Liz was just coming out of the bathroom in a different pair of pajamas, this time in a green print. In a moment of gut honesty Connor answered, "It's working, Grandpa."

It's working.

Chapter Four

Before Liz went to bed, she reached into her purse and wrote out a check. After signing it, she handed it to Connor, who was sitting at the kitchen table with the phone still in his hand.

He glanced at it. "What's this?"

"Before you give me trouble, I want you to know I already added the word *generous* to that list I'm keeping on you. You wouldn't know how to be anything else, but I wouldn't have accepted your offer to ride with you if I couldn't reimburse you every few days for my expenses."

She saw him hesitate before he folded the check and put it in his shirt pocket. "Thank you."

"I'm the one thanking *you* for not giving me a hard time about it. I like to pay my own way as much as possible." She walked over to the sofa and pulled out the bed. Once she got in, she finished braiding her hair. "How's Ralph tonight?"

"Good. Ned came for a visit."

"Did he see him?"

"No. He spent all his time with his parents. It's too soon for anything else."

"At least the doctor said he could visit them. That sounds like progress to me."

"Maybe." He got to his feet. "I'll grab my shower now."

"I tried to leave you plenty of hot water."

He stopped at the door to the bathroom. "Like I said earlier, you're too nice."

Liz frowned. He'd said that before in so many words. His words struck her like a backhanded compliment. He'd been in a relaxed mood until now. While she'd been showering, he'd had time to make other calls. Something had upset him. She didn't think it had anything to do with Ned.

After finishing her hair, she reached for the phone to call her parents. She told her dad what Connor had said about waxed reins. He told her Connor had a point and she should try the knotted kind when she practiced. See which one she liked better, since it was a personal preference. Maybe it would make a difference to her, maybe not.

They chatted a few more minutes before she hung up and returned Doc Rafferty's call. He wanted to talk about a difficult case.

"Thank goodness everything turned out all right in the end, Sam. Talk to you soon."

Connor had just come back in the room in a pair of gray sweats. "Was that Dr. Rafferty?"

"Yes. He thought he would lose a cow giving birth today. She had a closed uterus, but he got the farmer to help him roll her to untwist it. Then they had to wait for her to dilate. When that didn't happen, he had to perform a Cesarean in the freezing cold. But the little heifer is fine and so is mom. I should have been there to help."

"You can't do it all, not when you're on your way to winning a world championship."

"The way you talk, you make me think it's possible. I wish I could work the same magic on you."

He turned off the lights and climbed into the niche in one easy movement. "Why do you say that?"

"Because there's something disturbing you. If my desire to pay you back offended you in some way, we need to talk about it."

She heard a sigh. "You're way off base, Liz."

"Good. Since my check wasn't the reason, I can go to sleep with a clear conscience for tonight."

"A clear conscience. What would that be like…?"

"I said *for tonight.* You think I don't have demons driving me mad, too?"

"Name one."

"Out of which group?"

He looked down over the edge at her. "You mean you put them in groups like animal, vegetable and mineral?"

"No. My demons fall into other categories altogether. There's the bad, the awful and then the downright ugly."

Connor's rich male laughter rang throughout the trailer.

"Judging by your mood on the way to the bathroom, I'd guess tonight's demon has you rattled, but since you can still laugh, I'd only put it in the bad category."

He lay back down. "I have a dilemma, but it could involve you, so I'm going to tell you what has me worried."

"Go ahead." Connor had her full attention.

"Though we've talked on the phone a few times, I've only seen my ex-wife twice since our divorce two years ago. Last evening she phoned and left a message that she was coming to Las Vegas for a few days hoping to see me. She'll be staying at a hotel and is there now."

Liz cringed. "I see." Like she'd told her mother, Connor was still in love with his ex-wife and she with him.

"She knows the RV park where I always stay. Because she's a journalist and very tenacious, there are times when Reva doesn't care about crossing boundaries. She might show up at the trailer trying to find me. While we're in Las Vegas, the truck and the trailer are yours as much as mine. I just wanted you to be prepared ahead of time for any surprises."

"Thanks for the heads-up."

"I didn't know she was going to do this, Liz. I swear it."

"It's none of my business, but in case you're worried, I believe you."

"Thanks for being understanding."

"I'm glad you told me." She didn't need to ask him if he was all right. Hearing from his ex-wife had rattled him. "Since you're probably wide-awake now, do you want me to turn on the TV for you?"

"Thanks, but no."

On impulse she said, "Want to play a little five-card stud? I brought a couple of decks with me. I don't know about you, but cards have a way of settling me down when I've got stuff on my mind."

He'd reached the floor before she could blink and

turned the lights back on. "You're exactly what the doctor ordered." Excitement lit up his brown eyes.

Pleased by that positive reaction, Liz reached into her suitcase for the cards and walked over to the table. "That's because I *am* the doctor. Here. Take this pill. It will help." She threw him a Kit Kat bar.

Connor let out a happy yelp before they both sat down and started playing. After a dozen rounds they turned to Pineapple and then Crazy Pineapple, both variations of Texas Hold'em poker.

"You're good at this."

"Same to you. If nothing else, waiting around for a rodeo event to start has produced a ton of crack poker players. We could be dealers in Las Vegas after we're through with the rodeo."

Connor squinted at her. "Does your daddy know about this surprising side of his daughter?"

"Between my parents and your grandparents, who do you think taught me and Sadie how to play in the first place?"

He sat back so the front legs of the chair were off the floor. "I didn't know that. We'll have to get up a game after we're back from finals."

"Then you're asking for it," she teased to contain the rush his suggestion produced. "Sadie told me she outbluffs Jarod all the time."

He sat forward. "I have news for you. He lets her win to keep her happy, except when it comes to his favorite poker game."

The way he was staring at her brought out the heat to prickle her face. She put her hands palm down on the table. "Speaking as your doctor, I can see our card game has put you in a better frame of mind. We both ought to be able to sleep now."

Connor's grin was wicked. "You keep thinking that, sweetheart."

That image of him stayed with her long after she'd scuttled back to bed and put the covers over her head.

Soon it was dark and quiet. Her thoughts turned to the woman who still anchored for a television show out of Los Angeles. Did his good-looking ex-wife still go by the name Mrs. Bannock when she wasn't in front of the camera?

Liz knew nothing about her and had formed no opinion of her. Liz had been away at vet school during that year he'd been married. As she'd told him earlier, she'd had no clue that he'd gotten a divorce until months after the fact.

But tonight she decided Reva Stevens had a fundamental selfish streak. Even if they still loved each other, it was cruel to call Connor with the kind of news she'd sprung on him right before his first round of competition to win a sixth world title.

That insensitivity proved to Liz that his ex-wife didn't value his former achievements or what he was hoping to achieve now. Otherwise, she wouldn't have dared interfere with his concentration.

According to Connor, his ex didn't recognize boundaries if she wanted something. It sounded as if she wanted him back. Liz had no way of knowing if Connor wanted the same thing.

But couldn't Reva have waited until the pro rodeo finals were over? Ten crucial days out of his life to accomplish what no other bulldogger had done before? Liz decided his ex-wife didn't deserve Connor.

But in all fairness, Liz couldn't rule out physical attraction and chemistry, those potent forces a person might wish to escape because of other problems, but couldn't. Was that the case with Connor and his ex-wife?

In turmoil, she turned over on her back.

Before you start finding fault with Reva, better take a good look at yourself first, Liz Henson.

A LATE-MORNING SKY of high wispy clouds over Las Vegas greeted them as Connor pulled into the RV equestrian park at eleven. The temperature registered fifty-nine and was climbing.

This was his fourth year bringing Firebrand. To make things more familiar, every year he reserved the same spot closest to the arena and barn, and the same stall, in order to cut down on any tension for his horse.

Luckily the manager of the park had arranged to get him the stall next to Firebrand, as well. The surroundings might be new to Sunflower, but she'd grown used to being around Firebrand. As long as they weren't separated, both ought to do fine.

After he turned off the ignition, it occurred to him he hadn't awakened this morning with that sense of dread over the unknown that was coming once the finals were over. He could blame this elevated change in his mood on the attractive woman seated next to him.

He turned to her. "Shall we exercise the horses first?" To his amusement, she asked him the same question at the same time. They both chuckled before Liz jumped down from the cab first to walk back to the end of the trailer. In the side-view mirror he admired the way her feminine figure moved until she was out of sight.

He shoved on his cowboy hat, thinking this had all been too easy. Something was wrong for everything to have gone so smoothly this far. But as Connor got out of the truck, he realized that if there was a problem, it was because he was looking for one. It had become a pattern of his.

The other morning, after they'd stopped to visit his grandfather, Liz had picked right up on it and had gotten after him for it. That was the moment she'd come alive, treating him to a fiery side of her nature he hadn't witnessed before.

Last night he'd tensed up before telling her about Reva. But whatever reaction he'd feared, Liz didn't even blink. Instead, she'd made the rest of the night so much fun, he hadn't wanted to go to bed.

He rebelled at the idea that their road journey down here was over. The only thing helping him was the fact that they'd be living together for the next twelve days, and then there'd be the trip back to Montana. Though they'd been neighbors all their lives, he'd only started getting to know her on this trip. Connor was already looking forward to the drive home with her.

Together they backed their horses out of the trailer and took them on a walk before heading for the barn. With the finals starting on the fifth, the place was packed. Some of the competitors stayed here with their rigs. When they recognized Connor they shouted to him and tipped their hats to Liz.

The two of them led their horses into the barn and found their stalls. Connor emptied some bags of soft shavings around both stalls.

"This is really a nice setup, Connor. Every facility we need is here!"

"On the fourth we'll trailer the horses to the rodeo grounds and stall them there if you want, but for now this is a perfect place for them."

"I agree." She patted her horse's neck. "You like it in here, don't you, Sunflower? You'll have to thank Connor for these fabulous accommodations."

"She has already nickered at me. That's all I need." He put out the buckets for water and filled the hay nets. Buckets were a good way to measure the amount of water their horses were drinking.

"They're both nickering. Did you hear that?"

Connor smiled. "Firebrand's happy they're together."

"I think they're both pleased. Come on, little lady. Let's get your boots off and give you a good rubdown. Then I've got to get over to the center and take Polly around the arena. I'm afraid she's already feeling neglected."

Liz treated her horse the way she would a child. He watched her over the partition. It was touching to see and hear how she loved Sunflower. Given this kind of treatment, that horse would do anything for her. Never in his life had he wanted anyone to win a championship more.

"When you're through over there, doc, Firebrand needs a thorough going-over, too. I think he's jealous of all the attention you're giving his girlfriend."

Her gentle laughter was like an unexpected breeze on a hot day, refreshing him.

Within a half hour they left the barn and cleaned out the stalls in his trailer. The first rule with horses was to take care of them before you did anything else. Liz understood that. They worked side by side while he unhitched the trailer from the truck.

"After we've driven to the center to check out our other horses, let's go buy you some reins. When we get back here, you can try them out. I'm curious to see if you feel any improvement with them."

"Our minds must think alike. I was just going to ask if I could take the truck later to buy some."

"Would you rather go alone?"

"No—" She sounded surprised.

"Good." He'd wanted to go with her. "I know a reputable place to get what you need."

Her eyes swept over him. "For a change, why don't you shower first?"

"Do I look that bad?"

She grinned at him. "Even in a foot of muck you couldn't look bad, and you know it, Connor Bannock."

He swept his hat off his head. "Well, thank you, ma'am. That's the sweetest sweet talk I ever heard."

"Well, don't get too used to it. Your head's going to swell right up after your next championship. You'll be too heavy for Firebrand to prance around the arena with you in front of your thousands of screaming fans."

Connor's heart came close to palpitating out of his chest. "Are you a psychic, too?"

She shook her head. "Nope. I've been studying the statistics on you. Barring a catastrophic force of nature, you're favored to win. Nothing would make me or your parents happier. I'm sure they'll be looking down at you."

"How did they get into this conversation?"

"Once, when Ralph was giving me and Sadie some

barrel-racing pointers, they both came out to the paddock. They'd been watching you practice at the arena with Wade. We heard your dad say that no one worked harder than you, whether it was ranch work or training for the rodeo. They both said they were so proud of you they could burst. Of course Ralph agreed."

A lump as large as a boulder lodged in his throat. "It's kind of scary how well you know what went on at the ranch behind my back."

"We weren't there all that often, but I'll tell you this. Everything I heard about you would make you happy inside."

"You've forgotten Ned."

"I'm trying to, but there you go again, determined to stomp all over yourself. Those Corriente bulls from Mexico that you throw around have nothing on you."

He laughed before hurrying to get cleaned up. Come to think of it, he'd been doing a lot of laughing since they'd driven away from the ranch.

Once he'd showered and dressed in a clean shirt and jeans, he made them bologna-and-cheese sandwiches along with a fresh pot of coffee. "Nice," he remarked when she joined him a few minutes later smelling like a meadow of spring wildflowers. She was wearing jeans and a red-and-blue-plaid hombre shirt with horn snaps.

"Thanks."

He gave her another sideways glance. "It's a good thing I'm going out shopping with you. I'm afraid you won't be safe in those duds on your own."

"Throwing more bull, Bannock?"

"Just stating the truth, ma'am." He wondered how she'd react if he told her she was a knockout in that outfit.

She gave him the once-over out of dark-fringed green eyes. "That shade of brown suits you."

"And here I was afraid you wouldn't notice."

Her arched brows lifted. "You'd be surprised what I notice. Thanks for the lunch. I'll be out in the truck when you're ready to go."

LIZ COULD TELL Polly was happy to see her. She kept nickering. They took a walk around the arena to help her get used to new surroundings, then Liz stalled her again. "I'll be back later, I promise."

She gave the horse an apple, one of Polly's favorite treats, and then she left the tent area to meet Connor at the truck parked out in back. She'd been to Las Vegas several times with her parents, but for short periods. With the horrendous traffic, she was glad Connor knew his way around town. It gave her a chance to look at everything.

The marquees were dotted with the names of famous cowboys, cowgirls and celebrities who'd flocked here to enjoy the festivities of rodeo at its best. Entertainers were hosting special concerts at various venues across the city.

"Did I tell you I've seen half a dozen marquees so far with the name Connor Bannock up in giant letters? You own this city."

"Me and a hundred others," he mumbled, but she heard him. "Just remember one thing. Here today, gone tomorrow."

"This is your sixth year of being on top. That's not peanuts, as my father says. Seriously, Connor. You've honored me by asking me to drive here with you. It's a thrill of a lifetime, one I'll never forget."

When his hand reached out to squeeze hers, she almost had a heart attack. "I have news for you," he said. "Your company has been a bonus in ways I hadn't anticipated." He held on until he found a parking space in front of a local tack shop and had to let go. But his warmth continued to flow through her like sun-kissed Montana wild honey when you could find it out riding.

As they got out of the truck and entered the store, several wolf whistles reached their ears. Connor flashed her a speaking glance. "See what I mean? You need protecting."

You walked right into this, Liz. When he's back with his wife, you're going to pay for it.

She might have known Connor would be friends with the owner. He came out of his office, and after introductions were made he gave them the red-carpet treatment. Before they left with the reins Connor specified, the owner wished them luck and took pictures of them.

"This bulldogger here is the greatest of all time," he said, clapping Connor on the shoulder.

Liz nodded. "I already know that. We've been neighbors from the time we were born. I watched him growing up. No one could beat him, and no one will beat him this year, either!"

Another shocking thing happened when Connor put an arm around her shoulders and pulled her against him. "Mark my words, Stan. This year Liz will take the championship in barrel racing."

The older man smiled. "I'll be there in the front row, watching."

She eased away from Connor and hurried out of the store. It was one thing for him to grasp her hand in the truck from a surfeit of emotion to do with his parents. That, she understood. But the feel of his arm around her shoulders was something else.

He'd been paying her a supreme compliment in an effort to make her feel good, of course. To be held by Connor for a brief moment didn't mean anything to him and shouldn't mean anything to her. She needed to get over it. It was the unexpectedness of his doing it in front of someone else that had thrown her.

On the way back to the arena, they stopped to fill up with gas. Connor looked at her. "I want some gum. Can I get you anything while I'm in there?"

"Not for me, thanks."

"Be right back."

While he was inside the crowded station, her cell rang. When she saw the caller ID she felt a stab of guilt before clicking on. "Kyle?

"Hey, you—are you in Vegas yet? I thought I'd have heard from you by now."

She shut her eyes tightly. In truth, she'd forgotten all about him. "Sorry. I got in late last night and have been out shopping for some gear for my horse. I was going to call you this evening. Where are you?"

"Yellowstone. I had a delivery here and will be flying home in another hour, so I thought I'd try to reach you now."

"I'm glad you did."

"Are you nervous? Excited?"

"Both," she said as Connor got back in the cab and started the engine.

"I'll bet. I'm looking forward to next weekend. I've got three days off so I can enjoy the rodeo and spend some time with you after you've won the championship."

"Don't I hope," she said as they drove away. Liz might not be able to spend much time with Kyle after the rodeo if Connor wanted to get right back to the ranch.

"There's no doubt in my mind you'll win."

"Thanks for your support. It means a lot. Now, I'm afraid I have to hang up and start putting my horse through our routine. I don't want her to think I've deserted her."

"I think I'm jealous."

"Don't be. After Las Vegas, my barrel-racing days are over."

"Forgive me if I tell you I'm going to be glad you'll have more time for us. When is the best time to phone you?"

"Maybe it would be better if I call you."

"I'll be waiting. I miss you."

"Me, too." She wished it were the truth. "Thanks for the call. Take care flying back."

"Always."

No sooner had she hung up than Connor said, "Which one of your favorites was that?"

"Kyle."

"Where is back?"

"The airport in Bozeman. He's an air-cargo pilot."

"I presume he'll be coming to watch you compete."

"Yes."

"When?"

"On the last night."

"Has he ever seen you in action?"

She took a deep breath. "Not yet."

"He'll be blown away by the good doctor."

"You're good for my ego."

"Then we're even."

Connor...

He drove to their spot in the RV park. "Leave everything else in the truck and I'll lock it. First person to reach their horse gets a free Milky Way."

"You're on!" A good race was exactly what she needed to expend her nervous energy.

The two of them took off running. She was fast, but no match for him. They whipped past other people. When she tried to enter the barn, he turned around in front of her, preventing her from reaching the stalls.

"Connor—" She was out of breath. "You're cheating!"

"Is that what I'm doing?" He blocked every advance she made. There was fire in his eyes. Her pulse raced off the charts. "Sorry, sweetheart, but no Milky Way for you." He'd backed up to her stall.

"You're the one who's going to be sorry for this. I'll get you when you're not expecting it."

His smile was wicked. "Before or after midnight?"

"Maybe while you're mucking out the stall."

"Whoa. Just remember you'll be in there with me."

She laughed. "You're shameless."

"I'm not the one with the halo."

Was he trying to rile her with comments like that? Daring her to do something outrageous? While she was trying to figure him out, he went into Firebrand's stall. In a minute they walked their horses out of the barn to the trailer where they saddled up and put the new reins on Sunflower. Liz had no idea if she would like them or not.

"Let's find out how those work for you." Connor brought along her bagged set of barrels. Once they'd mounted, they rode around the park several times and finally headed to the arena. Some riders were there for pleasure; others were putting in practice sessions before the first night of rodeo events coming up day after tomorrow. Competitors would be out here every day from sunup to sundown to get in the needed workouts.

"I'll set these up for you."

"No, Connor. You need to practice."

"Wade will be over later and we'll work out then. Right now I want to help you."

"I didn't expect this."

"Well, you've got me, little princess, so use me!"

"Little princess—?"

"That's what Grandpa calls you behind your back."

"You're kidding!"

"I know a few things you don't know."

"I'm sure you do," she muttered. She was touched that he would share something that personal with her. "Thank you for your help."

"That's better. This is fun."

He was like a kid out there setting up the four red, white and blue pop-ups with weighted bottoms. After placing them in a diamond pattern, he got back on Firebrand to watch her from a distance. "Are you ready?"

"Yes!" Her heart raced because it was Connor watching her every move with his expert eye. She wanted to put on a good show in front of him.

"Let's go, Sunflower. Easy at first." She took off to do her ten-minute trot-and-lope drill around the barrels. At first, the new reins were a distraction, and she told Connor her horse could tell.

"Keep sticking with it, then give her a rest and come back this evening to try again. If they still don't suit you, then forget using them. The last thing I want you to do is lose your concentration because of them."

Good advice.

"You're looking great out there."

Sunflower seemed happy to be put through her paces after traveling in the trailer for such a long time. By now, they'd acquired a fair amount of bystanders watching them, but if she'd developed nerves, Connor was the source of them.

The king of the cowboys was taking his precious time to help her be the best she could be. Short of winning his love, which she could never have, she was the luckiest woman in the world to be sharing this special moment in her life with him. Liz wouldn't have missed this experience for anything on earth.

She leaned forward and patted the horse's neck. "Good work, Sunflower. We'll come out again later."

Connor gathered up the barrels and put them in the bag before they rode back to the trailer to remove all the gear. With that accomplished, they walked their horses to the barn and mucked out the stalls. A lot of nickering went on.

"It sounds like they're having quite a talk," Connor murmured.

"I know. Maybe Sunflower is confiding in him."

"Stop worrying about it, Liz. I could kick myself for suggesting you might like these reins. If I've thrown you off, I'll never forgive myself."

"Of course you haven't!" she cried softly. "I'm a big girl. I didn't have to buy them, and I plan on trying them again. You feel too much guilt over problems that don't exist."

"Is that what I do?"

"Yes. It makes you a very nice person, but a troubled one when you don't have to be. Let's go back to the trailer and I'll fix us some sloppy joes and salad."

"That sounds like heaven."

Once they reached it and went inside, Connor washed up in the bathroom while she washed her hands in the kitchen. As Liz got the hamburger out of the freezer to thaw in the microwave, she heard a knock on the door. A special knock. It was probably Wade.

She walked over to open it. There stood Reva Stevens in a fire-engine-red two-piece suit and heels. Her makeup was perfect.

Thank heaven Connor had warned Liz.

His ex-wife was a stunning woman with black hair that flowed to her shoulders and light blue eyes. She was beautiful and petite, standing shorter than Liz by several inches.

"I'm looking for Connor Bannock. This is his trailer, isn't it?"

"Yes. I'm his neighbor, Liz Henson."

"Oh…from Montana. You and Sadie are good friends."

"Yes. And you're Reva. Since Connor and I are both competing in the rodeo, he was kind enough to trailer my horse with his."

"Is Wade with you?"

"No. He came in his own trailer with his girlfriend. Connor and I just got back from the arena. He'll be out of the bathroom in a minute. Please come in."

"Thank you."

Liz went back to the kitchen area. At a glance, she could just imagine what Reva was thinking. The signs of two people living in close quarters were all over the place. If Liz were in Reva's shoes right now, she'd be having a major meltdown.

"Hey, little princess—later on tonight I want a re-match of Pineapple."

Reva had just sat down on the sofa when Connor emerged from the bathroom. At his announcement, Liz watched his ex-wife spring back to her feet.

Chapter Five

Connor hadn't had time to phone Reva yet. She looked gorgeous, as usual. He'd be a liar if he didn't admit to certain emotions flooding his system at the sight of her. Moving closer, he kissed her cheek. "It's been a long time."

"Too long," she whispered.

"I can see you've met Liz Henson."

"Yes." But her eyes continued to search his. "I've been waiting for your call."

"I was just going to phone you. We had to exercise the horses first."

"Understood. Can you leave now? I've got a rental car outside."

He turned to tell Liz he'd be back later, but she'd gone into the bathroom and shut the door. Frustrated, he said, "Let's go." He reached for his keys and followed Reva out the door of the trailer. She'd pulled the rental car behind it. He walked her to the driver's side to open the door for her.

She hesitated before getting in. "I know you like to drive. Do you want to?"

"No, thanks. I've been on a long road trip. You do the honors. But I don't want to go back to your hotel.

I need to put in another practice session later, so let's pick up a hamburger at the drive-through three blocks down the street to save time. We can park there while we talk."

When he got in the passenger side, she still hadn't turned on the engine. "Connor—this isn't what I had in mind when I phoned you."

He studied her for a moment. "Unfortunately, you chose the wrong time."

"If you loved me the way I love you, there'd be no wrong time."

She was right.

"I'll always love you, Reva, but we couldn't make our marriage work."

She moved closer to him and grasped his arm. He breathed in her fragrance. "Once you're through with the rodeo, we'll try again. I'll resign from my job and live with you on the ranch."

He shook his head. "After a week following our marriage, you grew so restless you couldn't get back to Los Angeles fast enough."

"That was then, Connor. I'm ready to start a family. I know it's what you want."

"Why *now?* Two years ago it wasn't what *you* wanted."

"I'm not getting any younger. A baby will change everything for me. That's why I came to Las Vegas, so I could tell you in person. I want you to think about it while you're competing. Kiss me, Connor. Please. It's been so long. Do I have to beg?"

Following her urgent cry, she threw her arms around his neck and covered his mouth with her own.

The physical side of their marriage had never been

the problem. As good as it felt to be kissing her again, something was off, but he couldn't pinpoint it right now. Out of the windshield he could see the trailer. Knowing Liz was inside, he broke off their kiss and grasped Reva's arms. She protested when he put her away from him. He could taste her lipstick.

"When the rodeo is over, I promise to contact you and we'll talk about this some more. But for now I need to concentrate, so don't phone me or come over."

Her eyes had filled with tears. "You promise?" After an extended separation, that ache in her voice had always affected him. Until now.

"I swear."

She nodded. "I know you're going to win. You always do."

"We'll see. Have a safe flight home." Avoiding another kiss from her, he opened the door and got out.

"I'll come back for the last night to watch you get that sixth world-champion gold buckle, and we'll go off together afterward for a long talk."

Already his thoughts were focused on the last night when he watched Liz take the championship. "We'll have to wait and see about that. Thanks for the support, Reva."

He closed the door and headed for the trailer. Before he reached it, he wiped any trace of lipstick off his mouth. The second he walked inside, the delicious aroma of sloppy joes wafted past him.

"You're back so soon?" Liz sat at the table eating her meal.

"Yup, and I'm starving." He put up his hand. "Don't move. I'll serve myself."

No sooner had he sat down, ready to dive in, than

there was a familiar knock on the door. "Come on in, Wade!"

His brown-haired buddy walked in. Wade was a good friend and a good hazer. They'd been working together since high school. Next to his grandfather and Jarod, Wade stood a close third in the trust department.

"Hey, Wade," Liz greeted him. "It's good to see you again."

"You, too."

"Are you hungry? There's plenty."

"It smells good, but Kim and I just finished a late lunch. Thanks anyway. After we put my horse in the barn, she took off and will come back later this evening, after Connor and I are through working out."

"I'll be finished eating in a minute." Connor glanced at Liz. "These are fantastic."

"I learned from Mom. She's never made a bad meal in her life."

"That must be one of the reasons your dad is always in a good mood."

Liz's mouth had an impish curve. "It's one of them."

Wade eyed Connor with a gleam in his eye. "Lucky man."

The green salad had a tasty dressing on it. While Connor munched, he could have added that if Millie Henson was as much fun to be around as her daughter, it was no wonder Mac Henson was a happily married man.

When he thought about it, Connor's grandparents had achieved that same kind of harmony. So had Jarod and Sadie. They'd gotten it right.

Before he couldn't mount Firebrand because he'd

eaten too much, he pushed himself away from temptation and cleared his place. "I'll do the dishes tomorrow."

"Promises, promises," she teased.

He smiled at her. "What are you going to do while we're gone?"

"I've got some housekeeping chores. Leave the clothes you want washed and I'll do them with mine. Then I'll leave for the barn and put Sunflower through another routine."

"When you're done, come on over to the chutes and livestock area. I want to know how those reins are working out for you."

"I will."

"What reins?" Wade asked when they went outside.

Connor told him, then he asked Wade, "What would you think if I started a stud farm using feral stallions?"

Wade stopped walking. He stared at Connor as if he was out of his mind. "Ferals?"

"Yeah."

"I know you're nuts about Firebrand, but you've got ferals on your mind at a time like this?"

"Why not?" Connor kept walking.

Wade hurried to keep up with him. "What's happened to you?"

"What do you mean?"

"I don't know. You seem different. Usually—"

"I'm wound up tighter than a bull on the rampage? You're right. I've been a pain for years."

"Hey, Connor—it's me. Tell me what's going on."

"I'm not sure. I'll let you know when I've figured it out."

A CROWD HAD gathered around Connor and Wade. Whether he was working with his horse or in serious competition, you knew you were watching the crème de la crème. Liz wouldn't disturb his concentration right now to talk about the reins, so she rode back to the barn to settle Sunflower for the night.

Once she'd mucked out both stalls, she went into the trailer to shower. After getting dressed, she got into Connor's truck and drove to the Vegas Style beauty salon they'd passed earlier in the day on Tropicana. It was open until midnight.

She'd been mentally preparing for this competition for years, but there was still one thing left to do that would give her a new sense of freedom. Cut her hair.

Why she hadn't done it in college, she had no idea. It was a pain to wash and braid. With a shorter hairdo she could shampoo and blow-dry it in a few minutes every night. No more braid flipping around whether she was on a horse or working at the animal hospital.

There were several clients ahead of Liz. While she waited, she thumbed through the latest magazines until she found several styles she liked. The hairdresser finally told her to walk over and sit in the chair. "What can I do for you?" she asked, putting the drape over her.

Liz showed her the pictures in the magazine.

The woman studied her for a minute before undoing the braid. "Hey, honey—you really want to cut off this hair? I know gals who'd kill for such a beautiful mane."

Liz chuckled. "I've worn it this way from childhood. It's time for a change, don't you think?"

"I don't know. It'll take a long time to grow back if you decide you don't like it."

"To be honest, that doesn't matter. After being in a

rut for so many years, I need something different." Her life was going to change whether she won the competition or not. She needed to change with it.

Her hairdresser tapped one of the pictures. "I think this cut will suit your face best and will be easy to take care of. It's a blown-out, straight variation of the layered bob with a casual sophistication. Some feathering and smooth curves that flip up give it a surprising contrast. The natural lighter streaks in your hair make it a great look for you."

"Let's do it."

An hour later, Liz used the hand mirror to inspect her hair front and back. "I love it."

The woman nodded. "I did a great job, if I do say so myself. With those bones, you're a real beauty, you know that?"

Liz flushed. No one had ever said that to her, except her dad. "Thank you."

"You could be in one of the shows around here."

Liz laughed out loud. "Not me. I'm just passing through." The hairdresser hadn't met Reva Stevens, who was a true stunner. No wonder Connor hadn't been able to resist her!

"Well, I'm glad you passed my way."

"So am I." Liz took off the drape. They went over to the counter. Liz handed over her credit card and added a tip. Already she felt lighter, as though she could fly around the arena on Sunflower.

After she left the salon, she stopped at a drugstore to buy a blow-dryer. Then she hurried back to the RV park in case Connor wanted to take the truck and be on his own for the night. No one was inside when she let herself into the trailer. He was either with Wade or his ex-wife.

The way Reva had looked at Connor earlier had broken something inside Liz. He'd been married to Reva and had loved her. His ex-wife hadn't shown up in Las Vegas for the fun of it. Though Connor flirted with Liz, and had given her compliments, she couldn't assume he'd let go of Reva completely. Liz needed to be careful that she didn't read too much into his attention to her.

With an aching heart she reached for a Kit Kat from the sack of candy, then changed into pajamas and turned on the TV to a British comedy rerun. Liz adored the snob named Hyacinth. The fabulous actress was out enjoying a riparian feast in the country with her poor, henpecked husband, Richard.

At this point in the film, Hyacinth stood on a pier, straining to hold on to the small boat carrying her husband down the river, but she couldn't last and fell into the water. It was so hilarious Liz laughed until her ribs hurt. That was when she heard a knock.

"Who is it?" she called out.

"Who do you think?" Connor's deep voice had Liz jumping off the couch.

"Just checking first."

"So was I," he answered before unlocking the door. That was the gentleman in him.

"I didn't expect you back this soon."

Instead of coming in, he stood there in his cowboy hat, staring at her through unreadable brown eyes. "I'm looking for Dr. Henson, but I seem to have the wrong trailer."

"Oh, stop it, Connor, and come in. I wish you had seen this show. It's one of my favorites."

"What is it?"

"A British comedy called *Keeping Up Appearances*."

She hurried back to the couch to finish watching, but all he did was lock the door and continue to scrutinize her from a distance. Unable to concentrate with his eyes on her, she turned off the show. "Is the change that shocking?"

Without a smile, he said, "I'm still trying to catch my breath."

"Is that good or bad?"

"Because I'm a man, it's good, but Sunflower might have trouble recognizing you."

A delicious shiver swept through her. "I'll wear my hat. She'll never notice. As for me, I won't have to fight that braid any longer. I don't want any distractions during competition."

He put his hat away and walked into the kitchen. "I could hear you laughing. For a moment I thought you must be entertaining someone."

"Only myself. Hyacinth, the woman on the show, is absolutely hysterical."

Connor smiled. "You have that amazing quality of being able to enjoy yourself no matter the circumstances. No wonder my grandfather loves having you around."

"You're full of compliments, but I sense you're a little down. Dr. Henson is in the office if there's anything you'd like to talk over."

"The fact that you're here is good enough. Let's not waste that new hairdo. How would you like to go line dancing with me tonight? I don't know about you, but it'll help me unwind."

His ex-wife's appearance had done damage. How much damage wouldn't be known until the rounds of competition started.

Liz's comment to her mom before this trip came back to bite her. *I'm thinking this will be my one and only chance to see who he really is and get over what has prevented me from moving on with another man.*

"I'd love to. Since I've already showered, I'll change out of my pajamas while you clean up."

"I guess I'd better do that if you're going to let me get close to you." A quick smile broke out before he disappeared.

Yup. That was the killer smile that had blown her away in her teens. But she was a woman now, and she'd been given glimpses of the troubled man inside his skin. Liz couldn't find the words to describe the feelings growing within her. But already she knew there was pure gold lurking inside him, shinier than all the gold buckles he'd accumulated during his life's journey this far.

She dressed in another Western shirt and jeans before putting on her suede jacket. He emerged from the bathroom wearing a new black shirt she hadn't seen. Talk about trying to catch your breath.

Her hat came last as they left the trailer for the truck. Once inside the cab he said, "This bar is in the north end. They have a great band and I like the kind of crowd it attracts. Do you mind?"

"I've been on the Strip before. Surely by now you know I trust your judgment to pick someplace different."

His gaze played over her features for a pulse-pounding moment before he started the engine and they drove out to the main street. The traffic was heavy but typical for Las Vegas. Before long, they turned off and wound around to Tiny's Bar and Grill. Though there was a crowd, they didn't have to wait to get inside.

Connor had been right about the band. It rocked. As they walked in, the people on the dance floor were doing the Watermelon Crawl. Liz found her senses throbbing to the music.

After being shown to a table where he helped remove her jacket, he ordered soda for both of them. The band was getting ready for another number. "I'm in the mood to dance."

"Me, too."

They got up and walked out to the floor. The next song turned out to be the Cowboy Boogie. The moment they started, Liz glanced sideways and saw her escort could boogie with the best of them. Many of the females in the room recognized the king of the steer wrestlers and glommed onto him in a big hurry.

Someone in the band announced that the famous Connor Bannock was in the grill. Everyone cheered. Liz loved it. He was electrifying when caught in the right mood, and he was definitely in the right mood. His eyes lit up when he realized she was well into it herself.

Liz danced her head off. She'd never had so much fun in her life. The whole crowd was living it up. Pretty soon they turned to the Sleazy Slide, and they must have danced to half a dozen songs before the band took a break.

After he cupped her elbow and led her back to their table, he leaned toward her, his eyes full of flattering male admiration. “I’ve never been with a woman who dances like you. Is there anything you can’t do?”

If only her heart would stop its sickening thud. “I can’t steer wrestle.”

“I’m being serious,” he ground out.

She drank her cola. “So am I. As I said before, my folks didn’t get a boy.”

He sipped his drink, viewing her mysteriously over the rim of his glass. “They won the jackpot.”

“Try telling them that. You never heard about the pony dad paid money for that he didn’t have. After I went to my first rodeo, I plagued him for one. Then I nearly drove the poor thing into the ground trying to make it go around tree stumps in the forest. I almost killed it.”

Laughter started deep inside him until his whole body was shaking. It brought tears to his fabulous brown eyes. “How old were you?”

“Oh, I don’t know. Maybe six. I gave them fits day in and day out for years. When I was nine, dad got me Magpie, whom I promptly crippled. After he got Dr. Rafferty to explain all the terrible things I’d done to him trying to make him run around more stumps and bumping into them accidentally, I had to nurse my horse until she was better. I think it was then I decided it might not be a bad idea to become a vet if my animals were going to survive.”

A smile laced his features, giving him a dashing look. “In the midst of it all, a barrel racer was born.”

“My dad was forced to train me so he would survive parenthood.”

“His hard work paid off.”

She averted her eyes as her throat closed up. "Let's hope so."

"You made it to the top fifteen in the world. Number two puts you in the top money earnings. As your father said, that's not peanuts." The band had started up again. "Let's dance."

It wasn't until they reached the open floor she realized the music had changed to allow everyone to slow dance. She felt a spurt of adrenaline as he pulled her into his arms and drew her close to his hard-muscled body. Their hats nudged against each other, but he didn't let that stop him from pressing his cheek to hers. She was burning up. Surely he couldn't help but notice.

When the song ended, he didn't let go. "This is nice," he whispered in a husky voice.

So nice she could hardly breathe. He continued to rock her in his arms until another song began. "I like your gold barrel racer earrings. They're unique."

"Sadie and Jarod had them made for me on the reservation to bring me luck."

"They're working so far."

Liz lost track of her surroundings. The whole time they clung to each other, his warm breath tickled the ends of her newly cut hair, sending rivulets of delight through her body. It was uncanny how they moved as one person.

"Do you have any idea how good you smell?"

"We both used the same soap, remember?"

"One of the great perks of rooming together," he teased. "I'm glad we've still got two weeks ahead of us."

And then what? Would he get back with Reva? But Liz chose not to think about that right now.

Connor lifted his head so he could look at her. "I'm waiting for you to say something back." If she wasn't mistaken, she heard a trace of vulnerability in his voice. "Have you changed your mind? Would you rather room with the other barrel racers at the hotel? It's a once-in-a-lifetime opportunity to rub shoulders with the best of them."

What to say to convince him she was happy with the decision she'd already made? "When Mom asked me why I decided to travel with you, I told her it was a once-in-a-lifetime opportunity to rub shoulders with the best of the best. That's *you,* Connor."

She heard his sharp intake of breath, which could mean anything, before he spun her around the floor. When the song ended, he grasped her hand and led her through the crowd to the exit. Silence punctuated the drive back to the RV park. By the time they reached the trailer, Liz sensed Connor had worked himself up into a mood she didn't understand.

He unlocked the door for her. "I have an errand to run. I don't know how long I'll be."

After giving Liz the thrill of her life, he was off to spend time with his ex-wife.

She knew he wasn't a player. Connor's grandfather had suggested he take Liz to Las Vegas with him. He'd probably told him to show her a good time. No one could do it better than Connor, even with Reva waiting in the wings for him.

"You don't owe me any explanation, neighbor. Thank you for a great evening out." She went inside and shut the door before locking it.

Liz checked her watch. Five after one in the morning. Too late to have a heart-to-heart with Sadie. After she got ready for bed and had crawled under the covers, she texted her best friend who would see her message in the morning.

I need to talk, but know it's impossible tonight. I'll try to reach u tomorrow. Suffice it to say, I'm in trouble.

No sooner had she pressed Send and turned out the light than her cell rang. She couldn't believe it and clicked it on. "Sadie?"

"It's not impossible because I'm wide-awake. Jarod drove to the reservation and is staying all night with his uncle Charlo's family. They're rebuilding the fence around their house. I stayed behind because I haven't felt good for the past two days."

"You're sick?"

"Yeah. Poor little Ryan doesn't understand what's wrong with me."

All of a sudden, Liz screamed with joy. "You're pregnant!"

"Yes! I just found out, but I told Jarod I was coming down with a cold because I want to surprise him when he gets back after breakfast."

"I'm so thrilled for you, I'm jumping out of my skin!"

"Me, too, but I'm *so* sick. The nausea is deadly. Still, enough talk about me. You said you're in trouble, and we both know why."

Her hand gripped the phone tighter. "I'm afraid so."

"Where's Connor?"

"With his ex-wife."

"Reva's there?"

"Yes."

"You're kidding me!" Sadie cried. "That woman refuses to leave him alone! Jarod's going to croak when he hears this."

"They're still in love, Sadie."

"So are you. I can hear it in your voice."

Liz closed her eyes tightly. "Yes. He's so wonderful, you have no idea."

"Of course I do. He's Ralph's grandson and Jarod's brother. There's no one like the Bannock brothers on this planet," she said, in so fervent a tone that Liz shivered. "I have no advice for you. Absolutely none."

"I didn't expect any. I just needed to talk."

"Go ahead and bawl your heart out. I did enough of that to you for eight years. It's my turn to listen."

The floodgates opened. "H-he's lost confidence, Sadie. It goes back a long way."

"Tell me something I don't know. I'm still working on Jarod."

Liz wiped the moisture off her face. "He feels guilty about his life."

"That sounds familiar, too. Blast Reva for showing up at a time like this."

"She can't help that she loves him."

"It's not the kind of love he needs. Jarod's worried about him retiring from the rodeo. He's vulnerable, and Reva knows it."

"I couldn't agree more."

"Thank goodness you're in Las Vegas now. How's the hotel? Are they taking special care of all you barrel racers, letting you loose in the casino?"

Guilt caused her to sit up straight up in bed. "No."

"What do you mean?"

Her pulse picked up speed. "Connor and I are sharing his trailer as our hotel while we're here."

At least a minute passed before she heard, "Liz—what's going on?"

"I'll tell you what I told Mom. After all these years of being haunted by him, he gave me an opportunity to get a real dose of him, one-on-one. I was convinced that driving to Las Vegas with him, staying with him in his trailer, would be a revelation and provide the cure I've been needing."

"Where's Wade sleeping?"

"He's driven down in his own trailer with his girlfriend."

Another silence. "My poor, dear, darling, foolish friend..."

"Sadie? You and I both know this was all Ralph's idea. He gave us this charm bracelet to hang on the truck mirror to bring us luck. Connor's trying to please him. He's been bending over backward for his wallflower neighbor."

"Wallflower—"

"The shoe fits, Sadie. I'll act grateful if it kills me."

"It's already killing you."

It was.

"You're in the worst trouble I ever heard of and the rodeo hasn't even begun yet. It beats my eight years of exile from Jarod. I thought you wanted to win the gold buckle."

"I do. Pray for me."

"I already am."

Chapter Six

Liz set her watch alarm for six-thirty in the morning. She wanted to take Sunflower on an early ride. It would give both of them a chance to work with the new reins. When she looked up, she could see Connor was in bed. He'd probably just gotten in from being with Reva and would need a ton of sleep.

After dressing quietly, she gave her hair a quick brushing. What a delight after having to take care of that long braid day after day for years! She bit into an apple, put on her hat and left the trailer. The sun was just making its appearance, a favorite time of the morning for Liz, as she headed for the barn.

When she reached the stalls, she let Sunflower finish off her fruit. Not forgetting the other horse, she slipped Firebrand a treat from her pocket. "Don't worry. Connor will be here before long."

Then she turned to her horse. "Come on, little lady. Let's give these reins another try and find out if Connor was right about them."

She led Sunflower back to the trailer. Once the mare was saddled, Liz levered herself into the seat and took off on a slow walk. Only a few people were out riding.

Slowly she ran through her routine. "Whoa," she

said every so often, pulling on the reins as Sunflower stopped and backed up. The more she worked with the reins, the more she realized she could get a good grip with those knots. The feel was definitely different.

When they returned to the arena, she started making her circles. After a little while, she increased her speed and could tell she had more control with these reins, giving her confidence. Better yet, her horse was getting the message and couldn't pull around a turn like she sometimes wanted to do because Liz had a stronger, better grip.

At the rodeo in Great Falls, Connor's eagle eye had seen the reins slide through her hands that one time. It took a champion to have noticed. Another slip like that could cost her a winning time when it came down to the wire. She owed him for helping her make a crucial adjustment in her gear.

Over and over again she practiced her circles with Sunflower, changing from a walk to a lope, one direction, then the other, then backing up. The knotted reins were what she'd needed to fine-tune her connection with Sunflower.

"By Jove, I think she's got it" came a deep, familiar male voice out of the blue.

She turned her head. "Professor Higgins!" she cried in a rush of excitement. How long had he been watching her? "You're a genius!"

"That's nice to hear first thing in the day."

Her heart melted at the sight of him astride Firebrand, his hat dipped low over his forehead to shield his eyes from the rays of the sun. In her mind, Connor had always been the ultimate American cowboy, but since their trip she'd learned he had many facets to his complex personality. He was such a marvelous man, she could hardly put her feelings into words.

"Do you want to hear something else exciting?"

A half smile broke out on his face as he rode closer. "Shoot."

"The thing we've all hoped for has happened. Sadie just found out she's pregnant, but Jarod doesn't know yet." Connor whistled. "She's going to tell him today, with a special surprise when he gets back from the reservation."

"What is it?"

"After they were married, she secretly asked Jarod's family to make her a basket cradleboard in the hope that one day they'd have a child. She has it hidden at Ralph's. I bet she ran over to get it and has put it in the middle of their bed so he'll see it first thing."

A stillness surrounded Connor. "He's going to die of joy."

"Oh, wouldn't you love to be a fly on the wall when she tells him?"

Connor let go with a whoop and tossed his hat high in the air. Pure love for his brother had inspired that maneuver. Naturally, because he was so athletic, he caught it again.

"I can't wait to hear what Crow name he comes up with after their baby is born."

He grinned. "Probably something like Howls Like a Wolf."

She laughed hilariously. "Or Bear Cub Who Makes Noise."

Connor sidled his horse right up to her. "When did you talk to her?"

"Last night, before I went to sleep. She would have

gone to the reservation with him, but felt too nauseous. I guess that's when she learned she was pregnant. The news about Sits in the Center will go out over the pow-wow drums at their next celebration," she teased. "Just think. You're going to be an uncle, and Avery will be an aunt!"

He nodded. "This will give Grandpa a reason to go on living." He smiled as he said it, but she heard a forlorn tone that crushed her, because she knew where it came from. Connor didn't feel he carried his weight as a Bannock. She couldn't bear it that he didn't know how remarkable he was.

"Ralph has three outstanding grandchildren carving out their own destinies. All of them help him get up every morning."

He studied her for a long time. "You're the one person I know who always sees the glass full. Not half-full or half-empty, but full."

"That's because it is. Have you eaten yet?"

"No. I heard you leave and decided it was my turn to muck out the stalls while you were working with Sunflower."

"That was a sneaky move on your part. You're afraid I'm going to get you when you're knee-deep in the stuff."

A chuckle escaped his throat. "The thought has crossed my mind more than once. Are you hungry?"

"I'm getting there."

"Let's drive out of town into the desert. I want to barbecue some steaks and cook up potatoes and onions. We'll take a trail ride. The horses need a break from their normal routines and it'll be fun for them. We'll come back in time for me to work out with Wade."

"Do you have a specific place in mind?"

"I thought we'd drive to Red Rock Canyon. It's not far, and there are trails running throughout with some awesome views. How does that sound?"

A whole afternoon alone with Connor now that they'd reached their destination? There had to be a reason he wanted to get completely away. *You wanted to get to know the real Connor. But you hadn't counted on his ex-wife to be a virtual presence. You are a fool, Liz Henson.*

She averted her eyes, unable to sustain his glance. "It beats spending time losing the little money I brought with me on the roulette wheel," she quipped. "Come on, Sunflower. We're very lucky our gracious next-door neighbor wants to show us something we haven't seen before. Let's see if we can't beat him and Firebrand to the trailer."

With a clicking sound, she took off like a shot. It was exhilarating to get into a full gallop. Liz wouldn't have done it if Sunflower hadn't already been warmed up. She reached the back of the trailer first, but that was only because Connor had decided not to make it a competition. She jumped down to open the doors.

Moving quickly, she walked her horse into the stall and filled the bucket with fresh water for her. She patted her neck. "If you run that fast for me during the events, we'll have nothing to worry about."

While Connor led his horse inside the other stall, she secured the lead rope and then left the stall. Before long he'd hitched the truck to the trailer and they took off.

No one eyeing them would see a thing wrong this picture, but Liz knew it was flawed. "Connor," she began. "I—"

"Reva went back to Los Angeles yesterday," he broke in before she could apologize."

So he wasn't with her last night.

"She won't return until the last night of finals. But I want to get something clear right now. You've been more than a neighbor to me for a long time, and I'm not using you for substitute entertainment."

"I know that," she whispered. "But I guess I'm overwhelmed by your attention. When Ralph asked you to drive me here and take good care of me, I never dreamed you would be so thorough about it. It makes me feel guilty, because I've done nothing to deserve it.

"Though you warned me about Reva, when she walked in the trailer I could see what she was seeing, and it hurt me for her sake. She couldn't have been happy that I was living in there with you. If your kindness to me, or your grandfather's, has done anything to cause trouble between you and your ex-wife, I couldn't handle that. I'd be happy to explain the way things really are to her."

"Have you finished?"

She lowered her head. "Not yet. Jarod and Sadie almost didn't get back together because of horrible misunderstandings. Look at them now! If I can be of any help to you where Reva is concerned, you know I'll do whatever I can."

"Now are you through?"

"No! I'm indebted to you and Ralph for getting me here. If I accept that job on the reservation, I'll be indebted to Jarod. I guess I'm having a hard time accepting the incredible kindness you Bannocks have showered on me."

He cleared his throat. "Let's get a few things

straight. In the first place, the problems between me and Reva started a long time ago and resulted in a divorce. The fact that you're using my trailer while we're here has no bearing on my relationship with her because she and I no longer have a relationship. A miracle would have to happen for us to get together again."

Though Reva might have pursued him this time, she knew in the core of her he was still hoping for that miracle.

"Second, you're under the false impression that my grandfather asked me to drive you to finals with me. But you're wrong. He had nothing to do with it. In fact, I know it shocked him when he found out. The truth is, I allowed you to make that assumption because I was afraid you wouldn't come otherwise."

Liz knew he wasn't a liar. Her body started to tremble from those stunning revelations. "Then why *did* you ask me to come?"

"Frankly, it's because I wish it hadn't taken so long for me to get to know you, but because of Daniel I was forced to stay away. Years ago Grandpa made me promise I wouldn't go near you. That's why you and I never really connected though we've lived next door to each other our whole lives. At Daniel's funeral I was determined to fix that problem, but our schedules have been hectic.

"Last month I saw you out riding in the Pryors, working on your form. Your discipline and work ethic is absolutely phenomenal. It struck me how crazy it was that two people who love the sport like we do, and have given our lives to it, have never gotten to know each other better. That's when I got the idea to invite you to drive to Las Vegas with me. But after you turned me down in Missoula, I'll admit I was nervous to approach you again."

Her emotions were in chaos. "I can't imagine you being nervous about that."

"Are you kidding? Grandpa's little princess? Sadie's best friend? Your parents' pride and joy? Montana's wonder woman?"

"Okay, okay. Stop!" She laughed in spite of her shock.

"I didn't want to make a mistake with you. Have I made one now by asking you to spend the day with me?"

"Of course not."

"That's good. Now I'm going to stick my neck out once more and ask you another question. Have you ever wished I'd asked you to go out with me?"

With her heart slamming into her rib cage, she lifted her head and eyed him directly. "You mean before you met Reva?"

He nodded.

"Sure." She flashed him a smile. "Every girl in the county wanted a chance to be with Montana's hot steer wrestling champion."

A shadow crossed over his features. "I'm talking about your wanting to be with the second son of the rancher next door."

What did he just say?

"But now that I think about it, Bobby Felton and Ricky Jarvis always hung around you at school, so the thought to be with me probably never entered your mind."

He couldn't be serious. But when she looked into his eyes, she could see that he was. *Connor, Connor.*

The tension between them was palpable. "Do you think you can handle the truth?"

"Try me." His intensity shook her to the bone.

"The times Sadie and I went out riding and Jarod just happened to show up though it was forbidden, I always hoped his younger brother would be with him, but it never happened."

A long silence stretched between them. "When we get back from finals, plan on my showing up. If I see you with Kyle or any of your other favorites, I'll lie low until I can catch you alone."

Gasp.

"SEE YOU TOMORROW at the Mack Center, Wade. Liz and I will be taking our horses over after lunch."

He nodded. "That was a good workout tonight."

"Yup. Firebrand's never performed better."

"I'm talking about you."

"Yeah?"

"Yeah." His gaze played over Connor without saying anything more.

After Wade left the barn, Connor took care of the horses. While he made certain they were watered and fed for the night, his cell phone rang.

Jarod!

He'd been waiting for this call the whole time he and Liz had ridden in Red Rock Canyon. With certain misunderstandings cleared up, their outing had been quite perfect.

"Hey, bro—I thought you'd forgotten me. How are you and Sadie doing?" He was waiting to hear the excitement about the baby.

"I just got back from the reservation. She's so sick, she can't lift her head off the pillow."

Connor grinned. "Must be the flu. It's going around."

"It's not that. She's pregnant, and I'm terrified."

He blinked. "Those two statements don't go together. How could you possibly be terrified over news that has to have made you a new man?"

"You don't know how sick she is, Connor. I've never seen her like this in my life."

"If it's that bad, then she should be in the hospital where the doctor can reduce the nausea with medication."

"I've already talked to her OB. He'd ordered medicine for her and I just gave it to her. But what if—"

"It isn't!" Connor interrupted him. "The doctor said her heart operation fixed the problem for good. Some women get really sick. Grandpa told us our mom had terrible morning sickness for a few weeks with Avery. Remember Prince William's wife? They had to put her in the hospital for a few days. Now they have baby George. Have you got any ideas for your baby's name?"

"I can't think right now."

"I don't think I could, either, if I'd just been told I'm going to be a dad. Congratulations, bro! This is the good news we've all been waiting for."

"You really think this is going to pass?"

"I think you need a good talk with your uncle Charlo."

"He'll tell me I'm a mess."

"That's your right as a new father. Have you told Grandpa or Avery?"

"No. You're the first."

Afraid not. Liz had gotten there before anyone else. Connor loved it.

"Did you find her in bed when you got back?"

"No. I found a flat-board cradle on my side. She was in the bathroom throwing up."

Connor tried not to burst out laughing. This was one situation his big brother, who was always in control, wasn't prepared for. "I'm sorry she's sick, but you know it won't last long. Give her my love and cling to the Crow courage that led you to the light during your fast."

He thought his brother might have hung up when he suddenly said, "How are you? How's it going with Liz?"

"Sometime I'll tell you, but not tonight. Go take care of your wife. I'll call you tomorrow."

Liz was already in bed when he returned to the trailer. He looked down at her. "I just got off the phone with the father of Little Sits in the Center."

She sat up. "I love that name you made up! Is Jarod thrilled out of his mind?"

"Not yet. Sadie has bad morning sickness. He's so in love with that woman he can't handle anything being wrong with her."

"Sadie's tough."

Connor had needed to hear that himself from the one person who knew Sadie better than anyone else. "I told him we'll call him tomorrow. We'll both talk to him. Since I'm too excited to sleep yet, how about some poker after I've showered?"

"I've got another idea. Have you ever played Boggle?"

"Can't say that I have."

"I'll set it up. You're going to love it!"

He had news for her. He loved whatever he did when they were together. In truth, he didn't want the finals to end....

AFTER HER WORKOUT at the Mack Center the next day, Liz took care of her horse, then left the temporary tented barn provided for the horses and headed for Connor's rig. They'd parked on the lot of the university's soccer field. That was where she would wait for him. To her surprise, she saw a cowboy lounging against their truck with his arms folded. When he saw her coming, he waved and started walking toward her.

"Dr. Henson?"

"Oh—you're one of the famous Porter brothers I met in St. George."

"Derrick." He smiled. "I'm glad you remembered that much. I was hoping to catch up with you. Are you finished for the evening?"

"Absolutely. I put Sunflower through her paces today. We both need a rest."

"With tomorrow being our first official event, I think we've all had a tiring workout." He shoved his hat back. "I saw Connor's rig, so I'll come right out and ask if you and he are an item before I go any further."

He was nice. Rather cute. Probably her age. Maybe a little younger. "I'm his neighbor. He was kind enough to give me and my horse transportation here. I'm using his trailer as a hotel during the events."

Derrick was a friend of Wade's. It was important she made her relationship with Connor perfectly clear with Derrick because it would get back to Connor at some point.

His eyes flared in response. "One question down. One more to go. If you don't have any plans for this evening, would you care to have dinner with me?"

Though Liz was flattered by Derrick's interest in her, she didn't want to encourage him when Kyle would be coming the last night of finals. On the other hand, maybe it wouldn't hurt this one time in order to give Connor some space. He'd mentioned that they'd get together after they got back to the ranch, but she had no idea how serious he'd been about it. Since they'd left Montana, they'd been together constantly. *What to do?*

"That's okay, Liz." His smile said it was, but her lack of a quick response wasn't kind. Surely it wouldn't hurt to go with him this once. They were all competing, and he was anxious as everyone else underneath. Theirs was a unique fraternity.

"No, no. I'd like to go. It will be relaxing. The errand I'd planned to do can wait. Thanks, Derrick. Give me a minute to go inside the trailer and I'll be right back out."

"Take your time."

Once inside she freshened up and changed into a clean blouse and jeans. After brushing her hair and putting on lipstick, she wrote a message for Connor and left it on the counter.

Connor,
Have made plans for this evening. Will see you back at the RV park later tonight. Liz.

Dispensing with her cowboy hat, she walked out and locked the door. Derrick was waiting for her in his white truck. As he was helping her in the passenger side of the cab he said, "I like your new hairdo."

"I'm flattered you even noticed. Thank you."

"You're impossible not to notice, if you know what I mean." After Connor's reaction, she'd decided she should have cut her hair sooner. Derrick shut the door and walked around to get behind the wheel. "I thought we'd go for my favorite meal, if you don't have a preference."

"I'm so hungry I could eat anything."

"Even breakfast?"

"Maybe you're psychic. If I had to choose to eat the same meal every day of life, it would be bacon, eggs and cinnamon toast."

"Even if I'm not psychic, I'm superstitious and always eat breakfast the night before an event the next day."

"With two gold buckles in your possession, your system must be working. Maybe it'll work for me."

He drove them through the park to the main street. "I watched a couple of barrel racers earlier. Then I spotted you. The control over your horse is superb."

"Are you trying to sweeten me up, cowboy?" she teased.

"Nope. I call it as I see it."

"You know how to make a gal feel good."

"Just being with you makes *me* feel good."

Hopefully he said that to all the girls. Liz ended up having a nice evening. Derrick worked on his father's sheep ranch in Rock Springs and was still single and enjoying the rodeo circuit with his brother. They mostly talked shop.

At ten-thirty they drove into the RV park. Connor

had brought his rig back from the center. The truck was there, too. He might be inside or with Wade, but it didn't matter. Just the thought of him sent a minor quake through her body.

"Tomorrow night a few of us are going to attend a party at the Bellagio, but we'll go to the South Point Hotel first to see the gold buckles given out." She knew all about the Wrangler NFR–hosted event. It was held in the ballroom of the main casino every night. "Would you like to go with me?"

She was ready for him this time. "I can't make plans that far ahead. Why don't we wait until tomorrow night to see what it brings?"

"Fair enough. I'll look for you after your event is over."

Liz gave a nod without actually committing herself. "Good luck to you and your brother."

"The same to you. See you tomorrow night."

Maybe, but she wouldn't be going out with him again. "Thanks for dinner. Don't get out." She opened the door and jumped down.

Liz felt his gaze on her as she approached the trailer and reached inside her purse for the keys. But before she could get it in the lock, Connor opened the door.

"Hey, Connor." With a smile, Derrick waved his hat to him before driving off.

There was no answering smile from her host. He locked the door behind her, looking the way her father had in her teens when he didn't know where she'd been and was worried. But her heart knocked against her ribs over the lack of animation on his face. "Is Sadie worse?"

For a few seconds he didn't say anything.

"Connor?"

"Sorry. What did you ask?"

"You look so upset, I thought you must have had bad news about Sadie."

"I'm sure she's all right or I would have heard from Jarod," he mumbled.

"Then what's wrong?"

He shot her a piercing glance. "Derrick's a player. I thought you'd already figured that out."

Was Connor jealous? Was it possible? She sat down in one of the chairs. "It was just one dinner with another competitor to talk shop."

"So *that's* what you were doing?"

"He approached me at the rodeo grounds and I didn't want to be rude, knowing he's a friend of Wade's and a little uptight waiting for tomorrow." It was the truth.

"Wade said he has a girlfriend back in Rock Springs, but I wager Derrick didn't mention her." His brows lifted. "Has he asked you out again?"

"For tomorrow night, but I told him I couldn't make plans."

"That was smart."

She couldn't believe this had come out of him. For Connor to be upset over Derrick thrilled her to the heels of her cowboy boots.

"I don't know what will happen in my event," she said. "But I want to see you get your buckle. For five seasons in a row you've had the winning time the first night of every competition. It's unheard of. That's why you're a legend already."

No compliment could nudge him out of his foul mood.

"Connor? Have you eaten yet?"

"No." He rubbed the back of his neck. "I wasn't hungry."

"Ah. So this is what happens to you the night before an event. You need food. That's why you're a grump. I'll fix you some eggs. They taste good anytime."

She put her purse on the couch and got out the eggs and bacon from the fridge. In a jiffy she found the frying pan and started cooking.

He stood there, watching her, with his hands on his hips. "What did you have for dinner?"

"Breakfast."

"He took you to breakfast?" The scowl on his face spoke volumes.

"It's my favorite meal."

"I know." His head reared. "Did you tell *him* that?"

She was beginning to believe Connor really *was* jealous.

"Only after he told me it was what he wanted for dinner. Why don't you sit down?" She made coffee and set a place for him. Pretty soon she'd served him breakfast and added some of the toasted English muffins he liked.

To her satisfaction he ate every bite.

"That was delicious. Thank you. Wade wanted me to go eat with them, but I didn't feel like it. When I got back here, I didn't feel like cooking, and I apologize for my behavior."

"The king of the steer wrestlers has every right to experience an off night."

"*You* never have one."

"Don't worry. My turn is coming, so be warned."

When he'd finished, she cleared his place. Then she

took some thin chocolate after-dinner mints out of her purse and put them in front of him.

"Where did these come from?"

"The restaurant. I thought you'd like them with your coffee."

"So you *were* thinking about me." He sounded happy about that.

"Of course. Since you and I left the ranch, it feels like we've been joined at the hip. I thought you might like a breather, but you knew I'd be back. I didn't want to return empty-handed."

It seemed those were the magic words. On that note, he undid the foil wrappers and gobbled the mint down, causing her to chuckle. "You remind me of Sunflower enjoying her favorite treat."

The light had come back into those dark brown eyes. "I like treats."

She smiled. "I know."

"If ever you feel like giving me more, make them chocolate."

"I know your tastes by now." Liz cleaned up the kitchen. Connor obviously wasn't up to partying. He'd done all those things with Reva once upon a time. She couldn't blame him for brooding over his situation now. "How did your workout go?" she asked over her shoulder. "Feel like you're ready?"

"I never feel ready," he muttered.

She leaned against the counter. "Neither do I. I'm so glad you admitted it first. Maybe you'll think this sounds crazy, but I feel at a loose end without Sunflower tonight. She's in a new place. Even with Polly there, I'm sure she's missing me and Firebrand. The barrel horses are in a different row inside the barn."

"Tell you what. Tomorrow night we'll bring them both back to the RV park and give them a shampooing. Might as well keep them here for the rest of the competition. It will be much quieter and friendlier for them."

"That would be wonderful," she blurted.

"You never wanted to move them there, did you?"

"I didn't know."

"Well, we know now." He got up from the table. "I'm glad there's a smile on your face. In the meantime, will *I* do for company?"

She turned away from him. "Always." The word slipped out before she could prevent it.

"Want to go for a swim? The indoor pool is open all night."

She'd forgotten there was a pool. "That'll be the perfect place to unwind. I'll change into my suit."

After finding it in the bottom of the suitcase, she hurried into the bathroom to change. Then she put her clothes on over it and grabbed a towel. Connor carried his suit and towel with him. They left the trailer and made their way to the building that housed the pool. Several guys were in the shallow end, talking along the edge.

When Connor left to change, she removed her clothes and got in at the deep end. Two men promptly swam over to her, forcing her to tread water. She figured they couldn't be a day over nineteen.

"You're that barrel racer we've seen out in the arena with Connor Bannock."

He had fans everywhere. "That's right. Are you two here to compete?"

"Don't I wish," one guy said. "I'm Bart. We're students at the university, but love the rodeo."

"Ah."

"We both work here during the day," the other guy said. "I'm Casey. We found out he was registered here and hoped to meet him and get his autograph. I saw you working with him earlier. You're a sensational rider, too."

"Thank you."

"Since you're friends with him, what do you think? He's so famous that after he wins his sixth gold buckle, we won't be able to get near him."

"I'm sure he'll give you one. Have you got something for him to write on?"

"Be right back!" They both charged out of the pool and disappeared.

"What was that all about?" Connor had plunged into the pool and emerged at the deep end next to her. The water made his hair look darker, giving him a different look she couldn't resist.

"Two fans who work here at the RV park and are dying for your John Henry. I told them you'd do it. Do you mind? You're their idol."

The way he appraised her sent licks of flame through her body. "As long as that was all they wanted."

They did some laps together, taking their time to reach the other end. Before long, the two guys came back to the pool carrying the things they wanted autographed. Liz turned her head toward Connor, who'd edged up close to her. His closeness caused her heart to thud.

"Go ahead and make their night with that thousand-dollar signature, cowboy."

"Come again?"

"That's what it will be going for down the road."

She stayed in the water while Connor bounded to the patio and talked to them for a minute. They were all smiles as he signed what looked like a poster and a magazine. Before they left she heard them call out, "Thanks, Dr. Henson. We didn't know you're competing, too. We'll be cheering for you tomorrow night, as well."

Curious how Connor always referred to her as *doctor* in front of other people.

"Thank you!" Liz waved while she waited for Connor to get back into the water. That was when the idea to "get him" took root. As he swam up to her, she did a strong kick, splashing him in the face, something he wasn't expecting.

He sputtered for a second. "So you want to play?"

"Better here than giving you a muck bath in the stall."

In a lightning move he caught her ankles and pulled her to the center of the pool, where he swung her around with her arms flailing, making her dizzy. "Connor—" she shrieked in laughter, helpless to defend herself. "Stop!"

He kept going. "Had enough?" His devilish smile shook her to the foundations.

"Yes—"

Connor towed her to the shallow end and sat down on the step, where he pulled her onto his lap so she sat across him with his arms around her. His eyes bored into hers. "You always seemed so untouchable to me. For years I've wanted to get close to you like this, to find out if you're really real. It's been such a long wait, don't deny me what I want right now. I couldn't take it."

She heard his ragged voice implore her before his

mouth covered hers. A moan escaped her lips. Surely this wasn't happening. The urgency of his kiss caught her off guard. He'd stolen her heart years ago, but right this minute he'd stolen her breath.

Mindless from the sensations he was arousing, let alone the warning bells, she forgot everything except her hunger for him. This incredible man was kissing her as if he really meant it. As for Liz, she *did* mean it with every fiber of her being and was letting him know.

When his hands roved over her back, drawing her closer still, she realized what she was allowing to happen. Afraid of her needs spiraling out of control, she wrenched her mouth from his.

"No more, Connor—" She refused to look at him. "I've crossed a line I swore I wouldn't do this trip. It's my fault, not yours." She tried to get away, but he wouldn't let her.

"Now look who's apologizing. Fault doesn't come into it. I caught this enchanting mermaid in an aqua bikini swimming in my territory. What else is a man to do?"

"Or a woman," she admitted. "But since we've had our fun, let's quit while we're ahead. Believe me when I tell you you're the best of the best, whether rodeo champion or second son of a rancher. It's my privilege to know you and be your friend. But tomorrow the competition begins in earnest for the last time in our lives. I don't want to do anything that distracts us from realizing our dreams. I know you don't, either."

She slid away and dashed up the step to the changing room off the patio. Her hands shook as she removed her suit and got dressed in her clothes. Sharing accommodations had made this moment inevitable.

Connor was waiting for her when she stepped outside the building. The temperature had dropped. They hurried toward the trailer in the distance.

"If you think I'm sorry for what happened back there, you'd be wrong."

Liz darted him a smile. *Keep it light.* "I enjoyed it, too." The unimaginable had happened and she was still reeling.

"Good. When we get back to the ranch, we'll pick up where we left off."

But with Reva waiting for his rodeo career to come to an end, was he trying to convince Liz or himself? Was that what his kiss in the pool was all about? "By the time we get back to Montana, the focus of our lives will have completely changed."

"Thanks to you, mine already has."

Her pulse sped up. "In what way?

"A feral stud farm. The possibility has taken hold of my mind. If I were to undertake a venture of that magnitude, I'd need a vet I could trust with my life. Would you be interested?"

She swallowed hard. His ex-wife was coming to Las Vegas on the last night. Liz was afraid of what it meant. To work with Connor for the rest of her life while the happily remarried couple lived next door?

Liz's conversation with her mother came forcefully to mind.

I'm convinced that driving to Las Vegas with him will be a revelation and provide the cure I've been needing.

And if it isn't?

If it isn't, then I'll have to take a serious look at my life and make changes.

That's what has me worried. Bannocks never pull up roots. That means you'll be the one who'll end up moving somewhere else.

A shudder swept through Liz as they entered the trailer. Millie Henson's words might just have turned out to be prophetic.

"That would mean stretching my practice in too many ways, but I'm flattered you would even consider me."

"At least promise me you'll think about it."

There was no reason to give him a flat-out no yet, not when he was actually considering her idea for using ferals. If anyone could do it, *he* could. "Let's get through the competition first."

"Agreed. Do you want to shower first?"

"Do you mind? Then I'll blow-dry my hair while you're in the bathroom. It's so noisy, it will keep you awake otherwise."

She grabbed a clean pair of pajamas and hurried into the bathroom. But after she'd closed the door, she sank down onto the floor and slumped over her raised knees for a minute while she tried to recover.

Love's first kiss.

Any other kisses before this didn't count.

She'd read about it in the fairy tales. Now she understood why it had brought Snow White violently awake. Prince Charming's passion had created a bonfire. Liz was burning up.

Chapter Seven

The day of the first round of the pro finals was upon them. "What do you think I should wear for the opening ceremonies?" While Liz cooked eggs and ham, Connor held up two Western shirts, one black, one brown.

She glanced at them. "Black will make a big statement."

"Black it is. Why don't you wear the royal-blue shirt I saw you hang up in the wardrobe? When we parade in front of the crowd with the other competitors from our state, every eye will be focused on you."

"You're throwing bull again." But her pulse throbbed from his compliment. Liz couldn't believe she was actually going to be a legitimate competitor in front of thousands of people at the Super Bowl of rodeos with Connor. Everything was starting to feel surreal.

"What? No argument?" he teased.

"Not today."

"Well, that was easy."

She chuckled. "Come and eat. I've made French toast, too."

"I love being spoiled rotten."

Liz loved being with him, period!

After breakfast, they cleaned the trailer, washed sheets and made beds. Then came the phone calls to and from family and friends. She received a text from Kyle wishing her luck. She sent him a message back with a thank-you. Keeping busy was the best way to handle the countdown.

At 11:00 a.m. Connor drove Liz to the South Point hotel to attend the Women's Pro Rodeo Star Celebration. There was a banquet program where they were handed out gift packs of an NFR ring, a jacket and a backpack. The finalists drew for the saddles.

Wade carried hers and put it in the back of the truck, then they headed out into the desert.

Later in the day, Connor fixed them lunch. After eating, they drove back to the trailer to shower and get ready. Once they'd reached the Center, Connor reached for the silver charm bracelet.

While he held on to one end, he motioned for her to catch hold of the other, their link to Ralph. "Shall we have a moment of silence?"

"Yes," she whispered, moved by his suggestion. Since driving with him, she wanted the best for him, not only for the rodeo, but for his very life.

He squeezed her hand before rehanging the bracelet around the mirror. She felt his warmth steal through her. "After our events, I'll wait for you here and we'll drive over to the South Point together. Later we'll load up the horses and take them back to the RV park." He leaned across the seat and kissed her cheek. "My bet's on you, Liz."

"I think you know how much I want you to win."

Within the next hour it was time to get in line for the parade. She'd watched it on TV for years. Incredible to think she was finally a participant. After the presentation of the American flag and the national anthem, there was the laser light and fireworks show.

It thrilled Liz to be riding alongside Connor. When their horses nickered back and forth, Connor flashed her a smile that turned her bones to liquid. He leaned closer to her. "They know something big is about to happen."

She nodded. "Sunflower is excited. I can tell."

"Firebrand has more nervous energy than usual, too." In the background, the music blared. "It's time," he said in his vibrant voice. "Ready?"

Liz heard the announcer introduce the contestants from each of the twelve pro circuit regions. A thunderous ovation greeted their ears when she and Connor rode out of the alley into the spotlight.

"From the State of Montana, give a huge welcome to Connor Bannock from White Lodge, unprecedented five-time world-champion steer wrestler hoping for his sixth on his champion horse, Firebrand. This triple-crown winner two years in a row has raised the bar."

The crowd went absolutely crazy with applause and cheers, raising the noise level. Liz heard thousands of people chanting Connor's name. She was so proud of him she could burst.

"New to this arena, also from White Lodge, is Liz Henson, number two in the standings of the world barrel-racing championship, riding Sunflower. When she's not competing, she's known as Dr. Elizabeth Henson, veterinarian." More cheers and whistles erupted. Sunflower fairly pranced. Sometimes she almost seemed human.

"Next is Pete Marshall from Ennis, sixth in the

world standing in tie-down roping on his horse, Foxy. This is his third appearance at the finals. Finally, let's greet Greg Pearson from Gardiner, number ten in the world standings in bull riding. This is his fourth appearance at this arena." The applause continued before they exited the stage and the competitors from the Prairie Circuit made their entrance.

Liz followed Connor to Firebrand's stall. His event would be coming up soon. "I'll leave you and Wade to get ready. Go for it, Connor. Go all the way."

His eyes searched hers. "I'll find you after my event is over to cheer you on. There's no one who's better at what you do than you. Just remember that, and forget everyone else. This is your time."

Those words sustained her as she put Sunflower in her stall. Anxious not to miss anything, she made her way through the crowds to get the best view of the steer wrestlers. They were walking their horses in preparation for their event. She watched Connor from a distance talking with Wade, no doubt assessing the steers for tonight.

When it was time for the steer wrestling, she moved to a spot by some of the rodeo livestock support staff. This was the first night of the competition, which meant Connor, who was number one, came last.

The first twelve bulldoggers clocked times from 3.6 to 4.2. She heard Shorty Windom's name announced. The Floridian put a 3.5 on the board. "That's the winning time so far!"

It was a terrific score.

"Next up is Clive Masters, number three in the winnings from Amarillo, Texas." He took off and was fast, tying with Sonny Anza from Ojai, California, for a 3.6.

The crowd grew louder as the Arkansas champion Jocko Mendez's name was announced. Number two in the winnings, he was Connor's competition. Liz's heart began to thud as she watched him take off, but he went too fast.

"Uh-oh. Hitting that barrier too soon wasn't in Jocko's plans for this first round. That'll cost him, but he could still be number one if his overall average beats everyone else's."

Seconds later she saw Connor enter the box. "Can the number-one–ranked, five-time world champion bulldogger, Connor Bannock, from White Lodge, Montana, beat the best time tonight?" A roar broke from the crowd in answer.

Her breath caught in her throat.

"He's in the corner of the box, scoring his champion horse, Firebrand. Will his luck hold? For five years he's had the winning time on the first night of the pro final rounds. We'll see if he can do it again."

Just do your best, Connor, because you are the best.

She watched him give the nod, and before she could blink, he was out of there, going thirty miles an hour. Moments later, he had that steer on the ground in a flawless performance. "Ladies and gentlemen—he's broken his own record with a 3.2! Your winner for tonight, Connor Bannock."

The crowd went crazy with excitement, but no one knew what his win meant to Liz. *Now maybe you'll believe in yourself, Connor.*

She turned around and headed for the stall to brush down Sunflower and talk to her. When it drew close to the time for her event, she resaddled her, put on the knotted reins and her show bridle using the O-ring snaffle.

Once in the saddle, she leaned over and patted her neck. "Okay, little lady. We're being televised. This is it. What do you say we do this for my mom and dad? Without them, this night would never have been possible. Let's do it for Ralph who always believed me, and let's do it for Connor. He got us here safe and sound."

Liz headed toward the alley where the other barrel racers were assembling. She waited before getting into line, since she wouldn't go until second to last. His words echoed through her mind. *There's no one who's better at what you do than you. Just remember that and forget everyone else.*

Taking his advice, she forced a calm to come over her and went through a series of mental calisthenics. Sunflower did a few sidesteps, knowing what was about to happen. She was so smart it was scary.

At the precise moment it was her turn, Liz made the clicking sound her horse recognized. They shot down the alley. This was a blind barrel. You couldn't see it until you came out into the arena. To Liz's relief, Sunflower rated perfectly at the first barrel, the way they'd been practicing, and they raced across the arena to the second barrel. Around they went. Her horse had never made a better turn. Now the last barrel! *Don't knock it over.*

Once they got around it, they needed to fly back to the alley, and fly they did. Like the wind! She heard the announcer give her time as 13.61. That was the best time she'd ever had! The crowd went wild.

"Good girl, Sunflower. You outdid yourself!"

Trembling with excitement, she walked the horse

back to her stall. Everyone called out, "Great ride," and congratulated her before she reached her destination and dismounted.

"I love you, little lady," she said, hugging her while tears ran down her cheeks. She pulled a treat out of her pocket and gave it to her. "I have the best horse in the world."

"That works both ways" came the deep masculine voice she loved behind her. "Sunflower has the best rider in the world. It's over. You won tonight's round and the competition is in mourning. Dustine, who's number one along with three others, knocked over barrels. She did an 18.90. All Las Vegas is betting on you to win the world championship."

She wheeled around, the moisture still glistening on her face. "*Connor*—you won, too!" she cried. "I'm so happy for you I could—"

"Burst?" he finished for her. "Congratulations." He reached for her and hugged her. "Tonight beats every rodeo experience I ever had. We should have been traveling to all our rodeos together."

Liz's father had told her he thought she and Connor were the best kind of company for each other.

"Hey, Liz—how about letting another cowboy give you a hug? That was a dynamite performance."

She could see Derrick over Connor's broad shoulder and eased away from him, though he seemed reluctant to let her go. "I'm sorry I wasn't able to watch your event. How did you do?"

"Not as good as you and the legend here." He smiled and nudged Connor's shoulder. "Sixth-best time for me and my bro isn't great, but we'll try to recoup tomorrow night."

"You have nine more tries," she said in an effort to prop him up.

Derrick smiled at her. "Are you ready to claim your gold buckle? I'll drive you to the hotel."

She wished he hadn't sought her out, wished she hadn't gone to dinner with him. Now he'd shown up at the wrong moment. Liz wanted to stay in Connor's arms indefinitely.

"You go on." Connor answered for her, but the light had gone out of his eyes. "I'll head over to the hotel in my truck to join Wade and my sponsors. See you there."

CONNOR HAD FELT euphoric until Derrick had shown up. *Hell.* When Connor had hugged Liz just now, she'd clung to him in a way that sent a shock wave through him. More than her win—or his—had caused a reaction like that. He could feel something profound happening to both of them. He couldn't be wrong about that, could he?

On the drive over to the hotel he received a text on his cell. He pulled it out. Way to go, lover. 9 more days. Can't wait.

He put his phone back in his pocket. At five to eleven he showed up at the casino where Wade and their road buddies were waiting for him. The Wrangler NFR announcer began the presentations. There was tons of laughter and a few tear-jerking moments as he and Liz picked up their buckles along with the other night's winners.

Connor got as close to Liz as he could. They exchanged an intense glance before they had to leave the stage so the main concert could begin. He could feel that she'd wanted to be with him. While the fans started to two-step the night away, he watched her join Derrick, who was eating her up with his eyes.

When they disappeared, he said good-night to Wade and Kim and headed back to the RV park to hook up the trailer. En route Jarod phoned to congratulate him.

"Sadie and I invited the Hensons and Zane to watch the whole thing on our big screen with Grandpa and Avery. Neither you nor Liz could do anything wrong. You know that?"

"Liz's performance was phenomenal."

"So was yours, bro."

"I got lucky. Jocko had a bad break. That was tough."

"He was too eager to beat you."

"He still could."

"But he won't! You should have seen our grandfather. He and Millie just sat there crying like babies from the moment of the opening ceremonies. When Liz's score flashed on the screen, Mac lost it. I never saw him break down before."

"I'm not surprised. She rode for him. Before we hang up, tell me how the mother of Little Sits in the Center is doing."

Jarod chuckled. "So-so. The medicine is helping, but she's in for a siege of morning sickness, I'm afraid."

"But nothing you can't live with."

"No, thank heaven. We'll all be watching again tomorrow night. Sadie's here with me. She sends her love to both of you."

"Tell her thanks. I'll let Liz know."

"You mean she's not with you?"

He bit down so hard he almost cracked his teeth. "Afraid not. She's…partying."

"Liz?"

Connor shouldn't have said anything. "I didn't mean it that way. In truth, I have no idea what she's doing with Derrick."

"Who is that?"

"The guy in the team roping with his brother. He's a friend of Wade's."

"Does that mean Reva's there with you?" he asked in a quiet voice. "Grandpa told us she called the house before you left. What's up?"

He sucked in his breath. "She wants to get back with me."

"As in married?"

"Yup."

"Are you with her right now?"

"She came for a night, but I sent her back to L.A. We'll talk when the rodeo's over."

After a silence, "Have you figured out what your heart's telling you yet?"

"Yeah," he said without hesitation. *Oh, yeah.* "Thanks for the call, Jarod. Tell Grandpa I'll phone him in the morning."

"Will do. I have no doubts tomorrow night will bring another top score for you. But if you're not happy with it, remember I'll always be proud of my brother. Take care."

"You, too." They clicked off. Connor was glad he had work to keep him from going crazy until Liz got home.

Another hour and he had the horses put to bed in the barn at the RV park, safe and sound, as Liz put it. He showered and got ready for bed. After he'd climbed into the niche he heard the key in the lock and felt his pulse pick up speed. When she came inside, Connor sat up.

"Welcome home."

Her head jerked around in his direction. "Hi!"

"I thought you wouldn't be in for hours."

"I'm not interested in Derrick and told him I wanted to get back to the trailer. No partying for me while I'm here."

At that news Connor's foul mood did a complete reversal. "Did he ask you out again?"

"He tried, but I told him I needed all my wits about me to concentrate on the rest of the competition. When he asked me to go out with him on the last night, I told him I already had plans with the man I've been seeing."

"You mean Kyle."

"Yes."

He released the breath he'd been holding. If she was in love with Kyle, she wouldn't have agreed to drive with Connor. "How did that go over with him?"

"Not well. He said he's not giving up."

"He's a player. By the end of the rodeo he'll have found someone else."

"I hope. Partying takes too much energy out of me. I don't know how everybody else does it."

"Not everyone won the gold buckle tonight, that's why."

After hanging up her jacket, she took the box with the buckle out of her purse and put it on top of his box sitting on the table.

"That's quite a centerpiece, Dr. Henson."

"If you perform the way you did tonight, that pile is going to grow, Connor Bannock."

"Shall we make a pact to win eighteen more and build a skyscraper?"

She flashed him a brilliant smile. "Why not? The dream to make it to the Dodge Ram and Wrangler Finals has come true for me. Now I have one buckle. Who says there aren't more to be won?"

With a mysterious look in her eye, she reached into her purse and tossed him what looked like an oversize silver dollar. "After your fabulous performance I knew you'd be waiting for your treat, so I asked Derrick to stop at the Quick Mart."

On another burst of adrenaline he unwrapped it and bit into the chocolate. His eyebrows lifted. "You know you're stacking up points with me, right?"

"I hope so. I'm so deep in your debt already, I'll never climb out."

Good. That's where I want you.

DERRICK THE PLAYER was in for a huge disappointment, Connor mused, and smiled secretly as he lay back against the pillows. He listened while she showered. Soon she emerged from the bathroom and turned out the light before getting into the pullout bed. "Does Kyle have a truck and trailer?"

"Why do you ask?"

"So he can drive you and Sunflower home. That's what he intends to do, right? But if he doesn't have the equipment, I'll be happy to trailer the horses back with me. Then you and Kyle can do what you want."

"Thank you for being your generous self," she said in a subdued tone of voice. "But to be honest, I haven't made plans that far ahead yet."

"Maybe he's planning to surprise you and fly you home in his plane."

"Whatever the case, it's not your concern. You have your own plans to work out."

With a frown, he moved over to the edge to look down at her. "Why do you say that?"

"Didn't you tell me your ex-wife would be coming the last night? You may not want to go right back to Montana after finals are over. Fortunately, you and I both have enough of a support group that we don't have to worry about our horses getting transported back home. In the meantime, all I want to do is concentrate on getting through the next nine nights. Now, if you don't mind, I'm exhausted and need to go to sleep."

On impulse he said, "You sound a little out of sorts."

"I'm sorry. I told you I have a bad night now and then. Forgive me?"

"You ask that after what you've had to put up with me? Want to talk about it?"

"No, thank you."

"Plan to sleep in. I'll take care of the horses in the morning and fix us a big breakfast. When you're up, we'll take them for a ride. How does that sound?"

"Wonderful." When he thought there wasn't any more, she said, "Connor?"

"Hmm?"

"You're too good to be true."

"No one ever said that to me before." It was the truth.

"If they didn't, they *thought* it."

Liz's mood was different tonight. Something was bothering her. Too many guys on her plate wanting her? He recalled an earlier conversation with her.

Who's the lucky guy in your life?

Dad says they're all lucky.

All? Why aren't you with your favorite?

They're all my favorites for different reasons.

Connor pounded his pillow, but no matter how many times he did it, he couldn't get comfortable. Hell, hell and hell.

Chapter Eight

On the seventh day of competition, Liz discovered they were running low on food again. For the past six days they'd enjoyed eating all their meals in the trailer between training sessions and doing laps in the swimming pool.

"Connor? Do you mind if I take the truck for a little while?" He'd just awakened. His tousled dark blond hair made him so handsome, she had trouble not staring at him.

"What's up?"

"We need groceries. I'm going to run to the market so we can fix breakfast. Later on we'll exercise the horses."

"I'll go with you."

"But you don't have to."

He smiled. "What if I want to?"

"After winning another buckle last night, you deserve a long sleep in." Three more boxes had been added to their centerpiece. Since the first night, Connor had won two more buckles and Liz had won her second.

Both of them were still among the top three finishers on the other nights, but the competition was tight and fierce. Jocko Mendez had copped two buckles since his disastrous first night. As for Dustine Hoffman, Liz's competition, she'd also won two buckles.

He jumped down from the niche. "I'm up."

"Once we leave the trailer, you run the risk of being besieged by your fans."

"If you'll protect me from the females, I'll ride flank to protect you from all your new ardent male admirers."

"You don't ever run out of that sweet talk, do you, Connor?"

"You bring it out in me, sweetheart."

Never in her wildest dreams had she imagined going grocery shopping with him. When they reached the supermarket, he grabbed a cart and they walked up and down the aisles together, choosing the items they wanted. His jokes provoked constant laughter from her. Shoppers could be forgiven for thinking they were romantically involved. If Liz wasn't careful, she'd start to believe it.

Living together in semiseclusion had been working for them so far. By avoiding other people and the distractions of Las Vegas itself, they'd achieved an easy relationship and a schedule that was good for them and their horses. But in four more days this artificial world they'd created for themselves would end.

When she and Connor got back to the trailer to put the groceries away, nothing could have upset her more than to read Kyle's text. He'd made arrangements to stay at the Luxor and had already purchased his ticket to watch the events on her last night of competition. He was prepared to rent a truck and horse trailer to drive her home—whatever she wanted.

No. She didn't want him to come. From the second

she'd driven away from the ranch with Connor, the idea that, in time, she might grow to love the pilot had shriveled. It didn't matter that Connor and Reva might be getting back together for good. Liz knew it was no use to go on seeing Kyle.

Until she found a man she could love with the intensity she loved her next-door neighbor, it wasn't fair to mislead Kyle or any other man. Her dilemma was so severe, she needed to talk it over with Sadie before she answered his text.

After she'd fixed a late breakfast for them, Wade came over so he and Connor could put in another practice session. Liz begged off, saying she had some washing to do but would join them in a little while. For once she was relieved to find herself alone, and immediately phoned her friend.

"Sadie?"

"Liz! I've wanted to call, but was afraid it wouldn't be the right time."

"You never have to worry about that. How are you feeling?"

"Well enough with the medicine I'm taking, but forget me. Your scores are fabulous. You keep this up and your average will mean you come out the winner."

"So far, my luck is holding."

"It's more than luck. Jarod says you'll win the whole thing."

"What did he do? Consult his uncle Charlo?" she teased.

"He doesn't need to. It's in Jarod's blood to have visions, too. He's had one about you, but told me I couldn't tell you."

Liz didn't know whether to laugh or faint. "Did he have a vision about his brother?"

"I asked him the same thing. He said no."

The way Sadie spoke sent a chill through Liz.

"I still have no advice for you about Connor."

"He and Reva will be getting together after finals, but he's not the reason why I'm calling." Connor had been having fun with Liz, saying and doing all the right things to make her feel good and desirable. She'd felt his passion, but their time together was almost up. "This is about Kyle." She explained what was wrong. "If you were in my shoes, what would you do?" The silence went on for a long time. "Sadie?"

Her friend finally let out a sigh. "Since you didn't want Kyle to drive with you to Las Vegas, I think you should tell him the truth. That this isn't the time for you to get together with him. Surely if you explain about family coming and your responsibility to Connor and the horses, he'll understand, even if he's disappointed.

"Tell him you'd love to go out with him after you're home. By then, all the stress of the rodeo will be over and you can find out if the two of you have a relationship worth pursuing. Maybe, when you see him after being with Connor, you'll be pleasantly surprised. Maybe not. In any event, it'll be easier to say goodbye to Kyle knowing you didn't let him spend all that time and money to come be with you."

"Agreed." It was the advice she needed, because she'd been thinking with her hormones. "You're right. Thanks for being the best friend I ever had."

"Ditto."

"Give Ralph my love."

"You know I will. We'll all be watching again tonight. Go knock 'em dead!"

After they hung up Liz made her daily call to her mom, who sounded happy. Whatever worry her parents might have because of her feelings for Connor, they could see her scores had never been better. *Connor had been good for her.* It was the rest of her life she had to worry about, but she refused to think of anything but finals right now.

Her next call wasn't going to be so easy, but she had to do it. Kyle was a great guy who'd been trying to make plans with her. Maybe he would never want to see her again, but she knew herself too well. Better to disappoint him now than to pretend to be happy to see him after he flew in to Las Vegas. She couldn't do that to him, not when she felt the way she did about Connor.

She answered his text with another one, asking if she could phone him in an hour about something very important. He said he'd be available in a half hour.

Once she put the phone away, she headed over to the barn and put Sunflower through a special routine to keep strengthening her hocks. Those precision turns required the greatest power and discipline from her horse. During the workout, Kyle called her back.

He was mostly silent after her explanation, but incredibly decent about it. She promised him she'd drive to Bozeman to see him as soon as she got back from Las Vegas. That was, if he wanted her to come. To her surprise, he assured her he would look forward to seeing her.

Why couldn't she be in love with him?

After lunch, Connor watched while she got out her doctor bag and gave both horses a thorough medical exam. Liz had been doing this every other day. So far, her check for soft-tissue injuries, as well as hoof and teeth problems, had turned up nothing. Their horses' hearts and lungs, their breathing and digestive noises sounded normal.

She nodded to Connor. "They're in excellent shape. We've been lucky so far."

"Thanks to you. I've never traveled with a vet before. Like I said earlier, if it hadn't been for Daniel, we could have been doing this from the time you graduated from med school."

Yup. That would have been about the time he got his divorce. But with his career in rodeo over in the next four days, it looked as though Connor would be getting a second chance to make his former marriage work.

She looked into his eyes. "I wonder how many times Jarod and Sadie have said those same words."

He rubbed the back of his neck. "They went through hell. We all did, but that time is behind us," he ground out. "What do you say we drive our children over to the center and put night number seven behind us?"

"I can't believe we're getting near the end."

"I know what you mean. Our horses are lucky. They don't think the way we do and have no idea when this whole business is going to end. Until it's over, they just keep going."

"That's what we've got to do. Just keep going for four more nights." Liz leaned over to pick up her medical bag. Her breath caught when she felt his hands slide up her arms to her shoulders. He squeezed them gently. His warm breath tickled her neck. "You're going to win. I feel it in my bones."

Jarod had predicted a win for her, but not for his

brother. That alarmed her in the most profound way. She wished Sadie hadn't said anything, and turned to Connor so he'd let go of her. Liz couldn't handle his touch right now.

"I've already won by making it to the finals and traveling here with you. So far, the two buckles are simply a bonus."

His expression sobered. "I don't think you know how good you really are." He always managed to say the right thing at the right time, denoting a selfless, generous nature she admired so much there were no words.

"I was just going to say the same thing to you." With her medical bag in one hand, she caught hold of Sunflower's reins with the other and started walking toward the parked trailer.

"Hey—what's the hurry?"

"I want to walk Sunflower around and hang out by the alley without feeling the stress so she doesn't build up too much tension about it. Then I have to leave for the Las Vegas Convention Center. Wrangler has set up my autograph time for six-thirty. I wasn't allowed to pick it. Unfortunately, it means I probably won't get back in time to watch your event."

He grinned. "If you've seen it once, you're not missing anything."

"Don't be absurd, Connor. No one knows how hard you work to get each ride perfect. Thank goodness I only have to do this once."

"You have no vanity."

Fire shot from her eyes. "I've got plenty, but not during *your* event! Promise you'll phone me after you've finished and let me know how you did."

THREE HOURS LATER, Liz's words still resounded in Connor's heart as he backed Firebrand into the corner of the box for his turn. On his right he caught sight of Wade mounted on his horse on the other side of the chute. He sent Connor a speaking glance, letting him know this steer was a wily one. It looked to be six hundred pounds or better. Connor had seen them all, from four hundred and fifty to six hundred and fifty pounds.

With an answering glance he acknowledged Wade's message, then patted Firebrand's neck. "This is it, buddy."

Connor gave the official nod and the steer shot out, releasing the rope barrier. Firebrand took off. Connor rode low and leaned to the right, sliding down his horse to hook his right arm around the steer's right horn. With his left hand he grasped the left horn to slow it down and braced himself with his feet. His body knew these maneuvers like the back of his hand.

But the steer unexpectedly bucked upward as Connor threw him to the ground, resulting in a sudden, powerful load on his chest muscle. It sent excruciating pain shooting through his chest and shoulder before running down his right arm.

In a flash he knew he'd sustained a serious injury.

Just like that, *he was finished.*

The shock of the physical pain was bad enough. But the knowledge that the end of his career had been cut short four days early by an accident tore through his gut as if he'd been ripped open by one of those horns.

While the arena workers took care of the steer, the emergency staff came running to carry him out of the arena on a stretcher. Only the announcer's voice commiserating over the injury sounded in the eerie quiet of the crowd who were on their feet waiting to know the outcome. Everything was surreal. He saw Wade's ashen face loom over him.

"Don't worry. I'll take care of Firebrand," he assured Connor.

"I know you will. Wade—" It was hard to breathe. "Wrangler set up a schedule for Fan Fest. Liz took the truck and is at the convention center right now signing autographs. Find her when she gets back here. She'll have heard about the accident, so help her. She *has* to place again tonight. Do you hear me?" Connor muttered through clenched teeth.

"I'll do whatever I can," Wade promised before Connor was carted away in an ambulance. Once he'd been lifted inside, the last thing he remembered was someone sticking him with a needle.

WITH HER AUTOGRAPH session finished, Liz pulled up in the parking area at the back of the Mack Center. Before she got out, she heard her cell ring. That was the call she'd been waiting for. Excited, she pulled the phone out of her purse. But her spirits plunged when she saw Derrick's name on the caller ID. What on earth was he doing phoning her? She'd made it clear she didn't want to see him again.

A strange feeling crept over her before she clicked on. "Derrick?"

"Liz? I just saw what happened to Connor and I can't tell you how sorry I am."

A cold, clammy sensation broke out on her skin. "What *did* happen?"

"Oh, hell—you don't know?"

"Know what?" Her voice shook.

"He got injured during his event and was taken to the hospital."

Her eyes shut tightly. "How badly was he hurt?"

"I don't know. I thought you—"

"I've got to go."

Blind with pain, she rummaged for her keys to drive to the nearest hospital, but suddenly her door was flung open. It was Wade. He reached in and put his arms around her.

She lifted tear-filled eyes to him. "Derrick just told me the news. Is Connor going to live, Wade?"

"Sure he is. He injured his chest and shoulder, but he'll be fine."

"Is that the truth?"

"I wouldn't lie to you about this."

"Oh, thank God," she whispered before slumping against him. "I've got to go to him as soon as I finish my round."

"While he was on the stretcher, he begged me to find you and make sure you won your event tonight. I promised him I'd follow through. Just sit there for a few minutes till the shock wears off."

"So he was coherent the whole time?"

"Yes."

"What went wrong?"

"The steer was as ornery as they come. As Connor was throwing him, it bucked upward, probably causing a torn muscle."

Liz moaned. "He must be in so much pain."

"Even so, he was worried about you. I'll go to the hospital with you after your event. I can promise that the only news he'll want to hear is that you placed in tonight's event or won it. That'll help him get better in a big hurry."

She couldn't bear it. That sixth gold buckle had been denied Connor. Her heart broke for him. "His family has to be devastated after watching what happened on television." Ralph would need a lot of support. He loved Connor so much.

"Connor has a great family who are there for him all the way and will help him get through this. He's survived many injuries on the circuit."

"But this finals was his last." Her voice broke.

"I know," he said quietly.

"It's so cruel. He's the best and would have won the whole thing."

"I'm convinced of it."

She sniffed. "But five world championships isn't bad, right?"

He smiled. "Right. Do you think you've recovered enough to go inside and get ready? I'll stay right with you."

"I'm thankful you're here, Wade. What I want to know is, are you all right? This has to have been heartbreaking for you, too. Connor couldn't have made it this far all these years without your help. He has sung your praises over and over again."

"That's nice to hear. I'll be fine. You know this business better than anyone. There's always a risk."

She nodded and wiped her eyes. "I'm feeling better and should get ready."

"Let's go."

Liz had found her legs and headed inside for Sunflower's stall. She knew how much Connor wanted her to win. Tonight she'd do her very best to keep the rodeo alive for him until it was over.

While Wade chatted quietly with some of the other contestants around her, she comforted herself with the thought that Reva would have heard about his accident by now. No doubt she'd be on a plane to Las Vegas before morning. It would thrill him to see her walk into his hospital room.

With his career over, he could concentrate on a new life with Reva that would bring him joy and, later on, a family like the one Jarod and Sadie had started.

"Okay, little lady." She spoke to Sunflower before mounting her. "Our turn is coming up. We've got to do this one for Connor."

Wade gave her a private nod before she walked her horse toward the spot where the barrel racers had started to congregate. She noticed several competitors were having trouble with their horses not wanting to enter the arena.

The swell of cheers from the crowd signaled that the first racer had finished her run. Liz watched the second racer gallop down the alley for her run. The audience roared with excitement. Sunflower sensed their turn was coming and took a few steps in anticipation, but they'd be racing next to last.

When Liz finally heard her name announced, she made her clicking sound and they bolted out of the alley into the arena. Her horse knew the cloverleaf pattern they'd done hundreds of times and did it to perfection. They skimmed the third barrel but incurred no penalty. Then they went flat out for home. She heard a time of 13.47 announced. Her best one, giving her a third gold buckle.

Overjoyed, she cried, "Good girl, Sunflower!"

Wade was waiting at her stall with a beaming face. "You did it again!"

"Thanks."

She dismounted quickly. No matter how big a hurry she was in to see Connor, she had to drive to the South Point for the awards and then return to take care of her wonderful horse. She gave her the attention she needed plus a special treat, then she moved over to Polly's stall and talked to her for a minute, also giving her a treat.

Wade joined her. "Follow me to the hospital in Connor's truck. Let's exchange phone numbers in order to stay in close touch."

"I was just going to suggest it."

With that done, the trip was a complete blur to Liz. Her heart rate was too high to be healthy, but it wouldn't return to normal until she'd seen Connor for herself and knew he really would be all right in time.

He had a private room on the third floor. The nurse at the station told them he was only allowed one visitor at a time. Apparently it had been like Grand Central Station, and their famous patient needed rest. He'd be undergoing surgery at 6:00 a.m.

"You go in first, Liz."

She bit her lip before letting herself inside.

Naturally he'd been given painkillers, and he lay there, still and pale beneath his tan. But when she approached the side of the bed, his eyes opened. Their beautiful brown color hadn't changed.

"You got a 13.47," he murmured.

"Yeah. How about that?" She pulled a chair up close to him.

"Where's my treat?"

"I'm a doctor, remember? You can't have food before surgery. Love that outfit you're wearing, by the way. Picked it up at the Western store, did you?"

His lips twitched. "I talked to everyone at home. By now they know you're a shoo-in for the world championship."

She fought the tears prickling her eyelids. "So tell me the bad news."

"The doctor is going to repair my pecta something."

"Ah. You've suffered from a violent eccentric contraction of the pectoralis major muscle that caused a rupture at the humeral insertion of your right arm. That's not surprising, since you used that arm to catch the horn of that blasted steer. According to Wade, it was an ornery critter."

His eyes smiled. "How did you get so smart?"

"It runs in the family."

"You're not kidding. Liz—" She could see his throat working.

"Don't say it. I don't want to hear it. Five world championships are more than any human has the right to expect in this life. You're already a legend. The steer caused all the trouble, not you, Connor Bannock. Tonight you went out in a blaze of glory no one will ever forget, so enjoy the downtime.

"This hospital will have to be cordoned off to protect you from thousands of fans dying to know how you are. Since you're much too modest, I'll set up a blog to let everyone know that their hero is alive and kicking. I'll even put up some pictures of before and after. You owe it to them."

"You'd do that for me?"

"After all you've done for me, I don't know how

you can even ask me that question. It'll be a good way to advertise your feral stud farm if you decide that's something you want to do. Now I'm going to leave so Wade—"

"Don't go—I don't want to see anyone else right now."

Heart attack.

"I didn't bring any cards for poker with me. What else do you have in mind?"

"Let's talk about you coming to work for me as my vet."

"So you *have* been considering the stud-farm idea."

"I'm thinking it might just work."

"Of course it will, if that's what you want to do. You know you can do anything if you're on fire for it. But it's time to give your mind and body a rest. I'll be back tomorrow morning after your surgery."

"I want you here when I wake up."

"If there's standing room."

"Stop teasing. Can I count on you?"

She could hardly breathe. Something in his tone of voice told her he didn't want to be alone. "Feral horses couldn't keep me away."

"I'm going to hold you to that. Are you going back to the trailer?"

"Where else?"

"I don't like the idea of you being there alone."

"I'm a big girl now."

"I know, but I wish you'd stay here tonight. I like the idea of Dr. Henson being here before, during and after my operation."

Beneath the banter she felt he was dead serious. She shook her head in bewilderment. *"Connor—"*

"I've gotten used to us being together. Haven't you?"

"Well, yes, but—"

"So you don't have a problem with that."

"Well, no, but—"

"Stay with me tonight."

While she felt a shiver run through her, he said, "Would you tell Wade to come in? I need to talk to him, but I want you to stay put."

The painkillers had done strange things to him. In shock over his behavior, she got up and opened the door. Wade was out in the hall talking to one of the nurses. "Connor wants to see you now."

"It took him long enough."

"He's not himself at the moment," she whispered.

Wade entered the room and moved to the side of Connor's bed. "How are you feeling?"

"Weird. Will you do me a favor and take Firebrand back to the barn at the RV park tomorrow?"

"Sure. Kim and I will exercise and feed him, too. No problem."

"Thanks. When the doctor releases me I'll take care of him until the rodeo is over."

"You won't be doing anything for at least six weeks," Liz interjected. "I'll see to the horses while you rest here in the hospital."

The nurse suddenly stepped in the room. "It's long past visiting hours."

"Uh-oh," Wade muttered. "We've been given our marching orders. Be a good cowboy and we'll see you tomorrow." Wade's blue eyes swerved to Liz. "I'll walk you out."

Making another impulsive decision because of Connor, she said, "I'm going to see if I can stay with him tonight. I'll arrange with the nurse for a cot."

The look Wade gave her sent heat rushing to Liz's face. "Then I'll say good-night to both of you."

Liz walked him to the door. "I told you he's not himself. Thank you for finding me earlier." She gave him a hug.

"You're welcome." The faint smile he gave her left her perplexed. Then he disappeared down the hall.

As she went back to sit in the chair next to Connor, the nurse came back in. Liz asked if a cot could be sent up so she could stay.

The other woman nodded. "I'll call Housekeeping."

"Thank you."

Connor's eyes filled with anxiety. "It was selfish of me to ask you to stay tonight. You need your sleep to be your best in the arena tomorrow night. You need to go."

Her heart pounded too hard. "I'm not leaving. I want to make sure you're all right. Don't worry. I'll get a good sleep on the cot."

He fastened his gaze on her. "If you're sure."

"Of course I am."

"How did you find out I got hurt?"

She moistened her lips. "On my way back from the convention center I heard my cell ring. I thought you were calling, but it turned out to be Derrick."

"He never gives up!"

"No…that wasn't why he called. He felt terrible about your accident and wanted me to know. He's one of your fans. I need to call him tomorrow and thank him for being concerned. I'm afraid that the minute he told me you'd been carted off to the hospital I had a panic attack and left him hanging."

"A real panic attack?"

"Yes. I went clammy. Wade found me at the truck and had to help me calm down so I could get ready for my event. He's a wonderful friend, Connor."

"He and I may not have survived to the last three nights, but I'm planning to give him the cut of my earnings I would have given him if we'd lasted all the way. I've made a ton of money this year. Without him, I'd be nothing."

That did bring tears. She looked down to hide them. "He'll be thrilled."

"He deserves it."

An employee from Housekeeping entered the room and put the folded cot against the wall. After he left, Liz stood and found a spot to set it up. She removed her hat and boots before stretching out on the skimpy mattress.

"This is almost like being in the trailer. I can even look down on you," Connor quipped.

Liz chuckled. "I'll admit, this is kind of fun."

His eyes never left her. "Do you mind not being able to take a shower or brush your teeth?"

She flicked him a glance. "I'll live for one night. Don't say it—"

"Say what?"

"That I'm too good to be true."

"I wasn't going to. You were sensational out there tonight."

"You saw it, even in the state you were in?"

"My friend Brian caught it on his phone camera and showed me the video after they brought me in. He just left."

"Thanks for the compliment. I told Sunflower we had to do our best for you."

"She's almost human, Liz. I'm afraid Firebrand feels deserted and could use her company."

"They'll be together tomorrow. I'll talk to him and give him a rubdown."

Connor sighed. "Will it really be six weeks before I'm normal again?"

"Afraid so. At least to begin with. But you really need to give it twelve. According to this sheet on the bedside table, you'll need to arrange for physiotherapy when you get home."

"What else?"

Liz scanned the list. "For the first three weeks you'll wear a shoulder sling and will have to avoid pendular exercises. Later you'll do gentle isometric exercises as your pain allows and be weaned off the sling. At six weeks you'll be able to drive, do light lifting and some swimming. At twelve weeks you can go riding again."

He groaned. "In twelve weeks I'll have forgotten how."

"That's okay. It's possible you'll be putting a whole new business together." *Or a whole new marriage.* "That doesn't require getting on top of a horse."

Jarod hadn't received a vision about his brother. Now she knew why, and sat there in shock.

Connor's cell phone rang, interrupting her thoughts. He frowned. "Will you see who it is?"

She reached for it. "It's your grandfather."

"Go ahead and answer it."

Liz clicked on. "Hi, Ralph. It's Liz. Your grandson is right here in the hospital bed and anxious to talk to you."

"I'm glad you're there. How is he really?"

The love in his voice was tangible. "He's in excellent shape. Connor is tough, like you." The older man laughed. "Once his tear is repaired, he'll be good as new."

"What time are they going to do it?"

"At six in the morning. He'll be able to leave the hospital by tomorrow evening or the next day. I'll be here for the whole thing," she assured him.

"Bless you." His voice cracked. "You two have made this old man proud. My cup has run over."

"So has mine. Here's Connor."

After passing him the phone, she disappeared into the bathroom to freshen up and give them some privacy before things settled down and she could rest. Hopefully more painkillers would kick in and Connor would finally sleep.

For someone who'd sustained a serious injury, he was babbling like a brook. It had to be the medication. He was hilarious, and she loved him so terribly she didn't know what to do with all her unlocked feelings running rampant.

After she'd stayed in there as long as she dared, she went back in the room, hoping he'd fallen asleep because he needed it badly. No such luck. The nurse had just finished putting something in his IV and was recording his vital signs.

"I thought you'd never come out of there." He sounded grumpy.

She couldn't prevent the chuckle that escaped. "I bet it felt good to talk to your grandfather."

"He's a fusser, but I told him I didn't want Jarod or Avery to come because I had you to look after me. You're a doctor, and you understand me, and you like me and my horse a lot. And you give us treats and entertain me better than anyone in the world."

The nurse flashed Liz a grin. "That's high praise." She mouthed the words before she left the room.

"Your praise is going to go to my head," Liz said, trying not to burst into laughter.

"They'll all fly here on the last day with your parents to watch you crowned."

"I didn't know they were giving those out. I thought it was a buckle."

"No…no." His voice was slowing down fast. "You should have been…nominated for the queen of the… rodeo."

"Queen?" He must have meant Miss Rodeo. There actually was such a person being feted in Las Vegas, but Liz couldn't understand where that thought had come from.

"You…don't…know how…beautiful…you…a…"

Even if he was delirious, she felt the impact of those words in every atom of her body. Was it the drugs talking, or were his feelings as strong as hers? She wanted to trust them, but Reva was still in the picture.

Realizing the medicine had taken effect, she pulled her boots back on and slipped outside to the nursing station. She asked that, when it came time to prep Connor for surgery, they would wake her up if she wasn't already awake.

With that request taken care of, she slipped down to the lounge to buy some chips and a cola out of the machines. Before she returned to the room, she called her parents to tell them what was going on.

The minute she heard their voices, they all shed a few tears of happiness over her results so far, but once

Connor's name was mentioned it was her father who said, "His disappointment has to be gut-wrenching."

Liz's heart was devastated for him. "Right now he's too doped up to feel much of anything. But in the days to come he's going to feel it."

"I'm glad my Lizzie girl is there for him."

Dad... "He's been so good to me, it's my chance to pay him back. I told Ralph I'd watch over him."

"I know. We've already talked to him and he was so grateful he could hardly get the words out."

"Ralph's a sweetheart."

"Honey?" her mom chimed in. "You need to get your rest. You've got three more big nights coming up."

"I know. Don't worry. Wade and his girlfriend are here for Connor, too. We'll take turns. I'd better go now, but I promise to call you tomorrow after his surgery. Love you both."

Once they'd hung up she texted Derrick to apologize for being abrupt over the phone. She wished him and his brother luck and told him she'd call him soon to talk.

A phone message had come in while she'd been with Connor. Kyle had heard the news and asked her to phone him back. But she couldn't handle an actual conversation with him right now, so she texted him with a brief report and promised to call him sometime tomorrow. Liz hurried back to Connor's room and walked over to the bed. He was out like a light. Her heart ached because the great champion had come to the end of a long journey. But a new one would be beginning.

Please, God, help him to find himself.

The hospital cot didn't do the job, but it didn't matter. She was exactly where she wanted to be, because she'd discovered that the cover of the book she'd always found the most compelling couldn't begin to compare to the substance of the man inside.

Chapter Nine

"Mr. Bannock?"

He opened his eyes. The lids felt heavy. "Are you ready for me?"

"You're back in your room. The surgery is over and you're doing fine. Your doctor will be in later."

"I can't believe it."

"Well, it's true" came the familiar female voice he longed to hear.

His eyes opened wider. "Liz—you're here!"

Her beautiful face smiled down at him. He could never get enough of the green sparkle coming from her dark-lashed eyes. "Where else would I be? I made you a promise. Don't you remember?"

"Everything's pretty hazy. Did you stay all night?"

"Of course." He noticed that the room was filled with flowers. "We've been joined at the hip for almost two weeks now. I wouldn't have deserted you."

He reached out to grasp her hand, needing her touch. "What time is it?"

"Twenty after ten in the morning."

"You should be out exercising Sunflower."

"I've got all day, but my first priority is you. On a scale of one to—"

"A two, Doctor. No more."

"That's good."

"They must have doped me up big-time."

"I spoke to the surgeon. Dr. Mason made a small incision so, in time, you probably won't see the scar. He said it was a textbook case, and you're going to be a hundred percent *if* you follow the rehab instructions to the letter.

"For your information, he's a fan of yours. In case you've reconsidered your retirement from the rodeo, he said that you're still young enough and in such good shape that in twelve weeks you could get back in training in order to win your sixth gold buckle next winter."

Connor squeezed her fingers before letting her go. "Afraid not. I meant what I told you. My rodeo days are over."

"It isn't me you need to convince. There's a world of fans out there that can't bear to think they'll never again see you fly out of the chute on Firebrand to wow everyone with your genius."

He scowled. "It's not genius, just stupidity."

Her features sobered. "You know what? We're all born into this world with a purpose and gifts. You have many gifts, and one of them has been to entertain people who can't imagine doing what you do. For a little while, it wrests them from their mundane existence to watch a champion.

"To me, it's like listening to a great concert pianist or a world-famous opera singer. How about watching a great skier win the downhill at the world championships? Or thrilling to the winner of a Formula I grand prix? You think those achievements are stupid?" Her hands formed fists. "The venue doesn't matter. It's the fact that someone has risen far beyond human expectations to make life exciting for the rest of us.

"At my autograph signing last evening, a twelve-year-old girl in a wheelchair came with her parents to get my signature. She'd been paralyzed in a car accident. Before that, she'd wanted to be a barrel racer. She told me of the pleasure it gives her to watch someone like me perform and thanked me through the tears. I've never been so humbled in my life.

"Don't you realize how exciting your career has been for Ralph, who's been doing his hardest to help his grandchildren realize their dreams? Because if you don't, then it's sad that you're so blind, Connor Bannock!" Her rebuke rang out in the room.

It reminded him of that first day in the truck, when she'd ripped him up one side and down the other. But this second chastening found its way to his inner core. While he was trying to recover, he heard voices at the door. It opened a little wider to reveal his ex-wife's silhouette. Wade and Kim stood behind her.

Those startled light blue eyes darted from Liz to him. "Conner? I got here as soon as I could. Am I interrupting something?" She sounded out of breath.

Before Connor could say anything, Liz reached for her purse. "Not at all. I was just leaving to get back to the trailer and take care of the horses. I'll call you later to see how you're doing, Connor. If you don't overdo today, the doctor said you could be released by evening." He watched her greet the others before her lovely body in her knockout shirt and jeans disappeared out the door.

Evening? *Hallelujah.*

Liz left the hospital at a run. Anything Connor had said to her last night was the effect of the medication. *You're a lovesick fool, Liz Henson.*

Bless Wade for transporting Liz's horse to the Mack Center early. When she called him later in the day to find out Connor's condition, Wade told her the doctor said he was coming along nicely, but he shouldn't overdo it from all the phone calls and visitors. She also learned that Reva had been with him all day.

Connor had given Wade a key to get into the trailer and bring him his toiletries and a change of clothes. That meant he didn't intend to come back to the trailer. With Connor no longer able to compete and Reva there, he had incentive to leave in order to be alone with her. No doubt they would go to a hotel when he was released.

Naturally Wade wasn't about to pass on anything that Connor might have confided to him in private. It was enough to know his ex-wife had dropped everything to fly to Las Vegas. After all, she'd never stopped loving him.

Liz decided to keep her horse in the stall at the Mack Center for the duration of finals to cut down on the transporting. But, even with her usual preparations, she knew her timing was off when she raced out of the alley that evening. Lack of concentration was the culprit. Her score of 13.77 gave her a fourth place for the night. Not good. That would bring her average down.

When it was over, she removed the saddle and blanket. "It wasn't your fault," she whispered to Sunflower. "I didn't get any sleep last night and my mind couldn't focus. Worse, I did the unforgiveable and got angry with Connor right after he was out of surgery today.

I've really lost the plot, little lady, but I'll do better tomorrow."

She walked over to the other stall and walked Polly around for a little while before heading for the truck to go home. The trailer was like an empty tomb without Connor. After her shower she went straight to bed with the remote and turned on another rerun of *Keeping Up Appearances.*

In this one, Daisy had run away from her sister's house and needed to be found. Normally Liz would be laughing her head off, but not tonight. Dissolving into tears, she turned off the TV and buried her face in the pillow.

She slept late. While she fixed herself some cereal, her first thought was to phone Connor and make sure he was all right. But, if she did that, she'd be interrupting him and Reva.

If Liz could just apologize for what she'd said to him yesterday, maybe then she'd be able to get through two more nights of competition and not fall apart. For years she'd had the ability to compartmentalize her personal and professional lives. Not this time.

Wade's knock on the trailer door had her rushing to answer it. "I was just about to call you. Have you talked to Connor today? Is he all right?"

His friend eyed her steadily. "When I left his hotel room a little while ago, he looked in pretty good shape."

No mention of Reva, no mention of which hotel. Liz found it difficult to breathe. "Thank goodness."

"Yup. He asked me to check up on you." That made her heart flip-flop. "If you don't like sleeping in the trailer alone, he hopes you'll go to a hotel and has asked me to take care of you."

Pain cut her to the quick. “Both of you have enough on your minds without worrying about me. I got a good sleep last night and intend to hang out here until finals are over. Once my parents fly in with Jarod and Sadie tomorrow, we’ll figure everything out to get the rig and the horses back to Montana.”

“I’ll tell him what you said. Do you want to go to lunch with me and Kim?”

“That’s very nice, but I’m eating breakfast now and plan to stay here until it’s time to drive to the center and take a little ride on Sunflower.” It was nearing the end of the ten-day competition. She didn’t want to wear out her horse.

He nodded. “Connor told me to tell you good luck tonight, but he knows you won’t need it because you light your own fires.”

She’d done that, all right, when her mouth had run away with her yesterday. He might have forgiven her once, but not a second time.

“Thanks for coming by, Wade. Thanks for everything.” She hugged him before shutting the door.

THE NINTH NIGHT of the NFR finals was about to begin. Connor wanted to watch it on the hotel’s big-screen TV uninterrupted. Reva had left the hotel where she’d stayed the previous night and moved to his hotel.

She was curled up on the end of the couch to watch with him. He sat up in an upholstered chair with his arm in a sling, his feet resting on an ottoman. To his relief, simple ibuprofen was doing the job for the pain. He hated taking drugs.

“I still don’t understand why you wouldn’t stay at the Mirage with me.”

He thrust her a glance. "Because we're not married, Reva."

"But somehow living in the close quarters of the trailer with Liz Henson is different?"

They'd skirted certain issues last evening after he'd been released. But bringing up Liz's name now meant she was going for the jugular. "We pooled our resources to come to the finals together. The Hensons are our neighbors and family friends."

"She's more to you than that, so don't deny it!"

"I'm not." *I'm not.*

Those blue eyes glistened with tears. They'd always gotten to him before, but no longer. "Have you slept with her?"

His anger flared. "Have you slept with your producer friend?"

She averted her eyes. "I asked you first."

"This isn't a game, Reva. You called me and said you wanted us to get back together. But two years have gone by. Aside from the issues that broke us up before, if you can't be honest with me about him, where will that get us?"

After a silence, "We've stopped seeing each other. Yes, there was a period where I thought I cared about him and we did have an affair, but it's over."

The revelation didn't touch him. "Why?"

"After I stopped seeing him, I found out he'd been keeping a secret from me. Ginger told me he's the one responsible for getting me moved to the afternoon time slot."

Connor *knew* it had to be something like that. "In other words, they're making room for someone else on the six o'clock news."

"Yes. That's like death to me."

"I'm sorry, Reva, very sorry. I know how much you've put into your career. With your track record, you have to be aware there are other networks in other cities that would grab you up in a minute."

She got to her feet. "If I went to work at another network, the same thing would happen because I'm not getting any younger. I've thought it over and want to give it up to be a wife and mother." She eyed him hungrily. "I want to be *your* wife again and have *your* baby."

"You don't want to be a wife to a cowboy."

"But the rodeo's over for you now."

He shifted in the chair. "You just don't get it. Forget the rodeo. Ranching's my life. Every aspect of it, from the horses to the cattle. During our marriage you made it clear you hated that life."

"But a baby would—"

"Do nothing to change your feelings," he broke in. "You have to love that life the way I do. It's not for everyone, as you found out. I couldn't live in Los Angeles. It's not what I do or who I am. I'm going to be starting up a stud farm. The ranch isn't the place for you and your special talents in front of the camera." He could hear Liz's voice. "You have a unique gift not given to everyone and need to use it, Reva. We were young and thought we could make it work. It pains me that we couldn't."

"So you're saying it's impossible for us?"

They stared at each other. "Isn't it? Be honest."

"How about *you* being honest. I asked you once. Now I'm going to ask you again. Have you taken Liz Henson to bed yet?"

He took a deep breath. "No."

That seemed to shake her. "So she's not the reason you don't want to get back together?"

"Stop trying to find a reason when we both know what it is. Our attorney defined it. *Incompatibility* in the truest sense of the word. But I'll give you another reason I couldn't have given you two years ago, because at that point I was too devastated to think."

"What is it?" she murmured.

"I'm no longer in love with you."

Reva backed away from him. "I know." Her voice shook. "I can tell."

"If you'll be honest with yourself, you'll admit you're no longer in love with me, either, only the idea of it. That's what broken dreams are all about. But I'll treasure the memories of those early days when anything seemed possible. Time can't take that away from us."

Angry color filled her cheeks. She reached for her purse and started walking toward the door. Connor got up from the chair and followed her. She turned to him. "There's a big difference between you and me. I'm afraid I'll never get over you. Goodbye, Connor." She kissed his cheek before walking out into the hall.

He watched for a minute and then closed the door. All he felt was a liberating sense of relief that, at last, this period of his life was over. And maybe he felt a little guilt, because his mind was already somewhere else. After going back to his chair, he increased the volume on the remote. The rodeo was halfway over. He'd missed the steer wrestling. Three more events until it was time for the barrel racing.

Connor reached for the coffee he'd been drinking

and finished it off while he watched each performance. Team roping was up next. Derrick was the heeler in the Porter brothers' duo. His aim was off tonight and he only roped one hind leg of the steer, costing them a five-second penalty. That was too bad.

As the time grew closer to Liz's event, his stomach muscles tightened into knots. They'd never cramped up on him this badly prior to one of his own events. Good old Wade was there, watching over her, and would keep in touch with Connor. While he sat there held in the grip of gut-wrenching nerves, his cell phone rang.

He glimpsed Jarod's name on the caller ID and clicked on. "If it had been anyone else phoning right now…"

"I hear you. How are you holding up, bro?"

"Ask me after Liz's event is over. Is everyone with you?"

"We're all glued to the TV, too."

"She had to be upset about last night's score. That was my fault for asking her to stay overnight with me at the hospital the night before."

"You mean—"

"When I told her I didn't want her to leave, she arranged for a cot," Connor cut in. "That was selfish of me. She couldn't have gotten a decent sleep on that thing."

"I have news for you. No one slept well last night."

Connor let out a heavy sigh. "If you've got any special Crow prayers for her…"

"Liz doesn't need them."

"You sound like your uncle when he's looking off into a place no one else can see."

"All you have to do is visualize her doing what she

does best and you'll have no worries. Take care of yourself."

"I am. Wade and Kim have been waiting on me when Liz couldn't."

"That's good to know. We'll see you tomorrow."

"Tell Grandpa I love him." Emotion overtook him and he started to choke up. "Tell him I'm grateful for everything he's ever done for me."

Jarod's voice sounded oddly husky when he said, "He already knows, but you can tell him yourself after we get you home."

After *we* get you home?

No way. There was only one person who was going to get him home. *Sorry, Kyle.*

He clicked off to watch the last of the bareback riding, but his nerves were making him fidgety. He rubbed his scruffy jaw while he waited for the barrel racing to start.

One of the workers rode out on the rake to groom the arena. Besides maintaining a consistent, level footing, the machine repaired and regraded the footing layer. Connor wanted everything perfect for Liz.

The sounds of the crowd swelled as the first twelve racers clocked their times. Liz was thirteenth out. He held his breath when her name was announced. Unable to sit still, he got to his feet and moved closer to the TV. Suddenly, she hurtled out of the alley. She swished around those barrels like she was playing a seamless game of Quidditch at Hogwarts from a Harry Potter film. No extra movements.

Sunflower was an extension of her. Elegance personified, that was Liz. His heart warmed in his chest to watch her gallop home. A huge roar went up from the crowd over her sensational score of 13.40, but no sound was as loud as his own cry of joy. She'd set the bar high for tonight's competition.

Dustine Hoffman was the last one out. She was a tough one to beat by anyone's standards. Her style reminded him of a pianist who moved her whole body back and forth while she played at the keyboard. Lots of elbow and footwork. Her long hair flew behind her like a pennant. She clocked a 13.44.

You did it, Liz.

He couldn't stay alone in this hotel room another second. Without hesitation he called the front desk and told them he was checking out. He asked them to send someone to carry his overnight case and to call him a taxi.

On the way to the RV park, he asked the driver to stop at the all-night supermarket where he'd shopped with Liz before. He found some fresh-cut daisies in a vase and paid for them, along with a bag of Snickers bars. In another ten minutes he let himself inside the trailer. The driver brought in his case for him. Liz had left a light on.

It felt so good to be home again, he didn't care about being sling tied for the rest of the month. The faint scent of her fragrance hung in the air. When Liz got back later, another buckle would be added to their centerpiece.

She'd left it in the middle of the table. He put the vase of flowers next to it, along with two candy bars. The rest he set on the counter. After he took another dose of antibiotic, he fixed himself a cheese-and-bologna sandwich with one hand. It was tricky, because he was right-handed, but he managed. Then he settled down on the couch to watch TV and eat.

Wade phoned. He was higher than a kite over her win. Connor told him Reva was gone forever. The revelation was met with silence. Connor took it to mean Wade was glad for him but didn't dare say anything.

Connor helped him out by telling him he'd moved back to the trailer, but asked him not to tell Liz. He wanted to surprise her. They chatted for a moment about the steer wrestling. Wade informed him of Jocko's win. "That's good."

"With you out of the finals, he stands a good chance of winning the whole thing. I admit he has a lot of try," Wade commented before they hung up. Yup. Jocko would no doubt win his first world championship.

Since Liz had to go to the eleven o'clock buckle ceremony at the South Point before coming home, it would be a while before she walked through the door.

It was a Friday night, so her favorite reruns ought to be on. He found the channel featuring the British comedies and discovered the show about Hyacinth would be on in five more minutes. He was curious to find out what Liz thought was so hilarious and decided to record it so they could watch it together after she returned.

The news bored him. With time hanging heavy, he found his electric razor and went into the bathroom to do something about his beard. After two days it was driving him crazy. He was almost through when he saw Liz coming toward him looking shell-shocked. She tossed her hat and purse on a chair.

"Connor—I didn't know. I—I didn't realize you were here," she stammered.

"Yup. I'm back." He finished the under part of his chin before shutting the razor off.

"But I thought you'd be staying at a hotel from now on."

"So you didn't miss me and wish I'd stayed away?"

Her brows formed a distinct frown. "I didn't say that. Don't put words in my mouth. I'm just surprised, that's all."

"The only reason I got myself a hotel room was to give everyone a break. I could just call room service when I needed something."

Liz looked away from him. Maybe he was mistaken, but he thought her face had lost a little color. "You should be in bed."

"I'll get there, Doctor, but since I need to sleep downstairs, do you mind spending the rest of the time in the niche?"

"No," she blurted. "I'll change the sheets on both beds right now."

"While you do that, I'll fix you a peanut-butter sandwich and a glass of milk. You need food after your outstanding win tonight."

Her chin lifted. "You saw it?"

He nodded. "Before I left the hotel. The arena hasn't seen a score like 13.40 in years. You're on the verge of walking away with the whole thing. My heart was in my throat when you and Sunflower flew back to the alley."

A fetching smile appeared at one corner of her mouth. He'd been waiting for some sign that she was glad to see him. "So was mine. I'm afraid there'll be no encore tomorrow night."

"Don't worry. All you'll need to do is your best. It'll be enough."

"Since when did you start seeing the glass as full?"

"Rooming with you has something to do with it. After you make the beds, we'll celebrate your victory. Where's your buckle?"

"In my purse."

"Be sure to add it to our centerpiece." Before she got out the clean linen, she took the box from her purse and put it on top of the others.

"Daisies!" Her eyes shone. "They're beautiful. Thank you, Connor."

"I wish they were roses, but no florists were open tonight. That makes four for you."

He fixed her a sandwich, but he couldn't keep his eyes off her feminine lines and curves while she used the ladder to get her work done. Once the beds were made, they ate and watched TV.

"I have one more surprise for you."

"You've done too much already."

"I did it for me, too." He turned on the program.

"You recorded *Keeping Up Appearances!*" The pleasure in her voice made it all worth it.

"I want to see what's so funny."

"She's a scream, Connor."

Halfway through the program, he could see what she meant. Hyacinth was being chased through a field by a bull. The faces she pulled and the contortions she went through in order to extricate herself had him laughing out loud. "They should pay her to come to the arena and put on this act. It would bring the house down."

Their gazes met. "It really would. You've made this a perfect night, but you look tired. Let me help you get ready for bed." She shot out of the chair to find him clean pajamas. In the end, he kept on the Western shirt he'd been wearing and put on the bottoms. While he was in the bathroom, she'd changed into her own nightwear. She put his medicine and water by the head of the couch. With teeth brushed and lights out, they got into their beds. He had to lie flat on his back to accommodate his sling.

This time, she was the one who looked down on him. Those fabulous green eyes and her smile healed every wound. He knew he would have to see her every day and night and all the seconds in between for the rest of his life, or it wasn't worth living.

"The doctor is in. If you need me in the night, just call out."

Lady, you have no idea what you've just said.

Chapter Ten

Liz's cell phone rang at 8:00 a.m. She clicked on. "Hi, Mom. I was about to call you." She'd just fixed breakfast for Connor and had helped him off with his shirt. His cut physique was something to behold. She trembled just thinking about him. Now he was in the bathroom getting ready for the day, but he'd need her help putting on a clean shirt when he came out.

"We're on our way to the airport. Zane's driving us in his car."

"I can't wait to see all of you."

"We feel the same. Our flight from Billings leaves in two hours. Connor's family will meet us there."

"Who's tending Ryan?"

"Jarod and Sadie drove him out to the reservation to stay with his uncle's family. They're crazy about him."

"I miss him. I miss all of you. Who's going to be with Ralph?"

"Besides the household staff, his brother Tyson."

"That's good. I'll give him a call before my event."

"He'll love that. It won't be long now, honey. We're scheduled to arrive in Las Vegas at two. Sadie called last week and said she and Jarod had made reservations at the Venetian for all of us. It was very thoughtful of her. You'll need to let your friend Kyle know where we're staying."

Liz took an unsteady breath. "Our plans have changed. He's not coming. I'll tell you why later."

"Oh, honey…" She heard her mother's dejection.

"It's for the best, Mom. Really, it is. Give me a ring when you've reached the hotel. I'm going to work with Sunflower early so I can spend time with you before we all have to head for the arena."

"I guess I don't need to tell you how proud we are of you. I didn't know I could cry so many happy tears. Your father's going around in a daze."

"I'm in a daze, too. Get here safely."

"We will. Love you."

Connor came out of the bathroom as she was cleaning up the kitchen. He had a dark green-and-black-plaid shirt in his hand. "Do you mind helping me into this?"

Oh, Connor. If you only knew.

Smothering a groan from the unassuaged ache she felt for him, she eased him into it with great care and buttoned him up. He was a heartbreaker, all right, from the sun-bleached tips of his wavy hair to his well-worn Justin cowboy boots, one of his other sponsors.

"You smell good," she commented.

His eyes bored into hers. "We wear the same perfume," he teased. "By the way, that long-sleeved navy shirt looks terrific on you."

"Thanks." She forced herself to step away from him. "Everyone will be at the Venetian after two."

"It'll be a great reunion. Wade and Kim will pick me up there. We have front-row seats at the arena right by our families."

A deep pain passed through her. "Connor—when

we started out, we had no idea what was going to happen to you. It kills me that you're not going to be performing in that arena tonight."

He studied her for a minute out of those intelligent brown eyes. "Do you want to know the truth? I'm glad things worked out exactly as they have. For the first time in my rodeo career, I'm going to be sitting in the arena with the people I love, watching someone I admire more than you could possibly imagine. That person is you."

She picked up a throb in his voice she couldn't ignore.

"Tonight, Liz Henson, you're going to win the world championship. I wouldn't miss this experience for anything on earth. It's been my honor and privilege getting to know the you who has been hidden from me."

She stood there without moving.

Did he just say, "It's been my honor and privilege?"

Had those words been meant as the most beautiful goodbye speech she'd ever heard? Had he and Reva decided to get remarried and make it work this time? If a person could die of heartache, she was a prime candidate.

He brushed his mouth against her cheek before he reached for his cowboy hat. "I'll wait in the truck for you. Mind driving me to the hotel on the way? I want Wade and Kim to have a day off from worrying about me, so I'm going to stay in Jarod and Sadie's room until our families arrive."

Despite her shaking body, Liz managed to get ready, then drive him to the hotel. She was glad he was going to rest in his brother's hotel room where he could enjoy room service. Her heart aching for him, she dropped him off and drove to the center to check on Sunflower. On this last day of competition, she walked her around on foot for a little while, with no expectations, in order to give her a rest.

"Tonight will be the last time, little lady," she whispered.

As for Polly, she needed some exercise, so Liz rode her around. This horse would be happy to get home where they could take some trail rides. She didn't like been cooped up. For that matter, neither did Sunflower, who had to be tired of ten days' competition.

After grabbing a quick bite to eat at a drive-through, Liz went to the hotel and discovered the families had just arrived. The reunion with loved ones was an emotional one. She had to fight tears. Around five o'clock they all left the hotel for the Mack Center.

She watched in despair over Connor, who was unable to compete. It wasn't fair. He drove away with Wade and Kim, his arm in a sling. The others left in a taxi, while she drove over to the arena with her father.

After she parked the truck, she leaned across and hugged him. "I love you, Dad. I would never have made it this far without you."

"Sure, you would have, but I'm glad you didn't have to. You've given me thrill after thrill so far in this life. And there'll be a lot more of that coming after the rodeo is behind you."

She knew what he was trying to tell her, but when you were in pain…

It was time to go inside.

"You really like the knotted reins?"

"Definitely."

"Connor knew what he was talking about."

"Yes."

"He seems to be in a lot better emotional shape than I would have expected."

She agreed, which was no surprise since he and Reva had probably reconciled for good. "Connor's tough, like Ralph and Jarod."

"Ralph calls you two his champions."

She smiled. "I know. I talked to him and Tyson on the phone for a few minutes, back at the hotel."

He grasped the hand closest to him. "Go out there tonight and have the time of your life."

She nodded, but it would be hard to do, knowing Connor was just a spectator this time.

"Whatever happens will happen, Lizzie girl. Just remember how wonderful the journey has been."

Especially the journey with Connor. A time out of time, never to be repeated.

As usual, her father gave the best advice. "I'll remember."

"We'll meet you out here after it's over."

They parted company and she headed inside to mount up one more time. The earthy scent of horses and cattle drifted throughout, making the National Finals Rodeo a full sensory experience she'd never forget.

Liz walked past the same contestants getting ready for their events. It was concentration time. She rounded the row of stalls, then gasped. Sunflower was lying against the side of her stall in a horrible position.

The first rule in a crisis was to avoid frightening her horse. At a glance, she could see Sunflower was stall cast. She'd gotten so tired she'd lain down, rolled against the wall and was trapped. Without enough room for leverage to stand up, she'd injured her legs.

"It's all right." Liz hunkered down and spoke to her, patting her neck. "I'm going to find help for you. Don't panic, little lady. I'll be right back."

She crept out of the stall and found the two assigned livestock helpers, who rushed forward. Between the three of them, they got Sunflower on her feet. During the whole procedure she spoke gently to her favorite horse, who was struggling with fright. If she panicked, she could go into shock.

"You're all right now," Liz said, over and over again. Carefully she ran her hands over Sunflower's legs. There was no bleeding, so she hadn't been in that position long, thank heaven. But those tendons would be sore.

Tears ran down Liz's cheeks as she flung her arms around her mare's neck. "You've given it your all, Sunflower. You're the best. No one ever had a better horse. Tomorrow I'm taking you home."

Joe, one of the older helpers she'd gotten to know, tapped her on the shoulder. "Your event's up next."

"I know. I'm going to have to ride Polly."

"Don't you worry about this horse. I'll stay here and gentle her until you come back."

She sniffed. "I'm indebted to you, Joe. Keep her warm with this light blanket." Liz threw it over her horse and gave her a treat.

"Everything's going to be all right, Liz. You go out there on your other horse and you'll do fine."

Fine wasn't good enough. *Jarod's vision hadn't foreseen this catastrophe.*

With a nod, she carried her gear and saddle to the next stall. "Polly? It's you and me in the spotlight now." She got the horse ready and walked her out.

Joe smiled at her as she passed. "Your horse is settling down."

"You have no idea how much I appreciate your help."

"That's what I'm here for."

"See you soon, Sunflower."

Once mounted, she headed for the area where the other barrel racers were assembled. The first one took off. She heard the roar of the crowd.

Liz could visualize Connor and her loved ones out there waiting to see her performance. Her heart plummeted to her feet.

Get hold of yourself, Liz. You need to put that picture away and visualize what you have to do for this go-round.

"Our turn's coming up, Polly. All we can do is our best. The first barrel is a blind barrel compared to the outside runs. We're going to take Dad's advice. We're going to run out that alley and you're going to hunt for that barrel as if your life depended on it."

She patted her neck. "You're going to hunt it and kill that turn. You've done it before in practice—you can do it again. Do it for Connor. He's done everything to help me win. Now we need your help, Polly."

IN THE STANDS, Connor looked down the row of familiar faces. Both families were spread out on the seats, with Wade and his girlfriend next to Connor. Jarod and Sadie sat on his other side by Millie and Mac. Zane and Avery sat next to them.

Where was Kyle, Liz's supposed favorite? How come he hadn't shown up yet? Maybe he was sitting somewhere else, but that seemed odd to Connor with her parents here.

Though they'd all enjoyed the other events and cheered Jocko, who'd taken over Connor's place as world champion this year, their group grew quiet, knowing the barrel racing was about to begin.

This was it, the moment Liz had been training for since she was a young girl. It was amazing her mentor father could function right now.

The noise of the crowd reached a crescendo as the first barrel racer entered the arena. Connor watched her and the subsequent four riders who appeared in quick succession. They clocked good times of 13.80, 13.77, 13.74. The other knocked over barrels for a five-second penalty. One by one, more barrel racers put up their times. 13.72, two 13.70s. The scores were stacking up.

"Dustine Hoffman, riding Cranky tonight, is next to last in the lineup. She's number one in earnings coming into the finals this year. We'll see if last year's world champion can do it again."

Connor gritted his teeth, knowing this was the rider Liz had to beat. He watched her shoot out of the alley, but he could tell she was being more careful than usual so she wouldn't knock over a barrel. Whoops. She took the third one a little too wide and finished with a 13.78. Not a winning time this go-round. His body sagged in relief.

Then came the announcement he'd been waiting for. It zapped through him like a bolt of lightning. "The winner in three rounds here at finals, with the best score on her first round, and second in earnings is up next. Liz Henson from Montana on Sunflower! Hold on. I've just been told there's been a change of horses. She's riding Polly."

Polly?

Connor broke out in a cold sweat.

"No—" Sadie cried in anguish.

He and Jarod shared a pained glance. Wade leaned closer. "Something has happened to Sunflower."

Yup. Polly, a reddish-brown bay with a black mane and tail, had never competed here, though Liz had trained her well. This arena was small and a horse had to be aggressive to careen around the barrels. She didn't have Sunflower's speed.

Connor got a sick feeling in the pit of his stomach. Instead of sitting with everyone, he should have gone back to the stall to be with Liz before the events started. But he'd been afraid he might distract her. With his arm useless right now, he'd never felt so helpless in his life.

If Liz was going to have a shot at this last round, it was because Polly wasn't exhausted after competing nine rounds in nine days.

Suddenly she galloped out of the alley. Connor was on his feet as she circled the first barrel. Polly shot across to the second barrel with unbelievable energy, circling it so closely, he couldn't believe she didn't touch it.

One more barrel to go, Liz. He started to feel light-headed with excitement and sat down again. Then the thing happened that signaled the death knell. She bumped against the third barrel.

Pain tore his guts apart. Unable to look, he closed his eyes in excruciating pain before hearing the ear-splitting roar of the crowd.

"You can open them now, bro. The barrel didn't tip over."

What?

Jarod wore one of his rare brilliant smiles.

It had to be a miracle! Most of the time in practice the barrels didn't fall, but during the competition you could count on them going down.

When Connor looked over at the score he saw a 13.67. His mouth went so dry he couldn't swallow, let alone talk. Before he knew it, the event had come to an end and her score stood.

Jarod turned to him. "She won, bro. She's won the whole shootin' match. I'd hug you, but we don't want to do any damage to that incision."

The others were on their feet, jumping up and down for joy. Wade said, "Kim and I are going to find her."

"Tell her I'll be right there."

Sadie and Millie were embracing while he made his way over to Mac and shook his hand. "I hope you know she won this championship for her champion father."

He wiped his eyes. "I was no champion, but Millie and I gave birth to one. Thank you for getting her here safe and sound. I believe it made all the difference. We're so sorry about your accident."

"I'd forgotten all about it." It was the truth.

Avery hugged him on his good side. "Mac was right. Bringing Liz with you gave her the kind of confidence to put her over the top. You were always my hero, but you've outdone yourself this time."

After she kissed his cheek, Zane shook his hand. "I've never been to a rodeo until tonight. To think you won five times in this arena is phenomenal."

"I got lucky."

He grinned. "Sure you did. I guess Liz just got lucky, too."

Millie turned to him and gave him a gentle hug. "Bless you for taking such wonderful care of our daughter despite the terrible disappointment to yourself."

His throat swelled. "I would have liked to be doing this for her a long time ago, but Daniel Corkin got in the way." At that remark, her eyes flared in surprise. "Shall we go find her in the back before we drive over to the South Point?"

On their way out of the arena it occurred to him that Kyle might have been here the whole time helping Liz. It wasn't a pleasant thought.

Wade intercepted him when they reached the stall area. "Sunflower got stall cast, but she'll be fine." Connor grimaced. He figured it might have been something like that. "My rig's out in back. Why don't I load Sunflower and Polly and drive them to the RV park for the night while you go on to the South Point with your family."

"I owe you more than you'll never know, Wade."

His blue eyes smiled. "It works both ways, and you know it."

Connor followed him but held back while he watched the crowd around Liz give her hugs and congratulations. He didn't see another man around. What had happened to Kyle?

While Wade was leading her horses out of their stalls, she swung around to say something, but stopped when she saw Connor. Though her face shone with happiness, he glimpsed a shadow of sorrow in her eyes. Because Kyle wasn't here?

He moved closer. "Well…shall we add up the earnings for the world-champion barrel racer? You've won over two hundred thousand dollars."

"That last barrel should have toppled," she said in a shaky voice.

"But it didn't. Now you've got enough money to finish paying off your loans, buy yourself a new truck and car and still have money left over."

A stillness enveloped them. "It was never about the money."

"Like I told you a long time ago, you're too good to be true."

Her features hardened. "Yup. That's me."

"Where's your favorite? The one who was flying down from Bozeman?"

If he wasn't mistaken, those green eyes glittered. "At the last minute there was an emergency and he couldn't make it. But we'll see each other after I get back home. He's going to help me pick out a new truck."

The hell he was.

"Then why don't we pile everyone in my truck and head on over to the casino where you'll be royally feted. It'll be a tight squeeze, but I'm pretty sure no one will mind. I'll ask Jarod to drive us."

LIZ COULDN'T BELIEVE it when Connor managed the seating arrangements so the two of them were in back with her parents. Since it was a bit of a squeeze, he told her it might be better if she sat on his left leg so his sore arm had more room. Jarod drove with Sadie and Zane up front.

It was like déjà vu, reminding her of the night at the swimming pool when he'd pulled her onto his lap. Only, at that particular time, they'd been alone, and for a few minutes he'd kissed her with such hunger she'd started devouring him back, unable to help herself.

The memory of those moments of abandon sent a wave of heat through her sensitized body. She needed to get off him, but Saturday night in Las Vegas at the culmination of the rodeo had made the traffic impossible. Crowds of people arriving at the hotel slowed their progress. Jarod dropped them off before going to find a parking place.

To neutralize her body's reaction to their nearness, she phoned Ralph, who sounded completely overjoyed by her win. She shed tears for the love in his voice before they hung up. When she got out of the truck, she still reeled from the sensation of feeling Connor's strong heartbeat against her back. Liz throbbed to her fingertips. That was the last time she would ever get physically close to him. Reva had first rights.

As soon as she flew back to the ranch with her family, she'd let Jarod know she planned to take the vet job on the reservation and rent a house there. It wouldn't take her long to make the daily drive to the clinic in White Lodge. She'd make both jobs work if it killed her!

For the next hour she sat with the other world-championship winners behind the master of ceremonies. Her loved ones watched from one of the tables in the audience, but the only person she could see was Connor, dressed in jeans and his black shirt, and of course his white sling.

Exciting as the awards ceremony turned out to be, it hurt that Jocko Mendez was getting the gold buckle meant for Connor. She couldn't erase the tragedy from her mind, not even when it was her turn to say a few words before receiving the fabulous gold buckle she would always treasure.

"I'm reminded of a quote by Victor Hugo, one of my favorite authors. He said, 'There is nothing like a dream to create the future.' I'm here tonight living my future due to my two wonderful parents, Millie and Mac Henson, sitting out in this audience. They sacrificed everything for me and my dream. Will you please stand?"

She knew her modest parents wouldn't like this part. "Mom and Dad, this buckle's for you. My dad was a fabulous bull rider in his twenties and taught me everything I know, including about being on the back of a horse."

When they got to their feet, the crowd clapped and cheered. After the noise quieted down, they regained their seats.

"There are many people to thank. First, my best friend Sadie Bannock, a horse lover who always believed in me. I also want to acknowledge my next-door neighbor from Montana who's been my absolute inspiration for years. Neither he nor his grandfather, Ralph, another rodeo champion, would let me give up when I blew it at my first junior rodeo competition years ago. He's my idea of the all-American cowboy, and he, along with his hazer, Wade Torney, got me and my horses safely here for this great rodeo. Connor Bannock, will you please stand?"

At the mention of his name, the place literally exploded. Everyone was on their feet chanting, "Connor, Connor," before they gave him a thunderous ovation. Slowly he stood as the clapping went on and on.

"To this five-time world-champion bulldogger goes my heartfelt thanks."

The second the awards were over, Liz slipped down

to the table with her box and hugged everyone except Connor. He eyed her strangely. "*I've* been your inspiration?"

"Don't be absurd, Connor. Of course you have!"

"Now she tells me."

"Come on, everyone," Jarod spoke up. "Let's all head over to our hotel so we can party."

Liz's heart shriveled. It was the midnight hour. With her dream fulfilled, she now had to figure out her new life.

"Connor?" He stood a little distance off looking undeniably handsome. She walked over to him. "I don't know what your plans are, but if it's all right with you, I'll go by the trailer in the morning and pack up my things. Wade said he and your handlers would trailer our horses home in their rigs."

To her shock, he shook his head. "I'm taking Firebrand and Sunflower home in my trailer."

"You mean Reva's going to drive?" She thought she might die on the spot from pain.

"No."

"I don't understand."

"Reva is out of the picture and has gone back to L.A. for good."

Liz started to feel faint. "You're not making sense. You were with her yesterday."

He nodded. "After I left the hospital, I had a talk in private with her. She'd already checked in to another hotel, but we met in mine."

She rubbed her palms against her hips nervously. "I see."

"I doubt it. Reva wanted us to get back together again, but I told her that wasn't possible because I wasn't in love with her anymore. I haven't been for a long time."

The blood pounded in Liz's ears. She didn't know what to say and swallowed hard.

"But how can you take the horses back when you're not supposed to drive?"

"I'll get one of the guys to help me."

"But if you fly, you won't have so much discomfort to your arm and shoulder."

"I despise flying unless I have to."

What? "I didn't know that."

"There are a lot of things you don't know about me, but Wade's waiting to drive me to the Venetian. I'll meet you there. We can talk about this later. My only concern is for you, though it's obvious you've got family to take care of you. But you should know by now I wanted to be the one to do the honors."

Liz was dying inside. "You already did enough by driving me here."

"Not nearly enough," he muttered, "but that's a conversation for another time."

TO HER ASTONISHMENT, he sought out his friends and they left the ballroom. Sadie and Jarod walked over to her. "Are you all right? You look dazed. What did Connor say to you?"

Liz stared at her friend. Tonight at the awards ceremony she'd talked about a dream that created the future, but Connor's dream had taken several unexpected turns. She was afraid he was already sinking into a depression.

"I don't know what to do. He insists on one of the

guys driving him back to the ranch with the horses, but that wouldn't be good for him."

Sadie blinked. "What about Reva?"

"That's what I asked him. He said it's over. She's gone back to Los Angeles for good."

"For *now,* you mean, until she comes after him again. That's been their pattern, and he continues to let it happen because he can't seem to help himself." Sadie looked at Jarod, who didn't say anything.

As far as Liz was concerned, they'd both just verified her tortured thoughts. Despite the fact that he'd kissed Liz with passion, she couldn't forget the way he'd looked at Reva when he'd seen her in the trailer. Liz hadn't been able to handle it and had ducked into the bathroom.

"Jarod? Is it true your brother doesn't like to fly?"

Once in a while he wore an inscrutable expression. "Is that what he told you?"

"He said he despised it."

Sadie grasped his arm. "Then *you* can drive him, darling. I'll fly back with Liz and the others tomorrow."

Jarod looked down at his wife and gave her a kiss. "Since Connor didn't ask me, I think we have to leave it up to him what he wants to do. Come on, mother of Little Sits in the Center."

Sadie stared at him with a smile. "Little Sits in the Center?"

"That's Connor's name for our baby. Didn't you know? Let's go. Everyone's waiting for us out at the truck."

But on the way back to the Venetian with her family, Liz couldn't shake off the feeling that Connor was in bad emotional shape. As soon as they'd all congregated in Jarod's suite, she walked over to his brother, who was standing next to Avery.

She hugged Liz. "I've never been so proud of anyone, ever!"

"Thanks, Avery. That means the world coming from you."

When Zane called to her, Liz was left alone with Connor for a minute.

"Connor? I've given this some thought. You shouldn't plan to drive home with one of the guys. Then you'll have to act all tough."

"I'll be all right."

Liz took a deep breath, deciding to plunge in. "You'll be a lot better if you let *me* drive us back. I'm the doctor, remember? Don't forget, I have a supply of your favorite medicine on hand—chocolate. We'll take it slow and easy to give you and the horses plenty of rest. You won't have to pretend anything with me. After all you've done for me, it's my turn to look after your needs."

The second his brown eyes ignited, she knew she'd said the right thing. "Have you asked one of the guys yet?"

"No. And, frankly, I can't wait to start back. I liked it better when it was just the two of us."

"I did, too." *It was heaven on earth.*

Chapter Eleven

"Thanks, Wade! See you back home. We'll settle up there."

Connor waved off his friend, who'd hitched up Connor's truck to the trailer and loaded the horses. Now it was time to head back to Montana with Liz at the wheel and no one else around....

If he thought he'd been nervous before he'd approached her at the arena prior to this trip to Vegas, that was nothing compared to his anxiety now. He'd allowed her to believe he was afraid to fly in order to gain her sympathy. It was a lie, although he actually did despise all the stuff you had to go through. Still, it didn't hurt if she was worried he had a bit of a phobia and had offered to drive him. He needed to be alone with her.

Liz started the truck. After Wade pulled away in his own rig, she followed them onto the road that would lead out of the RV park to the main street. This morning she was wearing his favorite red-and-blue-plaid hombre shirt. Now that he wasn't driving, he could stare at her profile and shape whenever he felt like it, which was all the time.

"How was Sunflower when you loaded her? Do you think she's still suffering?"

"She seems in pretty good shape. Our horses were nickering when Wade and I put them in the trailer."

Connor smiled. "I noticed. She was probably confiding her problems to Firebrand. You can tell they're glad to be together."

"I wouldn't doubt it. Fortunately she wasn't stall cast very long. We'll make the same number of stops on the way home so they won't get too tired." She eyed him. "Before we leave Las Vegas, do you have enough antibiotic to get home on, or should we stop and get more?"

"My other doc ordered me a two-week prescription."

He heard her chuckle over his little joke. "That's good. You need to take all of it."

"Yes, Dr. Henson."

"Any time you get tired of sitting in the same position, I'll pull over so you can get out and stretch your legs."

"I'll take my break with our children. Thanks for coming back to the trailer with me last night. I'm sure our families understood I wanted to get an early start this morning."

"To be honest, I did, too. There's nothing like a party when it's over."

"But it was a great party while it lasted, right? You're the world champion."

She darted him a searching glance. "So are you. Until your accident, it was the most wonderful experience of my life."

"Accidents happen, Liz."

He heard her deep sigh. "Did you ever see that old film, *An Affair to Remember?*"

"I did. That was one of my grandmother's favorites. While she cried over the last scene, Jarod and I made faces at each other. We were too young at the time to appreciate it. Years later I saw it again."

"Then you'll understand what was in my heart when I saw you lying on that hospital bed after you came out of surgery. As the vulnerable hero said to the crippled heroine, 'If anyone had to have an accident, why did it have to be you?' That was exactly how I felt."

His pulse sped up. "If the producers had made a sequel, we would have seen him helping her get back on her feet while she supported him in his fledgling career. That's the power of true love. So, tell me, what are you going to do with your buckle? Wear it or display it?"

"When I move out, I'll give it to my folks and let them decide."

His brows met in a frown. "What do you mean, move out?"

"I've decided I'm going to take that job on the reservation and rent a house there. Once I've talked it over with Dr. Rafferty, I'm sure I can make both jobs work."

He ground his teeth. "Does this mean my job offer is out?"

"Connor—you weren't really serious."

"Now you've wounded me again. I think this is the third time."

"If I have, please forgive me."

"I might, with one provision."

"What's that?"

"That you reconsider and come to work for me. You're the person who reminded me of an old dream and gave it a new twist. Something else you're going to learn about me is that I'm deadly serious when I decide to go after something I want."

Funny how she suddenly had to correct the steering.

Taking advantage of the palpable silence, he said, "Have you decided what kind of a truck you're going to buy?"

"After winning at the Dodge Ram finals, I guess I'd better get one of their models."

"That might be a good idea, considering you're their reigning barrel champion. Think how the words *Bannock Feral Stud Farm* will look on a big black one, unless Kyle thinks you should pick out a white one. Personally, I think black makes a statement. I'll have the same words put on this truck."

He watched her hands grip the steering wheel tighter. "Assuming you're not putting me on, how much would you pay me?"

"To work for me, one hundred thousand dollars to start, but it will be negotiable when the business starts to grow. I'll pay for your insurance, too. Maybe you and Doc Rafferty can work something out for part time at the clinic, but the job on the reservation wouldn't be possible. Jarod will have to understand.

"You can write off your new truck as a business expense. As soon as we get back to the ranch, I'll be sitting down with my attorney."

"You're serious…." She sounded shaken.

"I don't know what more to say to convince you. The ranch has plenty of land to erect an office, new barns with paddocks, breeding stalls, feed, everything I'll require. The only thing I don't have nailed down yet is the perfect vet. That's you. I bet you already know more about ferals than most vets out of med school. What we don't know we can learn together."

"Connor—"

"Hold on," he interrupted her. "All I ask is that you think about it while I sleep for a little while. The second you get tired, pull off the road. We're in no hurry."

He could tell she was getting ready to erupt in that endearing way of hers. "Is this the real reason you wanted to be alone with me?"

"It's *one* of my real reasons. I need time to explain everything, and that's what we've got while we're on the road. Time and the kind of privacy I require to talk it all out."

"So you're not really afraid of flying?"

"No. I hardly ever lie, but in this case it was an emergency. Do you hate me?"

She let out a sound of exasperation. "You could have talked to me about it after we flew home."

"But I was worried it might be too late and you wouldn't listen to me, not if you're excited to see Kyle. He might have other plans for you that could influence you one way or the other. How serious is it between the two of you?"

"Is this part of the job interview?"

"Yes. I need to know the truth. Are you going to get married on me just when I'm getting my business started, and then tell me you're moving to Bozeman?"

Silence reigned in the cab. "We're not that close. Though I like him a lot, I've decided I won't be seeing him anymore."

"But you let me believe that, about him helping you pick out a truck."

She sucked in her breath. "I guess I did."

"Can I assume you told him not to come to Las Vegas?"

"Yes, if you must know."

"Thank you for being honest with me. Now that you've laid one of my fears to rest, what else would stand in the way of your accepting my offer?"

He could hear her mind working. "Let me think about it. Tonight we'll be in Kemmerer. Before we go to bed, I'll give you an answer one way or the other."

"Promise?"

She darted him a frosty glance. "This time I'm not lying. Normally…I don't," she added.

"Anyone is capable of it, depending on the depth of their desperation."

"Are you telling me you were so desperate to get me alone, you resorted to a lie?"

"I told you. I was afraid." He laid his head back and closed his eyes. "Wake me up if you need me."

Liz found herself glancing at him many times before they reached Kemmerer. He'd called ahead to reserve a place at the same RV park for them to spend the night. The lines around his eyes and mouth told her he was exhausted, and rightly so after all he'd been through and suffered.

He woke up when they stopped long enough for her to walk the horses and clean their stalls. After she fixed him snacks, he went back to sleep and they were once again underway. The weather was cooperating. Cold, but no snowstorms. It made for easy driving for her.

The hard part of this journey home was his question, and it had been torturing her all day. *What else would stand in the way of your accepting my offer?*

Liz had one simple answer.

Reva.

Sadie had come right out and said it to Liz's face, *in front of Jarod,* that Reva still had a stranglehold on him. Jarod hadn't denied it. No one knew Connor better than his brother, so Liz knew what her answer would have to be.

Connor had a cowboy's heart.

There'd been a million songs written about the one woman a cowboy couldn't forget. It was the way a cowboy was put together. You couldn't fight it.

She'd wanted to see inside the cover. Now that the inside was exposed, it was time for her to move on. Her life depended on it.

After they'd parked for the night, she went into the trailer and pulled out the sofa bed so he could lie down. Once she'd made him comfortable and fed him, she checked on the horses and cleaned the stalls. With that task out of the way, she showered and put on her pajamas.

Flipping off the light switch, she used the ladder to reach the niche. But now the tables were turned, because she was exhausted and he was wide-awake, wanting to talk.

"You've had enough time to consider my offer. What's it going to be?"

She'd prepared her speech. "I'm honored that you have enough faith in me as a vet to help get your business off the ground, but I've thought it over and want to work on the reservation. Once you advertise, you'll find a great vet anxious to work with someone of your reputation. But not every vet wants to live on a reservation.

"I love it there and would like to think I could make

a meaningful contribution. The Crow love their animals and understand things about them I'd like to learn. Between my work there and at the clinic, I know I'm going to find fulfillment now that my barrel-racing days are over."

"In that case, before you go to sleep, there's something I couldn't give you in front of the others. If you'd come down for just a minute."

"It can't wait until morning?"

"I'm afraid not."

Puzzled, she threw off the covers and lowered herself to the floor.

"Come over here."

"I can hardly see you." She made her way to the side of his bed. He reached for her with his good arm and pulled her down next to him.

"Hold out your hand."

When Liz did his bidding, she heard a tinkling before he put the charm bracelet in her palm. She let out a cry of surprise. "What are you doing?"

"Since I can't do it myself, I need you to put it on your wrist for me."

"But Ralph gave this to both of us to keep in your cab for luck—"

"This bracelet *is* ours, and it did bring us luck, but instead of keeping it on the mirror, I want you to wear it. Put it on, please."

Liz felt all jittery. It took her forever to fasten it. "Okay. It's done."

She felt his hand circle her wrist and feel for the individual charms. "Ah. There it is. I've found the heart. Grandpa said it meant love of country, but between you and me it represents *my* heart."

A strangely warm shiver passed through her body.

"I lost it to you on the drive to Las Vegas. It happened that first magical night, while we were outside in the snow with our children wondering if they were enamored. Remember?"

"Yes." Her voice shook. "How could I ever forget one second of our time together?"

"That's when I realized I was enamored of *you*. The fact is, I'm so terribly in love with you, I can't take another step without you. Wear this instead of an engagement ring until I can buy you one. If I thought you didn't love me back, I'd never get over it. You do love me, don't you?"

That trace of vulnerability in his voice got to her every time. "Oh, Connor—"

"Oh, Connor, yes? Or no?"

"You *know* I do. I love you more than life itself and have done from a distance since the time I was a teenager."

"Now she tells me." He let out a yelp of happiness.

She tried to breathe, but he was squeezing her with his good arm. "When you asked me to drive to Las Vegas with you, I thought I'd die for joy and leaped at the chance to be with you, even knowing about Reva."

"I wanted you to drive with me and resorted to my first lie so you wouldn't refuse me. Yes, I married Reva, but that was a time of life when I didn't know who I was. Neither did she. It was a marriage that never took. Without substance, the physical side of it eventually fizzled. She's my past. *You're* my future, Liz Henson. Tell me you'll marry me, or I won't be able to handle it."

"I can't believe this is happening."

"Say it," he begged.

"Of course I'll marry you!"

"And be my vet?"

She laughed. "Yes."

"And be the mother of our children?"

The tears had started. "Yes."

"And love me forever, the way I love you?"

"Oh, yes, darling, yes, yes, yes!" Her whole soul was crying for joy.

"Thank God. Lie down next to me. I need to feel your beautiful body against me. The night you came up to the niche and we ate the Snickers together, I wanted you so badly it terrified me."

"I wanted you, too. Way too much." Her voice trembled.

"You're so beautiful, Liz. You have no idea." He'd said those words to her in the hospital. It hadn't been the drugs after all. "Come closer, sweetheart."

"I'm afraid I'll hurt your arm."

"You're the doc and know how to be careful. I'll let you handle me. You're the only one who can. But be warned that one day soon it'll be my turn. For right now, just kiss me the way you kissed me in the pool. You lit a fire in me that's never going to burn out. I love you and can't wait to make you my wife."

With those words he transformed her world. "There's nothing I want more," she whispered against his lips after devouring him. "Do you have any idea how much fun it is to do what I want to you?"

"Yup. Just keep it up."

Breathless and eager to accommodate him, she kept it up until the fire was blazing hot. "I—I'd better leave you alone," she stammered, realizing she wasn't being careful enough.

"Don't you dare move! Until we get married, and maybe for several months after, will you live with me in my trailer?"

"I'm so glad you said that," she cried into his neck. "It felt like home to me the minute we left my parents' house. I've never known the kind of happiness I've had with you, Connor."

In his hunger, he leaned over to kiss her again, forgetting about his handicap. "Ouch—this arm." He had to lie back.

She chuckled in spite of the desire raging through her body. "That arm won you five gold buckles. Just be patient, and in six weeks all your body parts will be working again in perfect harmony."

"I have news for you, sweetheart. They're all working right now."

"I know. I've got the same problem, so I think it will be better if I just hold you for what's left of the rest of this night."

"Promise you won't leave me?"

"What do you think?"

"I think I'm the luckiest man alive."

AT NINE-THIRTY THE next night Liz pulled up in front of the Bannock ranch house. For once, they were putting Ralph before the horses they needed to put into their barns. They wanted to surprise him. The others wouldn't be home until tomorrow.

When she looked over at Connor, she saw such a different man than the one she'd left with two and a half weeks ago, she hardly recognized him.

The lines and shadows of self-doubt, guilt and recrimination were gone. If you could ascribe such an expression to a man, his striking face beamed with excitement. "Let's go break the news to him, sweetheart."

"I'll grab one each of our gold buckles to give him for a souvenir."

His brown eyes glowed as he looked at her. "Trust you to know what will touch his heart more than anything."

"Your coming home safe and sound will be the answer to his prayers. These trinkets are just the icing on the proverbial cake." She leaned across to kiss him long and hard before alighting from the cab.

Montana had been visited with more snow, creating another fairyland. After she'd gone into the trailer for the boxes, Connor wrapped his good arm around her waist and they walked up to the porch. He kissed her again. "Remember being here?"

"As if I could forget."

"It seemed so right that you and I were going off together to do what we loved."

"I thought the same thing."

"It was meant to be."

"Yes, darling."

He unlocked the door and they went inside. They crept down the hall to the den, but it was dark. "He's gone to bed."

"Maybe we should come back in the morning."

Connor shook his head. "No…this news can't wait." As he grasped her hand, the housekeeper approached.

"You're home! I'm so sorry about your arm. You would have won the whole thing, Connor. Congratulations to both of you!"

"Thank you," they said before he kissed her cheek. "He's going to be so thrilled, you can't imagine!"

"We're the ones who are thrilled." He grasped Liz's hand and led her all the way back to Ralph's bedroom. They found him lying propped up in bed. He was reading a book by the light of the bedside table.

"Grandpa?"

Ralph looked up. The book fell out of his hand. "It's you. You're home!"

"I am. I brought someone with me."

He pulled Liz into the room with him. While Ralph stared at the two of them, they walked over to the side of his bed.

"We have some gifts for you." Liz handed him the two boxes, which he opened. "Those are yours to keep. You always had faith in us."

Tears spilled down his cheeks. "I heard your speech at the hotel. I've been crying ever since."

"We've got something else to tell you that'll make you cry even harder. Show him, sweetheart." She tugged on the sleeve of her pullover so Ralph could see the charm bracelet. "I've asked Liz to marry me."

His grandfather gasped.

"We made it official last night with this bracelet you gave us. It brought us luck and love. The kind you had with Grandma. It's the kind of love I've wanted with every fiber of my being. I know I've found it with Liz."

Ralph's eyes shone. "I know you have, too. My little princess. I always wanted you for my Connor. My dream has finally come true."

"I've loved him forever." Her words came out sounding like a croak.

"Come here and let me give both of you a hug."

After he let them go, he said, "Who else knows?"

Connor's eyes danced. "No one. You're the first. We'll tell everyone tomorrow when they're back."

"What are your plans?"

"We want to be married at Liz's church, but that's as far as we've gotten. We want it to be soon."

"Where will you live?"

"Here on the ranch. Until we build our own home, we'll live in my trailer."

A big smile broke out on his face. "You've brought me such wonderful news, I might expire from too much joy."

"Oh, please don't do that," Liz cried. "We're planning on you living a long time.

"We want our children to enjoy their great-grandfather for as long as possible. But now we're going to say good-night. We have to take care of our other children."

Ralph chuckled. "Your horses did themselves proud."

Connor nodded. "Especially Polly. She pulled through like a champion."

"I told her she had to do it for Connor, who couldn't compete for himself. I'm positive she understood me."

Ralph winked at her. "You've always had special powers in that department."

Liz watched Connor give his grandfather another kiss. "We'll come in the morning and have breakfast with you."

"Can't wait. We'll watch all the recordings and you can tell me everything that was going on behind the scenes. Especially the moment when that hooky honker pulled that stunt on you, son."

"He was a rank one, all right. Sleep well," Connor said, before ushering Liz out of the bedroom.

"What do you say we stall both horses in our barn for tonight? We'll put Sunflower next to Firebrand so they'll be happy."

"I was just going to suggest it. Who knows? Maybe they're engaged, too."

He threw back his head and laughed that deep, rich male laughter she loved almost as much as she loved him.

Once the horses were safely housed in the barn, Connor told her where to park his rig for the night. He helped her clean out the trailer stalls the best he could until they were able to go to bed themselves.

After showering, she cuddled up to Connor's solid, hard body. Talk about heaven. He only put on the bottom half of his sweats. It was too hard to deal with the top. "Darling? I've never seen Ralph so happy."

"Our news did it, all right. Can you imagine how happy everyone else is going to be when they hear?"

"My parents will be overjoyed."

"So will the rest of my family. Now they won't have to worry about me anymore."

"Mine won't, either. When I told Mom I was driving with you, she almost had a heart attack for fear I'd be hurt. That was because she knew Sadie and I had always been pining for love of the Bannock brothers."

"Unfortunately, the Bannock brothers had been warned off your land. I hope lightning won't strike me if I say Daniel Corkin's passing was a good thing. He put me and my brother through hell."

"Speaking of Jarod, do you want hear something kind of spooky?"

He plundered her mouth for a little while before he said, "I'm all ears."

"The first night I called Sadie from Las Vegas, she told me I was going to win because Jarod had seen a vision. When I asked if he'd had one about you winning, he said no."

"He's a lot like his uncle Charlo. I'm glad you didn't tell me, sweetheart."

She shivered. "I wonder why he told Sadie."

"They share everything. He probably told her not to tell you. But she did anyway, because she loves you and wanted to instill you with extra confidence."

"I'm afraid it did the opposite. For the rest of the time, all I did was worry about you. When Derrick told me you'd had an accident, it was like a nightmare come true. How specific are Jarod's visions?"

"Let's ask him tomorrow."

"Maybe we'd better not, or we might get Sadie into trouble."

"Don't worry about it. He loves her too much. I'm more inclined to believe he knew she'd tell you. Jarod wanted you to believe in yourself."

She cupped his face in her hands, kissing every feature. "With everyone believing in me, especially you, how could I lose? I fall more in love with you every minute. I wish—"

"So do I." His voice had grown husky. "Do me a favor and help me to love you any way we can until I can get rid of this sling."

"Well, as long as I've got your permission…"

"You've got it, Mrs. Bannock to be. In spades."

* * * * *

MILLS & BOON®

Buy the Regency Society Collection today and get 4 BOOKS FREE!

Scandal and seduction in this fantastic twelve-book collection from top Historical authors.

Submerge yourself in the lavish world of Regency rakes and the ballroom gossip they create.

Visit the Mills & Boon website today to take advantage of this spectacular offer!

www.millsandboon.co.uk/regency